D1446670

it's in his touch

A RED RIVER VALLEY NOVEL

Red River #2

Also by Shelly Alexander

It's In His Heart: A Red River Valley Novel

Greenwood Public Library
310 S. Meridian St.
Greenwood, IN 46143

it's in his touch

A RED RIVER VALLEY NOVEL

SHELLY ALEXANDER

This is a work of fiction. Names, characters, organizations, places, events, and incidents are either products of the author's imagination or are used fictitiously.

Text copyright © 2015 Shelly Alexander
All rights reserved.

No part of this book may be reproduced, or stored in a retrieval system, or transmitted in any form or by any means, electronic, mechanical, photocopying, recording, or otherwise, without express written permission of the publisher.

Published by Montlake Romance, Seattle

www.apub.com

Amazon, the Amazon logo, and Montlake Romance are trademarks of Amazon.com, Inc., or its affiliates.

ISBN-13: 9781503948075
ISBN-10: 1503948072

Cover design by Laura Klynstra

Printed in the United States of America

This book is dedicated to all who have fought the good fight, and to Dr. L. A. Smith because she does remember my name.

To my husband, who never let me give up.

And to the real Kimberly, the best friend a gal could ever ask for. Every new adventure on our list is a hoot. (But I'm still not jumping out of a plane—not even for you.)

Chapter One

"Drop the panties, or the octopus gets it." Angelique Barbetta held out the plush doggy toy, a bottle of bitter anti-chew spray pointed at its overstuffed head. She used the predatory tone usually reserved for courtroom opponents as she glared at her four-legged adversary.

A soft breeze whispered through the trees, wrestling autumn-hued foliage to the ground. The draft of cool air caught the silky neckline of her robe and sent a chill racing through her. Late afternoon sunlight filtered through the shedding branches, and a silhouette of the snow-capped Sangre de Cristo Mountains glittered in the background. Her long black hair was up in hot rollers, and a sudden gust pulled a thick tendril loose. She blew it out of her eyes, refusing to lose a staring match to a dog.

The ten-pound weenie dog's posture tensed, his tail wagged a fraction, and his jaw clamped tighter around the black thong panties he'd snatched from her suitcase while she was unpacking. Hence, the reason she'd scurried outside half-dressed and sporting curlers so big they could pick up a radio frequency from three states away.

Why'd she bring skimpy panties on an extended vacay to Red River—population 475? *Pfst.* Insulated long johns would've been a more practical choice.

She shivered against another nippy gust of autumn breeze.

It wasn't like she'd ever wear the string bikinis currently lodged between her dog's teeth. They'd been part of the risqué honeymoon trousseau given to her by her best friend, Kimberly, and the horde of female Barbettas. Of course, that was before she caught her fiancé, Gabriel, cheating. *While* Angelique was recovering from breast cancer.

Asshole.

Come to think of it, she should let the dog have them. Let Sergeant Schnitzel chew up the underwear and every last memory of what she'd thought she had with Gabriel.

Just like she'd *accidentally* let the dog chew up Gabriel's Armani jacket. And his Tumi briefcase. And the crack in his brand-new fifty-five-inch widescreen—a testament to his insecurity and belief that size really did matter—may or may not have been an accident. Golf clubs sometimes slipped out of one's hands mid-swing. It happened.

Sergeant Schnitzel whined, his tail wagging at lightning speed.

"Come on, Sarge. Drop 'em. *Please.*"

Jeez, she was pathetic. Had she really been reduced to begging a dog?

Okay, admittedly, destroying Gabriel's personal property had been a vindictive reaction, but her momentary lapse in emotional restraint was understandable. While she was in the process of moving out of their rented condo, Gabriel announced his shotgun wedding to her legal assistant, whom he'd knocked up. Now with the wedding just a few weeks away, he actually expected Angelique to attend, along with the rest of their law firm, because *cohesion* would look good for the junior partnership he'd just landed. So much cruelty at once probably would've pushed Mother Teresa over the edge. That was Angelique's story, anyway, and she was sticking to it, because Gabriel deserved it times ten.

She drew in a tremulous breath, the familiar sting of loss pinging off the walls of her stomach like a pinball.

Now instead of standing toe-to-toe with a skilled criminal prosecutor, she was throwing down with a weenie dog. Definitely pathetic. She glared at him.

The cocktail-sized wiener growled, enticing her to give chase.

"Sergeant Schnitzel, don't you dare run off again," she warned, eyeballing him with her best menacing look. That stare wilted even the most seasoned district attorneys and brought witnesses to tears on the stand. Unfortunately, it didn't intimidate this little pilferer of women's underpants. "I swear, no more satin pillows to sleep on, and no more fancy chew toys." She shook the octopus, its legs flouncing in the air. "And no more bacon-flavored treats either."

Sergeant Schnitzel whined and cocked his head to one side.

Victory within her grasp, Angelique stepped closer and slipped the spray bottle into the pocket of her red silk kimono—another installment of her intended honeymoon wardrobe. When she stretched out a hand to retrieve the slobbery undergarment, the dog charged, making a quick circle around her *Sesame Street* slippers. The dark-brown dachshund's lightning-fast movements stirred up a cloud of dust and autumn leaves around her legs and made the hem of her robe flutter. Sergeant Schnitzel darted across her toes, his collar snagging the hem and pulling the front loose.

"Hey!" She grabbed at the gaping front and cinched it closed to hide the black lace camisole and matching panties. What the heck. She might as well get *some* use out of all those lingerie shower gifts, even if no one but her and Sergeant Schnitzel would ever see them. "That's it! You're the main course at my next weenie roast!" Angelique yelled after the dog as he raced across the vacation property and disappeared over the wooden footbridge that joined her one-acre lot to the next.

"Maybe he won't come back." Kimberly, her closest friend since law school, emerged from the cabin and sauntered over to Angelique, orange and yellow leaves crunching under her steps. "I still can't understand why you didn't give that demon dog to Gabe the Douchebag."

Clad in leopard tights, Kimberly stood next to Angelique. Kimberly pulled her hot-pink mohair cardigan tighter, folding both arms across her well-endowed bust. A petite gal with spiked bleached-blonde hair, her excessive bust line didn't exactly match her five-feet-two-inch frame, and when she wore a fitted shirt . . . well, armed and dangerous was the only way to describe her. Really, many a man had never been the same after seeing her in spandex workout clothes.

"Sarge isn't a demon dog. He's just a little spoiled," Angelique said, as they both stared at the empty footbridge, Sarge long gone.

And who could blame her for that, really? He was the closest to a child she'd ever have, now that she planned to keep her body to herself and focus solely on a career.

She looked at the stuffed octopus and tossed it up, catching it again. "No way was I leaving Sergeant Schnitzel with *her*. Gabriel gave him to me right before I was diagnosed." Angelique's hand went to her chest and rested there. "That two-faced . . ."

Angelique caught herself. Gabriel and his new squeeze weren't worth the energy it would take to stay angry. She drew in a deep breath, and the fresh mountain air filled her lungs and steadied her emotions. "She got everything else that was supposed to be mine—my fiancé, his baby in her womb, even the dream house he and I were building together." Angelique's fingers fisted around the fabric at her neck. She tucked the toy into the other robe pocket. "The dog is mine."

"Not much of a prize, if you ask me."

"It's the principle of the matter," Angelique said, adjusting the flaps of her robe. She cinched the belt tighter and retied it.

"Would've been a nice wedding gift. Sergeant Schnitzel could be chewing up the Cheerleader's undies right now instead of yours."

Since Gabriel's new soon-to-be-wife was seven years younger than Angelique and perky from her twenty-four-year-old boobs all the way to her petite size five-and-a-half shoe, Kimberly had officially dubbed her the Cheerleader. Gabriel couldn't have cheated with someone more different than Angelique if he'd tried. The Cheerleader was blonde, had hazel eyes, and was sweet. Or so she'd pretended to be. A sharp contrast to Angelique's dark Sicilian features and barracuda personality.

Rolling one foot onto its side, Angelique looked down at her size nines.

"Well, I think he should be skewered and roasted over an open fire," Kimberly announced. The small diamond in her nose glinted against the afternoon sun as she ran splayed fingers through her spiky hair.

"It's not that big a deal. I just need to keep my lingerie put away where Sarge can't get to it."

"I meant Gabriel."

Angelique threw her head back and laughed. "That's why I keep you around."

"Because I make you laugh?"

"No, because you'll help me dispose of a body should the need ever arise."

It was Kimberly's turn to laugh. "What else are friends for? Just let me know, and I'll bring the shovels."

"Maybe I should go after him." Angelique sighed, her gaze returning to the footbridge.

"Maybe you should relax and let him find his own way back home. You came to Red River to work on an easy case and do some more recuperating in the process."

"Real estate development cases aren't my field of expertise, but it's pretty open-and-shut. The firm was doing me a favor. It'll be like a three-month paid vacation while Gabriel's wedding and honeymoon hype blows over."

"After what you've been through, you deserve it."

Right. The emotional scars of losing both breasts ran deeper than she'd ever expected.

Thank God she didn't have to go through chemo, too. Losing her hair would've added insult to injury and probably pushed her over the edge. Reconstruction had been an even bigger horror. If she'd known how painful it was going to be, she'd never have done it. But she'd been scared to wake up without breasts. Terrified, in fact. And the thought of intimacy with Gabriel if she wasn't a whole woman nearly *had* sent her plunging over an emotional cliff.

"Speaking of, I need to get busy and study the case file." Angelique walked to her pearl-white SUV and opened the door to get her briefcase and a stack of correspondence from the firm.

"Not tonight, sweetie." Kimberly snatched the bundle of papers from Angelique's hands as soon as she got close enough. "Tonight we focus on the bucket list."

Angelique couldn't stop an eye roll. Unfortunately, neither Kimberly's annoying bucket list nor reconstruction had been able to replace all that her illness had cost her.

When Angelique looked in the mirror for the first time after the first surgery, she'd cried a river. Now it was time to suck it up, build a bridge, and get the hell over it. Grief and self-pity weren't going to keep her from the partnership she deserved.

She'd stay in Red River through the holidays, then go back to Albuquerque and kick butt. Cancer and cheating exes be damned. Once she returned to the firm, the C word would never pass through her lips again. A partnership called to her from the not-so-distant future, chanted her name like a chorus. At least that's what she hoped she heard and not voices that required medication. Some days she'd wondered, because her emotions had been all over the place since the diagnosis.

What didn't kill her made her stronger.

Her new motto. Maybe she'd have it tattooed across her backside as a reminder that she'd be just fine on her own. Her large, obnoxious family believed it their duty to smother her with love, and she had a great career going. That would be enough to fill the emptiness left inside her by a disease that she carried in her flawed DNA.

———

Blake Holloway sat on his back porch steps and looked at the bologna sandwich he'd thrown together for Sunday dinner. It tasted like cardboard, but it was better than nothing. With a small grunt of disapproval, he took another bite and washed it down with a long swallow of ice-cold beer.

As he set the glass bottle on the porch, a small dachshund tore into his backyard carrying something in his mouth. The dog stopped about ten feet in front of him, and they stared each other down. Too well groomed to be a stray, it probably belonged to his nearest neighbor, a new renter who'd just moved in.

"Hey, little buddy. Come here." Blake tried to coax it closer with a kind voice.

The dog squatted like it was about to leap up and run away.

Tearing off a hefty piece of bologna, Blake held it out and laid the sandwich on a plate next to his beer. The dog inched forward, finally snagging the bologna after he dropped the . . . um, *black panties*?

Holding the tiny strings up for a quick look, he supposed they were women's panties. He'd used dental floss that would cover more. Probably be more comfortable, too.

He tore off another bite and coaxed the wayward pup into his arms. Blake pulled him closer, giving him a scratch behind the ears. Reaching for the heart-shaped piece of metal that dangled around the dog's neck, he angled it for a better view. The name "Sarge" and a New Mexico phone number were engraved across the first and second lines. Blake lifted the pup a little higher to read the last line in small script. "Love, G."

Blake dropped the tag and scratched the dog's chest. Sarge whined back at him.

"One more piece, and I'm taking you home." He wrenched off a generous piece and the dog inhaled it.

Blake polished off his beer and set out for the neighbor's cabin.

The babbling stream cascaded under foot as he trekked across an old footbridge, the rogue weenie dog bundled in his arms.

He'd stuffed the small wad of strings into his pocket before heading next door. Returning the dog wasn't a problem, but he just couldn't bring himself to hand over a pair of G-strings to a neighbor on their first meeting. Maybe he should throw them in the trash and pretend they didn't exist.

Halfway across the old bridge, a rotted board creaked under his foot, and he readjusted his weight, taking a quick sidestep around it.

Something else to add to his long repair list. The new cabin was an improvement over the crummy apartment above his downtown

Red River medical practice. He'd made do in the small converted loft over his business for two years, until he finally bought a real place of his own. For all the good it had done. The bank might force him out before he could unpack the moving boxes still strewn around his cabin.

Heat roiled in his veins.

Now that the Red River Community Bank, courtesy of its new owners, planned to call in most of the small business loans in town, he stood to lose both his practice and his new cabin. So did most of the business owners in this quiet little community.

The only lawyer they'd collectively been able to afford didn't exactly inspire confidence. The guy was still putting off a face-to-face meeting, rarely returned their e-mails, and said he practiced out of his home where telephone reception was sketchy.

A gust of wind rustled the trees on the riverbank, sending a spray of autumn leaves fluttering past. The small dog folded under Blake's arm barked.

"Get 'em, boy." Blake laughed and stroked the dog's head. "You're quite the guard dog, aren't you? Women's underwear and falling leaves should beware." Blake chuckled. "I feel safer already."

Blake stopped short to examine the rotting handrails. New paint wouldn't help. The whole bridge needed to be torn down and rebuilt. He sighed. If the bank owners got their way, he wouldn't live here long enough to repair anything.

So much for his dream to live a quiet life serving in a community where people weren't just file numbers. Doctors Without Borders would've been a wiser choice.

He lifted the dog and scratched it's head as he stepped off the bridge. "Stay away from that bridge, little buddy. You might fall through into the stream."

The dog's tongue shot out and swiped at Blake's cheek.

As Blake dried his jaw with the back side of his sleeve, the neighboring cabin came into view. Two thirtysomething women, one of them in a robe and sporting a gigantic head of hair, disappeared through the front door.

Lorenda, his Realtor and general know-it-all on every property in Red River, couldn't find out much about the new tenant. Amazing considering news spread faster in this town than an outbreak of influenza in the middle of winter.

As he reached the small flight of steps that ascended the wooden front porch, the autumn breeze kicked up, shifting a small pile of leaves. Underneath, an envelope lay on the ground. He picked it up and read the return address. His eyes scanned the expensive stationery, and every muscle in his six-foot frame went rigid.

Riggs, Castillo & Marone, Attorneys at Law—the same law firm representing the new bank owners. Henchmen tasked to drive out Red River's lifeblood of small enterprise so they could build a corporate-owned resort complete with high-rise condos that would be marketed to the rich and famous. Huh. And it was addressed to one Angelique Barbetta, Attorney at Law.

His head shot up, and he stared at the cabin in front of him. Surely not.

Clutching the small animal under one arm, he climbed the steps and lifted the letter-carrying hand to rap a knuckle against the door. Before he connected, the door swung open and a tall, black-eyed, curler-laden beauty charged out, bumping smack into him and the dog.

The dog whined and wiggled, obviously familiar with the woman who had her silky hair wound around soda can–sized rollers. Her eyes widened as she looked up.

"Whoa," Blake said, catching her by the arm as she staggered backward. "You okay?"

Stunned, she blinked, and his eyes locked onto hers. Like fine cut glass, her onyx eyes shimmered and held his, refused to let go. A slender, toned arm warmed his palm, and his brain forgot how to form words. Grasping at the front of her rather inviting Asian-style robe, her other arm anchored across her chest.

He released her and took a step back.

"I . . ." he mumbled. Like an idiot. "He yours?" Blake finally managed, giving the dog a gentle boost.

Something flickered in her big inky eyes before she turned them on the dog. Her hand pulled away from her neckline a fraction and hovered there. Her uncertain stare darted to Blake, then back to the pup. Finally she wagged a long, slender finger in front of the dog's nose, and Blake took note of the lack of wedding ring on that elegant hand.

"Bad boy, Sergeant Schnitzel," she scolded.

Sarge whined and buried his snout under Blake's arm.

An assertive female voice called from inside the house. "Did you find that ornery dog? He's probably just hiding in the bushes." The other thirtyish woman appeared in the doorway wearing an ensemble that even Blake knew was a fashion faux pas.

Blake suppressed a grimace. "Hi," he said.

"Hi, yourself. Who are you?" The spiky-haired blonde leaned against the doorframe.

"I live next door," he said. "Just bringing your dog home."

"We've never seen that dog before," the blonde challenged just before she narrowed her eyes at the canine. Sarge squirmed in Blake's arms and strained toward his master.

"Stop it, Kimberly," Sarge's apparent owner told her friend as she scooped him up.

Sunlight gleamed off her ebony hair, and several loose locks cascaded in a messy network around her long, slender neck. The strands of jet-black against her natural, tan skin caught him off guard. His mouth went dry, and his eyes anchored to the hollow of her neck.

The leopard-clad woman sighed and pushed herself off the door-frame. "Fine. I'll go check on dinner." She disappeared into the house.

The dog sneezed.

"There's poison oak all over the place." Blake gave Sarge a scratch behind the ears. "He may have gotten into it, but it doesn't have the same effect on canines. He'll probably just sneeze for a while, then he'll be fine."

"Thanks," said the dog's gorgeous owner. "He has a habit of running off. Sorry if he bothered you." She launched a string of admonitions at the dog, whose ears folded back in shame. Then she pecked his nose with a kiss and cuddled him tight against her chest.

He'd never envied a dog before now.

Blake shook his head, trying not to focus on the fluttering hem of her robe as a feathery breeze breathed life into the delicate silk. "No bother."

The silk robe hung close around her tall frame, revealing curves in all the right places. Well-defined calves appeared below the hem. His eyes traveled down athletic legs that disappeared into slippers that could easily double as furry puppets. Unfortunately, they'd probably scare unsuspecting children instead of entertain them.

"Did he, um . . ." Her cheeks pinked, eyes darted around. "Was he carrying anything?"

Ah, the owner of the mystery panties, no doubt. Stuffing one hand into a pants pocket, his fingers closed around the provocative "anything" in question. "Nope." He shrugged, trying to look innocent. He didn't have the heart to embarrass her by producing the panties.

She blew out a shaky gust of laughter. "Good! I mean . . . okay. Right." She took a step backward over the threshold. "Thanks." She reached for the doorknob and started to push the door closed. "It won't happen again."

"Wait," he said, and she stopped the closing door. He stared at her. Blinked once. Twice. Hell, he was the stupidest smart person on the planet. Sucking in a breath, he showed her the front of the letter. "I found this on the ground. Yours, too?"

Her eyes widened as they scanned the address, and she snatched it from his grasp.

"I must've dropped it when I unloaded the car." She looked at the letter, then back at him. "Thanks . . . again."

"So you're the one," he said, his voice low and simmering with quiet anger. And disappointment, which shook him a little. He hadn't been interested in anyone in a long time. Years, in fact. The demands of medical school and residency didn't leave much time for dating. And since he moved to Red River to take over his dad's practice, no one had snagged his attention. Not until he'd walked over that rotting footbridge and laid eyes on this . . . this . . . Damn it. What was she? Not someone he should be interested in, that's what.

A crease appeared between her eyes. "Beg your pardon?"

His gaze dropped to her perfect mouth. Yep, dumb as a stump regardless of what his med-school test scores said. *Get over it. She's biohazardous material wrapped in a pretty little package.*

"You're the bottom dweller who's going to help destroy Red River." The thought popped right out of his mouth before he could filter it through his malfunctioning brain.

At first her eyes rounded and those plush lips formed a perfect O. Then a stony expression slid over her flawless face, and she narrowed her eyes at him. "I'm afraid you'll have to communicate with me through your attorney."

The door advanced toward him again, but he reached out and stopped it mid-swing.

"That's just it. We're just simple folks who can't afford a high-profile lawyer like you to protect us." He studied her and didn't miss the flash of victory that raced across her face. "And you know it, too. We're easy pickings for someone like you."

A hand went to her hair and discovered the apparently forgotten rollers. Her look of humiliation and horror was priceless. Blake smirked. *Sucks to be you right now, doesn't it?* Which gave him little comfort, because the truth was, it had to be pretty sweet being her right now. She was in the catbird's seat, and it sucked to be her prey. Which was him.

"This conversation is completely unprofessional and inappropriate—"

"Damn right it is." He pulled the black strings from his pocket and held them up between two fingers. She blanched. "Women don't usually send their panties to me, especially if they're trying to put me out of business."

Chapter Two

Two hours later, Angelique followed Kimberly into the Rain Dance Casino just outside of Taos. Hundreds of slot machines dinged in a constant disjointed harmony.

Angelique stumbled after Kimberly in stilettos so tall they were a safety hazard.

"I'd rather be home watching *Sister Wives*." Angelique sniffed and pulled at the hem of her formfitting cocktail dress. "It makes me feel so much better about my life."

Kimberly headed toward the cashier. "You're just upset over your freakishly handsome neighbor. Don't let it bother you." Kimberly strutted along in her four-inch knee-high boots.

Through the skintight fabric of her dress, Angelique adjusted the snug waistband of her rubberlike undergarment. "I can't believe you made me wear this thing. We'll have to stop by the nearest fire station on the way home so they can pry me out of it with the Jaws of Life."

"You're five feet nine and all legs. That dress is made for you," Kimberly said as they exchanged cash for chips.

"Well, I'm wearing a steel-belted radial." Angelique scratched at her lower thigh. "And it's kind of itchy."

Kimberly grabbed Angelique's arm and tugged her over to the roulette table. "Roulette is on our bucket list, so we start here."

Angelique rolled her eyes. "Seriously, how many more things are on your bucket list? Because this is getting ridiculous."

When Angelique was diagnosed, Kimberly had a meltdown. She sat by Angelique's bedside for a week crying, cussing, then crying some more. Angelique didn't have the heart to tell the poor girl what an ugly crier she was, but it had provided some entertainment while Angelique regained her strength. As a coping mechanism, Kimberly made a list of all the things they were going to do together *while they still could*.

"It took forever to get that *temporary* electric-blue dye out of our hair. I walked around for a month looking like an ethnic version of Katy Perry," Angelique grumbled.

"The color complimented your olive complexion."

"That was the week I tried to go back to work. It probably set my partnership back another year."

Kimberly, clad in a black leather miniskirt and zebra-print sweater, stuck out a hip and planted her right hand on it. "We were celebrating the fact that you got to keep your hair. Besides, after two days, you decided it was too soon to return to the office. Remember?"

How could Angelique forget?

On Angelique's second day, she'd gone back to the office late to pick up a few files. Walking in on Gabriel balls deep in her legal assistant, Ciara Mathews, with her ankles wrapped around his neck, wasn't something Angelique would likely forget in this lifetime.

That's when the ship carrying Angelique's sex life had sailed without her. And when she confronted him, he'd actually had the nerve to blame his cheating on her, accusing her of shutting him out. Seriously? That torpedoed her USS *Coitus* and it sank to the bottom of the ocean somewhere between Bite Me Island and the continent of Go to Hell in a Handbasket.

The croupier set the wheel in motion and dropped the ball. Click, click, click—the rhythmic bouncing caused a ripple of anticipation around the crowded table.

"And pretending to be a cop so you could frisk that guy at Cold Stone Creamery almost got us arrested." The spinning wheel made Angelique a little dizzy, and she reached for the table to steady herself. "By the *real* police."

"Seemed like a good plan, mocha java chip and the feel of firm thighs at the same time." Kimberly shrugged. "That was much further down the list, but the opportunity presented itself."

The bouncing ceased and the croupier called out the winner, causing a squeal from a scantily clad woman at the far end of the table. She immediately placed her winnings plus a few more chips on the same number.

"What number is gambling on your bucket list?" Angelique couldn't hide the irritation in her voice.

"It's *our* bucket list, and gambling is number twelve." She put a hundred-dollar black chip on number twelve. "Right before having a fling with someone tall, dark, and hot-some. Preferably on an island, so come on, place your bet. I hear Barbados calling to us."

"I'm not having a fling. With anyone. Ever." Angelique ran her fingers across the round disks in her hand, finally selecting a red five-dollar chip.

"Oh, come on!" Kimberly hooted. "You'll be living right next door to Mr. Tall, Dark, and Hot-some for the next three months, and he wasn't wearing a wedding ring. He's perfect fling-worthy material only without the island." Kimberly looked thoughtful. "Did you get his name?"

"No, I didn't get his name, and you know why I'm not interested in a fling."

But he really had been tall, dark, and really, really hot-some. Probably six feet, which would be a nice fit with her five feet nine height. Wavy chestnut hair and blue eyes the color of the ocean. Not the same ocean her USS *Coitus* had sank in. That ocean was a polluted abyss. This ocean was beautiful, calling to her every time his gaze met hers.

Until he'd called her a bottom dweller.

Crap, had she really held a fifteen-minute conversation with Mr. Tall, Dark, and Hot-some wearing hot rollers, a kimono, and Cookie Monster slippers? Not to mention he was on the opposing side of a legal battle that she was just stepping into, *and* he'd seen her thong. Held it in his incredibly powerful-looking hand, taunting her with it like it was an incriminating piece of evidence before she managed to snatch it from him.

Gah!

Dammit, it had been a gag gift from Kimberly.

Nope. No fling. Especially not with a man from Mayberry, USA, whose idea of progress was probably replacing a four-way stop with the town's only traffic light. Instead of bringing the freaking thong panties to Red River, she should've packed Kimberly's other gag gift—a neon-purple battery-operated device called the Harley. Because that was as close to a fling as she would ever get.

She'd never give another man the chance to look at her bared chest and see revulsion in his eyes, newly reconstructed boobs or not.

Even though every doctor who'd examined her said it was nice work, she just couldn't see it. They were *fake*!

He might be fling-worthy material, but she wasn't. She looked down at her chest. *Who would want to get naked with this?*

Illness had cost her dearly. Stolen her chance for a family because no way was she passing this nightmare down to another generation. But no more. She was back in control of her destiny. And where a man was conspicuously absent, a partnership at Riggs, Castillo & Marone would stand in the gap.

And maybe good ol' Harley. If she got desperate, he could help her out from time to time.

"Even if I was interested, and I'm *not*"—Angelique pursed her lips at Kimberly before continuing—"he hates me, and I wasn't exactly impressed with him either." Except for the fact that her rusty girly parts sputtered to life and did a dance when she first laid eyes on him, and then proceeded to turn cartwheels by the end of their rather awkward conversation. "And what about the conflict of interest?"

"Sweetie, if you think you'd be the first attorney to sleep with a player on the opposing team, you obviously haven't spent enough time in the Federal Court building."

The croupier cleared his throat, looking a little intimidated by the angry red faces at the other end of the table. "Are you ladies ready, or should I start without you?" He was actually asking Kimberly's permission while gazing at her Grand Canyon–sized cleavage.

"We were born ready, darlin'," Kimberly said and winked at him.

Angelique placed the red five-dollar chip on a black diamond.

"That's it? Five dollars on black?" Kimberly huffed.

"Fits my mood and my appearance." Angelique glowered. "Dark and cheap."

"The bucket list says a hundred bucks at the roulette table. And not in nickel increments." Kimberly waggled all four fingers in a *come here* movement. "Give it up."

Angelique pulled a black chip from her stack and placed it on number seven. "Do you think people can go to hell for gambling?"

"Not unless they use the chip to commit murder." Kimberly shook her head. "You Catholics."

The croupier spun the wheel and dropped the little white ball. It tapped around the board, finally landing on Angelique's number.

"We have a winner!" the croupier announced and pushed a stack of chips in front of Angelique. She snatched all of them up and deposited them into her handbag.

"You go ahead and gamble away your future child's college fund," Angelique said. "I'm out."

She gave Kimberly a fake smile and scratched her leg again. Did something bite her? Maybe she was allergic to the rubber under-garment that was squeezing the life out of her with every passing moment. The freaking thing was probably bulletproof.

Angelique wandered over to a vacant group of slot machines and sat down. Crossing her legs, she looked at the complicated winning combinations listed on the front of the machine and tried to figure out the payoffs.

"Hello," said a wheezy voice from behind her. A chubby man in his late fifties slid into the chair next to her. Cheap cologne singed her nostrils, and Angelique gave a little cough. "Is this seat taken?" He ogled her crossed legs.

She tugged her skirt down, but seeing as how it was the size of a Band-Aid, she gave up and angled her legs to the other side, away from Mr. Aqua Velva's bulging eyeballs.

"Um, no, be my guest."

Angelique retrieved a twenty-dollar bill from her handbag and slid it into the machine. When she tapped the button, the wheels spun, landing on a cherry and two bars. The red number of credits in the upper-right corner decreased by four.

A strange itch started just below her collarbone, and she rubbed it. Now both of her legs were itching. Darned if she'd wear latex underwear again. As Angelique reached up to press the button again, Aqua Velva put his hand on the back of her chair and leaned toward her.

"You looking for company, little lady?"

Angelique turned a gaping mouth on him. His comb-over fell forward a fraction, and he wiggled bushy brows that met in between his eyes. His leer slid over her. "You look expensive, but I can afford it."

She reeled backward, a mixture of revulsion and hysterical laughter bubbling through her lips in an indiscernible string of sounds. She grabbed for the machine to prevent falling off the stool and punched the Play button by accident.

The first wheel stopped on seven, then the next seven slammed into place. Angelique's heart skipped as she turned back to the machine. The last wheel slowed, and a seven slid into the window. The siren on top of the machine started to wail, and she looked around, alarmed, wondering what she'd done wrong.

"You won!" Kimberly ran over. "Hot darn, now we can afford that arctic dog-sledding trip. I think it's number forty-three on the list."

"How much for the two of you?" Aqua Velva whispered to her, a glint of anticipation dancing in his eyes.

Kimberly turned an appalled glare on him. "Beg your pardon?"

Angelique leveled a nuclear stare. "You've got to be kidding me."

He stood, snugging his leisure pants up under a ten-inch beer belly. He looked at Angelique's chest with a sneer. "Not a lot to offer up top in your line of work, sweetheart. I'm a boob man myself."

His words hit her like a dagger to the heart, the pain radiating to her core. She fought back tears. Tried to beat them back down and bury them like she had when she caught Gabriel naked with the Cheerleader, and when he announced his engagement with a baby on the way. She'd done it, too. Stayed strong, a pillar of strength. Not a sign of weakness from her.

She gasped for air, the tears threatening to spill over. A few deep breaths and she sucked up her resolve, and the cast-iron attorney who showed no fear to the enemy regained control. If she could weather the tragedy she'd already been through, this catnip-wearing asshole wasn't about to get a single tear out of her.

She stood, hardening her stare into steel. Fear coursed over his face, and he backed into one of the slot machines.

"I'm so far out of your league, I'd turn you down even in that perverse little imagination of yours." She took another step toward him, but Kimberly grabbed her arm.

"Come on, sweetie. Let's collect your winnings and get out of here." Kimberly's tone was soothing, motherly.

"Good idea," Angelique seethed through clenched teeth. "It smells like rotting garbage in here."

———

Angelique sat in her pearl-white Lexus SUV wearing a baseball cap and giant sunglasses. Parked against the curb in the middle of Red River's business district—laughable, really, considering Red River wasn't exactly a metropolis—she perused the buildings that lined both sides of Main Street.

An uncomfortable rash had crept up her neck in the middle of the night and now covered most of her legs, arms, and face. She rubbed it, trying not to use fingernails. Frick, it itched.

When she woke up this morning in agony from head to toe, she'd looked in the mirror and screamed at the unsightly splotches of red that greeted her. Kimberly charged in, panicked, and screamed too, covering her mouth with both hands.

Great. Sarge had even barked and growled when he first saw her.

While Angelique eased into a pair of yoga pants and a zip-up hoodie with nothing on underneath, Kimberly found the number and address to Red River's town doctor. After Angelique had assured Kimberly that she'd be fine on her own, Kimberly returned to Taos, and Angelique stared at the information Kimberly had scrawled on the scrap of paper. The address was familiar. Too familiar.

Crapola.

Dr. Blake Holloway was located in one of the structures her clients planned to tear down.

She'd pinched the bridge of her nose—one of the few spots on her upper body that didn't hurt—before punching in the number, and made an appointment for eleven thirty that morning under the name Angie Marone.

Double crapola.

Gabriel's last name had just popped out. It was the first alias she'd come up with on the fly, while the receptionist smacked gum in her ear.

Pulling down the sun visor, she regarded herself in the small mirror. Incognito was the look she'd been going for. If her ill-mannered neighbor had already figured out who she was, it was only a matter of time before everyone else in town did, too. But really, she just looked like a slightly creepy stalker, hunched behind the steering wheel to scope out the buildings of downtown Red River. Blowing out an exasperated breath, she flipped the visor up again.

The long, eclectic strips of office buildings that lined both sides of Main Street were so obviously the pulse of this sleepy little town. The tourists weren't hard to spot. They wore some sort of sweatshirt or windbreaker announcing their favorite college football team from Texas or Oklahoma because Red River's tourist population was largely from those two states. People meandered down the narrow sidewalks, popping into the German pastry shop, the bistro on the corner, the hardware store, the pharmacy . . . the town doctor's office. Even the local chiropractor's office. His name, Cooper Wells, DC, was etched on the door.

Ouch. That one hurt. She'd gone to high school in Albuquerque with Coop and represented him in an unfortunate legal situation a while back.

Which of the businesses that occupied these outdated structures belonged to Mr. Tall, Dark, and Hot-some? She wasn't sure because she hadn't bothered to ask his name. Seemed pointless after his glaring hostility. Maybe he was the accountant on the north side of the street.

She gave her head an involuntary shake. Nah, didn't seem the type.

Glancing to the other side of the street, she scanned the storefronts. Definitely not Red River's seamstress. Her eyes scanned farther down. Aha! Al's Plumbing and Septic Removal. Had to be him. None of the other establishments seemed to fit, and whoever said a plumber couldn't be hot as a summer day in the Mojave Desert?

She'd reviewed the file last night for the first time, the partner's notes citing that the community would be better off if the old, dilapidated structures were torn down, and replaced by a state-of-the-art resort and condos. The local economy would flourish, and the proprietors forced to move could find better locations, which would help their businesses rebound in the end. Some establishments would close, but those would be no real loss to the community since all the same goods and services could be acquired in Taos.

With the new resort, which would feature activities for both winter and summer, new small business ventures were likely to flood in from other upscale resort towns, creating a whole new sector of business owners. New blood with new ideas for the future, instead of the old, antiquated business district that could barely sustain the off seasons after the ski slopes closed every spring.

After reading the file, she could almost hear the birds chirping, the deer frolicking in the meadow on the outskirts of town, and the streets humming with content residents who were grateful for all the changes to their quaint mountain town.

Sounded legit. Except that small towns were often resistant to change. Progress scared them.

She stiffened her spine. Not her problem. She had a job to do, and an easy one at that. Her neighbor was right. The only attorney the townspeople could afford practiced out of his two-room cabin somewhere deep in the woods and had barely passed the bar on his fifth try. A little tidbit of information her firm had dug up and added to the file.

The locals would get over it. Move on. She was doing the very same thing in her own life. So could they.

But one thing niggled at her conscience. Buried deep in the client's notes was a legal document stating that the resort developers had also bought out Red River Community Bank. The same bank that held mortgages for most of the business owners in town, and those loans were about to be called in. The proprietors would be forced to pay up or sell, probably at a fraction of what the real estate was actually worth. Her expertise was in criminal law, not real-estate law, but she knew how big businesses operated, and they never looked out for the little guy. Some of these small business owners had leveraged their homes to buy a share of the building, and they stood to lose both.

A wave of guilt hit her.

Looking up at Wheeler Peak's soaring presence, its natural beauty disappeared for a moment and the snow-capped face seemed to frown at her. Loomed over her like a disapproving taskmaster.

Nope. Definitely not her problem. All she had to do was keep it professional, not get personally involved with this town or its residents. Easy. She could do it. Sure she could. She'd spend a few months up here, make sure this deal went through, and a partnership at Riggs, Castillo & Marone would be waiting for her back in Albuquerque. She'd feel like Caesar returning to Rome after a victory.

She swallowed.

Caesar died a horrible death, with no friends or loved ones watching his back.

She thumped her head against the steering wheel, sending her cap askew. *Okay, get your game face on. This isn't personal, it's business.*

Straightening her hat, she pulled the keys from the ignition and threw them into her purse. Careful not to move too quickly and send more shockwaves of pain over her tender skin, she slid out of the SUV and locked it up. With every step, her clothing rubbed over the fiery rash, and she gingerly picked her way across the street toward the door labeled "Dr. Blake Holloway, MD."

The first order of business was to get some meds for this hellacious rash and then get out of town and back to her cabin before someone figured out who she was and came after her with a dagger.

Chapter Three

Blake walked Ms. Nelson out of exam room A and escorted her toward the front desk, where the waiting room brimmed with female senior citizens. The seventy-seven-year-old and her club of widowed pinochle players made appointments in his office every week en masse, mostly because they were lonely without their husbands. Colorful quilts decorated the walls of his office, all handmade by their quilting group.

He handed Ms. Nelson's file to his thirtysomething receptionist, Nadine, who tossed it aside and scurried around the counter in hot-pink breast cancer awareness scrubs to run interference. She had his back. Thank God, because the pinochle posse could get a little too touchy-feely for his comfort. The whole pinching-his-butt-when-he'd-turned-to-retrieve-a-tongue-depressor incident had . . . well . . . nearly scarred him for life.

"Dr. Holloway," Ms. Nelson crooned as he pried her fingers from around his arm. "Are you sure it's not contagious?"

Since high cholesterol and arthritis weren't known to spread, he was pretty sure she just wanted attention. "I'm positive it's not contagious, Ms. Nelson. Take your usual medications and use your walker if you need it. You'll be fine." He communicated a nonverbal cry for help to Nadine.

She stepped up for the handoff, and Blake placed Ms. Nelson's hand on Nadine's arm.

"Do I need a prescription? Maybe I should make an appointment for tomorrow." Ms. Nelson batted her eyes and reached for him again, but Nadine went for the block and clasped the old woman's hand with an affectionate squeeze.

Nadine lifted a penciled-on eyebrow at Blake, the red pen behind her ear moving as she chewed a wad of gum. Heavy eyeliner stretched both eyes into catlike formation, her dyed jet-black hair making the thick makeup look even more severe. Blake didn't mind. If she kept him from getting pinched again, her semi-Goth look was fine by him.

"No new prescription, and you don't need to come back in tomorrow unless something new comes up." He slid a glance at Nadine, whose artfully drawn eyebrow rose even higher.

Something *always* came up.

"Nadine, why don't you help these young ladies to the door?" Blake said.

"I want a raise," she whispered over one shoulder as she turned Ms. Nelson toward the door. "Come on, you beauties, your chariot awaits." A murmur of approval rose from the silver-haired horde. "You first, missy." Nadine led Ms. Nelson to the door and handed her off to the Red River senior center's bus driver, who loaded them into a white passenger van.

Nadine waved from the front door until the van drove away, then she let it swing shut.

Blake chuckled. She pretended to be a hard-ass, but deep down, she was a softie just like him. That's why he'd hired her. When he traveled out to the Native American reservations to see patients or set up a free vaccination clinic in one of the impoverished villages in the area, she was the first to volunteer her time.

Kaylee, his newly graduated nurse who was so full of energy and enthusiasm he could barely keep up with her, emerged from the back office and handed him a file.

"Okay, Doc. A new patient's up next. Just moved here. Looks like a bad case of poison oak." She bounced on the balls of her feet. "Just like the vacationer we had yesterday. Poison oak always gets the newbies, right?" Her words hummed with energy. "By the way, I finished inventory on the meds cabinet, and we're running low on a few vaccines. I made a list." She glanced at her watch. "We're almost five and a half minutes behind, so can I help catch us up somehow? Am I doing something wrong?"

He placed a hand on her shoulder. "Take a deep breath, Kaylee. We've got lunch after this, so the world won't end if we're a few minutes behind schedule."

Her shoulders deflated.

Blake looked at the file and read the name. Angie Marone. Yeah, had to be a newbie to the area. In a town the size of Red River, he knew just about everybody, but this name was new. He walked to the exam room and opened the door a fraction.

"So, Doc, is there anything you want me to do over the lunch hour?" Kaylee followed him.

He turned back to her, the door cracked a bit. The paper on the exam table crinkled, the waiting patient moving around inside.

"I could clean the bathrooms. Or maybe restock the break room," Kaylee offered.

"Kaylee, why don't you take a real lunch break?" He gave her a fatherly look. "You know, walk across the street and have lunch at the Gold Miner's Café with a friend." Couldn't be too hard in this town to bump into someone she already knew. Really well. "Go find your boyfriend or gossip with a girlfriend over a tuna on rye." Jesus, he might even pick up the tab just to get her out of the office for an hour. Her initiative and drive made him feel about two decades older than he should.

"Are you sure? Because I can work through lunch."

He pointed the file toward the front office, his other hand still on the doorknob. The paper rustled from inside the room again. "Positive. Go. Now." He turned and pushed the door open.

⸻

Angelique sat up straight when the doorknob jiggled, and a crack appeared in the door. Yes! It was finally her turn. But the door only opened about an inch when it stopped, and muffled voices sounded from the hallway.

She bit at her nail, waiting for the doctor to come in.

Judging from the average age of the patients who had been in the waiting room, the doctor was probably ancient himself. A simple office with country quilts adorning the walls instead of modern décor gave the office an elderly feel. Warm. Inviting. Cozy. And old. Had to be old, because who else would practice year-round in a one-horse town like this? Maybe she should've driven into Taos, but it was just a rash. A darned irritating rash that lit her skin on fire and made her look like a leper, but still. How hard could it be to treat? Even an old-timer who was probably ready for retirement could handle an ailment like that.

Sitting on the papered treatment table in a hideous Pepto-Bismol-pink gown, she swung her crossed ankles and tried to keep her mind off the incessant itching.

She hated pink. Hated it. With a passion.

Old Dr. Holloway could write her a script for an ointment, and she could slip back to the cabin with the townspeople of Mayberry, USA, none the wiser.

More voices from the hall. The door creaked open another half inch. Sounded like the doctor giving orders to a nurse, but the voice wasn't old. It was young and masculine and . . . She strained forward to get a better look through the crack. The scratchy sound of Velcro prickled through the room as the fastening gave way at the back of her neck. The gown slipped forward and she grabbed at it, pinning it to her chest right above her nipples, just as the door swung fully open and a wide-eyed Mr. Tall, Dark, and Hot-some stared at her, his gaze sinking to her barely covered breasts.

Her lungs locked, and both arms covered her chest. Plenty of doctors had seen them, but *him*? No way. She forced herself to breathe, clutching the gown to her front.

Wearing a pair of khakis and a black mock-turtleneck, he had a stethoscope draped around his neck and a file in his hand. Confusion knitted the space between his magnificent blue eyes. Glancing down at the fake name on the file, he looked back at her. His surprise was gone, and a blistering glare scorched her already searing skin.

She suppressed a groan. So much for Al's Plumbing and Septic Removal.

"You." She made it sound like an accusation. Drawing first blood was always a good tactic in the courtroom. Throw the first punch, knock them off balance. Only it was hard to keep the upper hand when she was the one clutching an ugly medical gown to a splotchy reconstructed chest with no bra underneath. She pulled the gown over her shoulders, the movement setting off a firestorm of sensations over most of her body, none of them pleasant.

At her grimace, a wry smile turned the corners of his mouth

up a fraction, and her gaze hovered there, taking in his chiseled jaw, planed cheekbones, and incredible good looks for a second . . . or two . . . or five . . .

"Yes, me." The not-so-old Dr. Blake Holloway entered, closed the door behind him, and leaned against the cabinets that lined one wall. Tossing the file on the counter, he crossed one ankle across the other and folded both arms over his broad chest. "Hello, *Ms. Marone*. Oh, wait. That's not actually you, is it?"

"Look, I just need to get some medicine for this rash——"

"Poison oak," he corrected authoritatively, which rankled all the more. "Told you it was all over the place."

She glared at him, which caused his smile to broaden until straight white teeth glinted at her. Really? She'd half expected an empty space there, with the country bumpkin routine he'd poured on so thick while returning her dog . . . and her panties. She looked away, even more heat rising up her neck. Was it hot in here?

"Whatever," she finally managed, and scratched at her cheek. "Can you give me something, *Doctor*?"

"Sure, *Angie*. Let's have a look first, though." He pushed off the counter.

She eyed him suspiciously. His fitted shirt hinted at sculpted biceps and shoulders, and a steady pulse beat at the base of his corded neck. When he turned to the sink to wash his hands, she stole a look at his backside. Khakis slung low on narrow hips, they molded to muscular thighs and a really, really nice ass.

He grabbed a paper towel to wipe his hands and turned abruptly, leaving her staring at his crotch.

She inhaled, slow and labored with a dash of dread.

Please, please, *please*. He *didn't* just catch her staring at his ass and now his . . . Slowly, her gaze slid up his torso, over the gradient slopes of well-defined pecs with a perfectly formed hollow in between and finally to his squared jaw and sapphire eyes. One brow slightly raised, the corner of his mouth quirked upward into an almost-smile.

Hell's bells.

Retrieving two purple latex gloves from a dispenser, he pulled them on with a snap. When he advanced on her, she stiffened.

"Okay, enough. Disagreements aside, I'm a doctor. Believe it or not, I'm a fairly good one. Only two of my patients have died this week."

Her head swiveled toward him, but a mischievous twinkle danced in his baby-blues, and she almost relaxed. Almost.

"Very funny, Dr. Kevorkian."

"I double as a comedian at Cotton Eyed Joe's across the street." Gentle fingers grasped her chin and tilted her head to the side. "You should catch my act before the place is torn down."

He examined her neck and cheek, his breath whispering across her skin.

She shivered.

"Are you serious this time?" she asked, trying to steady her breathing. Having Mr. . . . correction . . . *Dr.* Tall, Dark, and Hot-some invade her personal body space, even with good reason, was as unnerving as getting a pap smear. She kept a splayed hand over her chest.

"About Cotton Eyed Joe's getting torn down? Absolutely. You know that as well as anyone. What you don't know is that Cotton Eyed Joe's is the social core of this town. If you take it away, you'll break the local spirit. The heart of the people who live here."

"No, I mean . . ." Her teeth ground together because she hadn't been talking about Cotton Eye . . . whatever. And he darned well knew it.

He tugged at the hand that was anchored to her chest, but she didn't allow him to move it. He sighed in a way that said she was trying his patience.

Good.

"I need to see your hands and forearms." His voice was the model of professionalism.

Hesitating, she held her hands out for him to examine. Even through latex gloves, his touch was consoling. Nurturing. He moved to her feet and lifted them. Again, his gentle touch soothed her. Made her trust him, like everything would be okay no matter the problem. Pulling out the table extension so her legs rested straight in front of her, he leaned in and examined her calf, running caring yet disciplined fingers down to her ankle where the rash stopped.

Her skin pebbled under his touch. When he turned her leg out and examined the inside of her knee, an electrical current jolted up her leg, down the other, and pooled between her thighs, a part of her anatomy she liked to call the Land of the Dead.

Okay, snap out of it, dummy. That part of her life—the part that made her tingle in unmentionable places and required taking her shirt and bra off in front of a member of the opposite sex—was over. Hence, the nicknaming of her neglected girly parts.

She let out an exasperated breath, trying to ignore both his bleeding-heart sentiment and the warm current flowing through her body that was trying to seek out the Land of the Dead and coax it from the grave. "Do you really do a comedy routine?"

"Nope." He straightened, peeling off his gloves with the same flare he'd put them on and tossing them into a red bin. "Your creepy puppet slippers protected your feet, so at least you can wear shoes."

"Liar."

He gave her an offended scoff. "Am not. Your slippers were definitely creepy."

Real mature. "What are you, five? I mean you lied about being a comedian *and* a doctor." Whatever. She wasn't going to sit here and argue with him. "Are we done here?"

"I never lied about being a doctor. You didn't care to ask." He walked to the counter and grabbed a prescription pad and pen. "Is that how you justify what you do, by not getting personal? Keeping your distance?" He scribbled something down and tore the small piece of paper loose with a rip.

She slid off the table, making sure the gown didn't open in the back. "For your information, I'm not tearing anything down."

"You're helping them do it." He handed her the prescription between two fingers, just like he'd done her panties. When she hesitated, satisfaction flared in his eyes.

"I have a job to do, just like you." She snatched the script away. Same way she had the panties.

"Except that I save lives and you destroy them. Get dressed and I'll meet you at the front desk, *Ms. Marone*."

She flinched at the name, and he studied her for a moment before disappearing out the door.

Blake stood at the front desk and scribbled notes into *Ms. Marone's* file. Leaning against the counter, he tried to concentrate on his work instead of the woman who was still in his exam room getting dressed.

The waiting room was empty, and Nadine's nails clicked against the keyboard as Blake scratched words onto the examination form.

What just happened? He'd never spoken to anyone like that, especially not a patient. Not even during his residency when a female patient twice his age had thrown herself at him. No one had ever evoked such raw attitude from him. No one except *Angie Marone*.

He raked a hand over his face.

"Tough patient?" Nadine asked.

"No, pretty ordinary." Except that Angelique Barbetta, aka Angie Marone—whoever that was—was anything but ordinary.

The patient in question emerged from the hallway and approached the front desk, each step and movement calculated and guarded. It *was* a wicked case of poison oak. Her legs had been exposed beneath the hem of that Asian robe thing she'd been wearing, so the outbreak there was understandable. Her chest, neck, and cheeks had probably contracted it from the dog after she'd scooped it up and let it rub all over her.

Obviously, it had hurt too much to wear a bra, and he averted his eyes from the taut nipples that strained against her hoodie and her formfitting yoga pants that left nothing to the imagination. Actually, his imagination was springing to life, and he was having a hard time beating it back down. Sort of like a game of Whac-A-Mole at an arcade.

She limp-walked up to the counter, and a ping of compassion swelled inside him. Damn that Hippocratic oath. He jotted down the last of his notes and handed the chart to Nadine.

"What do I owe?" Angelique asked Nadine without so much as a glance in his direction.

"Let me figure up those charges." Nadine's black-polished nails clicked against the keyboard some more.

"This one's on the house." He leveled a stony look at Angelique.

She shook her head and winced, pulling at the neckline of her hoodie. "Thanks, but I'll pay."

"No," he deadpanned and headed for the door. "I'm off to lunch, Nadine." He threw a detached look over his shoulder at Angelique. "Just use the lotion three times a day, and stay away from poison oak."

He pushed through the front door of his office into the bright noonday sun with Angelique on his heels. Just like a Rottweiler. Probably why she was a good attorney. Had to be good if she was hired by the conglomerate real estate developer that was trying to buy out all of downtown Red River.

"Wait!" She limped onto the sidewalk after him, and he turned. "How long will this last?"

"You'll see a noticeable decrease within a few days." He shrugged. "Should be totally gone within two weeks at the most."

An old Ford truck tooled by and beeped. He turned to wave at one of his patients.

"But I don't even know what poison oak looks like. How do I know how to stay away from it?" She seemed desperate. City girl. Figured.

Scrubbing a hand over his face again, he sighed. Heavily. He was going to regret his next words. He already knew it. "Since I live next door, I'll come over later and chop it down. At least I can cut down the vines right around your cabin."

A middle-aged couple exited the pastry shop a few doors down and walked past holding hands. They pushed canvas sun hats onto their heads. She waited for them to pass before responding to his offer.

"No thank you. I can do it myself."

Stubborn, pushy woman. He pinched the bridge of his nose where a dull throb started behind one eye. "Wearing what, exactly? You're obviously extremely allergic to the stuff. Unless you have a hazmat suit handy, you'll be eaten up head to toe." His stare fell to her full nipples, clearly visible through her microfiber hoodie. Dropping both hands to rest on his hips, he looked down the street. A motorcycle club motored past, turning onto the street beside Cotton Eyed Joe's.

Avoiding her stare, he studied the black-leather-clad bikers. They parked along the side street and walked up the wood stairs to Joe's with bow-legged struts.

Hell. Had he really just asked her what she'd be wearing? *And* said the words "eaten up head to toe"? A distinct image of black strings popped into his throbbing brain.

Definitely regretting the offer.

"I'll be done here by four thirty. Expect me around five fifteen. You don't even have to come out of your cabin."

Before she could protest, Cooper Wells emerged from his chiropractic office next door.

Angelique recoiled, her countenance shrinking. She wrapped both arms around herself.

He held the door for his very pregnant wife, Ella, and she waddled out after him and shielded her eyes against the bright sun.

"Hey, man." Coop notched his chin up at Blake. Coop popped a trendy pair of sunglasses onto his nose and shook a sandy tousle of loose curls off his forehead.

Ella was Red River's very own celebrity. A strawberry-blonde, rock-star erotic romance writer who had turned Coop's life upside down last year. Coop hadn't been the same since. Thank God, because that boy had needed some straightening out.

Ella, looking ready to pop, leaned against a metal post.

Coop ran to her side.

"Don't touch me," she warned through clenched teeth. "That's what caused this to begin with." She waved to a woman across the street who stood in the door of a souvenir shop. The woman waved back.

Coop backed off like she was a rabid animal ready to bite, and Blake got a little scared. Growing up an only child, he wanted what Coop and Ella had—a family to come home to at night. He'd even been a little jealous last year when they tied the knot, and four months later, she called asking for a referral for an ob-gyn in Taos. By the look on Ella's face, now he wasn't so sure he envied Coop.

Coop glanced up and did a double take. "Angelique?"

She turned around, a thin smile on her lips. Instead of the granite jawline and determined black eyes, her expression was sad. Mournful. Her hand went to her abdomen for a moment, then dropped to her side.

"Hey, Coop. How are you?" A delicate tremor shook Angelique's voice.

Huh.

Coop ran over and tried to hug her, but she held up a palm, warning him off. "Sorry." She pointed to her face. "Poison oak. It hurts to hug."

"Did you drive in from Albuquerque for the weekend? If I remember correctly, you were buying a vacation place up here the last time I spoke to you," Coop said.

She squirmed, avoiding Blake's inquisitive stare. "My plans changed. I'm renting a place out in the Mountain Shadows subdivision."

I'll be darned. Ms. Hard-Ass didn't seem to want anyone to know the truth. Probably wise. The residents of Red River stuck together, and if they found out what she was really doing here, they might come after her with pitchforks.

"Babe," Coop said to his wife, the clear skies and bright sun making Ella squint when she looked up. "This is Angelique Barbetta." He walked to Ella and placed his sunglasses on her. She pushed them up the bridge of her nose.

"Nice to meet you in person." Ella tried to straighten, but sagged back against the pillar. "Thanks for helping Coop out last year."

An off-road Jeep meandered by and honked. Both Blake and Coop waved back.

Angelique nodded. "Sure thing. I love my job, especially when my clients are innocent."

Now that was rich. What about when her clients were hurting innocent, hardworking folks? Blake crossed both arms and leaned against a light pole. Angelique pretended not to notice the weight of her own comment and his exaggerated reaction to it, but oh yeah, she'd noticed. Deep scarlet crept into her cheeks, and she swallowed.

He couldn't stand it any longer. He *had* to say something, because this might just be interesting. "So you two know each other?"

"You bet," Coop said with a boyish smile. He stroked the space between his wife's shoulder blades, and she gave a tiny whimper of approval. "We went to high school together."

Blake slid a glance at Angelique, who looked guilty. Well, at least she did have a conscience, albeit a guilty one. "Really?" Definitely interesting.

"Weren't you going to lunch, Dr. Holloway?" Angelique asked with a sharp tone in her voice and a plastic smile on her lips.

No way was he leaving now. He wouldn't miss this for all the attorneys at the bottom of the sea. "Nope, I'm good. I bet you two know some really good stories about each other."

Coop laughed, then hid it behind a cough when Ella threw fiery darts at him with her eyes. It was no secret that Coop had been a player before he met Ella. "Angelique was good enough to take my case last year, even though she lost a bet to me in eleventh grade, and I made her go out with a geeky member of the chess team." He shrugged. "Thanks for not holding a grudge, Ang."

"No problem." Angelique smiled a genuine, hearty smile that spread across her blotched face.

A smile that stole Blake's breath, knocked it right out of his lungs, because it was the first time she'd done it for real in his presence. The smile lit her pretty face, and it matched the rest of her soft, curvy body. Warm, lush.

Fascinating.

"I got you back when I kicked your tail on the volleyball court, remember?" Angelique said, the joy in her voice threading through each word.

And for a fleeting moment, Blake glimpsed the real Angelique Barbetta. The one hiding under steel armor.

This time Coop really did laugh. "I'd forgotten. The girls' volleyball team challenged the boys' varsity baseball team to a match during assembly. You wiped the floor with us poor schmucks."

Ella straightened and put both hands to her lower back. Applying pressure sent a wave of relief across her face. "How long will you be in town? If you're that good, Angelique, then we need you. I can't play right now, and our team is dropping in the city league rankings." She shot another testy glare at Coop.

"Not my fault." Coop shook his head.

"You and your brother are getting your butts kicked every match." Ella crossed her arms, resting them on her perfectly round stomach.

"I noticed," Coop said. "We'd be winning if you could still play."

"Uh, *pregeeeers.*" She pointed to her stomach.

"That kind of *is* my fault." He put both hands on his wife's basketball-shaped midsection and rubbed affectionately.

Blake could swear Angelique's breath swooshed out. He studied her. No. No way. He had to be mistaken. Not the maternal type.

"So what do you say, Ang?" Coop asked. "You up for some volleyball?"

"Well, I'll be in town for a while, but—"

Ella clasped her hands together, and her tone turned competitive. "Angelique, you have to. We can't lose another game."

"Well, I . . ." Angelique bit her lip. "Sure. I suppose."

Ella and Coop whooped.

Blake laughed. It would be interesting to see her on the court. Maybe she'd let her armor slip again and the real Angelique would come out to play. He pushed off the light pole. "Better take care of that poison oak rash by Friday night, because that's when you and Coop play my team."

Before her scalding glare could melt him like hot wax over an open fire, he turned, said good-bye to the Wells family, and jogged across the street.

Chapter Four

The pantry door nearly rattled off its hinges when Angelique slammed it shut. She set Sarge's bowl and dog food on the counter and closed her eyes, still simmering over *Dr.* Holloway's arrogance. Honestly, she was more irritated with herself for sticking around to chat it up with Coop and his wife like she was one of the townsfolk. She doubted they would be so friendly if they knew her real purpose in Red River. Now she was committed to a community volleyball league?

Sarge cocked his head to one side and whined, wanting his dinner. Getting involved with the local folks was a bad, bad idea. Bad.

She fed Sarge, walked him, and showered. After applying the lotion she'd picked up at the pharmacy with a cotton ball, she pulled on a soft pair of black leggings and a steel-gray cashmere sweater, then settled in at the oak kitchen table to pore over the Red River Resort Development file, as it was labeled on a color-coded tab across the top.

Running a thumb across the tab, she wondered if the Cheerleader had typed it. Helpful as always. So helpful, in fact, Angelique hadn't seen the deceit behind the Cheerleader's perky smile, her strokes of admiration, her willingness to do personal errands for Angelique and Gabriel, her enthusiastic volunteering to work overtime to help Gabriel when Angelique had to take so much time off from the firm.

By the time she'd studied every document in the file, three hours had passed. She took off her reading glasses and rubbed both eyes. The owners of the resort development firm had bought the local bank as a separate investment. Red River Community Bank didn't fall under the umbrella of the development company, so it was perfectly legal. They'd done their homework, hiring consulting firms to conduct studies and provide irrefutable reports that would sway any judge in their favor. This resort project was good for the community.

On paper.

There was just one tiny fly in the resort's progressive ointment. One little loophole that could bring the entire project to a halt unless the opposition's incompetent attorney overlooked it, which he obviously had.

The thing that pricked at her conscience the most was watching her old friend, Cooper Wells, and his wife walk away hand in hand and stop to hug the pastry shop owner who'd been cleaning his front window. While she'd sat in the waiting room, the fiftyish seamstress from three doors down popped in with a homemade cake for Nadine's birthday, and they chatted about their kids' dance recitals and little league teams. She'd listened to a group of silver-haired widows sing Doc Holloway's praises and pay homage to his volunteer work all around northern New Mexico. Then she'd watched the very same Dr. Tall, Dark, and Hot-some hustle across the street, only to stop and hold the door for a group of tourists who all wore Texas

Longhorns shirts as they exited a quaint little souvenir shop. Jeez, he'd practically done every good deed except save a puppy.

Hell's bells.

She slammed the file shut. Actually, he *had* saved a puppy. Hers. She gave Sarge, who was curled at her feet, a disgusted look. "This is all your fault. You realize that, right?" Sergeant Schnitzel took a contended deep breath without opening his eyes.

She pushed the chair back, careful not to wake her four-legged baby, and went to the kitchen. Her bare feet shuffled against the cool tile floor, and she uncorked a bottle of pinot noir from a local winery. Digging around in the cupboard, she found a wine glass and filled it.

The rich bouquet soothed her weariness, and she breathed it in before taking the first sip. A robust flavor drenched her taste buds and warmed her insides as it slid down her throat.

The firm had rented a nice cabin for her. Decorated in a rustic motif, it was warm, inviting, and quite charming. Luxurious cocoa leather furniture with brass studs adorning the edges filled the den. A vaulted ceiling soared overhead with strategic windows inset for natural lighting to filter in. An artistic log staircase hugged the right side of the den and ascended to a large master suite in the loft. Not cold and modern like the décor Gabriel had insisted on for the new house they were building before his indiscretion.

Another sip and the tension between her shoulder blades eased a bit.

She should probably make an appointment with Coop for that, but she'd already committed to more personal contact with the locals than was prudent. Maybe she could find a way to get out of the volleyball match. She sighed, grabbed her reading glasses and file, and wandered onto the back porch.

Easing into one of the Adirondack chairs, she pulled her legs up until they were crisscrossed and tossed the file onto a small side table that stood between the two chairs. With her glasses perched atop her head, she savored the hearty wine. The sun sank behind the jagged mountain peaks, hues of purple, pink, and orange jettisoned across the sky, and the chilly autumn air nipped at her toes.

It was beautiful up here. Peaceful and soothing to the soul. So much so that she wasn't feeling very eager to disrupt the tranquility of Red River. A good legal fight usually got her juices flowing, the smell of victory bolstering her professional ego. The little town of Red River was outgunned. A fact that would typically have her zeroing in for the kill. Short. Sweet. Easy. No need to prolong the agony of her adversary.

Not this time. This case was her first since returning to work after all the surgeries and recuperation. Maybe the big C had taken away her zeal to go the distance against any opponent. Stolen her competitive edge or soured the taste of adding another notch to her belt of wins. Sucked everything but actual life out of her. Even though she'd never admit it to another living soul, she hadn't been the same since her diagnosis.

Pulling on her wine again, she sighed. *Cancer.* She hated that word. It had cost her so much. Just about everything she thought was important. Was it possible that it had given her back some humanity? Allowed her to see past the thrill of the attack, the gratification of winning, and focus on the living, breathing people affected by her legal expertise?

She'd never gotten personally involved with a client. Didn't care if they were innocent, guilty, or somewhere in between, because it didn't matter. Determining innocence or guilt, fairness or injustice, wasn't her job. Representing her clients, winning cases, that's what she got paid to do. And she did it well, because losing wasn't built into her DNA.

But when she thought of Red River's kind seamstress who wore a permed bob twenty years out of date, and the rotund pastry shop owner who had hollered a loud hello to pedestrians with a distinct German accent, and Cooper Wells, DC—even if he *had* made her go out with Simon the chess team captain in eleventh grade—and . . . and . . . Gah! And Dr. Tall, Dark, and Hot-some, who made the local elderly women feel like they were beauty pageant contestants, well, it just didn't feel like a victory at all. It felt like shit.

She polished off most of the wine and sulked at the powdered mountain peaks.

A hacking sound broke the spell, and her head swiveled toward it just as Blake rounded the side of the house, swinging a machete with his gloved hands. He stopped and took her in.

"Hi," she finally said, curling the wine glass against her chest.

His chin hitched up a fraction. "Hi."

The wine fogging her senses, she drank in his masculinity. A pair of faded Levi's with a frayed hole in one knee fit him to perfection. He was earthy and powerful in a red flannel shirt, unbuttoned with a white T-shirt underneath, and suede-leather hiking boots. So the opposite of Gabriel's polished appearance, which usually entailed wearing Armani on at least one part of his body at all times.

Blake just stared right back at her, and she wanted to know what he was thinking. About her. Wait. No, no. She probably didn't want to know, because they probably weren't nice thoughts.

"All the poison oak out front is gone. I bagged it and put it in the trash at my place. There's just a little left back here."

"Oh." She blinked. "I didn't hear you out front. I was working on the case."

His expression dimmed a shade.

Hell's bells. Why'd she have to bring it up? She glanced down at her glass. The wine. Definitely the wine.

"How's the medication working, Ms. Barbetta?"

Right. Formality. Got it.

"It's easing the discomfort. Thanks." Fidgeting with her glass, she downed the rest. "Um, would you like a glass of wine? It's the least I can do."

"I haven't eaten yet, so I better not drink on an empty stomach." He gave the machete an absentminded swing, grazing the grass with its tip.

"Okay, well." Were her words slurring? "I haven't eaten either." Probably why her words were slurring. "I was just about to throw together some shrimp linguini." She was? Yes, of course she was. She'd bought all the groceries she'd need for at least two weeks, she just hadn't actually planned out when to cook it all. "It won't take long, and I'm not a bad cook. Not as good as my Italian mom or grandmother, mind you, but I know my way around a kitchen." She bit her lip, the only way she could stop the incessant rambling. And jeez, it hurt. "Um, would you like to join me?" Seriously? Had she just invited a man who disliked her to the bone inside for dinner? A man she was going to have to squash like a bug in court.

Oy vey.

Something flickered across his face, then disappeared.

"You know what, it's okay." She stood and raised one palm toward him. "Bad idea. Sorry—"

"Yes." He stood still as a marble statue, the faint rise and fall of his solid chest his only movement. Except his ridiculously blue eyes. Those babies skimmed down her legs before returning to meet her gaze.

"Um, what?"

"Yes, I accept your dinner invitation. Unless you're already changing your mind." One corner of his mouth turned up into that same sexy almost-smile that'd made her quiver in unmentionable places while sitting on his exam table. "Or unless you've already torn down the kitchen to make room for a hotel."

She narrowed her eyes at him.

A full smile spread across his face, and her knees weakened a little.

"Just kidding. Actually, I'm starving, and I don't do much cooking myself. A home-cooked meal would be nice for a change." He looked around the backyard. "I have a little more work out here, though."

"Okay, well." She was already kicking herself. That freaking delicious pinot noir. "I'll get started on dinner while you finish up." Turning to go inside, she stopped and looked back at him. "It's shrimp, you know. Are you sure you don't mind having bottom dwellers for dinner?"

Something new flared in his eyes. Like a satisfied hunter who watched his unsuspecting game walk into a baited trap.

"I'd love to taste bottom dweller for dinner."

Her breath hitched, and a prickle raced across her skin.

"We can go back to being enemies tomorrow," he said. "I promise."

Forty-five minutes later, a delicious aroma caressed Blake's nose and made his mouth water. He discarded his work gloves and machete on the chair next to the back door. Beside the chair, a thick file folder lay on the table with neatly typed lettering across the tab. He leaned over to read the words. Red River Resort Development.

Huh.

With the sunlight almost gone, he peered through the window. Settings for two trimmed the table to the left, while his hostess stirred the sweet-smelling concoction over the kitchen stove to the right. He reached for the folder, then hesitated.

Damn his conscience. Why'd he always have to be the nice guy? Didn't nice guys finish last? He'd likely be practicing out of an RV parked down by the river when she was done here, and he felt guilty about breaching a tiny little line of ethics that was right in front of him practically begging to be breached.

He grabbed the file and knocked.

"Come in." Angelique's voice lilted through the door.

He turned the knob and entered. Breathed in the hearty scent of sautéed something and almost melted. Whoever said the way to a man's heart was through his stomach was smart. Definitely a woman. A very savvy woman. He looked around the kitchen at the various dishes in progress. Probably an Italian woman.

Funny, he wouldn't have pegged her for the domestic type at all.

Sarge greeted him at the door with a wagging tail and innocent eyes. Blake laid the folder on the bar that separated the dining area from the kitchen. "You left this outside. It looked important." He bent to give the dog a scratch.

When her eyes locked on to the file, she blanched. She dropped what she was doing, scurried over to retrieve the file, and tossed it into a drawer, slamming it shut.

"Would you like a glass of wine?" She returned to the kitchen island, where she scooped salad onto small plates.

Her long, slender legs didn't seem to end, and a loose sweater slid off one shoulder, exposing bare skin. When he didn't answer, she stopped mid-scoop and lifted an eyebrow in his direction.

"Sure." He showed her both hands. "Do you mind if I wash up first?"

When she lifted a finger to point, it tremored, even though her expression was as cool as the evening breeze outside. "Around the corner." She pointed an index finger, salad tongs still in hand. "Down the hall, first door on the left."

He nodded and followed directions. Rolling his sleeves up to his elbows, he scrubbed like only a doctor would, then splashed some water on his face. After drying off with a hand towel, he returned to the kitchen, where she was setting their meals on the table. She waved him into a chair, noticeably not at the head of the table. She saved that position of power for herself.

Sad that every move obviously had to be calculated, strategic.

He eased into the designated chair and took a drink of wine. So did Angelique. Several small, nervous little sips, in fact.

She placed a napkin in her lap and twirled linguini onto a fork. "I hope you like Italian."

Her lips closed around the fork, and his throat turned to chalk dust. "I do. Very much." Then he gave himself a mental kick in the pants and said, "I like anything that's home-cooked. I don't get a lot of that."

The savory aroma made his stomach growl, unlike his usual meals scraped together at the Red River Market—the town's only grocery store. They required little more than punching the keypad on his microwave or smearing mustard across a slice of store-bought bread.

"Your mother didn't teach you to cook?" She forked up salad and sipped wine again. Fork, sip, fork, sip.

Hmm. Ms. Badass Attorney was nervous. Because of him. That could work to his advantage if this legal situation got ugly, which it was likely to do.

"My parents divorced when I was young. I grew up outside of Phoenix with my mom. She was a nurse and worked long shifts at the hospital. So no, there wasn't much cooking in my house."

When his mother did have spare time at home, it wasn't spent in the kitchen. Silent and smoldering in bitterness over her five miscarriages, she'd pushed his father away more with each lost child until he finally left. Once they divorced, she completely withdrew into herself. It had been like living with a stranger. A lonely only child, his youth had been quiet and isolated. He'd spent a few holidays and long weekends every year in Red River with his dad and cherished those visits because they were the only time he felt like he belonged to a real family. Those few weeks in Red River each year had been his refuge growing up.

Now the people of Red River were his family, along with his dad, stepmom, a few aunts and uncles, and a smattering of cousins. Probably the reason he wanted to get married and have a houseful of kids. He wanted a family of his own.

He forked up his own pasta and nearly moaned when the savory morsels touched his tongue. "Mm," he said with his mouth full. "This is really good."

At the compliment, the rigidity of her shoulders eased. "So how'd you end up in Red River?" She passed him a basket of warm bread and slid a saucer of shaved butter toward him. Very Martha Stewart.

"My dad grew up here. He moved back to Red River after he and my mom split." He took a drink of wine and buttered a piece of bread. "So I did my residency in Albuquerque and bought out his practice a few years ago when he retired."

She hesitated. "Your dad was a doctor?"

He nodded, suppressing another moan as he chewed another generous bite of shrimp linguini. Italian-flavored bottom dwellers weren't bad. He glanced at Angelique. Not bad at all. "Yep, he is a country doctor, too. He volunteers on most of the Native American reservations in the area. Gives him something meaningful to do in his retirement."

She stilled. Stared at her plate, picking at noodles and chewing on her bottom lip. "The tribes allow him to do that? My firm collaborated on some legal work for one of the tribes last year, and the leaders are pretty particular about letting in outsiders."

"My stepmom is half Navajo." He shrugged. "That helps."

"So acting like Florence Nightingale is a family tradition, then?"

He stopped mid-chew and locked his stare on to hers. He swallowed, then stabbed at his salad. "If helping people who are ill and too poor to travel long distances for medical care makes me a target for smart-ass remarks, then so be it. At least I can sleep at night."

"It was a joke, Doc." The chandelier light glinted off her big black eyes.

"Oh," he said back, because that was the most intelligent word he could think of with those onyx gems shimmering at him.

"But for the record, I sleep just fine." She swirled more noodles onto her fork.

In what? He almost asked out loud, because if the panties were any indication . . .

"There are two sides to every story, Dr. Holloway." A long, slender finger traced the edge of her wine glass. "Think of it this way. You're trained to give medical attention to anyone who needs it, regardless of who they are, what wrongs they may have committed against you or anyone else, right?"

Hell. He already knew where this was going. He nodded, feeling like he was on trial.

"So if a criminal came into your office, or needed your services in some way, you wouldn't turn them away?"

"Absolutely not. It's against the oath I took. I may not like it, but I'd do it anyway, because it's the job I swore to do."

Turning a palm up, she lifted her bare shoulder. "I live by the same set of rules, just a different profession."

"But after I treated the criminal, I'd call the police and turn him in."

She laughed, a wine-laden huskiness threading through the sound. "Touché. But you don't get to determine who deserves medical treatment and who doesn't. It's the same thing in our judicial system. Everyone is entitled to representation, just as they're also entitled to medical care."

"Still doesn't change the fact that the little guy usually loses because the system is stacked against him."

She looked away, fingered the stem of her glass, then regained her composure.

Obviously, he and the rest of the business owners were in trouble. Angelique Barbetta didn't seem to have a shred of mercy when it came to doing her job.

"So what am I supposed to do? Walk away from a job that's all I have left . . ." She paled, snapped her mouth shut, and pushed her glass away. Obviously the wine was talking for her, and it had just said too much. "I can't just leave a client who has legal rights hanging because a few people deem the case as unfair." She shook her head. "It's called progress, Doctor."

He swiped the napkin across his mouth and tossed it on the table. The chair scraped against the wood floor when he shoved it back. "It's called ruining the livelihoods of good, hardworking, salt-of-the-earth people."

Like him. He was one of the small-town folks who stood to lose everything, and then where would he be? He wouldn't have the capital to start over here. He'd have to move back to a big city where he could make some real money to pay off his medical school loans. A big city where doctors were robots and patients didn't have names, they had file numbers.

He stood, his chair clawing against the wood floor again. "Thanks for dinner."

She stood, too. "I'm not trying to upset you. This is just a friendly debate."

He scoffed. "Easy for you to say when it's not your life at stake."

"Tonight was supposed to be a truce, remember? Enemies tomorrow, friends tonight," she said.

He had no idea what possessed him to do what he did next. Her eyes widened as he closed the space between them.

His hand went to her neck, and she drew in a rocky breath but stood her ground. He'd expected nothing less from her. With the tip of an index finger, he traced down her creamy neck and across a strapless shoulder, her skin quivering under his touch.

"There's something you should know," he mumbled, staring into her dark eyes.

"Wh . . . what?" She trembled, and her voice shook.

So he affected her, the same way she affected him. Another sliver of intel he could file away for future use. Leaning in so his nose almost touched hers, he put a finger under her chin and tipped it up so her eyes met his.

"I'm not giving up without a fight." He brushed a thumb over her bottom lip.

A rush of desire hit him so hard his chest constricted. Before he caved in like a bamboo hut in a typhoon and caught her up in his arms, he pulled away and headed to the door. The last thing he remembered was the rubber soles of his boots squeaking across the floor, the back door slamming with a thud, and the regret of never being able to feel her body against his.

Chapter Five

By Friday afternoon, Angelique was ready to call Coop and Ella to beg off from the volleyball game, using her poison oak outbreak as an excuse. Unfortunately, before she made the call, they'd shown up on her doorstep to give her the team uniform and saw for themselves that the rash was nearly gone. So roughly three hours and twenty-two minutes later—not that Angelique was counting—she pulled on a pair of black athletic leggings along with the red team shirt that said "Red River Chiropractic" across the back, grabbed Ella's handwritten directions to the Red River Community Center, and drove into town.

This time of year Red River was cold but not brutal. The kind of weather that made a person long to bundle up inside a warm blanket and sip wine in front of a fire while soft jazz played in the background. Snuggling deeper into her purple fleece jacket, she got out of the car, thumbed the remote lock, and plunged both hands deep into the insulated pockets. The Lexus beeped, and the parking lights flashed behind her as she walked into the community center.

She stopped short and stared at the bleachers full of spectators. Families, couples, kids, even the local fire department filled the stands, chattering and laughing. Like a family.

A lump started to form in her throat. This was entertainment in a small town that didn't even have a movie theatre. Her hands still shoved into deep pockets, Angelique glanced over her shoulder, seriously contemplating a quick, inconspicuous exit before anyone noticed her. Before anyone could ask prying questions about why she was really in Red River.

A sharp, earsplitting whistle, the kind blown between two fingers, rang out, and Ella Wells waved both arms in the air like a person marshaling airplanes on a tarmac.

Great. So much for making a quick escape. She forced a smile and waved back. As Angelique approached Ella and Coop, most of the spectators stopped to look at her, a new face in this tight-knit community. She smiled at a few, and they smiled back. Friendly and neighborly.

"You ready?" Coop asked when she reached them.

"Heck yeah, she's ready," Ella answered. "And you guys are going to kick some butt out there." Her voice turned to a competitive growl, and Angelique liked her instantly. Angelique was the same fierce competitor on the court, on the high school debate team, in law school, in the courtroom, and in life. That trait had scared off some friends in high school and college and deterred more than a few guys she'd wanted to date. Losing wasn't in her makeup, and Ella seemed to be a kindred spirit.

Coop tried to introduce her to some of the townsfolk sitting around them, and several shouted a friendly hello, until Ella interrupted.

"She can meet everyone after the match, Cooper. Get ready to play."

When Coop said, "Yes, ma'am," and laid a sultry kiss on his pregnant wife, Angelique felt a pang of envy.

The ref blew a whistle.

"Let's huddle up," Coop said.

Angelique took off her jacket, and Ella snatched it from her. Ella started to chant their team initials—RRC. "RR*C*, RR*C*, RR*C*." Half the stands chimed in.

But then another mantra started from the other side of the bleachers. "Doc Hollo*way*, Doc Hollo*way*, Doc Hollo*way*." Angelique scanned Dr. Tall, Dark, and Hot-some's cheering section, mostly a gaggle of women of all ages. She rolled her eyes. Blake and his teammate emerged from the stands and took the court, Blake giving an encouraging slap on the back to his partner.

"We have to watch out for Doc Holloway. He's a good spiker, but he's playing with his cousin, Perry. Nice guy, but not exactly an all-American athlete, you know what I'm sayin'?"

Angelique peeked over Coop's shoulder at Blake's cousin. About the same age but much shorter than Blake, Perry was stocky—to put it politely—and he wore a boyish grin that said he probably was the nicest guy in the county. Another Robin Hood act of charity. No wonder Dr. Tall, Dark, and Hot-some was going under. He didn't play to win. A guy like Blake could've had any number of tall and agile teammates, but he'd obviously given preference to his short and stout cousin, which was kind of . . . nice.

What? No. *No, no, no.* It was foolish. A true competitor always played to win. Right? Angelique nodded at Coop. "Got it."

"Their strategy is mostly for Perry to set it to Blake, then Blake pounds it over. If we play smart, we can take them. Pretend we're back in high school and the smart-ass baseball team is on the other side of the net."

Angelique nodded. "I can do that." Piece of cake, because a smart-ass really was on the other side of the net.

They clapped and ran onto the court, squaring off against the other team.

Blake broke off his conversation with Perry mid-sentence to stare at Angelique. Not Coop. Just her. One side of his mouth slid up into that almost-smile. A playful lock of wavy chestnut hair drooped across his forehead. Wearing loose-fitting black nylon warm-ups and a fitted black compression shirt, he looked . . . well, hot-some. Tall and lean, his arms and shoulders all rolling hills of masculine flesh. His chest, defined with a swale in the center that beckoned to be touched. Kissed. Her tongue would fit nicely in that crevice . . .

Angelique nearly jumped out of her skin when the ref blew the whistle again and threw the ball to Blake.

The ref instructed them to shake hands, so all four players met at the net. Angelique shook hands with Perry and then turned to Blake, who wore a smile that could charm a block of ice. "Good to see you again, Ms. Barbetta." He shook her hand but didn't let go, as Perry and Coop returned to their places on the court.

She looked at their clasped hands, his engulfing hers. Strange that as his warmth blanketed her flesh, it also sent a shiver through her entire body.

"I wasn't sure you'd have the guts to show," said Blake. "Seeing as how you're here to disrupt the lives of most of these folks."

Her eyes rose to meet his. His expression remained pleasant, but his words cut her.

For the first time in a long time, a *real* grin so broad it almost made her cheeks hurt spread across her face, and she felt it to her bones. The joy of competition burned in the pit of her stomach, and adrenaline pumped through her veins. She dislodged her hand, set her jaw, put her hands on both knees, and stooped in an agile pose, ready to play. Hard.

"You'll wish I hadn't shown up once I'm done wiping the floor with you boys."

Blake's smile faded.

"I'm very competitive," Angelique explained.

"No kidding? I wouldn't have guessed that." He walked backward to the serving line, the ball lodged under one arm. Eyes never leaving her.

The ref blew the starting whistle. Blake bounced the ball twice, zeroed in on Angelique, and took a fast step to the line as he sent a perfect serve flying over the net.

Angelique bent into a nice dig and popped it up in the air to Coop. Coop got under it and set it high, offering the ball up on a platter. She went in for the kill. As she plowed it over the net, Blake and his counterpart went up for a block, but the ball whizzed over their heads, landing within the boundary lines. Coop and Angelique high-fived, as Ella screamed her approval from the stands.

Hands on knees, Angelique and Blake faced each other at the net.

"You're gonna lose," Blake taunted her.

"I'm sorry, are you talking to me or your imaginary friend?" Angelique gave him a thin smile, trying to ignore the broadness of his shoulders and how his corded neck rippled when he spoke.

"You don't like losing, do you, Ms. Barbetta?"

Losing sucks. "Doesn't bother me to lose once in a while."

"Don't you have someone to sue around here?" Blake glanced at the stands.

Ouch. That was a low blow, even if it was true. "Why don't you go cure something important, like your own bad case of diarrhea-of-the-mouth?"

"I would, but you'd probably sue me."

The ref threw the ball to Coop.

"You are so going down, Dr. Holloway."

Her words drew a naughty smile from Blake. "Is that an offer?"

She bit her lip at the images her poor choice of words evoked. Heat rose up her neck, exposed because of her upswept hair. Blake laughed at her. *At* her, dammit.

Coop waited for the whistle and then sent a nice serve flying right at Perry. Perry's hit came down a little too far from the net, making it impossible for Blake to spike it over. The ball caught on the top edge of the net and bounced back at Blake.

The ref declared a point for RRC, and Ella started another round of chanting in the bleachers while she yelled a demand for more of the same. Coop and Angelique obliged, scoring five more points before losing the serve to the other team.

The game went back and forth, the spectators chanting louder and Ella getting more obnoxious with every point.

Angelique had to laugh. "Coop, maybe you should tell your wife to calm down. She might work herself into premature labor."

Coop's expression turned a little fearful, and he raised both brows. "Yeah. You want to be the one to tell her that?"

Angelique looked at Ella for a second, her face as red as her hair from yelling while she rubbed her rounded belly. There weren't many things on earth as beautiful as a woman close to labor, ready to bring forth a new life. Not many things scarier either. Angelique gave her head an exaggerated shake. "Nope. I'm good."

Coop nodded. "That's what I thought." He clapped and returned his attention to the opponents on the other side of the net. "Let's play."

They did, and finally, with RRC one point shy of winning, Coop called a time-out.

Angelique wiped the sweat from her forehead with a sleeve and tossed her ponytail over one shoulder. Her breathing heavy, she put both hands on her hips and waited for Coop's instructions.

"We're almost there. All we have to do is win back the serve, and the game is ours," Coop said, the anticipation of victory flowing through his voice. "We just have to keep Blake from spiking it."

She glanced up at Dr. Tall, Dark, and Hot-some, who had the ball lodged under one arm and his other hand on his hip. Nice trim hips that angled up and out into wide shoulders. He smiled in her direction, confidence oozing from his stance. Overconfidence. From a man who had to have the help of a dog to get into her panties.

She nodded to Coop. "We have to keep hitting it to Perry, but they need to be hits that he can't return."

Coop smiled. "Exactly."

They broke huddle, and Angelique took her place against the net.

Blake stood behind the serving line and spun the ball on his fingers. He hesitated for a second, then jogged forward to meet her at the net. The crowd went silent, and Blake leaned in.

"By the way, I have something of yours," he half whispered and patted his pants pocket. "That dog of yours wandered over to my house early this morning." His smile turned wicked.

No. Way. How could Sarge have gotten ahold of another pair of panties?

Before Angelique could respond, Blake jogged back to the serving line. When the whistle blew, he popped a serve right over the net and straight at her. Her mind still reeling over the object in his pocket, she sent the ball flying out of bounds. A point for Dr. Tall, Dark, and Hot-some. She glared across the net in disbelief. He smiled back. The next few serves went about the same, until it was game point for Blake's team.

Ella let out a few bloodcurdling screams about making the other team eat the ball, and Coop huddled up with Angelique.

"You okay?" he asked.

"Yeah." Angelique nodded, brushing a sleeve across her forehead. Kicking at the floor with the tip of her shoe, she squeezed her eyes shut and drew a deep breath. "Sorry, I just haven't played in a while." And the way Dr. Tall, Dark, and Hot-some's gaze kept drinking her in like a tall glass of water didn't help her concentration.

"No worries." Coop squeezed her shoulder. "Let's mix it up a little. Just as he steps forward to serve, let's switch places. I'll set up the spike for you this time. They won't be expecting that."

Angelique smiled big again and felt it down to her toes, her competitive edge finding its way home. The thrill of victory coursed through her. "You got it." They clapped and did just what they'd planned. When Angelique went up for the spike, Blake and his teammate followed for the block. Angelique hammered the ball straight down over the net, and it slammed into Blake's nose.

Blood squirted out, and the good doctor fell back onto the court clutching his face.

An "ohhhh" rippled through the crowd of spectators, and Angelique stared in horrified silence as Coop and Perry ran forward to help Blake.

Oy vey.

Guilt welled in her, because she'd probably just broken his nose.

More people gathered around Blake. Angelique stepped toward him to offer an apology, but she couldn't get close enough because of the cluster of women trying to help. For a moment, Blake disappeared under the crush of protective females, but Coop insisted everyone back off so Blake could breathe, and the crowd thinned.

Ella walked up and stood with Angelique.

"I . . . I'm sorry. I didn't mean to hurt him." Angelique wrapped both arms around her midsection.

"Tough break, but he'll be okay." Ella gave her a pat on the back.

A tall, thirtyish woman joined them. She chuckled. "Yeah, poor baby. Life is rough for a guy like him."

Blake, gracious and kind, fended off the advances of all the ladies trying to help him.

"Angelique, this is Lorenda." Ella made the introductions.

One of Blake's female fans pulled off her jacket and placed it under his nose, and then she put her hand on his thigh. He politely pushed it away, and relief washed through Angelique. She turned her attention to Lorenda.

"Hi, Lorenda. We spoke over the phone last year. Your dad showed me a few cabins up here."

Lorenda issued a warning to her two elementary-aged stick-brandishing sons. "Sorry," Lorenda said, turning back to Angelique with an easy smile. "I do remember. Hope you're doing well now."

Ella's expression turned quizzical, but Angelique didn't offer up an explanation.

"Nice to meet you in person," Angelique said.

Coop offered Blake a hand and pulled him to his feet. Blake's ocean-blue eyes hovered on Angelique as Coop led him over to their group.

Angelique flinched at his wounded expression. She tried to stiffen her spine. All's fair in love and volleyball, right? Blake Holloway was nothing to her. Just a guy who lived next door. A guy she didn't even know very well and didn't want to get to know because it was a conflict of interest.

Okay, a ridiculously good-looking guy. A single doctor who just happened to be well acquainted with her provocative undies, but still.

"Maybe we should move the party somewhere else." Ella hitched a thumb toward Blake. "You know, before Doc Holloway's fan club starts throwing their panties at him to use as handkerchiefs."

The air rushed out of Angelique's lungs. When she glanced at Blake again, his eyes danced back at her. She bit her lip. Heat singed the tips of her ears like fire, and she shifted from one foot to the other and back again.

His hand went to the pocket he'd patted earlier, and he plunged it deep inside.

Eyes rounded, she sent him a silent plea. *Please, please, please don't*. Not here.

She fought a sigh of relief when he withdrew an empty hand.

"I'll take Blake across the street to the clinic for an ice pack, and then we'll meet you guys at Cotton Eyed Joe's," Coop said to Ella.

"Angelique, we always meet up after a match for drinks," Ella said. "You're coming, right?"

She shook her head. Vehemently. "No, I can't. I've got to—"

"She's coming," Blake interrupted. "I need a ride home, and she lives next door," he said, his tone a bit nasal from the swelling. He hooked a thumb in his pocket that housed her undies. "Besides, *Ang*," he said with emphasis, "we need to discuss that little scrap of a problem regarding your dog."

Blake's gaze found Angelique the moment he walked into Cotton Eyed Joe's, an ice pack pressed to his schnoz. She took a drink from a longneck bottle of beer, then tossed her head back and laughed at something Ella said. Her silky black hair was pulled up into a ponytail, wispy tendrils framed her face, which was flushed from physical activity. Her ebony eyes glistened with amusement that lit her expression. Happy and at ease, she chatted across the table with Blake's cousin, Perry.

When she looked up, the color drained from her face and the merriment in her eyes dimmed. Jesus, he'd never met anyone as competitive as her. She turned into a shark as soon as she stepped onto the court. It was in her stance, her posture, and the steely set of her jaw when she put her hands on her knees in front of the net and challenged him. No wonder she was so good at her job. She probably ate prosecutors alive in the courtroom. Then had the witnesses for dessert.

Yeah. He should tear down the rickety footbridge with his bare hands to put more distance between them. Tomorrow.

Warning bells should be going off in his head right about now because her killer instincts would likely ruin his business and steal his plans for the future.

Blake waved to Dylan McCoy, one of Joe's full time bartenders, and held up two fingers as he and Coop walked past the long bar. Dylan acknowledged him and set two frosty mugs on the tap, pulling the handles.

Blake should protect himself and everyone else in town by exposing Angelique's purpose here. Unfortunately, her purpose wasn't what he wanted to reveal. The minute she'd walked into the community center gymnasium wearing those skintight athletic clothes, he'd wanted to peel every stitch of formfitting material off her tall, curvy body and feel her exposed skin flush against his.

The old wood floor creaked underfoot as he and Coop made their way to the large group in the back of the room. Soft country music lilted through the cavernous space, and peanut shells crunched under each step. Angelique stole twitchy glances at him as he walked toward the table, and his eyes never left her. Not once.

Train wreck waiting to happen. Don't even sit by her, idiot. Flashing red and blue lights whirled inside his head. *She's a complication you don't need in your life*. Here in Red River he had all the things he'd lacked during his lonely youth and the years of residency that consumed him twenty-four-seven—an entire town he could call on any time of the day or night, an extended family, a practice where he knew his patients by name. Life was good. He *liked* his life.

He was also fucking bored. And a little complication named Angelique Barbetta had him using the warning bells and flashing lights for target practice.

An insecure man would probably not just walk but run from a woman like Angelique. A smart man, too. Blake smirked and walked up to the table. *He* should run from her, but he wasn't insecure, and right now, he wasn't acting too smart.

Coop claimed a seat next to his wife, and Blake eased into the chair next to Angelique.

Mistake. Big mistake.

A raw satisfaction surged through him when deep scarlet replaced the white blanch in her cheeks. Uh-huh. General Patton wasn't as indifferent as she'd like him to think.

"Hey, cuz," said Perry from across the table. "Tough game tonight. We'll get these guys next time." Perry motioned his beer bottle toward Angelique and Coop and took a swig of beer.

Angelique stared at her beer bottle, examining the label like it was an important legal document.

"Mmm. Can't wait." His nose throbbed as he adjusted the ice pack. A few more minutes, and maybe it would go completely numb.

Angelique slid a tentative glance his way. She looked up at him from under long black lashes, and a miniscule quiver moved across her chin.

"Sorry." Her eyes darted to his swollen nose for a split second. "Is it broken?"

"Just bruised." Blake shook his head and winced.

Her hand flew to her mouth. "I really am sorry. Can I do something to help?"

He gave her an assessing look. "I'm sure I can think of something." She looked away, and the blush on her cheeks deepened. He shifted the ice pack to the other side. "Are you that vicious in the courtroom?"

Her lips thinned. "Competitive," she corrected. "Yes, I am."

Miranda, Cotton Eyed Joe's manager, delivered frosty mugs to Blake and Coop and set an array of appetizers around the table. "Hey, Doc," Miranda said. "What happened?"

"I had a run-in with an overzealous volleyball." He shot a glance at Angelique, who meticulously traced the beer label on her bottle. "It won." He clinked mugs with Perry and chugged a third of the glass. Maybe it'd help the pain.

Miranda shook her head, her black curly hair swishing behind her. "Some people consider the strangest things fun."

Miranda took a handful of pink breast cancer ribbons out of her apron. "It's October. Cotton Eyed Joe's is selling pink ribbons for five dollars. All proceeds go to finding a cure for breast cancer." Several people around the table took out their wallets and handed five dollars over to Miranda. She passed out the ribbons.

Angelique handed her a twenty. "You can keep the ribbons."

Blake studied her. Her posture had gone rigid, and she twisted the bottle around in her hand.

"You sure?" Miranda asked while everyone pinned the ribbons to jackets or hats.

"Positive." Angelique's expression turned to stone. "I don't need to wear a ribbon to support breast cancer victims."

The table hushed for a second.

"Suit yourself." Miranda put the ribbons back into her apron. "Let me know if you guys need anything."

Angelique took a long swallow of beer and set the bottle down a little too hard. The silverware clinked next to the bottle. When she let go of the beer, a slight tremor echoed through her hand.

Blake studied her profile. She was young, probably too young for breast cancer. But women were getting it earlier and earlier, and she'd had health issues that she wasn't willing to talk about. Any kind of cancer was a bitch, but a young woman having to go through breast cancer was just cruel. He'd seen some of his female patients go through it, and it messed with a woman's head.

"I really need to get home." She fumbled around on the back of the chair, trying to retrieve her purse. After digging another twenty out of her wallet, she tossed it on the table. "It was nice meeting you all." She glanced at Blake but refused to hold his gaze. "Do you still need a ride, Dr. Holloway?"

"Yeah, if you don't mind." He really didn't care if she minded. He chugged a little more beer and got up. Instead of tearing down that bridge and keeping his distance, he needed to spend a little more time with her. Maybe then he could figure out how to chip away the armor she hid behind and find the real Angelique Barbetta.

Chapter Six

The ride to Blake's cabin was thick with silence, both of them focusing on the dark, winding road ahead. Because really, what could she say? She'd pummeled the guy's face with a volleyball and then acted like a compassionless witch when the waitress tried to give her a pink ribbon. Refusing it was a knee-jerk reaction. She hadn't been able to wear a pink ribbon since her diagnosis. It branded her a victim, cursed like an outcast among people her age. Especially happily married people with a baby on the way, like Ella and Coop. She might as well wear a scarlet letter.

But her harsh reaction had startled a few people, and she didn't miss the look of surprise on Blake's face.

Hell's bells.

Approaching Blake's cabin, she slowed and flipped the blinker up. The ticktock filled the deafening silence of the car as she turned into his driveway.

"You can pull around the back." He pointed to the left of the midsize two-story cabin where the gravel drive snaked around to the rear of the house. "I never use the front door."

She followed the meandering gravel path and pulled up next to his red Chevy Silverado truck. She tugged the gearshift into reverse and gripped the steering wheel, the dash lights casting a glow on them both just enough. "Look, I'm sorry about your nose, but—"

"And my shirt." He pointed to the bloody stain that covered his logo on the front. "It's Under Armor. Custom printed for my team. Very expensive." He took the ice pack from his nose with slow and deliberate movements.

She tapped a fingernail against the steering wheel. "Well, you played dirty by mentioning my panties." And he had. It'd rattled her, and then it had pissed her off. But it was a pretty savvy tactic, she had to admit. She would've used it if she'd been in his shoes.

"Anything to win, right?" His gaze wandered over her face.

"Like I said, I'm sorry. Really." She bit her lip for a beat. "I'll even have the shirt cleaned for you. Or better yet, I'll buy you new team shirts."

"I don't want your money, Angelique." Blake faced her, the silhouette of his wavy hair and athletic build illuminated just enough for her to appreciate. "Money isn't everything."

But winning was. Some wins were sweeter than others.

"And there are some things money can't buy." He still stared at her.

Like a good win. And my life. Couldn't he just get out of the darned car so she could go crawl into a hole somewhere? Because she really just felt like being alone to sulk after she'd busted up his nose and then snarked at their server.

"Put the car in park, Angelique, and come inside." He unlocked the door and pulled the handle, planting one foot on the ground. The interior light came on, and she flinched.

"I can't. I've got to go."

He turned back to her with a teasing smile. "I'll tell everyone what you're really doing in Red River." He patted his pocket. "And don't you want these back?"

She glared at him. "That's cheating."

He shrugged. "If it's the only way I can win with you, then I'm good with it."

She stared him down like a courtroom adversary. Only he didn't crumble under her scrutiny like witnesses did. Raising an eyebrow, he gazed back at her, his sea-blue eyes caressing her cheeks, down her nose, anchoring on her mouth for a brief moment before returning to meet her stare.

She swallowed, her lips parting a tad. The movement lured his stare back to her lips, and for a second, Angelique wanted him to kiss her. Wanted to satisfy the need that swelled in her nether regions, the need to feel him, the need to experience his taste firsthand. The need to feel like a woman again.

Without looking away, he reached for the gearshift, pushed it into park, found the keys, and killed the engine. "Come inside. I don't bite."

Too bad.

What? Wait. She shouldn't. Should she? The feelings stirring inside her weren't part of her plan. They were exactly what she *didn't* need right now.

Of course she shouldn't go in.

"Okay." Her tone was wary, and the tip of her tongue darted out to trace her bottom lip. "Just for a minute. Then I'm leaving."

His mouth twitched into a smile.

"But for the record," Angelique warned, "*I* bite when backed into a corner."

He laughed, pointing to his nose. "Yeah, I got that. No corners, okay?"

She followed him onto the porch and shifted from one running shoe to the other, one shaky hand clasping her other arm for warmth against the chilled night air and shielding her from the heady testosterone that wafted off of her host in waves. Unlocking the door, he stepped inside and flipped on the lights. Besides the array of unpacked moving boxes that littered the den, his cabin . . .

Well, his cabin screamed single straight guy, doused with a generous helping of hillbilly yokel, from the top of its steeply pitched roof all the way to its rustic, unvarnished wood floors. She scanned the open floor plan that merged the kitchen, dinette, and den into one room with just a bar and half wall separating the rooms.

Faded framed wildlife photographs hung in the den, slate-blue paint dulled with age covered the walls, and old rustic furniture filled the place. A rather disturbing stuffed moose head with giant antlers and macabre glass eyes stared at her from the dinette.

And he called her Cookie Monster slippers creepy.

"Coffee, wine, or beer?"

"Coffee would be nice." She set her purse and keys on the credenza next to the back door.

Blake went straight for the coffeepot. "I haven't had time to unpack everything or fix the place up."

She walked to the fireplace while he put together the ingredients and flipped the switch to the on position. A pair of antique cross-country skis hung crisscrossed over the vaulted stone face. The fireplace was the focal point of the entire cabin. The hearth held a basket of chopped wood—hence, the nice guns Dr. Tall, Dark, and Hot-some sported every time he flexed his arms—and huge mason stones angled up into a chimney that soared past the upstairs loft and into the vaulted ceiling above.

The cabin she'd planned to buy up here a year ago had a similar fireplace that was double sided and could be used from the bedroom side, too. She'd fallen in love with it, imagining her and Gabriel sharing a king-size bed while a roaring fire and a glass of wine kept them company.

Her eyes went to the door to the left of the fireplace, and she imagined Blake tangled in sheets.

Don't go there, stupid. She blinked the image away.

After a few gurgles, steam swirled from the top of the machine as dark-brown liquid started to stream into the pot. The aroma filled the room, and it suddenly became cozy. Intimate.

"Is this a double fireplace?" she couldn't help but ask.

"Yeah. How'd you know?" He retrieved two mugs from the cupboard.

Her hand went to her collarbone and rested there. "I almost bought a place up here very similar to this a while back. Probably the same builder."

"How do you take your coffee?"

"Cream. Two sugars."

He measured out sugar into a spoon, preparing the coffee to her specifications. "What happened?"

She turned to him and shook off the wistfulness that threatened to stir up too much emotion. Emotions she'd put behind her and refused to let control her anymore. When she didn't answer, he paused and looked up at her.

"The cabin. Why didn't you buy it?"

She caressed the area just over her breasts. "Bad timing."

Another dream that had slipped through her fingers after the diagnosis. She sucked up her resolve. Cabins came up for sale all the time in Red River. Another opportunity would present itself. Except that Red River wouldn't be the same quaint community it was now. Not after she was done . . . winning the case. So why didn't the usual thrill of imminent victory course through her, the euphoria of an inevitable conquest?

He stared at her for a moment before pouring half-and-half into the mugs. Metal clinked against ceramic as he stirred. She wandered over to a bookshelf. A single item sat on one shelf—a pink Power Ranger doll, well worn like a favored toy that'd been outgrown and now sat on a shelf, lonely and unloved. One arm was missing; the other limbs were scratched and twisted into odd angles. Battered and bruised just like her.

"I like what you've done with the place." She turned and stood in front of the moose head.

He didn't miss her jab. "It came like this. Obviously, I haven't gotten around to buying my own furniture. Except a new bed."

She shot a look at him and looked away just as fast. Studied the ghoulish moose head, whose eyes seemed to follow her around the room. Anything to avoid making eye contact with Dr. Tall, Dark, and Hot-some over the topic of his bed, especially since she'd just been visualizing that very thing. With him in it.

"Interesting choice in knickknacks." She joined him at the kitchen bar and pulled out an Amish-style barstool.

"You mean Harry?" He nodded toward the moose.

"You named it?"

"How could I not?" He walked around the bar. "He's hard to ignore." He set both mugs on the counter and took the seat next to her. "Harry's gotta go when I get around to redecorating."

She chuckled. "Good call, but actually, I meant the pink doll." She threw a glance over one shoulder toward the bookshelf.

He nodded, taking a sip of coffee. "That's one of my most prized possessions."

"An old pink Power Ranger doll?" She grabbed her cup and blew on the piping-hot liquid.

He stared down into the caramel-colored coffee like a fortune-teller would a crystal ball.

They sipped in silence for a few moments. "This is good." She tried to break the uncomfortable silence. At least it was uncomfortable for her. Blake seemed to be completely at ease. His laid-back, nonchalant demeanor kind of irritated her. Is that what life in the country did to a person? No worries, no fast lane, no ambition.

Boring.

"A patient gave the doll to me during my residency." He stared down into his cup. "A little girl named Jenna who was in the hospital with end-stage leukemia."

Angelique didn't know what to say. She stared into her cup. "That part of your job must be hard."

"It's the hardest part." He let out a heavy sigh. "All of a sudden their hospital bed is empty, or they miss an appointment and you know they're never coming back. They've become like friends or family or a little sister, and they're just gone."

She studied his profile for a moment. An army of doctors had poked and prodded her. They'd saved her life, but she'd bet not one of them remembered her name like Dr. Blake Holloway did his patients.

He rubbed a hand over the shadow of stubble on his chin. "There are a lot of people I *can* help, and that's how I move on." He took another languid sip of coffee, but the tension in his shoulders didn't slack. Setting the cup down, he swiveled his stool toward her and was dangerously close to entering her personal space. "What about you? How do you move on after a case is over?"

Kind of like her doctors. It was easy to move on to the next file waiting on her desk if she stayed emotionally detached from the clients.

"I just think about the next win," she said honestly. A fact that had given her a sense of pride until Blake walked into her life carrying her runaway dog and thong panties.

She pushed her mug away. "Thanks for the coffee, but I should go. My parents are driving in from Albuquerque tomorrow afternoon, and I have a few things to do before they arrive." *Like what?* Okay, not really, but she really should leave before he pulled on more of her heartstrings.

"It must be nice to have a close family," he said.

And the pluck of another string thrummed in her chest at the mention of her family. Great. She looked at him. Studied the firm set of his jaw, the trace of sadness in his eyes that matched his tone. "No brothers or sisters?"

He shook his head. "Nope. Just me."

"You're obviously used to being alone, having a lot of quiet time." Angelique chuckled. "*Quiet* isn't in my family's vocabulary."

"Quiet and alone are overrated. Trust me, too much of both can be . . . dismal." He rubbed his jaw.

"Your dad lives in the area, doesn't he?"

Blake shrugged. "My dad's pretty introverted. He and my stepmom stay close to home unless he's working in the free clinic on the reservation. We do have a close relationship, though. I see them at least every other week."

"Perry's your cousin. And you have other family here. What about them?" she asked.

A warm expression lit his face and replaced the sadness in his eyes. "My family is small. I didn't grow up around them, but it's nice to have them around now. Perry is such a great guy. But all in all, we're a pretty laid-back bunch."

Wow. Angelique couldn't beat most of her family off with a

stick. Quiet and alone time had been a valuable commodity in the Barbetta household during her youth. Her two brothers and sister, now scattered around the western part of the United States, came home to visit all the time, and even though her parents moved to Albuquerque in the seventies before she was born, they kept in close contact with their relatives in New York and Florida. Angelique still loved the obnoxious Barbetta family reunions. Some years the get-togethers were cringe-worthy, like when she was twelve and her sprouting boobs had been her six aunts' favorite topic. But still. There was never a time when Angelique was lonely for familial companionship.

Except when she woke up from surgery. Even then, with her entire family around her for support, the loneliness and desolation that had engulfed her after losing the most feminine parts of her body had seemed insurmountable. Her mother and grandmother had been through it and tried their best to help Angelique cope, but she'd still felt alienated and alone for a time.

She offered a sympathetic smile. "At least you're not completely alone anymore. Sounds like life is looking up for you." She regretted the words as soon as she said them.

He drew in a breath, resting his jaw in the palm of his hand. An index finger tapped against his cheek as he studied her. "It was until recently."

Angelique set her mug down. "I should get home." She turned to him, holding out an open palm. "You have something of mine."

Her thigh brushed against his, and he rotated her stool, his thighs framing hers. Heat pulsed through her. With two gentle fingers, he clasped a stray lock of her hair. She drew back ever so slightly, until his stare captured hers, and she saw the kindness there. The warmth. Even forgiveness.

She swallowed. Stilled. And let him tuck the strand behind her ear, his hand lingering there.

He stared down at her open palm, and then his eyes traced back up to her lips. "I lied."

Her brow furrowed. "You what?"

"I lied about your dog," he said. "I don't have your panties." When he spoke the P word, his eyes turned smoky.

"You cheated?" Her mouth gaped. *"Again?"*

He inched closer, now both his arms and legs braced at her sides like a cocoon. "You almost broke my nose, so we're even."

Her breath caught as his heat washed over her. "You asked for it," she whispered.

A wicked smile turned up his lips. "Yep."

Before she could recover, he threaded one hand behind her neck and pulled her into him. His startling blue eyes held hers, their noses brushing just the slightest bit. His breath caressed her mouth, her skin, and for a moment the room melted away, and only the two of them existed in the universe. Her brain screamed, *No, no, no!* But even as a dozen reasons why this was a bad idea zinged through her mind, her double-crossing body leaned into him just a smidge. Her hands smoothed along his rock-hard thighs, over narrow hips and a taut abdomen. They found his chest. Just as solid as the rest of him.

She sighed.

A caressing thumb stroked across her bottom lip, his hand cradling the side of her face, angling her head to fit with his. Another gentle brush of his thumb to her lower lip coaxed her mouth open to wait for his. Her eyes fluttered shut under the tender touch, and she forgot to breathe.

A determined scratch sounded at the back door.

She blinked backed to reality, and Blake growled under his breath.

Another scratch, louder this time, had her jerking out of his grasp, and her eyes darted toward the sound.

A muscle in Blake's jaw twitched, but his eyes didn't leave hers. "I think your dog is paying another visit."

"My dog?" Her brows drew together before realization dawned. Her eyes squeezed shut. "Oh," she whispered.

He pulled himself off the barstool.

Good. She breathed deep. Kissing him would've been a mistake, right?

Right. Lips still burning with unrequited desire, she traced them with a fingertip. Rubbed them together to snuff out the pull of lust his touch had ignited.

He opened the back door. Sergeant Schnitzel darted straight to Blake, his tail wagging and his jaw clamped around a pair of her mint-green lace panties. The mutt completely ignored her while offering up her unmentionables to Blake like a prize.

Oh, for God's sake. "Sarge!" she hissed. "Give me those this instant."

The dog didn't even glance in her direction, his attention devoted to Blake.

She pinched the bridge of her nose. How the heck was Sarge getting ahold of her underwear? Did she leave a crack in her lingerie drawer? That long snout of his could probably wedge into the slightest gap and push the drawer open.

Her breath hitched. Thank the angels in heaven she didn't actually bring good ol' Harley. She really would have to serve that dog up on a bun if he got ahold of that thing. Didn't women usually hide their tools in their lingerie drawer?

When Blake held out his hand under the dog's mouth, Sarge dropped the ball of lace right into his palm. Blake scratched him behind the ears. "Good boy."

"Good boy?" Angelique stood. "I'm going to give him away if he keeps this up." Even though he did just save her from making a serious mistake. Sarge's timing was impeccable.

Blake held the green swatch in his hand, and Angelique's face burned like hot coals. "I kind of like his visits."

She stuck one hand on a hip. "Well, I don't." She held out the other hand. "Give me my . . . things."

She grabbed for the panties, but he moved them out of her reach. "If you want these back, you'll have to trade for them."

She narrowed skeptical eyes at him.

Clenching them into his fist, Blake crossed both arms across his chest. "I'll make you a deal." He raised a brow. "You're good at that, right? Cutting deals."

"Give them to me," she seethed through clenched teeth.

"I will if you'll agree to let me show you something."

"I beg your pardon?" she blurted, her stare dropping to his crotch for a nanosecond. "I don't make deals like that."

A scoff intermingled with his laugh. "Don't flatter yourself. I want you to see what this community stands to lose if your clients get their way."

His arrogant smile pissed her off. She hadn't been in a courtroom battle for a year now. Maybe she was due for a good scrap. "You know what?" She grabbed her purse from the credenza and tossed it over one shoulder. "You keep that pair." She snatched up Sergeant Schnitzel. "I've got plenty more where those came from." She stomped out the door and down the porch toward her car.

When she got to the driver's door, she glanced up. Blake leaned against the doorframe, arms crossed over that firm chest and a lazy smile on his lips.

"I can't wait to see them all. Sarge's visits are better than a Victoria's Secret catalogue."

Oh, he did not just compare her panties to an X-rated catalogue! She pulled open the car door. She thrust herself behind the wheel. Planting Sarge in the passenger seat, Angelique fired up the car and punched the gearshift into reverse. A cloud of dust filled her rearview mirror as she headed home, determined to stop her underwear from making any more public appearances.

Chapter Seven

After a fitful night of thinking about a certain irritating doctor who was as hot as a summer day in July, Angelique dragged herself out of bed at the first hint of dawn. Her parents were set to arrive after lunch, and Kimberly planned to drive in from Taos for the night, no doubt wielding the dreaded bucket list, but that wasn't for several more hours.

Coffee. She needed coffee to clear the cobwebs from her sleep-deprived mind. Maybe fresh mountain air from a good run would kick-start her stiff muscles and dispel her grumpy attitude. Or a new neighbor. That'd probably work just as well, but since Dr. Tall, Dark, and Hot-some wasn't likely to move anytime soon, she decided on the run first.

She went to the window and leaned against the seal, pulling the sheer organza curtain to one side. Past the stream and footbridge that led to Blake's cabin, her upstairs view made the top of his pitched roof and the stone chimney visible above the autumn palette of trees.

The truth was, he'd probably be moving sooner than either of them expected. Because of her. Letting the curtain fall back into place, she shook her head.

It's not because of me. It was her client's doing, and it was her job to represent her client. Period.

Angelique pulled on Nike thermal tights and a hoodie, and went for a run, trying to get her head back in the game, to stay focused on this thing she came here to do.

An hour later, she showered, dressed in her favorite fitted jeans, and paired them with a hooded red sweater, the color that always made her feel in charge. Tugging hot rollers out, she tossed them aside and ran a brush through her hair. She stood in front of the full-length mirror in her bedroom and checked herself. Her long black hair hung in messy curls, the warm color of the sweater enhancing her dark features. She'd lost a little weight during her illness but still filled out her jeans with rounded hips and trim but muscular thighs from running.

She sighed. Why could she not see herself as attractive anymore? When she walked into a room, at least a few heads used to turn, and it'd been flattering. Now paralyzing fear gripped her in a crowd because she was certain the only thing people could see was a woman so insecure that she'd caved and had plastic surgery. And what kind of woman does that?

The scared kind. The kind who wants to be whole again but doesn't know how.

Grabbing a tube of lip gloss off the dresser, she swiped it across pursed lips. A frosty scarlet gloss shimmered back at her, and she leaned in close to the mirror. Gabriel's favorite. Her rhythmic breaths fogged the mirror.

The same lip gloss the Cheerleader had purchased after hearing Gabriel compliment Angelique about it. The color had been forever burned into Angelique's memory when it shimmered across the Cheerleader's puckered lips as she screamed for Gabriel to screw her harder, Angelique frozen in his office doorway.

Jamming the wand back into the tube, she went to the trash can and tossed it in. She brushed her hands off with finality.

"Gone the way of Gabriel's widescreen TV."

It took two Kleenex and a wet rag to completely wipe the red color off her lips, but when she was done, her lips were like a fresh canvas. She fumbled through her makeup bag, cosmetics flying in every direction. Finally she withdrew a natural, earth-toned tube. She removed the brush and stared at it.

There. A new color. Different. Fresh. Real.

Sarge greeted her at the bottom of the stairs, so she gave him a pat on the head and picked up the Red River Resort Development file.

Open it. Do your job. Then go back to Albuquerque like a champion.

The file and what it represented pricked at her conscience. That file held the key to her future—a prestigious partnership. What she'd wanted her entire professional life, worked hard for. Even made a few enemies to attain it, and it was the thing that would fill the emptiness now that she'd decided to keep her body to herself and let go of the possibility of having a family of her own.

It also held the future of a lot of honest and friendly folks. People who'd become real to her. People who were already accepting her into their close-knit circle.

The people who came in and out of her life because of the legal cases she dealt with had always seemed like a surreal videogame, and she held the controller. Moved them around their world like avatars on a screen. When she won, because she always won, she paused the game until the next case came along and then restarted it. Simple. Detached. Not a lot of emotion, because really, she wasn't a shrink, and emotions could be dangerous in her line of work.

She tossed the file back in a drawer and slammed it shut. Out of sight, out of mind, at least for a few hours. "Be good, Sarge. I have to get out of here for a while." She grabbed her purse and keys and left the cabin. Searching out a strong cup of coffee was a worthy mission, and it provided a good excuse to get out of the cabin where the Red River Resort Development file haunted her.

She'd thought the one-horse town mentality of Red River would wear thin. Instead, it was growing on her. She found it . . . charming. Warmth spread through her chest, filling an inexplicable void. Her time in Red River gave her a sense of . . . what was it?

Contentedness.

Big mistake. Letting a case get personal was stupid. Any good lawyer knew better. *She* knew better. Yet here she was, following Highway 38 west through Bobcat Pass, on her way into town to find some coffee and some . . . company.

She flipped on the radio and tried to find a jazz station. Static. Static. Country and western. Static. More C and W. Static again. Sighing, she shut the radio off.

Cracking the driver's window, the fresh mountain air filled her lungs. Cleared her head. Instead of the natural scent of pine, maybe a crowbar would do a better job knocking some sense into her. She'd almost kissed Dr. Tall, Dark, and Hot-some.

"Stupid, Barbetta," she mumbled.

A relationship of any kind was not her goal, not even a one-time thing. It couldn't be. Not anymore. The thought of having to explain her fake breasts to a man, having him touch them, kiss them . . .

Her hands tightened around the steering wheel. It was even difficult to let her surgeon do follow-up exams. The thought of anyone else seeing them made her nauseated. She punched the button on the door, and the window rolled down another inch. She sucked in a breath.

Maybe she'd never see Blake again.

Pfft. The chances of that were about as good as Sergeant Schnitzel leaving her underwear alone. As if it wasn't already hard enough to avoid someone in a town this size, he had to be her neighbor.

She had a plan for her future. A solid plan.

Until a nuisance who looked as good as a Michelangelo sculpture walked into her life carrying a pair of her panties.

Nope. She wouldn't keep Blake Holloway or Mayberry, USA, in her life any longer than necessary. And really, just why was *Dr.* Holloway still single, anyway? Must be something wrong with him, or some cheerleader would've already snatched him up.

Angelique really, really disliked cheerleaders.

Yeah. Dr. T, D & H-some probably had some sort of inherent flaw that chased the ladies away. Okay, she could feel better now. She *did* feel better now. Sort of.

It would help if the pang of disappointment stopped reverberating in her chest. She rubbed the area just below her collarbone.

Nope.

The Red River city limits came into view, and she slowed. Where was she going, anyway? Seemed like a loaded question at the moment. If she couldn't figure out where to park in a town of 475 people, then it shouldn't come as a big surprise that her professional focus seemed to be derailing like a locomotive jumping its track at full throttle.

Slowing her speed, she tooled onto Main Street. She meandered through downtown Red River, and the Ostergaards' German pastry shop next to Coop's office caught her eye.

Yes! Fresh coffee. Precisely what she needed.

She slid into a parking spot against the curb and got out.

She took a step but stopped. Leaned against her SUV and took in the long strips of businesses on both sides of Main Street. When she had first arrived in Red River, they had looked old and dilapidated. Obviously designed decades ago, the two-story red barn facade and red brick trim offered a look of Old West nostalgia. It fit. Belonged like the Eiffel Tower belonged in Paris. The imitation model in Las Vegas just wasn't the same. And a new state-of-the-art resort wouldn't replace the sentimental charm that kept tourists coming back to Red River year after year. Wouldn't be the pulse of the town for its year-round residents.

The streets fairly deserted on an early Saturday morning, she strolled across and stepped into the pastry shop. A string of bells jangled to announce her arrival, and the sweet scent of fresh pastries made her melt inside.

A rotund man with a cheery smile and rosy cheeks, presumably Mr. Ostergaard, appeared from the back room, wiping his floury hands on an apron. "Allo," he said with a heavy German accent.

"Hi." She looked into the cabinet that housed a half dozen different pastries. The display wasn't even half full.

"Vhere are you visiting from?"

Her insides twisted, his accent a connection to his heritage, just like her parents had kept thick New York accents and mannerisms from the old Italian neighborhood even though they'd moved to Albuquerque decades ago. The vernacular, the gestures, the food. They all said *family*. Roots. The traditions of culture that wouldn't be forgotten no matter how many generations removed. Unless the place was torn down to make way for a new resort that would attract chains like Stardust's Coffee—corporate-owned chains with which a mom-and-pop shop like the Ostergaards' bakery couldn't complete.

"I live in Albuquerque."

"Ah! Vhat can I get you?"

She perused the delicious-looking pastries. "How about a honey cinnamon pecan scone."

"Goot choice!" He dropped his voice to a whisper. "Cheese Danishes are our best, but my wife makes those, and she hasn't felt well lately. Scones are our next-best recipe."

Angelique smiled at him. "In that case, I'll take two. And a coffee."

His chest puffed out as he served up the scones and rang up her total. She pulled a bill out of her wallet and put a generous tip in the tip jar.

Mr. Ostergaard's equally portly wife appeared, wandering in from the back kitchens. And just like that, Angelique's heart twisted like a pretzel. Mrs. Ostergaard wore a light-pink terrycloth head wrap with a dainty dark-pink breast cancer ribbon embroidered on one side. The exact same head wrap Angelique's oncologist had given her in a hot-pink gift bag during the initial consultation. Really? A gift bag? With a pink sparkly bow and everything. That day she'd vowed never to wear the hateful color again. Thankfully, Angelique never had to use the *thoughtful* gift.

But Mrs. Ostergaard did. The wrap covered most of her balding head, leaving only a remnant of unhealthy skin visible at the bottom. But it was enough for Angelique to know that Mrs. O had breast cancer and was getting treatment for it.

"Allo," Mrs. Ostergaard greeted her.

Angelique smiled and reached for a wad of napkins before settling into a chair.

She took a bite, and the buttery scone melted on her tongue the same way her mother's Italian desserts did.

She looked up and found the Ostergaards staring at her expectantly. Angelique stopped mid-chew.

"Um . . . it's really good," she said around a mouthful of cinnamon, honey, and pecan. Swallowing, she said it again. "The most delicious scone I've ever tasted."

At the compliment, they both let out the breath they'd been holding. Angelique almost laughed. She *had* to introduce the Ostergaards to the Barbettas, because they were four ethnic peas in a pod.

"I should bring my parents by." *Real smart, Barbetta.* Her parents didn't know the details or the repercussions of her work in Red River either, and if they found out, they'd probably try to ground her. "You'd like them." *Way more than you'd like me if you knew why I'm here.* "Although, my mom might try to mutiny and take control of your kitchen."

The Ostergaards blinked at her, expressions blank, bodies frozen in place.

She shrugged. "You know how pushy New York Italians can be."

"Ah!" They both threw their hands up in understanding. Angelique's simple phrase explained an entire culture with just one sentence. They busied themselves with straightening tables and chairs that were already perfectly aligned. "Then ve'll get along just fine." Mrs. Ostergaard grabbed a broom and started sweeping the spotless floor.

The strand of bells jingled as the door swung open. Angelique looked up and nearly choked on a bite of scone. Her coffee tilted off balance, and some of it splattered onto the spotless floor.

"Hi, Angelique," Gabriel said. His tall frame perfectly filled out the Ralph Lauren slacks she'd given him last Christmas. The first two buttons of his tailored dress shirt were unbuttoned in an attempt to look elegantly casual—which he pulled off like a champ—and the sleeves were cuffed up just below his elbows. "You're looking well."

"Oof!" Mrs. Ostergaard scurried over with some paper towels. "Let me clean this up, and I'll bring you another cup."

"No need, Mrs. Ostergaard." Angelique stared at Gabriel.

Mrs. Ostergaard swiped at the liquid with a cleaning rag.

"Vhat can I get you, sir?" Mr. Ostergaard asked Gabriel.

"Nothing, thanks," Gabriel said.

The silence grew thick as Mrs. Ostergaard finished cleaning up the mess and disappeared into the back room.

Angelique clutched the marble tabletop with her free hand, her knuckles turning a sick shade of white. "What? You missed your weekly quota of doling out misery, so you came all the way to Red River to find me?" Angelique offered a fraudulent smile to her ex-fiancé. "Really, Gabriel, you should find another hobby. Your attachment to ruining my life is getting a little weird."

Cheating on her was one thing, but she drew the line at him disturbing her date with a hot buttered scone. He should be thankful she wasn't on a date with Ben and Jerry. She may have actually gotten violent.

"And how did you find me here, anyway?"

"I was passing through town on my way to the cabin." He slid both hands into his pants pockets. Smooth. *GQ*. Simulated like a lifelike robot. "We rented it for you, so I know the address. I saw your car parked out front. Not a lot of places open this early in a town like this. The streets must roll up at dark." He gave the inside of the bakery a repugnant once-over. "It wasn't hard to find you."

"Don't you have something better to do, like marry my pregnant legal assistant?" She took a deliberate bite of scone and closed her eyes in appreciation, savoring the taste. "Mmm, this is so good. Really. You should try one." She transformed her expression into granite. "Then get out."

"Come on, Ang." Gabriel's voice sounded vulnerable. He was so good at that, making himself look the wounded party. Garnering sympathy with that good-guy demeanor, glad-handing the partners and associates at office parties and PR events. He never showed the real Gabriel to anyone. She'd seen glimpses of it. The false facade, the artificial persona he created to rise high in social circles and climb the corporate ladder. Only she had seen how shallow he really was. It was all about him, even down to how their new house should be decorated—sterile chrome with black and red contemporary furniture imported from Denmark, even though he knew she hated the ultramodern look. Besides, what kind of a man cared so much about interior decorating?

Maybe he was gay. It would serve the Cheerleader right. Angelique took another vicious bite of scone. Unfortunately, he wasn't gay. Just narcissistic enough to insist that even the style of furniture conform to his tastes.

"I need a few minutes of your time. Something's come up at the firm."

"They couldn't have sent someone else, Gabriel? *You* had to come here?"

She purposefully left him standing, but he pulled out the chair across from her anyway. He graced the seat with a casual side-slouch. One arm slung over the back of the metal chair, he'd perfected the move, thinking it made him look confidently in charge.

Dammit, it did.

Well, two could play the game. Angelique puckered her lips—because that had been the part of her body that Gabriel complimented the most—and took a slow drink of coffee. Swallowing, she closed her eyes and wrapped those very same shiny lips around a piece of scone. And this time she did moan. Out loud. She slowly chewed and swallowed the delectable morsel. When she opened her eyes again, Gabriel's lips had parted, and his gaze was anchored firmly to her mouth.

"You should try one of these. They melt in your mouth," she said, ignoring his disconcerted look. He didn't respond. His eyes didn't leave her lips. "What's this about, Gabriel? Did you come here in person to tell me it's twins? Because that would be so like you."

Gabriel turned a little red and cleared his throat.

"Angelique." He looked away. "I'm not here to rehash the past. It's not personal, it's business."

"Why does that not surprise me? Of course you didn't drive all the way up here to apologize or to check on my well-being." Because he didn't care about what she'd gone through. He'd only thought of how her illness had affected him. Angelique drank more coffee. "So what *do* you want?" She wiped her hands on the napkin, then tapped her nails against the table.

Gabriel shifted in his chair and looked a little less comfortable. Angelique's skin prickled. The same feeling came over her in the courtroom when the prosecution was about to produce a surprise piece of evidence that would look bad for her client.

"Is there someplace we can talk privately?" Gabriel asked. "It's in your best interest, Ang."

A red flag the size of Alaska flew high and bright. "As a matter of fact, there's not, so you might as well spit it out." No way was she bringing him to her cabin.

Another worried look flickered across Gabriel's normally composed countenance. He cleared his throat again. "A few inconsistencies have come to my attention." He paused, letting her absorb his words.

"And?"

"I thought you might be able to shed some light," he said.

"I might be able to, if I knew what the hell you're talking about. How about you just tell me what you came here to say?"

"Certain client files have gone missing," Gabriel said.

Ah. *And the firm thinks the woman scorned is responsible.*

She smirked. "Seriously, Gabriel? You think I'd stoop that low because of *you*?"

"It would be perfectly understandable under the circumstances. You were under a lot of strain with your health—"

"Don't you dare patronize me. And don't ever blame my illness for your poor case management."

"I just want the files back. No harm, no foul," said Gabriel.

She studied him. "What makes you think I took them?"

"Ang, you were very angry when you moved out."

"I had every right to be. What does me moving out of our condo have to do with missing case files?"

Gabriel ignored her comment. Denial was a beautiful thing for someone like him, who always seemed to seamlessly shift the blame to anyone but himself. Unbelievable. After all she'd been through, the way he'd cut her heart out with a dull knife and left her bleeding, he could still walk in here with no conscience and hack at her some more.

She swallowed. Beat down the dizzying effect of his painful accusations. Taking a long drink of coffee, she hoped the warm liquid would squelch the coldness in her stomach. It didn't.

"Some company funds also went missing." Gabriel didn't meet her eyes.

Angelique would've laughed at the preposterous accusation if it hadn't been so serious. He wasn't just talking legal espionage, he was suggesting she embezzled money from the firm.

"And you think I took it?" Her voice rose a notch.

Mr. Ostergaard reappeared and stood behind the counter. "Is everything okay?"

Angelique pinched the bridge of her nose, then turned to the shop owner. His reddish-blond eyebrows bunched together, he gave her a worried look. "It's fine, Mr. Ostergaard. We're discussing business. Would you like us to leave?"

Mr. Ostergaard shot a distrusting scowl at Gabriel. "*Nein.* There're no customers here. I'll be in the back if you need me." He gave Gabriel another scowl before leaving.

Angelique turned back to her ex-fiancé. "I'm not a partner yet. I don't even have access to the company accounts. You know that." Gabriel studied the floor tile like a textbook. And then she knew. "But you do, and it's your case files and account funds that are missing."

"You had access to my computer. I wasn't home when you moved out."

A lightbulb zinged to life, sending jolts through Angelique's brain. She was the easiest person for Gabriel to blame because of the momentary lapse of control she'd displayed while moving. The television, the jacket, the briefcase. It wouldn't be that hard to get the firm to make the jump from property destruction to embezzlement, and Gabriel would look like the victim.

What a pinhead.

"Tell me, Gabriel, does the firm know yet?" Because if they hadn't discovered the missing funds yet, they soon would, and her instincts told her that Gabriel was desperate to do some damage control before the security breach came out and whispers started circulating around the firm about him, the Golden Boy.

His hesitation and inability to look her in the eye answered her question.

"Considering the state of mind I was in at the time, I probably would've thrown your computer against the wall, not stolen account numbers and access codes. Besides, I'm not the only one who's had access to both your computer and the case files, Gabriel."

Gabriel shrugged. "You're the only one who had a motive."

She let her stare burn through him for a quiet moment. "You were so charming at first. So good at wooing the partners." Her tone turned a little whimsical as she remembered those early days when Gabriel had been brought into the firm.

He looked confused at the sudden change in subject and at her shift in tone.

"At a client dinner or cocktail party, you could have them reeled in within minutes with your charisma. I actually admired your way with people because you were so much smoother in social situations than me." Her voice went hard again, each word so brittle, as though they could snap in two with just a twitch of her lips. "But people are like trees, Gabriel. If you're with them long enough, they drop enough leaves to reveal their true self." She leaned back in her chair and considered him. "I was planning to put our wedding plans on hold, but then my mom insisted I go in for a routine mammogram because of our family history, and that changed everything. All I could think of was surviving."

Gabriel's mouth opened and shut. Nothing came out. Obviously, he was still trying to wrap his brain around the fact that Angelique had actually had second thoughts about him.

"By the time I found you with Ciara, I'd seen how little depth you really have."

Gabriel's stare turned to ice. "Cattiness is beneath you, Angelique."

"I'm curious, Gabriel, if I hadn't caught you, which one of us would you have chosen? Me or her?" A thought popped into her head. A disgusting, repugnant thought, but one that seemed to fit Gabriel's overinflated self-image and sense of entitlement.

His beady eyes—which used to remind her of expensive gray cashmere, but now looked like nothing more than two cold, empty chips of ice—darted away.

"Ah, you would've tried to keep both of us."

"Your illness was tough on all of us." Gabriel's gaze flicked around the room, never quite meeting hers. "Everyone suffered."

"Right." She laughed, then gave her head a soft shake. "Thank you for saving me from making the biggest mistake of my life."

Gabriel's tone went callous. "The files and the money. That's why I'm here."

Snatching up her purse, she headed for the door. With a hand on the doorknob, she turned back. "I didn't take either the files or the money. If you don't believe me, press charges and battle it out with my attorney." Her lips thinned into a predatory smile. Gabriel knew this was the kind of fight she lived for, and there was no one better at legal standoffs than her.

"Wait, Ang." He switched his tone in a nanosecond, and the charisma was back. "We can talk this through like reasonable adults."

"Really, Gabriel?" She couldn't believe his absurdity. Well, actually she could. "This is the opposite of what we do. We defend people from unfounded accusations where there's no evidence of guilt. I suggest you look closer to home, because I'm not the bad guy here. I think there's someone in the firm who wants one of us to look like the culprit."

Pulling the door open, she stepped onto the sidewalk and saw Blake two doors down trying to unlock his office door. Obviously stuck, a bundle of keys dangled from the lock, and he jiggled the doorknob. A loud click echoed around the deserted street as the key turned, and the door swung open just as he looked up at her. She stopped cold and stared at him and his slightly swollen nose. Their eyes locked, and his expression warmed. And then Gabriel followed her onto the sidewalk, ruining the moment.

Angelique saw an opportunity. That was her gift and one of the reasons she was a good trial lawyer. She could see the tiniest crack, the tiniest opportunity and capitalize on it fast before the witness, the judge, or the prosecution figured out what she was doing.

"Hi, sweetheart." She smiled at Blake, whose expression went blank. Putting a sway in her hips, she walked to him. "You're late. What took you so long?" She lowered her voice to a sensual purr.

Before Blake could expose her maneuver for what it was, she wrapped her arms around his neck, launched herself flush against him, and planted a red-hot kiss on his parted lips. He hesitated, but then his powerful arms circled her waist and he returned the kiss. With fervor. Her brain clouded over as she molded perfectly into his embrace, the warmth of his mouth making her lose focus on the world around them.

A throat cleared somewhere in the background.

Angelique sighed deep and dreamy as she broke the kiss and stared up at Blake. That was . . . that was . . . What exactly was it? Stupid? Irresponsible?

Hot.

Yes, yes, that was it. She licked her lips as he smiled down at her without loosening his grip.

"Uh, Angelique." Gabriel's stunned voice broke the spell Blake had just cast on her.

She plastered on a smile and turned back to her colleague, or ex-colleague. She wasn't exactly sure yet. But most definitely an ex. Snuggling next to Blake, she snaked her arm around his waist and gently poked him in the back with one finger. She gave him a wide-eyed smile, and he got the hint, because a sculpted arm encircled her shoulder.

"Sweetheart." She smiled up at Blake, and one of his eyebrows lifted. "This is Gabriel Marone."

"Marone." Blake looked down at her thoughtfully, a wicked twinkle in his eye. "That name rings a bell."

Of course it did. Of all the names she could've used as an alias on her first visit to Blake's office, why'd she have to pick one so lame? She blinked at him and kept the fake smile firmly in place. He made an odd sound when her fingernail stabbed into his back. Then she rubbed it affectionately. A silent plea.

"Must've been a patient from a long time ago." He shook his head.

Gabriel sized him up like a prizefighter at a boxing match. He rarely let his shallow, selfish side show, but he wasn't able to hide the territorial posture at the sight of Angelique with another man.

She hugged Blake close, putting her free hand on his chest. "Gabriel, I'd like you to meet Blake Holloway, Red River's medical doctor." Silence descended. Gabriel's eyes darted between her and Blake, and Blake's chest expanded a little in a protective posture.

"He's my . . . boyfriend." She coughed, choked, and clutched at her throat.

Chapter Eight

Blake rubbed the space between Angelique's shoulder blades, trying to make it look affectionate. No idea what she was up to, he decided to play along. He shouldn't. He should let her wallow in whatever trouble she was obviously in with this guy. But that sex kitten kiss she'd just laid on him had taken him by surprise. Stiff as cardboard when she first threw herself at him, but then she'd softened and molded against him, deepened the kiss and seemed to get lost in it. A little sigh of pleasure had even slipped through her lips.

Until this joker interrupted what was quickly turning into a nice little morning fantasy on Blake's part.

Gabriel Marone. Huh. They obviously had history if she felt comfortable using his last name as a cover. Not to mention, Sergeant Schnitzel's tag said, "Love, G."

"You okay, babe?" Blake kept rubbing her back, keeping up the charade.

Her gaze flew to his, and he gave her an innocent blink. She definitely had some explaining to do when he got her alone. Just twelve hours ago, she was running from his kiss. Now she was pretending to be his girlfriend and mauling him with her plump lips. Lips that tasted sweet like honey and shimmered like the silk panties Sarge had been good enough to share with him.

"Fine, thanks." She cleared her throat again. "Just a little dust in the air."

He glanced at the tall, sandy-haired guy she'd introduced as Gabriel Marone. He had a smooth, cool smile that didn't match the detached look in his eyes. Blake already didn't like the immaculately dressed asshole because he knew the type. Polished on the surface, not much underneath. And the possessive way he looked at Angelique made Blake want drop-kick the guy and his overpriced Rolex right out of town.

Still. This little game was like a gift from heaven. An opportunity Blake just couldn't pass up because now she owed him. And he might be able to play this card during the legal battle with her client. His arm tightened around Angelique's shoulder again, and she narrowed those ebony eyes at him. He flashed a cheeky smile and pulled her even closer.

Gabriel's eyes flared with greed as they raked over Angelique, his pleasant smile as fake as his persona. "Well, I'm glad to see you've moved on, Angelique. Congratulations."

Angelique leaned her temple against Blake's shoulder with a miniscule hesitation that only Blake could detect because her soft body had just gone as rigid as granite against his side.

"Thank you." She coughed again. "We're very happy."

Blake looked down at her, and the tip of her nose glowed scarlet. She refused to meet his gaze. Oh, heck yeah. This was the most fun he'd had teasing a girl since high school when Carla Jacobs dove into the pool at a swimming party and came up without her top. Flimsy bikini top strings were a thing of beauty for a sixteen-year-old boy.

Gabriel's smile was thin and artificial as he scanned both of them with assessing eyes. "How long have you been together?" He wagged a finger between himself and Angelique. "It wasn't that long ago that we were engaged."

Blake's entire body tensed. Ex-fiancé. Clearly why she needed a pretend boyfriend. Even better for her that Blake was a doctor. He didn't have an ego about it, but by the look on the ex's face, that fact came in handy right about now.

Angelique stammered without actually forming a complete sentence. Probably weighing her response carefully. He'd noticed that about her. He doubted she was the quiet type, unless she found herself on shaky ground or around strangers. Smart as she was, she was careful with her words and didn't let strangers in easily. The impression he'd gotten in just the week he'd known her was that she vetted everyone through tactics second only to the CIA, Secret Service, and Homeland Security before letting them into her inner circle of trust. Smart girl. So how did this joker get past her bullshit radar and talk her into almost marrying him?

"Long enough to know I'm a lucky man." Blake caressed down her arm. Angelique looked up at him, but instead of giving him a warning glare, her eyes said, *Thank you.* Then her gaze dropped to his lips like she could've kissed him again. Like she was thinking about it.

"What brings you to Red River?" Blake asked her ex. "You're not dressed like a vacationer." *And what do you want with Angelique, if you're not together anymore?* Because his visit obviously had Angelique on edge. *Angelique.* The woman who could deflect flaming arrows with just a single glare.

"Business," blurted Angelique. "Gabriel's one of the partners from my firm."

An office romance gone bad. That must've been awkward, especially with his name on the door. That meant Gabriel was the boss, and she was his employee.

Gabriel nodded. "I had some business matters to discuss with Angelique, and I wanted to see her in person." His stare dropped to her chest. Studied her like something that might bite if he touched. "She gave me . . . us . . . the firm quite a scare with that brush with breast cancer."

Angelique went rigid again, and Blake tightened his grip. His hunch had been right on target. Her aversion to pink ribbons made sense now because she'd been down that rabbit hole way too young. He loosened his grip and gently caressed her shoulder, keeping her flush against his side.

"You look good *now*, Ang," Gabriel said.

Angelique's already taut body went so brittle, Blake thought it might shatter against his touch. "Gee, thanks, Gabriel. That means so much coming from you." Her words dripped with sarcasm, which seemed to go right over her ex's head.

What an obtuse jerk. He'd just implied that she didn't look good while she was ill, with no indication that he'd insulted her to the core. Blake wondered how Gabriel would feel if he'd had testicular cancer.

Angelique swallowed, but didn't speak. Her face was like stone, completely lacking emotion. But a slight tremble coursed through her body, and Blake's sympathetic physician's heart knew she'd just been wounded. The human body was resilient, the human spirit even more so. But there was only so much a person could withstand without breaking, no matter how tough and solid they were.

A silent beat passed while Gabriel stared at her like a salivating dog who wanted another alpha dog's bone. Blake's hand lifted from her shoulder and stroked her hair.

"She looks better than good." And she did. She was gorgeous, and Gabriel had obviously let her slip through his grasp. The tension in her shoulders released a bit, and the palm of her hand molded against his back. She squeezed gently, and Blake wasn't sure if it was a warning or a thank-you. "The mountains agree with you, babe." He leaned down and planted a quick kiss on her lips. Her black eyes flashed up at him as her lips parted, and he gave her a wicked smile.

She's mine now.

The words almost slipped from his mouth. He stilled against the thought, because for a moment he'd actually believed them. Slipping into the role of her boyfriend and lover felt right. Like she belonged right here in Red River. With him.

Only she didn't.

Her soft palm against his back transformed into a pinch, and he suppressed a flinch. Uh-huh, that was definitely a warning. Maybe he was laying it on a little thick, but so what? He might as well milk this because he had the upper hand, and that probably wouldn't last long.

"You were just leaving, right? It's quite a drive back. You'd better get going." Her entire demeanor changed when she turned back to Gabriel.

Gabriel's feet shuffled in place, and he rubbed the back of his neck. "Think about what we discussed, Angelique."

"Oh, I will. And you think about what I said." Her tone was cautious.

"I'll be in touch, Ang," said Gabriel with a little too much familiarity. The guy obviously hadn't let go of her. Was probably here in person instead of just picking up the phone because he was looking for a chance to reconcile. Someone really needed to explain the modern-day technology called phone calls and Skype.

"Don't bother, Gabriel. Deal with the firm's security breach." She put her free hand against Blake's chest and snuggled into him.

Nice. Blake draped both arms around her, and Gabriel's eyes clouded over.

"I've got everything under control here." Angelique leaned her cheek against Blake's chest, and her warm breath seeped through the cotton fabric of his red Henley.

Even better.

"You're getting married soon. You'll have your hands full with a pregnant wife half your age to keep happy, so let me handle things here. I'm doing just fine." Her steely voice sent a rocket straight to her target's heart.

Bull's-eye. Gabriel flinched when her missile hit home.

"Have one of the partners keep me posted on the situation and any new developments. No need for you to worry about it with so much change going on in your life."

Gabriel gave a reluctant nod, stepped off the curb, and walked to a slate-gray RS-7 that'd been waxed to such a high sheen it could blind a person if the sunlight hit it just right. A car like that cost an easy six figures. And just like its owner, it was slick.

Gabriel glanced over his shoulder before climbing in.

Angelique waved. So did Blake. Gabriel didn't.

He slid into the driver's seat. The roar of the racy engine was a strange sound in a town like Red River where most everyone drove pickup trucks or SUVs. As Gabriel pulled away from the curb, Blake took Angelique's upper arm and guided her through his office door.

Angelique hesitated at the threshold of Blake's office. Did she really want to fight this battle now? Her head was still spinning from Gabriel's accusations and his backhanded compliments. Not to mention Dr. Tall, Dark, and Hot-some's heroic gesture to participate in her charade. He'd played the part masterfully. So much so that her double-crossing body had responded to him, causing her brain to short-circuit and confuse reality with fantasy.

A warm palm against the small of her back guided her all the way in. At his touch, warmth spread over her like a campfire on a cool autumn night. No, she definitely didn't want to explain her illness to him and all it entailed. But here she was at his mercy, and she did owe him some gratitude. She could at least thank the man who'd taunted her with her own panties, then swooped in like Superman and rescued her from more humiliation at Gabriel's hands.

Well Superman *was* hot, so she really shouldn't feel too guilty about her girly parts turning summersaults worthy of the Olympic trials while she snuggled against his chest.

Oy vey.

As the door thudded shut, she turned to face him. A chill prickled over her, replacing the warmth. Crossing his arms over a hard chest, he leaned back against the door and waited.

She fidgeted, looked around the waiting room, studied the handmade quilts hanging on the walls that gave the room an air of down-home hospitality. When he didn't speak, but just stood there with a brow arched high, she hugged herself. Was it chilly in here? Okay, it was the weekend, but a little heat wouldn't hurt. The lights were still off, the only source of sunlight streaming through the half window of the front door and the skylights overhead. A large plant in the corner cast an awkward shadow on the wall.

Hugging herself, she tried to regroup, tried to stop her world from spinning off its axis, but she wasn't used to being the one on trial. Wearing an opponent down with cold, patient silence was *her* tactic! She locked gazes with him. He still waited, quiet and composed, as though he had all day. Frick, it was Saturday morning. He probably did have all day. Heat crept up her neck and settled in the tips of her ears. At least she wasn't chilly anymore, and hell's bells, he was almost as good at standoffs as she was. He should've gone to law school instead of becoming a doctor.

"What?" She refused to give in first.

"Seeing as how I'm your boyfriend and all, I thought you could fill me in on what just happened out there."

She sputtered. Fidgeted some more. *I owe you big.* "Okay." She finally caved and rolled her eyes like a child who just got sent to the principal's office. "I was engaged to Gabriel."

"I figured out that much. What else?"

"And . . ." She stumbled over the words, took a deep breath. "He cheated with my legal assistant, and now they're getting married. I'm sorry for using you like that. I just wanted him to see that he's not important to me anymore."

"I'm not talking about your history with him. He's an ass, and you're better off without him." Blake's chin hitched up. "Why was he here bothering you? Dialing your phone number seems like it would've been much easier than driving up here from Albuquerque."

Angelique bit her lip. Blake was her adversary, or at least her client's adversary. Thanks to Gabriel showing up and giving out her personal 4-1-1, Blake already knew way too much that he could try to use against her. A good attorney would do that, find something personal, something that made their opponent vulnerable and twist it to their advantage. No way was she going to tell him about the missing client files and money.

She shrugged. "Some things need to be handled in person."

Okay, that was a weak excuse, but he'd have to accept her answer whether he bought it or not.

Pushing off the door, he advanced on her. She backed up a few paces, then stood her ground. When he reached her, his hand lifted to her cheek and rested there. A gentle thumb brushed across her skin. And oh, how she wanted to lose herself in that touch. The strength of it, the tenderness. It made her heart ache with longing, and she swallowed, steadied herself.

"There are only two things I'm concerned about." Just a breath away, his words caressed her cheeks. "Him leaving you the hell alone is one. Especially since he's marrying someone else."

"I'm a big girl, Doc. It's not your problem," she whispered, her eyes searching his. An earnest warmth glowed in the aquamarine pools.

"You made it my problem when you claimed me as your boyfriend." His mouth twitched up, and his eyes anchored to her lips. "You're welcome, by the way. I'm glad I happened to be here at the opportune moment instead of Clifford, the maintenance man who cleans my office on the weekends."

Blake's fingertips traced her jawline.

"I could've made do with Clifford," Angelique whispered. But no. No, she couldn't have.

"Clifford's about six inches shorter than you and is as big around as he is tall. I don't think clinging to him would've made a big impact on your ex-fiancé."

His hand found her neck and stroked.

Oh, yeah. Blake made a much better fake boyfriend than Clifford. And the look on Gabriel's face had been priceless. Almost comical.

She swallowed, her throat closing up. "Wh . . . what's your other concern?"

"That was one helluva kiss you laid on me." His thumb made its way to her mouth and traced the outline of both lips. Traitorously, they parted at his scorching touch.

"Was that a concern?" Pulse humming, her breaths came short and quick.

Closing the small space between them, his nose brushed hers. With the side of his index finger, he tipped up her chin so that their eyes locked. Gaze cloudy with desire, he looked as though he intended to devour her.

"Were you thinking of him, or me?" he asked, his voice so thick with lust that Angelique went a little weak in the knees.

Catching her around the waist, Blake hauled her against him and covered her mouth with his. He drank her in, slow and sweet. And oh, mama, she let him. His spicy taste overwhelmed her senses and clouded her mind. Melting into him, her arms instinctively circled his neck, and she opened her mouth against his onslaught, his tongue mingling with hers, searching, caressing, until a small moan escaped from somewhere. It sounded distant, like it didn't belong to her, but it did. And it communicated her pleasure and how much she enjoyed the feel of him, because he pulled her closer. One hand pressed into the small of her back, while the other found its way to her hair and anchored there at the back of her head. Her purse crashed to the ground, but neither of them flinched.

Digging her nails into his shoulders, she clung to him. Couldn't get enough of him. It had been so long, so freaking long since a man had wanted her physically. She moaned again. When Blake's hand released the back of her head, she broke the kiss and let her head fall back. Her eyes shut, he trailed hot kisses down her neck, and his hand found her breast.

She froze. Held her breath until her senses returned. Coldness filled her lungs, and she suppressed an anguished groan. No one had touched her there intimately since . . .

"Breathe, Angelique," Blake whispered, concern threading through his voice as his hand fell away from her breast.

She opened her eyes and gasped for air. His handsome face etched with concern, he searched her expression. Placing both hands flat against his chest, she pushed back, but he didn't release her.

The heat, the passion, the lust that danced in his eyes slowly transformed into something else. *Oh, God no. Not pity.* Her heart sank, then squeezed with anger.

"Let me in. You don't have to go through this alone," he said, like she was a charity case.

She pushed harder against his chest, breaking his embrace. Running a hand through her tousled hair, she tried to gather her wits. Finally, she reached for her purse and turned on him like a lion. "What do you know about it?" She headed toward the door.

"Obviously, more than you think. I'm a doctor. It's my business to know." There was sadness in his voice.

Great. He really did see her as a victim.

"Like I said, Doc. I'm not your problem." Angelique jerked the door open and hustled to her car.

Chapter Nine

Angelique's lips still burned from the heat of Blake's kiss. She leaned against the windowsill and watched Sarge torture an unsuspecting tree. Tracing her bottom lip with the tip of one finger, her eyes fluttered shut.

Sarge scratched at the door, and Angelique opened it to let him in. Kimberly's red Jeep crunched into the drive, so Angelique held the door open until her BFF pulled up and jumped out. She blew through the door carrying a purple leopard-print overnight bag.

"Hey, girlfriend!" Kimberly plopped her Bohemian-style purse onto the counter. All the metal objects dangling from it clanked together. "So it's either belly dancing or line dancing tonight. Take your pick. They're interchangeable on the bucket list."

Angelique rolled her eyes, loading a few dirty dishes into the dishwasher. "Really? Those are my only choices?" She picked up a pot and started to scrub it with a Brillo pad. And wondered how long her lips would feel swollen and bruised from the onslaught of

Blake's sizzling kiss. Her bottom lip puckered involuntarily, and she drew it between her teeth.

Kimberly studied her. "Okay, what?"

"*What*, what?" Angelique looked up at her friend and frantically scrubbed a small pot like it had radioactive waste on it. Only the running water and steel wool against metal filled the silence between them. Unless, of course, Kimberly could hear the lust Dr. Tall, Dark, and Hot-some had stirred through every fiber of Angelique's body.

Tapping her foot, Kimberly waited for an explanation until her eyes finally widened. "Oh. My. God." She gasped, and Angelique returned her attention to the pot. She really, really needed to get this pot clean.

"You got laid, didn't you?"

"*What?*" Angelique's head shot up, but she kept on scrubbing. "No!" *Not even close.* So why was she acting like a skittish college girl who'd just lost her virginity?

"Did too." Kimberly planted both hands on her hips. "You're totally doing someone. Who is it? No, wait!" she yelled, holding up a hand. "Let me guess . . ." Then she gasped again, a conspiratorial smile on her face. "It's your hot neighbor, isn't it? I told you he was fling-worthy!"

"We're not having a fling," Angelique hissed, concentrating on the pot. But oh, she'd wanted to when he'd salvaged her dignity by pretending to be her boyfriend, when his lips were on her neck, when his hand slid up that sensitive area over her ribcage. Until his palm found her breast and she panicked like an adolescent playing spin the bottle for the first time.

"Uh-huh. Well, if you scrub that pot any harder, you'll wear a hole in it." Kimberly reached over and flipped off the water. "So spill, or I'm making you do number fifty-six on the bucket list, which is skydiving, and I know how much you hate heights."

"It's not that I dislike heights, it's just that I can't understand why any rational person would willingly jump out of a perfectly good airplane." Angelique pulled a head of lettuce, a cucumber, a bag of Roma tomatoes, a few stalks of celery, and a purple onion out of the refrigerator.

"I'll push you out if you don't tell me what's going on."

With both arms full, Angelique dumped the load of veggies on the counter. "Mom, Dad, and Nona will be here soon, and I want to have lunch ready. Can we talk about this later?"

"No." Kimberly started tapping her foot again.

Angelique let out an exasperated sigh. *"All right,"* she said, and filled a large pot with water, salt, and olive oil. Then she put it on the stove and turned on the burner. "At least make yourself useful and make the salad."

Kimberly grabbed a kitchen knife from the butcher block and laid the vegetables out across the island. "I'll chop, you talk."

Hell's bells. Angelique drew in a deep breath and tried to figure out where to begin. "Turns out Dr. Blake Holloway lives next door."

Kimberly's mouth hit the floor. "You're doing the town doctor? The one who brought your thong home?"

"No!" Angelique pinched the bridge of her nose. "No, I'm not doing anyone."

"But you want to," Kimberly said in a singsong voice.

"No, I most certainly do not." Angelique bit her lip, because since this morning when she and Blake had made out like two teenagers with their clothes still on, she'd wondered what it would be like to run her hands over his *bare* chest, down his sleek, muscled back to the firm butt that his worn Levi's cupped so nicely. But then he'd want to do the same to her without clothes on, and when he got to her fake boobs . . . She shuddered with fear. "I just . . . we . . ."

"Totally pushing you out of the plane." Kimberly pointed the small knife at her.

"*Okay.*" Angelique gathered her thoughts, then recounted the whole bizarre mess with Gabriel at the bakery.

Kimberly chopped and diced more urgently. "We'll sue him for defamation, and then we'll file a civil suit. He'll be wearing rubber boots from Walmart instead of eight-hundred-dollar Italian shoes by the time we're done with him."

Angelique filled another pot with sauce and set it on the stove. "And Blake . . ."

Kimberly arched a brow while dicing a stalk of celery.

"*Dr.* Holloway happened to be handy, and I kind of pretended to be with him."

Kimberly's chopping ceased completely when Angelique described the kiss.

At the memory, Angelique busied herself by stirring the sauce as rapidly as she'd scrubbed the pot. "Don't tell Mom I'm using sauce out of a jar."

Kimberly did a turning key motion to her lips. "It's in the vault." She grabbed an apple from the fruit bowl and took a big bite.

"And all of that was *after* I almost broke his nose in a volleyball game," Angelique said as she hid the empty marinara jar at the bottom of the trash can.

"Holy shit," Kimberly said, mouth still full of apple chunks. "Red River is like a soap opera. I'm gone a few days, and all hell breaks loose."

Angelique took up Kimberly's position in front of the chopping board and viciously attacked a carrot.

"Sweetie." Kimberly put her hand on Angelique's arm that wielded the knife. "That carrot is dead now—you can rest easy."

Angelique stared down at the carrot, then put the knife down. She rubbed a hand over her cheek.

"Maiming the guy might make it harder to get him into your bed."

"I wasn't trying to get him into my bed," Angelique said through gritted teeth.

"Well, you should've been." Kimberly threw the apple core in the trash. "It's just like competitive diving."

Angelique started to speak, but her mouth just hung open. "Wait. *What?*"

Kimberly snagged a ripe banana this time, never able to satisfy her voracious metabolism. "Coaches make their divers get right back up on the board after an accident, so they're not consumed with crippling fear that will prevent them from performing again."

"Uh-huh." Angelique eyed the meat-tenderizing mallet on the counter . . . maybe a good whack would bring Kimberly back to planet earth because Angelique still didn't know what diving had to do with Blake Holloway.

"You! Sex! Men!" Kimberly hollered as though it should be obvious. "I'm the coach and you're the diver. You can't just stop because of the bad break you caught with health issues. And because Gabriel was a shallow idiot." She smacked and swallowed. "You do realize Gabriel was a shallow idiot long before you had breast cancer, right?"

Yes, yes, Angelique did realize that. It had taken her longer to see through his smooth, well-dressed facade of perfection than it should have. Looking back, the signs were there. She just hadn't wanted to see them, which made his betrayal all the more humiliating.

"He would've still been a shallow idiot even if you'd never gotten sick, so stop thinking all men are going to react to it like he did."

Angelique went to the stove, stirred the marinara sauce, and then turned the burner on low. "I am not having this conversation."

Kimberly ignored her. "If your hot neighbor is a doctor, then he of all people will be understanding about the surgeries. Give him a shot."

Angelique wished she could, except it was so much more complicated than that. Doctor or not, what if he didn't want to get naked with the bride of Frankenstein? And another rejection like the one Gabriel had doled out was more than she could withstand. She'd had her limit of heartbreak for one lifetime. She wasn't opening herself up for that again.

Even if Blake was understanding, she didn't want his pity, and they wanted completely different things in life. They had nothing at all in common. Not to mention the fact that he hated everything she represented.

Dr. Blake Holloway just wasn't an option.

A knock sounded on the front door.

"That's probably my parents, so don't say anything about Gabriel. It'll just upset them."

Kimberly polished off the banana and pitched the peel into the trash. "Fine. We'll plot his demise later."

Angelique hurried to the door, and her mom rushed in full of hugs and kisses. Her mom's salt-and-pepper hair was cropped short, and it still held quite a bit of jet-black for a woman her age. The familial resemblance was unmistakable.

"Glad you made it, Mom. How was the drive up from Albuquerque?"

"Beautiful as always this time of year." Her mom's New York accent was still noticeable even after all these years in the Southwest. "We even saw a herd of big horned sheep coming through the pass." She looked around. "The firm rented you a nice place."

"That's because my baby girl deserves the best." Her dad walked in carrying two Health Shack grocery bags. "Hi, sweat pea! We picked up some groceries in Taos." He set the bags on the counter and gave her a bear hug. His waistline had expanded several inches since he retired a few years ago, but he still had a full head of hair and a keen mind. "You're looking good." He chucked her nose like she was five years old. "What's this?" He squinted through his bifocals at the fading red patches on her neck.

"Just some poison oak." She waved off his concern and hustled to the stove to throw some pasta into the boiling water. "I got some medicated lotion for it."

"Well, I'll cut that down for you before we go back to Albuquerque in a few days," her dad said, concerned. "I never knew you were allergic to it."

"Neither did I, but there's no need. My neighbor already came over and cut it down."

Kimberly coughed. When Angelique shot her a shut-up-or-die look, Kimberly busied herself with chopping the rest of the veggies.

"Where's Nona?" Angelique asked, returning to the counter to unload the groceries. "Did you forget her in Taos?"

"I tried, but the woman followed us here anyway." He snatched some antipasto from one of the grocery bags and popped it in his mouth. "She runs fast for an old lady."

Her mom made an annoyed clucking sound and swatted him on the arm with a wooden spoon that she'd grabbed from a utensil jar on the counter.

Dad rubbed his arm.

"Nona's still in the car," her mom said. "A couple of old codgers flirted with her in the geriatric section at the health food store. She's trying to type their numbers into her smartphone but keeps dialing the fire department accidentally."

"Accidentally my right butt cheek," Kimberly scoffed. "She just wants to talk dirty to those good-looking firefighters."

"At my age, I'll take whatever action I can get." Nona walked through the door. She looked at least a hundred and ten years old. With a slight hunch to her shoulders, she shuffled along without a walker, insisting she looked younger without assistance. Soda-bottle glasses magnified her eyes into saucers, her silver hair held a bluish hue, and her New York accent was thicker than the traffic in Manhattan during rush hour. "I won't be needing to dial 911 for a while." She put a hand under her back-combed hairdo and fluffed it, the pungent odor of Final Net wafting around. "I have a date."

"Way to go, Nona." Angelique gave her a high five as she walked past to shut the door. Nona often forgot such trivial details. Details like putting the car in park, which was why her driver's license had been revoked.

Mom sputtered. "You don't even know the man! What if he's a criminal?"

"Well, I have the solution," Kimberly announced, and everybody groaned.

"Please, God, let it not be another crazy idea on your bucket list," Angelique said, because skydiving was looking better and better.

"I'm so underappreciated by this family," sulked Kimberly, crossing both arms over her breasts.

Another groan rounded the kitchen.

"I can forgive and forget, if you'll go line dancing tonight." She put an arm around Nona's shoulder and squeezed. "Saturday night in a town this size? Cotton Eyed Joe's is sure to be jumping, and Nona can invite her date."

Great. Just what Angelique needed. More interaction with the people she was about to help put out of business. Thank the angels in heaven her parents wouldn't be the least bit interested in line dancing.

Mom clasped her hands under her chin. "Oh, that sounds like fun. Of course we'll all go." She looked at Angelique. "There's nothing else to do up here, right? We might as well join in with the locals."

Angelique's heart hit her feet like a brick. Everyone in the room stared at her expectantly. "Sure. Sounds like a hoot."

Cotton Eyed Joe's on a Saturday night in October was Angelique's worst nightmare. The place was decked out with obnoxious pink ribbons. The napkins were pink. The waitstaff wore pink. Pink martinis littered every table. A handful of pink cowboy hats and pink cowboy boots even made an appearance. When the offending color whizzed past Angelique's table from the dance floor, she whistled to the server and ordered a second beer before she'd finished the first.

Uh-huh. The pink craze that settled over every community in America this time of year was enough to drive her to two-fisted drinking.

She surveyed the room. *Everyone* wore a tacky pink ribbon. Everyone except Angelique. Even her parents and Nona had coughed up money for a ribbon, ignoring Angelique's protests. Angelique sighed. Mom and Nona had been through the surgeries, too. Why couldn't they see that a pink ribbon didn't show support? It branded them a victim. Weak. Unable to move on. Unwilling to climb out of the ditch into which the disease pushed its unsuspecting and undeserving prey.

While Mom and Dad filled her in on the Barbetta family gossip, Kimberly bopped to country and western music. Well, more like her girls bounced, which garnered several ogles from the male patrons. Nona sat at a separate table with her new gentleman friend.

Every last boot-wearing, cowboy-hat-tipping, C&W-dancing person at Joe's was *happy* to be part of the festivities. Everyone but Angelique. She was ready to chug both beers and get out of Tombstone to avoid both the color pink and another confrontation with Doc Holloway. She almost snorted.

Oy vey. Maybe she should order a third beer, because all this frenzy over the color pink was making her crazy. Who picked that awful color anyway? Why not chartreuse?

Angelique drew on her mug, a pull starting low in her belly when Blake walked through the front door. His gaze zeroed in on her just as quickly, even through the boisterous crowd of patrons. All brooding and sexy, his eyes turned to smoke and the muscles in his corded neck flexed as he stared at her.

He started at the opposite side of the room and made the rounds. Angelique tried to ignore him. Tried not to snatch glimpses of his broad shoulders and easy smile as he greeted just about everyone there. Tried and failed miserably, because his quick, subtle glances in her direction made her skin sizzle and a certain spot between her thighs tingle.

Frick. If only she had three hands, she could drink until Dr. Tall, Dark, and Hot-some was just a blur and the pink turned to red.

Blake rounded the room, slow and methodical, shaking every hand. And, oh, how the locals seemed to love Doc Holloway. His smooth, country-boy manner had all the men slapping him on the back and all the women puddling at his feet. As the town's only medical doctor, he probably knew just about everyone and their secrets.

Including hers. She'd revealed a weakness when he touched her breast. A vulnerability that she hated with every ounce of her being. If the tables had been turned, she would have looked for a way to exploit that vulnerability. But not Doc Holloway. Even though she was the enemy threatening to help tear down his whole life, his Hippocratic oath had kicked in and he'd shown her compassion. Kindness.

A waitress scampered over to him like a puppy dog and coaxed a five-dollar bill out of him in exchange for a pink ribbon, which he pinned to the collar of his blue pinstriped button-up shirt. Angelique chugged on her beer as he took a seat at the end of the bar where he chatted with the bartender, Dylan, and his cousin Perry. Dylan and Perry laughed, but Blake just nodded, smiled, then returned his heavy-lidded stare to Angelique.

She pretended not to notice and nodded at something her mom said about her nephew's pediatric appointment. Really, it was a little hard to concentrate on her nephew's butt rash while surrounded by enough pink to make her nauseated and with Blake watching her every move.

It made her squirm. Made her feel self-conscious in the knit dress that showed off her tall, curvy figure. It also made her want to invite him into the parking lot and rip that crisply pressed shirt of his open without unbuttoning it first.

She looked at the frosty mugs in front of her. Jeez, she wasn't usually such a lightweight. The local brew must be potent because all she could think of right now was Blake hiking her dress up, but still leaving it to cover her breasts.

Now, there was a thought. Sex might be a possibility if she left her shirt on.

No. No. She actually shook her head. Blake wasn't her type. Not that she actually had a type anymore. Too bad she wasn't interested in women. She wouldn't feel half as insecure about her body if she was undressing in front of another woman. But she was as straight as Blake Holloway was beautifully masculine. Which meant she was really, really straight.

Lorenda came over, introduced herself to Kimberly, and waved them onto the dance floor. "Come on! I love to line dance. Doesn't require a partner."

"I'm with you, girl," Kimberly said, and they both dragged Angelique onto the dance floor just as a new song started.

"I have no idea how to do this," Angelique sputtered. "And I'm not wearing boots."

"Just follow everyone else," said Lorenda. "You'll get the hang of it."

Okay, four hands would come in handy right about now. If she could drink with all four hands at once, it might give her enough liquid courage to do this. Angelique watched the other dancers for a minute, then joined the fray. It took a few minutes to catch on, but before she knew it, she moved in step with the other dancers, sliding and turning to the beat. Laughing when she made a mistake, letting the music take her body along with the rhythm. She grooved and moved like she'd been line dancing her whole life. She quickly saw the appeal, because it was easy and fun.

Her formfitting burgundy sweater dress allowed her to move easily to the music, but her flat-heeled black shoes were a little binding. So she kicked them off at the table and ran back to reclaim her spot in between Lorenda and Kimberly. By the time they'd danced straight through three songs and worked up a little sweat, they were laughing like three teenage girls at a slumber party.

Dr. Tall, Dark, and Who? *That's right.* She didn't need a man to have fun.

Finally, the DJ announced a break from line dancing and put on a slow song for couples. Angelique and Kimberly took a seat at the table, inviting Lorenda to join them. Lorenda called over a server and ordered another round of drinks.

And here came Blake. No, no. Yes. No. *Yes.*

Relief washed through Angelique as Blake made a detour and headed toward the restrooms. And disappointment, too.

A soft country song came on, and a burly man wearing a long sandy-blond ponytail and looking to be in his midthirties came over, the spitting image of the country singer Trace Adkins. He approached Kimberly and took off his hat. "Ma'am, would you care to dance?"

Kimberly sized him up. "Sure, but I'm not going home with you," she announced, almost like it was a challenge. She did that to men. Tested them to see how quickly she could scare them off. Worked nearly every time.

"Fair enough." His amber eyes twinkled at her, like he knew her MO. "I'll settle for a dance or two, then."

Kimberly left her chair and took his arm. "And keep your big male hands north of the border. *Capiche?*"

"Yes, ma'am." He led her onto the dance floor and swung her into a fluid waltz.

Two square pegs who'd become fast friends. Angelique sighed and looked at her mom and dad, who even cuddled to the soft music.

"Sweetheart, why don't you ask one of these single men to dance," her mom said. "It's just a dance, after all."

"I was just coming to claim a spot on her dance card," said a voice from behind her, and her heart skittered. The voice slid over her like hot caramel on an ice cream sundae. She swallowed, and despite the sweat she'd worked up on the dance floor, a shiver lanced through her.

Greenwood Public Library
310 S. Meridian St.
Greenwood, IN 46143

Chapter Ten

When Blake walked up behind Angelique, it took every ounce of self-control he could muster not to touch her. A small ripple of satisfaction pinged through him when she startled at his voice, then an infinitesimal shiver slid over her.

Funny, since she was flushed from line dancing, and it wasn't the least bit drafty inside of Joe's.

He'd promised himself he wouldn't go near her tonight. Any contact he had with her should be to weaken her case or outmaneuver her legal strategy. Nothing more. But every time she shimmied her shoulders and shook her rear end in perfect rhythm with the music, his mouth had grown drier until he could almost spit cotton. Not even Joe's best brew could quench his thirst for her. Her long legs, only half covered by a short dress that revealed every curve, had flexed and teased him with every ridiculous step while she line danced with Joe's usual Saturday night crowd.

"Sorry, but I'm all danced out," Angelique said, taking a long swallow of beer without looking at him.

The older couple at the table had to be Angelique's parents because the resemblance was remarkable. When Angelique didn't make an effort to introduce them, Blake did the honors himself. "I'm Blake Holloway. Angelique's neighbor."

Blake could swear he heard Angelique's teeth grind, even over the music. He couldn't hold back a smile.

"Thanks for cutting that poison oak down. Who knew she was so allergic?" Her dad offered his hand, and Blake shook it.

"You folks up here for a visit?" Blake asked.

"Just a few days to check on our girl." Mrs. Barbetta smiled at her daughter, and Blake's heart warmed. Nice folks. Strong family ties. Angelique was luckier than she realized.

He looked at Mrs. Barbetta. "Can I steal your daughter away for a dance?" Better to go to the person with the most power. Mom.

Angelique shook her head. "I don't think so, I'm a little tir—"

"Oh, go on, dear. It'll be fun, right Frank?" Mr. Barbetta, his mug half to his lips, humphed when his wife's elbow connected with his ribs.

"Yes, of course. Go have fun, sweat pea," her dad said.

Angelique turned to Blake, her brow knitted and eyes flashing. The dark irises shimmered under the lights. When his gaze drifted over her flushed face, the tension in her expression eased. Her breath hitched, and her lips parted.

Perfect.

"What do you say, Ms. Barbetta?" His mouth curved into a knowing smile. "We can dance and talk shop at the same time."

Her eyes rounded, and she glanced at her parents. Ah, so they probably didn't know exactly what Angelique's business in Red River entailed.

Finally, she eased out of her chair and faced him. "One dance."

Smiling, he held out his arm and led her onto the dance floor. The song was slow and smooth, but she tensed like a plank of wood when he pulled her into his embrace. A light sheen of perspiration glittered across her neck and chest just above the zipper of her knit dress. The soft skin at the base of her neck pulsed.

"I'm not really a country and western dancer," she mumbled. "So easy steps, okay?"

He eased her into a simple two-step.

"Could've fooled me. You were doing a pretty good job line dancing."

"Well, that was line dancing. You don't have to follow someone else's lead. You can do it all by yourself."

"But it's so much better with a partner." His voice went husky, and he smiled at the slow burn that appeared over her sculpted cheekbones.

Changing directions, he scooted her across the dance floor in a slow cadence. Unable to accommodate the shift, she stepped on his toes. Her pink cheeks deepened to a flaming scarlet.

"I told you I don't do country and western. You don't listen."

"Well, talk slower. Maybe I can follow along," he smarted off.

She glowered at him.

He had to laugh. "You're doing just fine." He rested their clasped hands against his chest. "Don't worry about your feet. Close your eyes and feel your way through the steps."

Her body solidified into granite.

He sighed. "I'm serious. If you concentrate on the way my body shifts and moves under your hands, your feet will follow."

Her eyes rounded.

Ah, crap. That *did* sound kind of sexual, because he could easily picture his body moving and shifting with hers. And her hands. Yes, her hands would definitely be all over him.

"This . . ." She swallowed, her eyes darting around the room. "This really isn't a good idea."

"Probably not." He shifted their direction to maneuver around a corner of the dance floor. "But here we are, so let's just go with it. See where the music takes us."

She searched his expression. "What do you expect to gain? Do you think if I succumb to your charm, like all the other women in Red River, I'll give in and let you win?"

Maybe. But it was more than that. He wanted her to stop looking at him like just another case to win and see him as a man. Her attraction to him was obvious, and God help him, he wanted to get to know the woman under that impenetrable shell of hers.

"Did you just say 'succumb to my charm'?" he teased her and felt oddly gratified when annoyance flashed in her eyes.

"I did. Would you like me to explain the meaning?"

"Oh, I know what it means. They did make us learn a few vocabulary words in medical school. I just wanted to be sure that's what you said, because . . ." He smiled down at her. Slow, lazy, drawing out the moment because of how much it was going to irritate her. "Now I know you think I'm charming."

She nearly growled.

He tightened his hold on the small of her back and pulled her closer. "Not everyone has an ulterior motive, Angelique." He kind of did, but he was also bent on getting to know her as a woman. "Knock off the badass lawyer routine, drop the armor, and just be. Who knows, you might even have some fun."

"I'm not here to just *be*," she said through clenched teeth. "Or to have fun."

"I'm well aware of that." He turned her to the left, and she missed a step.

He tugged her closer, and she studied him for a moment.

"Just concentrate on the music and the movement under your fingertips." He looked deep into her shimmering eyes. Saw the moment she decided to trust him, and her eyelids fluttered shut for several beats. Long, glossy eyelashes swept the soft skin under her big ebony eyes.

He rested his cheek against her temple and breathed against her hair. A delicate tremor slid over her, and he swallowed a moan.

What was he thinking? *This is trouble, idiot.* Pulling away a fraction, he looked down at her. After a few beats, her eyes drifted open, and she swallowed.

"Where's your pink ribbon?" Blake asked.

"Pink is tacky." Her expression went hard. "And I'm not a weepy female who wallows in grief and self-pity."

Yeah, he got the not-a-weepy-female part loud and clear. Like a blinking neon sign. The kind that induced migraines. He pulled in a strained breath.

Another slow shift and they drifted in a different direction. "I haven't told anyone why you're in Red River," Blake said. "But they'll find out eventually. Rumors spread pretty fast in this town."

Her jaw hardened. "Is that supposed to be my problem?"

"The business owners involved in the case sort of designated me the leader. I'll keep it quiet as long as I can."

"Why would you do that, and why should I care?"

Because I'm an idiot? "I'm trying to keep it quiet because I'm hoping for a resolution before it gets ugly." *And so I can spend more time with you before you're run out of town by an angry mob.* They might even run him out of Red River if they thought he was protecting the person who was there to ruin their town. "And I think you do care."

The melody slowed to a close, and they stood in place, still toe-to-toe.

"Well, you're wrong, Doc. I care about doing my job. That's it."

He glanced around the room, absorbing her words. Several couples left the dance floor, while others walked on. Kimberly was already partnered up for the next dance. An elderly couple had joined Angelique's parents and were deep in conversation.

Angelique tried to pull her hand off his chest, but he kept it anchored just over his heart. He looked down at her, and his eyes dropped to her mouth. The lush pink lips parted.

No, pink wasn't in the least bit tacky. It was gorgeous and tempting.

"You can't win," she whispered, a hint of regret twined into her words.

He wasn't usually the confrontational type, but the future of Red River was too important to walk away from without a fight. Or without seeing where things might lead with Angelique, if he could just buy a little time.

"Some things are worth fighting for."

"I'm meeting with your attorney soon, and he's not up to the task."

"It's just a preliminary meeting, right?" His attorney's last e-mail said he'd set a meeting with Angelique to size up the situation so he could plan a strategy. When Blake volunteered to attend, his attorney said it wasn't necessary. Said it was routine for opposing attorneys to meet before the case really got going.

"Yes, but . . ." She pulled a lip between her teeth.

"What?" He wanted her to open up to him. And not just to get information that could help his case. He wanted her to trust him.

"Don't you get it? I'm the best at what I do."

"Modest, too."

That coaxed a glimmer of something to form in her eyes. Not anger. Not irritation. But something he couldn't quite identify because it was almost akin to regret.

Her gaze hovered on their clasped hands. "Why are you going to make me humiliate you and your friends?"

"Because deep down I don't think you really want to do that. And what kind of man would I be if I didn't fight for what's mine?"

Another song started, this one a little faster. He wasn't sure Angelique could handle a quicker two-step, so he just swayed in place. Her body followed his in rhythm.

"I'll win. Guaranteed. Advise your friends to take the buyout deal my clients are offering."

"Your clients are offering a fraction of what our properties are worth."

"At least you'll come out of it with something, and you can start over."

He shook his head. "It's not that simple for some of us." A few of the proprietors would retire. Some had owned their office space long enough to pay it off and could start over in a different location if they wanted. But most, including him, had mortgaged their properties and would likely end up flat broke or bankrupt when it was over.

And she'd be gone from Red River and from his life, probably forever.

No. No, it wouldn't be possible for some of the business owners to start over. She'd studied the file and knew that several of them would be wiped out financially.

Blake's heartbeat thrummed under her palm, his hand engulfing hers. She'd come to Red River with a very simple agenda—win an easy case for a mega client that would catapult her into a partnership. A task she should be able to complete in her sleep. Unfortunately, her sleep had been invaded by a tall, incredibly well built country doctor, and the simple task had suddenly become very difficult.

Because you're letting it get personal.

Angelique looked up into Blake's baby blues, and her throat nearly closed because they skimmed over her entire face. Slow and smooth like the music. Like his molten lava voice and silky touch, saying so much, even though no words left his mouth.

His eyes turned from smoke to fire, and they nearly burned her up with their heat. The air around them snapped with energy. Hot. Sexy. Very, very dangerous.

She wanted . . . him. But . . . she couldn't imagine . . .

Closing her eyes, she dislodged her hand from his and stepped back. "This is highly irregular."

"Two people dancing is irregular?" Blake asked, an innocent smile on his lips. Wickedness in his eyes.

She may already be on thin ice at the firm because of Gabriel and his ludicrous accusations. Her career had taken a few heavy hits lately. Flirting with the enemy camp wouldn't likely help. Thankfully, Gabriel hadn't paid enough attention to this particular case or Blake to know she was crossing some boundaries. This case didn't revolve around Gabriel, so he wasn't likely to give it a second thought. But her biggest fear wasn't for her career.

The way her girly parts turned flips when Blake was within shouting distance had her quaking in her little black patent leather slip-ons. Even more frightening was the fact that he made her heart skitter and thump. The fact that she wanted to wrap herself around Blake every time she saw him was the problem. It would lead to taking off her shirt with him in the room, because resisting his touch, resisting the desire in his eyes, was wearing her down and quickly becoming impossible. Terror settled in her gut and nearly paralyzed her.

"I—" Her voice was cut off by her own strangled gasp for air. "I can't do this," she finally managed to eke out.

He took a step toward her. "Angelique."

"No!" Her feet moved her another step backward. She turned and darted for the bathroom.

Angelique locked the bathroom door and stood in front of the mirror, the music dulling behind the closed door.

"You. Are. Suchanidiot," she seethed at herself in the mirror. "Get your act together."

A knock sounded on the door as she rolled her head around on her shoulders. She stared at herself again in the mirror.

The knocking turned into a pound, but not in a rhythm like most people would knock. It was more like an odd bang, boom, bump.

She took a deep breath, went to the door, unlocked it, and plastered a smile on her face before stepping out into the hallway, where the music overwhelmed her senses again. And she came face-to-face with a life-size inflatable pink ribbon and a poster girl for breast cancer. The fortyish woman with a curly bob was dressed in Pepto-Bismol pink from the top of her pink cowboy hat, to her flouncy pink square dancing dress, all the way down to her pointy pink boots. She struggled to drag the mammoth ribbon toward the dancehall but lost her grip on it.

Angelique's head snapped back to avoid getting slapped in the face by the runaway ribbon.

"Oh, sorry! This darned thing got away from me and kept hitting the bathroom door," Pepto Cowgirl said. "And every time I bend over to grab it, this silly dress hikes up and shows too much of my behind. Not a pretty sight, you know what I'm sayin'?" She moved to the other side of the ribbon to get a better grasp on it. "What we do for a good cause, right?"

Was there no escaping the cursed ribbons? They were even stalking Angelique in the ladies' room.

"Hey, where's your ribbon?" blurted Pepto Cowgirl.

Before Angelique could make an excuse, Pepto Cowgirl pulled a ribbon from the pocket on her dress and pinned it to Angelique's sweater.

Angelique looked at the ribbon on her chest like it might bite her. "I don't—"

"It probably just fell off, sugar. Just let me know if you lose it again." She patted her pocket. "Plenty more where that came from."

Angelique gasped for air because it had suddenly become scarce. An anger as deep and vast as outer space welled up inside her until she thought she might implode. She reached up and fisted the ribbon in her hand. But before she could rip it off and tell this . . . this . . . *person* to watch who she went around pinning disgusting ribbons onto, a voice sounded at the entrance of the hallway.

"Hey, Donna." Blake came up beside them.

Just his voice soothed the ache in her heart and the knot in her chest.

"I see Red River's postmaster is working hard for the cause." He spoke to Donna, but his warm eyes and knowing smile stayed firmly on Angelique. "Let me get you some help for that thing." He turned and whistled through the entrance to the dancehall, and two young men bounded over to pick up the ribbon.

"I need some fresh air." He smiled at Donna. "It's getting stuffy in there." Then he turned to Angelique. "You're looking a little pale, ma'am. Want to join me outside for a few minutes? You look like you need to cool off."

Yes, please. Anything to get away from all the pink before it suffocated her.

She nodded.

"Thanks, Doc," said Donna, and she flounced into the dancehall in pursuit of her giant ribbon.

They were just silly little ribbons. Why did they hold so much power over her? But they were like pink kryptonite, and she hated them. Hated herself for hating them.

Angelique looked up into his glittering eyes, and oh . . . my . . . God. Her resolve crumbled on the spot, because understanding gleamed in them. Something she'd never gotten from Gabriel. She'd just *succumbed to Blake's charm*, because really, how could she not? She sent him a silent thank-you with a blink and a smile because he really was pretty amazing for rescuing her again. If he hadn't intervened, she'd most certainly have said something she would've regretted to one of Red River's obviously dedicated and hardworking civil servants who had done nothing wrong except try to be friendly to a stranger.

His gaze wrapped around her like a warm quilt that she could curl up and stay in . . . forever. Her heart stuttered.

His smile broadened and those baby blues twinkled, like he could read her thoughts. God, he was sex on wheels. Angelique traced her bottom lip with the tip of her tongue.

A middle-aged man pushed through them, muttering, "Excuse me," and entered the men's room.

He reached up and unpinned the pink ribbon from her sweater dress. "I can walk you back to your table if you'd prefer." His gaze searched hers.

She shook her head and swallowed. "I can't go back in there."

He placed a hand on her hip and rubbed with the palm of his hand. His breath smoothed over her cheeks, warmed her soul. She put a hand on Blake's chest, and for a second, she thought he would kiss her. She wanted it. As much as it terrified her, she still wanted him.

Blake's gaze shifted over her shoulder to the back door. "Let's go out the back way."

Chapter Eleven

The back door of Cotton Eyed Joe's swung shut with a thud, but Blake didn't look back. Instead, he veered right and pulled Angelique along the back side of Joe's, her fingers twined with his.

He was crazy. Or stupid. Or both. But when he walked into the hallway to find the men's room and saw a mixture of emotions colliding in Angelique's expression while she gripped that pink ribbon, Blake's protective instinct had engaged.

Blake didn't slow his pace. He still wasn't thinking. Didn't know exactly what he was doing or where he was going. All right, maybe he did. He wanted to be alone with Angelique and have it out once and for all. Or slide his mouth and his hands all over her. Either was fine by him.

Tugging backward, she stopped him. "Wait. Where are we going? My parents and Kimberly are inside." Foggy breaths swirled around them in the frigid night temperature, and she bundled into herself against the cold air.

He pulled her a few more steps, a dim street lamp on the far side of the parking lot helping him find his way on the shadowed walkway against Joe's. "Send them a text. Tell them I'm bringing you home. Later."

She stopped them again and looked up at the clear night sky, stars twinkling down on them. Shivering against the cold, she rubbed her upper arm with her free hand. "I . . ." She looked at him again. "It's not a good idea, Blake."

That one word, his name whispering through her lips, was his undoing. He wanted to hear it tumble out of her mouth when she orgasmed with him deep inside her. Pulling her into him, he anchored one hand around her hip and the other at the nape of her neck. He eased her up against the back red brick wall of Joe's. One knee slid between her thighs and coaxed them apart. She trembled in his arms, and her small, balmy gasp brushed across his cheek. Her warmth curled around him, and he pinned her hips with his. Warmth turned to heat as she responded to him, her hips pressing against his erection.

His pants had grown two sizes too small the second he stepped through the door at Joe's and felt her presence before his eyes even found her. When he scanned the crowd and snagged her with his gaze, he'd grown granite-hard instantly.

When he pressed his hips into hers, she gasped again. A little deeper this time, and he suddenly felt very overdressed. Wanted to peel every piece of clothing off both of them and feel the heat of her bare skin against his.

"Call me Blake again," he whispered against her lips, the tip of his nose caressing hers. Their rapid breaths engulfed them in a cloud of fog.

"What?" she panted out when one of his hands found the hem of her dress and slid under it, fingers flexing into her thigh.

His other hand caressed the side of her neck, traced her jawline with his thumb. "You've never called me Blake. Except when you introduced me to your ex and pretended I was your boyfriend, so that doesn't count."

"You're still not my boyfriend."

He nipped at her bottom lip, and it separated from the top, quivering. "Say it." Moonlight glinted off her black pupils.

She swallowed. "Blake," she finally whispered in a small voice.

It drove him insane with need because *Dr. Holloway* was just another case to her. A legal rival. Blake was a man.

His mouth closed over hers, not slow, not cautious. Just raw desire as his tongue sought out hers, and a sexy little noise escaped from the back of her throat. Blake groaned and sank against her, an ache starting somewhere below the belt and spreading through his entire body. He'd wanted her all night. Couldn't control his need for her, even though he'd tried. Now, pressing her hard against the brick wall, he wanted to get rid of her dress and see if she felt as soft, as good as he'd imagined she would. Remove the soft layer of fabric that dulled her blazing heat against him. When the tension in her body finally softened and she sank into the kiss, threading her arms around his neck, he wanted to take her right there against the wall.

But no. Not in a dreary back parking lot with the stench of Joe's garbage a few feet away.

When his mouth left hers to feather kisses along her neck, her skin pebbled under his mouth. Short, desperate breaths ruffled his hair, nuzzled his ear, sending a convulsive charge straight through him to his aching prick. She whimpered out his name again, and his cock roared, the roughness of his pants all the more bothersome. His fingers traversed up her thigh to cup her ass, and oh yeah, she had on a pair of tiny panties that weren't as big as the span of his palm. The soft lace tickled his fingertips.

"I don't think I've had the pleasure of seeing this pair." He smiled against the soft curve of her neck. Just enjoyed the feel of her in his hands, her tall frame fitting so perfectly against his. "Sarge is disappointing me."

The back door of Joe's opened, and he froze, her fevered body flush against his, her hot, wet breaths feathering across his neck. He turned, shielding her with his body. Cheesy fluorescent light and a catchy Rascal Flatts song poured into the parking lot. A couple seriously under the influence sloshed out along with the light and the music and staggered in the opposite direction toward the inn across the street.

When they were out of earshot, Blake looked down at her. "Send the text."

She hesitated. "My phone's inside."

He reached into his back pocket and withdrew his. He handed it to her.

It took her a few moments to decide. Seemed like an eternity to Blake. But just when he thought she'd push him away and walk back inside, she surprised him and reached for the phone. Typing in a message, she looked up at him a second before hitting Send, her eyes glassy with lust and worry.

Blake stroked her cheek with the back of an index finger. "You're beautiful, Angelique. So beautiful." He traced her bottom lip with the pad of his thumb, and her lips parted for him. Called to him. God, he wanted her. Even if it wasn't forever, he'd take whatever time she was willing to give him.

She dragged in a ragged breath, and her eyes clenched shut. "It's just that . . . they're . . . they're not—"

He placed a finger against her lips, silencing her. "I know."

They're not real. He'd known that was a possibility after finding out she was a survivor. Figured it was likely because of the way she'd reacted the first time he touched her breast. He didn't care. It didn't matter to him, but it mattered to her. Would matter to any woman. She'd lost part of herself. The part that most defines a woman's femininity and mental self-image.

His lips grazed hers. "Hit Send."

Pulling a plump lower lip between her teeth, she did what he asked.

Besides the neon beer signs in Joe's front windows, darkness shrouded Main Street as Angelique let Blake lead her toward his office. In the thick silence, Angelique could swear her heartbeat was audible. She wasn't ready for this, was she? But Blake's hands touching her, his mouth on hers, and the way his eyes had devoured her all night had made her feel like a desirable woman again. Something she hadn't felt in a long, long time.

His phone beeped, and he glanced at it. "It's for you." He handed the phone to her, and they stopped in front of his office door.

She read Kimberly's text as Blake fumbled with his keys. A Jeep turned onto Main Street, flicking on its high beams. Blake turned to the light and found the right key.

Go, girl! I'll take parents home.

You kids have fun!

XXOO ;-)

Angelique responded with I won't be out long, because hell's bells, how much time could they really spend in his office?

A few seconds later another text popped onto the screen.

Damn sure better be out late. HAVE FUN!!!

;-)

After a few jiggles, the sticky lock turned with a click, and Blake pulled her through the doorway. A small security light illuminated the interior just enough to get her bearings, while he locked the door behind them. Grabbing her hand, he grazed the back of it with his lips, and then led her down the hall and into his private office.

"This way." He led them through a door in the far corner of his office, then up a narrow wood staircase. The ancient wood creaked under their steps.

"What's up here?" She felt her way along the wall through the dark. Her grip tightened around his hand.

"My old apartment," he said as they reached the landing. "I lived here for a couple of years before I bought the cabin."

"Do you own it?"

He turned the doorknob and it opened, unlocked. "Yeah, I own both floors. For now."

Angelique drew in a sharp breath and closed her eyes. "Me coming here. It doesn't change anything."

"I didn't expect it to." He stepped aside and let her enter.

Shutting the door, he flipped a switch, and light flooded the small kitchen behind him.

The studio apartment was old, seriously in need of renovations, but sentimental with a warm feel to it. Original wood floors, scarred with age. Brick walls, old style like back in her parents' old neighborhood in Brooklyn where they used to visit family. The single-paned windows had rattled when he shut the door. No furniture, except an old velour recliner that had seen better days and a tube television with rabbit ears.

"I kept the bare minimum here when I moved to the cabin. Comes in handy when I need to take a break between patients."

Angelique walked to the window and took in the grand view of Red River's historic business district, small house lights dotting the foothills, and the silhouette of Wheeler Peak soaring in the distance with a full moon hanging over it. The computer-drawn sketches of the new resort didn't compare to the nostalgia of what was already here. Of what would no longer exist if her clients got their way. The whole thing, the apartment, the lofted view that it offered of Red River and Wheeler Peak—it was . . . It was . . .

Totally. Freaking. Gorgeous. Just like the owner.

With some renovations, the apartment would be exquisite. "I never knew Red River was so beautiful at night. Seeing it from up here gives it a totally different perspective. It's amazing."

"I planned to remodel both floors after I paid off my student loans. Medical school was expensive." He tossed his keys on the counter that separated the den from the small kitchen. They skidded across the butcher block laminate. "If I'm still here by then."

Guilt threaded through her, because he wouldn't be.

She turned around to face him. Dread and regret beat at her chest for what she had to do to this town. "You know if I don't do my job, they'll just find another attorney who will." Her voice shook, each breath becoming a little heavier. She had to convince him, wanted him to know why she had to finish her work here. Recusing herself from this case wouldn't stop the resort developers from getting what they wanted. Only one thing could stop them. One tiny little thing that Blake's incompetent attorney hadn't discovered yet. That's why her clients wanted her to push the deal through before someone found the loophole in the law.

"It's not over 'til it's over." He kept advancing on her. "Do you really want to talk about it right now? Because I don't. I don't really want to talk at all." He stepped into her space. "Unless you're going to say my name again. Preferably in the form of a scream coupled with the words *yes* and *more*."

A shudder raced through her. Earthy maleness wafted off of him like testosterone in overdrive.

The Land of the Dead between her legs was now very, very much alive. Coaxed out of its tomb like Lazarus. Her entire body and soul reverberated with desire. She wanted him. Wanted him to touch her and make her feel like a real woman again. But . . .

There were so many reasons why this was a bad idea. Countless, in fact. Her lawyer brain kicked in, making a mental list, building a case.

His gaze roamed over her heated face, and he lifted one hand to trail a finger down her neck. Her breath caught.

Reason One: Conflict of interest, dummy.

"You're so beautiful." His index finger lingered at the notch between her shoulder and neck.

She swallowed.

Reason Two: No one's seen you naked since Gabriel, and you know how well that went.

His finger traced her collarbone and cut a line down the center of her chest. Tugging down the zipper in the front of her dress a few inches, his finger caressed the skin between her breasts.

"Does that bother you?"

She shook her head, another breath lodging right under his fingertip.

"I've wanted you since the first time we met." His gaze started at her eyes and traveled down to her feet. He ate her up with his stare. "Even with your giant curlers and creepy puppet slippers." His finger caressed farther down until it connected with her bra.

Heat thundered through her veins.

"Even after I found out why you're here."

Reason Three: You have fake boobs!

Fear lanced through her and stabbed her in the gut.

"I don't care about the surgeries you've had," he said like he read her thoughts.

She tried to steady the tremors that coursed through her. It wasn't too late. She could still bolt for the door. "Um, here's your phone." She held it out, trying to delay so she could think this through.

Without taking his hungry eyes off her, he grabbed the phone and tossed it onto the lonely chair.

"This won't change my professional decisions," she said, but he put a palm at the back of her neck and hauled her against his firm chest. Hard. Male.

All mine. For the next few hours, she reminded herself.

"We'll see about that," he said and captured her mouth with his. *Reason Four: Wait. What was three again?*

She melted into him because he tasted so freaking good. Felt so good molded against her. Angling her head, he deepened the kiss.

Oh, to hell with four.

One arm slid around his neck, and the other hand caressed his jaw. Hard and masculine just like the rest of his beautiful body, with just the hint of stubble. His curious hands explored her, leaving a trail of heat everywhere they touched. Traversed the curves and valleys of her body until every cell blazed with frustrated desire. Just about the only place on her body his hands didn't seek out were her breasts.

When his mouth left hers, she wanted it back. Fisting a handful of his soft hair, she pulled gently, trying to guide his lips back to hers like a heat-seeking missile locking on to its target. He laughed against her throat, then nipped at her earlobe. A jolt of desire shot through her, and she let out a small but urgent moan. Her head fell back.

"Blake."

He cupped her bottom, pulling her against an awe-inspiring erection. She laced one leg around his thigh.

"Blake, what?" His voice ragged, his heavy breaths caressed her moist neck and sent convulsive shivers through her from head to curling toes.

"Blake, *yes*," she whispered.

In one fluid movement, he cupped her bottom with both hands and lifted her. Her legs instinctively clamped around his waist. As he carried her into the bedroom, she rested her forehead against his.

"I won't touch you anywhere you're not comfortable. It's your call, not mine." His voice was soft, kind. Loving. No wonder most of Red River's female population threw themselves at him. She nodded and closed her eyes.

The bedroom was empty except for an old brass-framed bed. Shades up, the full moon filtered into the room and lit half of his face as they walked past the window. She stroked his illuminated cheek with her fingers, the light stubble prickling the tips. Gently, he lowered her to the bed, the springs creaking their approval.

Heart thundering, she settled back into the soft quilt.

It had taken every ounce of courage she possessed to undress in front of Gabriel after the first surgery. Shirtless and alone, she'd spent a good hour looking at her scars in the mirror before letting him into their room. Staring at her reflection, she'd felt like the bride of Frankenstein, all pieced and sewn together with body parts that didn't belong to her. She'd finally let him in, expecting loving words of encouragement and soft caresses of acceptance. Instead revulsion and pity had flashed in his eyes. His rejection was a kick in the gut, causing more emotional scars than those left on her body.

Blake's thoughtfulness and gentleness were already so different than Gabriel's actions. But what about when she took her clothes off and Blake saw her in the buff? Sure, the finished product didn't *look* like mutilated flesh. They looked pretty real, until you got up close and personal. Then they reminded her of a kindergarten paper doll that had different body parts cut out and glued together that didn't actually belong.

Thank God the light was out.

He lay next to her on his side and splayed a hand on her tummy. "How much feeling do you have left?"

She knew what he meant without having to ask, and the fact that he'd cared enough to ask made her heart ache with gratitude. Still, she hesitated. "Not much on top." Her voice shook a little. "I can feel more over the ribcage." She swallowed, because her mouth had gone dry. "You know, under my arm."

"Do you still have pain?" His hand slid up her torso to the zipper. It whizzed as he tugged it all the way to the bottom of her minidress. The soft knit material fell away, exposing her bra and panties. The moonlight cascaded across her legs, leaving the rest of her in shadows. For that she was grateful. With a wiggle of each foot, her flat Mary Janes thudded against the hardwood flooring.

"Some." She pointed just right of her breastbone. "Right here."

He placed his hand back on her bare tummy, fingers spread wide. An intimate warmth ignited under his palm and spread through her. He leaned in and kissed the spot she'd indicated.

"Can you feel that?" he whispered against her skin, and placed another wet, warm kiss in the same spot.

Her skin pebbled and everything inside her tightened with arousal. Not so much from the kiss, because she had no feeling in that spot, but because of his tenderness, his gentle thoughtfulness. She nearly had an orgasm right then.

"Not much," she breathed out. "But it's still nice."

His hand drifted up her torso, detoured around her breast, and slid her sweater off one shoulder. His mouth moved to the flesh just above her breast. "That?"

More moist kisses caressed her, and her head bobbled up and down like a puppet on a string. "I can feel that a little." Her words came in heavy breaths, and she clutched at his shoulders.

He moved to her shoulder, tugging the lace bra strap away. Hot breaths against her skin made her want to scream, but she bit it back, letting his essence, his touch settle over her. When his mouth touched the small indention between her collarbone and shoulder, she couldn't hold back the whimper that clawed to get out. He smiled against her shoulder. "You can feel that."

"Yes," she breathed out.

Gently, he dislodged her arm from his neck and threaded his fingers through hers and pinned her hand to the bed above her head to give him better access. His mouth traveled downward, around her breast, over the side of her bra, to her ribcage just under her breast and arm. When he suckled the skin, tracing the well between each rib with the tip of his tongue, she arched violently against him.

"Oh, God," she gasped, barely able to speak without screaming.

"This spot seems to be your favorite. So far." He suckled down her top rib again.

With her free hand, she grabbed for the hem of his shirt. Wanted to feel his bare chest against her, but he'd sunk too low, so she threaded one set of fingers through his hair. "Yes," she said, her tone urgent. "I like that spot."

Releasing her hand, he dropped lower, his tongue and lips working their magic along her side all the way to her waist. She couldn't breathe.

"You're so damned sexy," he said, just before nipping at the skin around her belly button. "You drive me crazy."

She wanted to tear his clothes off and look at him. But at the moment, her brain couldn't command her hands to push him off of her. Not with his mouth and tongue exploring her . . .

His soft kisses lowered to the triangle between her thighs. Warm, moist breaths through the thin lace that rubbed against her made her insides clench and beg for more. Now both hands anchored in his hair.

"*Blake!*" Her voice was urgent, demanding.

"Blake, what?" He teased her. Taunted her to the point of cruelty.

"Blake," she rasped out, and swallowed. "*More.*"

When his mouth left her, an empty coldness covered the spot where his moist warmth had been, but only for a moment. He stood and had his shirt unbuttoned and discarded by the time she could raise up on both elbows to watch him. He kicked off his hiking boots and retrieved a wallet from his back pocket. With a toss it landed on the bed.

Holy jeez, he was beautiful. Hard. Sinewy.

She drank him in shamelessly while he unbuttoned his Levi's. A muscled chest and sculpted arms flexed against the moonlight. The sight of his hardened body turned her insides into liquid fire, heating her all over again.

But nothing prepared her for the final revelation. When his pants and boxer briefs fell away and he kicked them to the side, she drew in an inspired breath.

Awe-inspiring indeed.

He held out a hand, and she took it, rising off the bed.

"Now you," he said, and slid his hands under the edges of her gaping sweater dress. He pushed it down her arms, and it swooshed to the floor when she pulled the sleeves over each hand. His eyes raked over her, and his breath turned ragged. "I knew you'd be this gorgeous."

"You've been fantasizing about me without clothes on?" she teased.

"Twenty-four-seven." His arm encircled her, and he traced the length of her spine with his fingertips. "Have you thought about me?" The other hand dipped inside her panties to caress her bottom. She shivered.

Heck yeah. "No," she said, her eyes fluttering shut.

"Liar." His mouth found hers, just as the other hand plunged into the back of her panties and lowered the swatch of lace. With a small kick, they flew in the same direction as his pants. Deepening the kiss, he slid his hands up her back to the fastening of her bra. Heart thumping, she tensed.

He broke the kiss and placed one on her temple instead. Rested his mouth there so affectionately that Angelique's heart squeezed. Gabriel hadn't been half as loving and considerate *before* her illness. Afterward, he'd turned into a stone-cold bastard. Kimberly was right. Gabriel had always been a prick, and her illness hadn't made him that way. It had simply exposed it.

"We can stop."

That's all Blake said. Three simple words revealed the depth of his character. The deep well of compassion running through him. The love he had to give to the right person.

They had tonight. That was enough. Had to be. She could never give him what he would surely want in the future if they started a real relationship. Relationships either led to marriage and kids, or they led to heartbreak. She couldn't risk either. But tonight she wanted to be his.

She shook her head. "No." Her eyes lifted to meet his. "I don't want to stop." A stinging thought paralyzed her for a fleeting moment. Maybe *he* was having second thoughts. "Unless, you do. I'd understand if you did." She tried to pull back, but he held her firm against his chest. The muscles flexed under her fingertips.

"Does it feel like I want to stop?" Voice husky, he dropped a hand to her ass and pulled her hips tighter against his magnificent erection.

Laughter bubbled through her lips. "I'm just nervous. I haven't . . . well, it's just that . . ." She fell silent for a beat. "I don't want to stop," she finally said.

His strong hands slid up her back again and found the fastenings. With a quick flick of his expert fingers, the bra was gone, and their bare bodies melded together like hot wax pouring into a mold. Her bare breasts pressed against the hardness of his chest, and she felt . . . sensual . . . like the same woman she'd been before she'd given her body over to be butchered. And she wanted him. She didn't care how, she just wanted him in her, driving her to the cliff of desire then pushing her over into oblivion. Just this once.

Careful to stay out of the moonlight, she stepped backward, away from him, and grabbed his hand, pulling him with her. His breaths quickened, and he followed her onto the bed. The box springs groaned again, and so did she when his clever hand found her curls and parted them. He stroked, gently at first, as his mouth captured hers. As his thumb circled that small spot between her legs that unleashed fire into her limbs, she squirmed with pleasure. He anchored one of her legs with his to open her to his very capable fingers.

And oh, what excellent fingers.

"Blake," she whimpered.

His index finger slid into her while that thumb still stroked the little nodule of pleasure.

"Blake, what?" He pressed his finger deeper.

"Yes!" Her entire body arced into him. Desperate, before she lost her mind, she grasped his impressive length in one hand and stroked up and down the expansive flesh.

His groan filled the room.

Reaching for his wallet, he retrieved a gold square and ripped it open with his teeth. She took the condom from him and rolled it on. Her hand caressed down his thickness with deliberate strokes while his lips sought out hers. Finally, the condom was on, and Angelique tightened her grip.

With a quick, smooth motion, he had her pinned beneath him, his knees nudging her thighs open. Placing his erection at her entrance, he sank into her just an inch. She clawed at his shoulders, her hips rising to meet him, but he didn't go any farther.

When she opened her eyes, disoriented and frustrated, he watched her with lust-glazed eyes.

"More," she whispered. He smiled, triumphant and self-satisfied.

"You're beautiful, Angelique." And he sank fully into her with one stroke.

Her entire body convulsed into an earth-shattering orgasm, and Angelique knew she'd never be the same again. The response his body coaxed from hers was mind-bending as he rolled his hips into her, heightening the sensations that exploded inside her.

Their fit was pure perfection. Nothing like Angelique had ever known. They moved together, finding that perfect rhythm that only happened once in a lifetime. The fruition of partnering with the one person in the universe who was made just for you.

In mere minutes, her insides began to contract around him, and she clung to him with every ounce of strength she had.

"Jesus, Angelique, you fit me like a glove," he said, his voice hoarse, his breathing hard, his heart pounding against hers.

He slid a hand under her bottom and gripped, reaching even deeper inside of her with each new stroke.

A shriek of pleasure that may have sounded like Blake's name pierced the lusty haze that shrouded her mind. She plunged over the cliff of ecstasy again, her entire body writhing under him, and dragged him over with her.

They lay still for a long time, their heartbeats and breaths intertwining until they became one. When their breathing steadied, Blake rolled over onto his back and pulled her with him. One arm around her shoulders, the other stroked her hair.

"You okay?" he asked.

Still speechless from the unbelievable response he'd elicited from her body . . . twice . . . she nodded and placed a gentle kiss on his chest. Then she nuzzled her cheek into the same spot, one hand caressing his pec.

A band of crickets struck up a tune somewhere in the apartment.

"Thank you," she mumbled against his chest. "For being so . . ." *Sweet. Hot. Big.* ". . . understanding."

His fingers gently caressed her hair, and he placed a soft kiss on her forehead. "Only a wuss wouldn't be."

When she circled his nipple with one finger, his manhood twitched. She smiled, turned her lips on the other nipple, and drew it into her mouth. Another remarkable erection sprang to life and pressed against her hip.

"How many condoms do you have with you?" she asked, then nibbled at the taut nipple again.

"Enough." He pulled her on top so she straddled him. "I promise you'll leave here tonight sufficiently satisfied."

"I'm counting on it," she said, as he placed one hand at the nape of her neck and pulled her mouth to his. And she really was counting on it, because this would be the only time they'd be together as lovers.

Chapter Twelve

A sense of contentment that Angelique had never imagined cloaked her like the warm quilt she and Blake had just left behind in his old apartment. She wasn't ready to let go of either Blake or the fulfillment he'd just given her. But she had to.

Sadness crept in to push out the warmth in her soul. And that old quilt? She could snuggle into it and stay forever, especially if Blake were in it too.

When they pulled into her drive, every light in the cabin was out. The same quiet peacefulness that had settled over her when she was in Blake's arms blanketed the landscape at this late hour.

"Pull around to the back. Looks like everyone's in bed," Angelique said. Thank the angels in heaven because she really didn't want to answer an onslaught of questions from Kimberly, especially with her parents visiting.

He parked and killed the engine.

"I'm fine from here. No need to walk me to the door."

Of course he ignored her. He got out and met her on the other side of the truck. As they walked up the path toward the back door, his fingers threaded through hers. They climbed the steps in silence, except for the nocturnal insects that came alive every night. And Angelique's heartbeat. It pounded in her ears. She jumped when an owl hooted from a nearby tree.

She should tell him now, tell him it had to be over before it ever really got started. A clean break would be the least painful for the both of them. Their lives were on separate paths, and they wanted different things in their futures.

Not true. Actually, they probably did want at least some of the same things. A family. Kids. Only she couldn't have what she wanted, but he still could. Better to end it before her heart was broken all over again, because he'd already taken a piece of her soul tonight. Nothing would ever fill it the way he had with his tender lovemaking.

At the door, Blake pulled her into his arms and kissed her. Soft and sensual. He let out a satisfied sigh as he deepened the kiss, and it wrung the same involuntary response from her.

Finally he broke the kiss and brushed a strand of hair off her forehead. "You better go inside. You're too loud for us to get started with your parents inside."

She blew out a shy laugh.

He found her lips again, caressed them with his own. Pulling back just a breath, she traced his bottom lip with the tip of her tongue.

His arms tightened around her, and one hand sank to her butt. He molded her against his male firmness. He really was hard all over. Impressively so.

"Seriously," he whispered against her lips. "You better go inside before I take you back to my place."

That would be fine with her. Except that it wouldn't.

"See you tomorrow?" he asked, staring down at her.

She hesitated. Tensed. And he went still.

"Blake, this is getting too complicated. I have to meet with your attorney next week."

He dragged a hand over his jaw and hauled in a breath. "We'll figure it out."

With a shake of her head, she pushed out of his embrace. "There's nothing to figure out. I'm a very good attorney. Do you know what that means?"

He shoved both hands into his pants pockets and looked out over the shimmering night sky. "It means you're going to win, and this town will change forever." He looked at her again. "And my work here will be over."

"It means you won't like me very much when I'm done here. It wouldn't be the first time someone loathed me for being good at my job," she said, her voice shaky. "You can do good work and help people anywhere, Blake."

He smirked. "It's not as simple as you keep trying to make it sound."

"Life never is. That's why this can't be." She waggled an index finger between them.

He stared at her for a second, then backed off the porch. "I'll see you tomorrow."

———

Misty images of Angelique panting his name and asking for more undulated through Blake's dreams until he woke up in the purple haze of dawn with the quilt tenting.

Best night's sleep he could remember in . . . well, ever.

He pulled himself out of bed, showered, and started working on a few repairs around the cabin. A leaky faucet, a few new nails in the back porch steps. His machete made quick work of the poison oak around his cabin so Angelique wouldn't get another rash when she came over. If she came over.

Oh, she'd come over. He'd make sure of it.

The work kept him busy, but his thoughts didn't stray from the hardheaded Italian beauty living next door. He hadn't been able to focus all morning because of last night's images of Angelique in the clutches of an orgasm while under him . . . on top of him . . . even when she'd pulled on his T-shirt and they'd gone into the kitchen for a drink of water, they'd somehow ended up against the wall making good use of another condom before finally collapsing into bed again.

She'd been every bit as beautiful naked as she was dressed. Of course he hadn't seen her with the light on, but the plastic surgeon who had done her reconstruction was obviously good, because in the moonlight they looked natural and better than most real breasts he'd seen. Which was a lot, considering he was a doctor. He'd wanted to touch them, taste them, but she'd have to make that move eventually.

Hopefully there would be an eventually. Stubborn-ass woman.

By late morning, the mist had burned off, and the sun hung high and bright in the cloudless sky. Unable to stay away from Angelique any longer, he tossed his tools in the shed and headed across the footbridge.

As he walked up to Angelique's cabin, Blake heard Sarge bark from the backyard. As he detoured around the side, Angelique and Kimberly's voices pierced through the quiet morning air. He stopped and listened to them chat on the back porch.

"I told you Dr. Tall, Dark, and Hot-some was fling-worthy," said Kimberly, apparently slurping a cup of coffee.

The corners of his mouth quirked up. They'd named him?

The robust scent made his mouth water for both the coffee and Angelique, and he suddenly wanted to curl up in a blanket with her and sip from the same mug. Right before he took her back to bed and made her scream his name all over again.

"It was one night," Angelique said. "That's it."

"Doesn't have to be," her friend argued.

Damn straight it didn't have to be, and he'd have to remember to thank Kimberly.

"My work here makes it impossible." Angelique called to Sarge.

"Have you considered telling the firm to piss off? I mean, really, after Gabe the Douchebag was caught screwing your legal assistant on company property, they should've asked for his resignation, but they didn't, and now he's trying to pin his financial discrepancies and his case file mismanagement on you."

Blake bristled. Tried to focus on the cedar siding of her cabin, counting the rings in the wood to keep himself from rounding the corner, demanding Gabriel's address, and driving all the way to Albuquerque to relieve him of his ability to chew for a while.

"Gabriel can't back up his accusations," Angelique said.

"What if the firm believes him? They haven't held him accountable for any of his behavior so far."

"I'll figure something out. I'm not about to let him ruin my chances for a partnership to save himself." Angelique went quiet for a second. "He sent me a text this morning."

Blake's fists clinched.

"Said he wanted to drive back up here to my cabin and talk about *the situation*." Angelique emphasized the last two words. "Alone," she added.

"Jeez, he's a real piece of work," Kimberly snorted.

"I told him I had nothing to say unless one of the partners was present. I also warned him that if he came to the cabin, I'd call the police and the firm and tell them he's harassing me." She laughed. "He didn't respond."

"Figures," Kimberly said with a smirk. "He's too chickenshit. So you're just going to go back to Albuquerque and work side by side with that jerk?"

Good girl, Kimberly.

For being so smart, Angelique wasn't using her brain. Gabriel wouldn't leave her alone. He'd make her life miserable every chance he got and probably try to get her back in the sack, too. The raw jealousy in Gabriel's eyes when Angelique introduced Blake as her new boyfriend had been impossible to miss. He knew the type. Rich boys who always wanted what they couldn't have.

Angelique's armor had slipped last night in the back parking lot at Joe's. He'd been happy to relieve her of it completely for a few hours, along with the rest of her clothing and another sexy pair of panties. The armor was firmly back in place this morning, and her false bravado was going to earn her more humiliation and another broken heart if she didn't take Kimberly's advice. She just didn't see it yet.

So maybe he could convince her of that before it was too late. Before Red River residents discovered her mission here, or before she won the case and went back to the firm where her ex would keep hurting her. Either that or he really was going to have to make the two-and-a-half-hour trip to Albuquerque and kick some lawyer-ass.

He'd probably get sued, but it would be well worth it.

Another little piece of intel may have escaped her notice. Blake was pretty smart and resourceful himself and didn't mind playing dirty once in a while. Like using her panties against her. If her shrieking his name and having so many orgasms he'd lost count was any indication, she'd thoroughly enjoyed herself last night. Great sex was a powerful weapon that he could use to save Red River if he had to.

But first, he needed to save Angelique from herself, and he hoped that *she* was worth it.

He rounded the corner, and Angelique blanched. Sarge ran to him, tail wagging full speed. Blake bent to give him a scratch.

"Morning, ladies," Blake said, picking up a stick. He threw it across the yard, and Sarge tore after it.

Kimberly plopped a hand on her hip. "That dog wouldn't play fetch with any of us if we wrapped the stick in bacon." She shook her incredibly wild head of hair, and not one strand moved. "Hi, Doc," she said, and looked at Angelique's pale face, rounded black eyes, and parted lips. "Bye, Doc." Kimberly scurried into the house.

"Hi," he said to Angelique when the door banged shut.

"Um, hi." She looked down, suddenly very interested in her creepy puppet slippers.

He sighed. Yep, she was going to make this difficult. He walked up onto the porch without waiting for an invitation and leaned against a wooden post. "I was out looking for more poison oak. Your place looks pretty clean."

"Thanks," she said and clamped her mouth shut. She cradled the blue coffee mug in both hands and stared into it.

The back door opened, and a single hand slipped through the crack, extending a mug of piping-hot coffee. "For you, Doc," Kimberly offered, her voice muffled behind the door.

Kimberly was obviously in his corner, and he'd take all the backup he could get. He grabbed the mug and resumed holding up the post.

The hand disappeared, and the door shut.

He took a sip as Sarge ran onto the porch with the stick between his teeth and dropped it at Blake's feet.

"Incredible," Angelique whispered, and shook her head at the dog.

Blake grabbed the stick and threw it again. Sarge lit out after it. "Last night *was* pretty incredible."

Angelique sputtered. "I wasn't talking about last ni—"

"You didn't think last night was incredible?" Blake sipped at the hot coffee. "Because I got the distinct impression that you had a good time." He let a beat go by. "A *really* good time. Was I wrong?"

Light pink colored her cheeks. "Yes!"

He arched a brow.

"I mean no." Her hand jerked when she said it, and coffee sloshed out onto the porch. *"Crap."* She wiped a hand against her fitted jeans.

The pink in her cheeks deepened.

Pink wasn't the least bit tacky. He'd have to convince her of that one day soon.

"It doesn't matter because it can't happen again." The armor slid back into place.

He rolled the caramel-colored liquid around in his cup. "Why not? We both enjoyed spending time together. I'll even promise not to make fun of your slippers anymore. Unless they give me night-mares, which is entirely possible."

The corners of her mouth twitched, and a hidden smile danced in her eyes. It took a second, but her self-control won, and the smile never fully formed. She looked out over the backyard, Sarge carrying the stick toward them. "I just can't. It's impossible on so many levels."

He shook his head as Sarge scampered up onto the porch again. Blake grabbed the stick and threw it for another round. "Compli-cated, maybe. But not impossible. Complications can be worked out. It's called compromise." And that was the problem, wasn't it? She didn't like to compromise. She liked to win.

"Professionally, it's not possible."

"And what about personally?"

She wouldn't look at him. Wouldn't answer him.

"Is this about your ex?" Blake didn't even want to say his name.

"No." A muscle in her jaw flexed. "This has nothing to do with him."

"I get that it's difficult because of our legal situation, but if it's not about your ex, then what *is* it about?"

Her hand went to her chest, her palm flattening against her breasts. "What if it comes back?" A tremor threaded through her voice.

Ah. She still hadn't let go of the fear. He'd seen it in some of his patients. Once they let themselves slide down into that hole, it was hard to climb out. "What if it doesn't?"

"It wouldn't be fair to put anyone through that again. I couldn't stand to see the resentment in your . . ." Her voice trailed off as she looked out over the expansive backyard. ". . . someone's eyes."

"If you're comparing me to Gabriel, don't. I deserve a little more credit than that, and aren't you being kind of arrogant?"

"Beg your pardon?" Angelique gaped.

"I'm a *doctor* for Chrissake. And I'm a grown man, unlike that little boy you were engaged to. Maybe you should let me decide for myself whether or not I want to get involved with you, instead of making the decision for me."

Angelique hugged herself, drawing inward. Away from him. Disengaging. "I couldn't go through the rejection again. Everyone has a breaking point, and I think that would be mine."

"You're willing to be alone the rest of your life?" Alone sucked. Emotional isolation had destroyed his mother, robbed her of every ounce of joy. Pushed everyone in her life away who wanted to help, including him. That wasn't living. It was hell.

"I've got my family." Angelique looked at her feet. "And my career, of course."

"For being so tough, you're a chicken."

Her gaze snapped to his. Finally. Whatever worked. Her eyes darkened.

"You got a raw deal with your illness. That's no excuse to stop living."

Anger flashed in her eyes. "You couldn't possibly understand what it was like. What it took from me. And it's none of your business."

"You're right, it's not." But he wanted it to be. Damned if he didn't want *her* to be his business in all of her stubborn glory. He ran a hand through his hair. "My mother died of breast cancer when I was in med school," he blurted. *Hell.*

Angelique's mouth fell open.

"You got a second chance, Angelique. Don't waste it." He set his coffee on the small table by the chair and walked off the porch. Stopping, he tossed a look over his shoulder and stuffed both hands in his pockets. "Maybe if you focus on people instead of wins, none of this would be so complicated. Because it seems pretty simple to me." He strolled toward home.

He really needed to practice what he preached, because he'd let his life get a whole lot more complicated by getting involved with such a headstrong woman. Give him a case of appendicitis to diagnose, and he was a genius. Give him a strong-willed woman, and he became a blithering idiot who was begging for trouble.

Chapter Thirteen

Angelique took a drink of the new concoction in her martini glass and smacked her lips. She had to admit, Mixology 101—number fifteen on the bucket list—wasn't so bad. Putting her lips to the rim, she drew on the fancy glass again and let the mixture slide down her throat. Yes. Yes, the amateur bartending class was actually quite fun. Much more relaxing than gambling or arctic dog sledding. And Angelique needed a little relaxation after her confrontation with Blake a few hours ago.

Blake. Since when did she start calling him by his first name? Oh, yeah . . .

Heat crept up her neck, and she tossed back the rest of her cocktail.

After losing his mom to breast cancer, why would he be interested in Angelique? Why would he chance putting himself through that again, unless he pitied her? Gah!

She and Kimberly stood at one of the bar-height mixing tables at the Andalucia Vineyard and Winery, Kimberly studying the cocktail recipe chart like it was part of the bar exam.

Angelique's phone rang. Well, shouted the ringtone of Jack Nicholson yelling, "You can't handle the truth!" She looked at the number and growled.

"Douchebag?" Kimberly asked, looking up from the recipe chart.

"How'd you know?" Angelique let it go to voicemail.

"The grizzly bear snarl kind of gave it away." Kimberly returned her attention to the chart.

Angelique waited for the phone to beep, and then she listened to the message.

"Ang, it's Gabriel."

It irritated her that he still called her Ang.

"We need to talk." His voice was desperate. "Monthly finance reports are due soon, and I need my case files. I've got work to do for those clients. If the money and the files don't turn up soon, I'll have to tell the partners, and they'll want an explanation. Call me back. Soon." His last word turned angry.

Hmm. Gabriel wasn't giving up, and a desperate Gabriel could be bad news. What if he really did try to pin this on her? How convenient since she wasn't around to defend herself.

She tossed the phone back into her purse. "Next weekend would you help me with something?" she asked Kimberly.

Kimberly poured ingredients for the next cocktail. "Does it require shovels and Gabriel's lifeless corpse?" She covered the metal cocktail shaker and shook the daylights out of it. The tip of her tongue clenched between her teeth on one side of her mouth, she concentrated on the ice pinging against metal.

"Um, no. No bodies, and remind me never to piss you off."

Finally the shaking stopped—thank God, because it made Angelique a little dizzy—and Kimberly poured her newest mixture into fresh glasses. "It won't be as much fun as duct-taping Gabriel and forcing him into my trunk, but you know I'd do anything for you." She threw two olives in each drink.

Angelique snagged one of the new cocktails and sipped. Okay, gulped.

Flipping the chart to the next recipe, Kimberly started organizing bottles of vermouth, gin, and bitters. "So what is this thing you need help with next weekend?"

The tasting room filled with a buzz of tipsy chatter from the dozen and a half people who had signed up for the Sunday afternoon class just to get schnockered. Really, did no one go to church anymore?

Angelique hiccupped.

"I got a second chance. You know, with my health." Hadn't Blake said that? She'd gotten a second chance, unlike his poor mother. "I think I have a way to pay it forward. There's this nice German couple in Red River, the Ostergaards. They own the pastry shop on Main Street. Mrs. Ostergaard is going through chemo."

Angelique put her empty martini glass down and picked up Kimberly's drink. Plucking out the cocktail pick, she pulled the olives off with her teeth one at a time. She gazed at the late-afternoon sky through the tasting room windows and chewed.

"Maybe it's a stupid idea." *Since the Ostergaards won't be in business much longer.* "But when a person's ill—like big C ill—a small gesture can boost their morale. Help them get through one more day." Angelique knew that all too well. Some days she'd felt like an arcade duck at a county fair all shot up with holes. The physical and mental battles started on day one of the diagnosis.

Angelique hadn't been able to forget the image of a rosy-cheeked Mrs. O wearing a head scarf to cover her balding head. The sight had melted Angelique's heart into a puddle right there on the bakery floor, and that's where it still lay.

"I got off easy with only oral meds as treatment. I can't imagine what it would be like to go through chemo or radiation."

Kimberly stopped mixing and studied Angelique. "That's the first time you've said you had it easy. The first time you've looked at the bright side of your illness. Did Dr. Tall, Dark, and Hot-some have something to do with that?"

"No." *Yes. Dammit.*

Angelique's fate after the diagnosis could've been much worse, and she was finally beginning to see that. Thanks to Mrs. Ostergaard. And Blake. Angelique shook her head. Hell's bells, she needed to stop thinking of him as *Blake.* She needed to stop thinking of him period. Except that Blake Holloway was *all* she thought about anymore. Somehow, he'd invaded her mind, her body, and her life, and she wasn't sure how to walk away from him. Wasn't sure she could.

"I thought we could help the Ostergaards bake. Their display cabinets were kind of bare, and I think it's because Mrs. O is ill."

A warm smile lit Kimberly's face, and she stared at Angelique. "You're so sweet."

"I've been called a lot of things in my life, but *sweet* isn't one of them." Another hiccup, this one a little louder, and Angelique giggled behind one hand. "Most people just think I'm bitchy and intimidating."

"Okay, then you're one classy bitch. I'll drive in next weekend, and we can bake our brains out for the Os."

Angelique knocked back the rest of her drink. "I knew I could count on you." She hiccupped again.

Kimberly eyed her. "Think you should slow down with the cocktails? I'm just having a taste of each recipe since we have to drive home."

Angelique gave her head a decisive shake. The alcohol was nice. Liquid courage. She'd pop over to Blake's cabin when they got home and make him understand why she had to sever their . . . their . . .

Hell's bells. There was no *their*. *Their* didn't exist. Not really. They were just a one-time thing. Just sex. Nothing more. Just hot, sensual, passionate, mind-altering sex. That she was never going to experience again. Her whole. Entire. Life.

"Give me another one." She held out her glass and hiccupped again. "I'll drink. You mix and drive."

Kimberly placed her untouched drink in front of Angelique since she was now the designated driver, and Angelique sucked half of it into her mouth, swishing it around before she swallowed.

"Do you think I'm intimidating?" Angelique leaned on the table because the room was a little tilted.

"Not at the moment, sweetie." Kimberly took Angelique's glass and led her to a chair. She dashed over to the hors d'oeuvres table and brought back a small plate of food and a tall glass of water. "Eat and drink this while I finish up."

"Seriously." Angelique grabbed a cream cheese roll-up and nibbled at it. "Do I scare people?"

Kimberly inhaled. "Let's just say you have an authoritative persona, a characteristic that would be applauded if you were a man."

Another hiccup escaped Angelique. "That sounds like a smooth way to say I'm bitchy and I scare people."

"I say this with the utmost respect, but when it comes to your professional life, you're like a bulldog in lipstick and stilettos. You're the best at what you do, so roll with it. It's a gift and a privilege to have your skills. Don't let the opinions of others diminish that just because you don't have a penis."

Angelique laughed and popped a cube of cheese into her mouth. She chewed. "Yet another reason I keep you around," she said around a mouthful of protein. "You like me the way I am."

"Keep eating," Kimberly said over her shoulder as she returned to the mixing table. "You're going to need it to fight off a hangover."

Angelique sighed, munching on another cube of cheese. Blake seemed to like her just the way she was. A lot. Especially when they were naked. But he wouldn't once he saw her in action.

She didn't see another way out of this, though. If she walked away from this case, she'd likely lose her partnership, and her client would find another lawyer to get the job done. Then what would she have left? A big fat nothing, because she didn't have a future with Dr. Tall, Dark, and Hot-some, no matter how well they danced the horizontal two-step together. Even if he did seem to . . . enjoy her company . . . a lot . . . she couldn't stand to see another man recoil from her if her illness came back. She had four more years before she hit the five-year mark and could rest easy. And even then, she doubted she'd ever really *rest easy*.

Nope. She needed to get her professional act together, see this through, and go back to Albuquerque where she belonged. Except that when she thought of Albuquerque, it didn't feel like home anymore. Didn't make her feel all warm and fuzzy inside like the cozy cabin in Red River and the friendly people that she inevitably bumped into every time she strolled down Main Street.

Angelique lowered her forehead and thumped it gently against the table.

And a certain country doctor with eyes and abs that made her toes curl wasn't waiting for her back in Albuquerque, either. He was right here in this tiny town that was growing on her with each passing day. Unfortunately, both he and the town would be gone once she completed her objective and moved on.

Angelique's dog showed up on Blake's doorstep late Sunday afternoon, another prize clamped between his teeth. This pair was red.

Thank you, Sergeant Schnitzel.

Perfect excuse to hike across the footbridge again and knock on her door. Might earn him another chance to get her to see reason. Even if she accomplished her objective here, the firm she worked for back in Albuquerque probably wouldn't be as loyal to her as she was to them. Her ex's unchecked behavior had proven that, so why couldn't she see it?

At any rate, he wouldn't be able to keep her true purpose for being here a secret much longer. So he'd spent the last few hours devising a fallback plan because, yeah, he was getting desperate. If she'd give him a chance, he could show her what Red River had to offer. What *he* had to offer.

When Mrs. Barbetta answered the door and he'd set Sarge down in the kitchen, she'd made Blake an offer he couldn't refuse—dessert and coffee. Good neighbors. He took another bite of tiramisu and licked a dab of mascarpone cheese from his fork. Really good neighbors.

"This is delicious, Mrs. Barbetta," he said, taking another bite. Like a delicious piece of edible art; he'd had to restrain himself from moaning while he inhaled it.

"Oh, let me get you another piece." Mrs. Barbetta stopped cleaning the kitchen and reached for the pan of tiramisu.

He waved her off. "Thanks, but I've had plenty." Angelique's parents didn't know when she'd be back, and Blake couldn't sit there all day eating dessert no matter how good it tasted.

Mrs. Barbetta continued to yammer at him as if he were a long-lost son, while Mr. Barbetta worked a crossword puzzle across the kitchen table from him. Nona slipped something from a flask into her mug when she thought no one was watching.

"What's an eight-letter word for aggravation?" Mr. Barbetta asked. He was obviously a nice guy. A good family man. The Barbettas had spent the last thirty minutes talking about Angelique and her siblings, and Blake admired their strong family ties. Hoped to have the same in his life soon.

"Son-in-law," Nona offered.

"Very funny," Mr. Barbetta said. "Aha! Nuisance." He glanced up at Nona. "Good word." He scribbled it into the boxes.

By the time Mrs. Barbetta refilled his mug the second time around, he'd been asked for an effective treatment for the butt rash on their infant grandson who lived in Denver, and Blake knew which cousin hadn't yet come out of the closet.

"Come on!" the entire family had wailed over the cousin's failure to report his gayness, hands flailing about in dramatic Italian fashion. "Does he think we're stupid? Or, God *fa-bid*, narrow-minded?" Everyone protested at once.

Blake sat at the end of the table polishing off the last of his generous slice of tiramisu, Sarge curled on top of his foot, when someone's cell phone rang.

Mrs. Barbetta answered it. "Kimberly?" She listened into the phone. "Is she sick?"

Blake stiffened. He was a doctor after all, sickness was his business, and it sounded like they might be talking about Angelique.

More listening. "Uh-huh . . . okay, I'll start a fresh pot now." She hung up and sighed. Then she started making another pot of coffee by grinding an enormous mound of fresh coffee beans.

"What's the matter?" Mr. Barbetta asked.

"It's that silly bucket list those two girls cooked up when Angelique was ill. They went to some bartending class, and Angelique drank a little too much. She's not sick, just tipsy, and she can't stop hiccupping. They're just a few minutes away."

Oh yeah, this Blake had to see. Ms. Badass Attorney hiccupping like a little girl who'd drank too much soda pop.

"On second thought, I'll take another piece." Blake held out his saucer. When Mrs. Barbetta enthusiastically dished up another generous portion, he ate slower, savoring both the flavor and the anticipation of seeing Angelique.

He pictured the latest installment of the dog's panty capers that were currently tucked into his front pocket. *Excellent* neighbors.

About halfway through the second piece of dessert, a meaty sounding engine rumbled down the long drive and pulled up behind the house.

Blake chewed, sipped. Couldn't stop a smile from curling onto his lips. He sat back in his chair and waited as Sarge went to the door, wagging his long, taut tail with anticipation.

The door swung open and a red-faced, giggling Angelique entered with Kimberly right behind her. And damn, Angelique looked like a supermodel. Her shimmering black hair was pulled back into a knot at the base of her neck, and large gold hoops dangled from each ear. Tall and all legs, she wore a black miniskirt the size of a Post-it note. A belt hung low on the swell of her hips and draped over a red turtleneck sweater that covered every inch of her torso but clung to each curve so perfectly that it left nothing to his imagination. A pair of high-heeled suede boots that ended just below her knees made his mouth water. She was gorgeous. And hot. And . . .

His brain cramped with desire because all he wanted to do was take her home and make love to her until she yelled his name again.

He broke into a spasmodic choke. Jesus, had he really just thought that with her father sitting in the same room? Blake's eyes filled with water from the lack of oxygen in his lungs. And his brain, apparently. Must've collected below his belt because, yeah, he really did just think those exact words along with wondering what color panties she had on under that sex kitten outfit. Frankly, he was getting attached to his weekly panty ration.

Thanks again, Sergeant Schnitzel. Great dog.

Angelique's eyes landed on him, and she stilled, her expression going stony. As he regained his composure, he stared back at her, letting a hint of a smile settle on his lips. A silent beat passed as they stared at each other.

She hiccupped.

His smile broadened, and her eyes narrowed at him.

"Howdy, Doc," Kimberly said, slinging her leopard-print purse onto the counter. "How's it hanging?" She pulled out a chair next to Blake and motioned for Angelique to sit.

Mr. Barbetta looked up from his crossword puzzle. "You'll have to overlook Kimberly's crudeness, Blake. She's from Taos." He said it like that was explanation enough, and Kimberly rolled her eyes.

Angelique's expression darkened as her eyes settled on the chair, a look of uncertainty capturing her features.

"Come on, sweetie." Kimberly crooked a finger at her. "You need to sit, especially in those heels."

Uh-huh, thought Blake as his eyes scanned every inch of her.

Finally Angelique acquiesced and sat, looking like she might as well be jumping to her death. Sarge barked at her side for attention, and she gave him a playful scratch behind the ears just before another hiccup erupted from her painted lips.

"I take it the class was a success?" Nona asked.

"You know Angelique," Kimberly said as she and Mrs. Barbetta prepared more coffee and dessert. "She's an overachiever."

When everybody had a full mug and piece of dessert, they all sat around the table. Angelique was rigid, looking everywhere except at Blake.

"It's Italian roast." Mrs. Barbetta motioned to her coffee mug.

"What else would it be in this family?" Kimberly said, attacking the sweets in front of her. "At least Angelique didn't get mistaken for a hooker during this bucket list adventure."

"*What?*" Mr. Barbetta scowled.

"We went to the casino last weekend, number twelve on the bucket list, and some sleazeball propositioned Angelique." Kimberly scarfed down half of her tiramisu in two bites.

"I'll kill him," Mr. Barbetta huffed, and Blake had to agree. He'd like to find the guy and teach him some manners.

"I handled it." Angelique finally picked up her coffee with both hands and blew on it.

Kimberly snorted. "The douchebag's probably still walking with a limp."

"Watch your language, young lady, we have company," scolded Mrs. Barbetta.

"Yes, ma'am." Kimberly winked at Nona, who rolled her fly-like eyes behind thick lenses.

Angelique's eyes squeezed shut with irritation, and frankly, Blake's head was starting to hurt from the constant volley of barbs. An evening at the Barbettas' was a cross between *The Godfather* and *Moonstruck*, but he had to admit, he loved every minute of the insanity. It was so . . . family-ish, and he was damned tired of being alone.

"So, Dr. Hollo—" *Hiccup.* Angelique covered her mouth with the tips of her fingers and tried to hide a tiny belch. "—way."

Dr. Holloway, huh? He preferred Dr. Tall, Dark, and Hot-some.

Returning the cup to her lips with both elbows resting on the table, she talked into her mug. "To what do we owe the pleasure?"

Oh, this was going to be good.

He gave her a steady smile. "Just bringing your dog home again. He paid me another thought-provoking visit. He's quite the scavenger hunter." His stare lingered over her lips as they parted. She searched his eyes for a hidden meaning, found it, and then she turned an incredibly attractive shade of red. Kind of matched the panties in his pocket. This pair probably covered more real estate than the black thong. Not much, though.

"Who knows why that dog does what he does." Nona polished off her second helping of tiramisu.

His stare lingered on Angelique's blushing face, and his tone turned just a bit husky. "A man can only imagine," Blake said, and Angelique dropped her fork. It clattered against the saucer, and she silenced it by slamming her open palm straight down on top.

"Are you okay, dear?" her mother asked. "I'm sure that gentleman at the casino didn't mean anything. He was probably trying to pay you a compliment."

"He asked me how much, Mother," Angelique said through clenched teeth.

"That's it." Mr. Barbetta wadded his napkin and tossed it on the table. "Enough with the bucket list nonsense. It's trouble waiting to happen."

"Oh, come on!" Kimberly half shouted. "Security walked us to the car."

"Actually, I have an idea for your bucket list." Blake spoke up, and all heads turned to look at him. "It's perfectly safe, I'll be there, and you'll be helping a lot of underprivileged children."

"Oh, that sounds fantastic." Mrs. Barbetta clasped her hands under her chin. Kimberly nodded, and Mr. Barbetta mumbled something about it being okay with him as long as a man was around for protection.

Angelique glowered at her father, smoldering like Mount Vesuvius. Just as hot too.

"Tuesday evening after work then." Blake looked around the table.

"I'll be in Taos," said Kimberly.

Mrs. Barbetta smiled. "Angelique can go with you, Blake."

Angelique stabbed her mother with a sharp glare. "No, I can't."

"Sure you can, dear." Her mom stared back like it was a Sicilian mafia standoff.

Blake held back a satisfied smirk. "Great." He wiped his mouth and stood. "Thanks for the dessert and coffee, Mrs. B." He looked at Angelique, her eyes simmering up at him through silky lashes. "I'll pick you up Tuesday at five."

Chapter Fourteen

Blake was punctual, Angelique would give him that. When Tuesday evening rolled around, he'd knocked on her door at five o'clock sharp. She could've refused to go with him. *Should've* refused to be alone with him. But she did owe him for pretending to be her boyfriend, so she'd reluctantly climbed into his double-cab pickup.

"So, where are we going?" she asked as they tooled along Highway 518.

"Beautiful out, isn't it?" He avoided the question and pointed to the west. "New Mexico is famous for its sunsets, but they're the best here in the northern part of the state."

The truck climbed another hill, the last rays of evening sun slinging a palette of colors across the sky. A few clouds feathered through the stains of purple, orange, and pink, casting a lavender hue on the timbered mountains that surrounded them.

Her gaze followed his finger, and a sigh slipped through her lips. "It *is* beautiful up here."

"Prettier than Albuquerque?"

"You lived there, right? You should know the answer to that."

He blew out a laugh. "I only lived there during my residency, and I rarely saw anything but the inside of the hospital."

"So did Sarge really bring you another pair of my panties, or were you lying again?" she asked, shifting her gaze to him instead of the mesmerizing landscape.

He smiled, tossing her a smug glance. "They're red."

"That freaking dog," she said, staring at the road again. "I should've left him with Ga—" She snapped her mouth closed, clipping off the rest of Gabriel's name. Too late. Blake went rigid, and coldness filled the cab of the truck. The silence grew thick, except for the rhythmic beating of the tires against the road.

"Do you still care about him?" Blake finally asked.

Angelique drew in a breath. "Of course I do."

Blake's hands tightened around the steering wheel and turned a chalky shade of white.

"He's a good dog. He just has a few irritating habits."

Blake relaxed. "I was talking about your ex-fiancé."

Angelique knew exactly what he meant, but she wasn't sure she wanted to share that information with Blake. Give him false hope for a future that could never be. But somehow she wanted Blake to know the truth. Didn't want him to see her as the fool she'd been for getting involved with Gabriel to begin with.

What the hay. She'd already breached every personal boundary she'd set for herself. She didn't have much left to lose, except the resort development case, and that wasn't going to happen.

"No." She shook her head. "I'm not sure I ever really did, at least not enough to spend a lifetime with him." She fingered the ends of her hair.

"Why did you agree to marry him?"

"It's hard to meet new prospects when you're so absorbed in a career. I suppose he was convenient, and one of the only men I've ever met who wasn't threatened by me." She laughed. Not a deep, hearty laugh, but a weak, cheerless laugh that rang hollow.

"I think he's very threatened by you." Blake flipped up his sun visor and turned on the headlights as the sun disappeared behind the mountains. "Probably why he cheated." Blake paused. "And he probably showed up in Red River in person because he wants you back."

Angelique scoffed. "He's getting married in a few weeks. She's young, attractive, and don't forget pregnant with his baby."

"He's also smart enough to know it was a mistake to let you go," Blake said. "I'm a man. Trust me, I can read other men fairly well." Blake slowed the truck and flipped up the blinker. The ticktock filled the cab as he turned onto a narrow, winding back road. "He still wants you, and if he can find a way to have you both, he'll try."

She wrinkled her nose and shivered at the repulsive thought. "I wouldn't give him another chance even if the Cheerleader was out of his life for good."

Blake laughed, deep and loud. "The Cheerleader?"

She couldn't stop a satisfied grin from spreading across her face. "Kimberly came up with the nickname." Angelique shrugged. "If the pom-poms fit."

He smiled, broad and full and contagious in the last hint of daylight. That smile, so authentic and pure that it made Angelique's insides dance the rumba, her heart thrum, and she smiled so wide it made her cheeks hurt.

"Your description of her proves my point. He still wants the best of both worlds—you *and* his new fiancée. She's safe and doesn't challenge his inflated ego, and you're . . ." He glanced at her, lust blazing to life in his sapphire eyes. "Well, you're you."

Her whole body grew hot.

What she ever saw in a man as self-absorbed and inconsiderate as Gabriel was a mystery to her now that she'd met Blake Holloway, who thought of everyone first and put himself dead last.

She studied his profile.

The Cheerleader and Gabriel deserved each other. The only thing they possessed that Angelique envied was the fact that the Cheerleader would feel the kick of an unborn child in her stomach, the sensation of a baby nursing at her breast, and she probably wouldn't appreciate it the way Angelique would have if that part of her life hadn't been ripped away.

"As for your Rottweiler personality," Blake said, "there are other ways to put it to good use, you know."

The moment of basking in his shower of compliments gone, she glowered at him. Rottweiler? That was barely a step above bottom dweller. "Is there a compliment in there somewhere?" She folded both arms across her chest. "Please tell me there is."

He chuckled. "Relax. It *is* a compliment."

A few miles down the isolated road, a community of lights appeared in the distance. He pointed to them. "That's where we're going."

Angelique looked into the distance at the twinkling streetlights. "Where are we?"

"The small reservation where my dad and stepmom live. They're expecting us."

Angelique drew in a sharp breath. "You're taking me to meet your parents?" Her hands went to her hair to smooth it. "You could've warned me." She adjusted the black sweater she'd pulled on with her favorite jeans and fawn-colored UGG boots.

"You look fine."

He turned left at a sign marking the reservation land and entered a small community of shabby adobe houses, some mere shacks. Maneuvering through the potholed dirt roads, he parked at a building labeled "Infirmary." An aging Chevy Suburban and a few cars were parked out front, and the windows of the infirmary glowed with fluorescent lighting. Pushing the gearshift into park, he killed the engine.

He leaned over the console and took her hand, caressing the back of it with the pad of his thumb. "You could do amazing things with your skills in an area like this, Angelique. It wouldn't be very lucrative, but some things are far more rewarding."

His earthy scent filled her mind . . . and her heart, and at that moment her resolve was ready to crumble like a house of cards in a windstorm.

"I . . . I'm . . ." She swallowed. "I'm damaged goods." She had no idea why she was spilling her most intimate fears and secrets, but she couldn't stop. Her throat started to close, and she pulled her hand from his grasp. "I'm no good to anyone. My career is all I have left." And the only thing she could completely give herself to without risk. Her future health was too uncertain, a relationship too much of a gamble. And even if she found a man who would be loyal, a man like Blake, it wouldn't be fair to put him through that. "I won't let anything"—she glanced away—"or anybody take that away from me."

Blake sighed. Didn't move. Just studied her through the dark. Waiting. She wasn't sure for what, but he obviously had the patience of a saint because he didn't falter. He just sat quietly, looking in her direction. Waiting for . . . something.

"Look," Angelique said as she wrung her hands. "I owe you. A lot, actually, for playing along with my charade when Gabriel was in town. And for keeping my job a secret so the locals don't make my time here difficult, and for my dog and the whole ridiculous panty thing, which you still haven't given back to me, by the way. And . . . and . . ." *And for the best sex I've ever had . . . will ever have.* She rubbed her neck with the palm of her hand. "I don't know why you brought me here." Actually, she could make an educated guess, and it probably had something to do with playing her heartstrings like a violin. "But let's just do this thing, and we'll call it even, okay?"

The evening had grown completely dark, but the smile in Blake's voice was clear as a sunny day in springtime. "I'll give you your panties back, but it's going to take a lot more than an evening drive to a poor village to make us even."

She turned toward the door and reached for the handle.

"And, Angelique." His voice had grown husky.

She turned back to him because, really, what woman in her right mind could resist the obvious desire that twined itself in every throaty syllable.

"You're anything but damaged goods. I'm just not sure what else I can do to prove it to you except this."

And just like that, he pulled her half across the console, scooped her into his arms, and laid the sweetest, dreamiest kiss on her lips.

Blake led Angelique into the decaying building he and his dad had converted into a clinic two years ago.

Angelique's parents and Kimberly had unknowingly helped him initiate Operation Prod the Badass Attorney's Conscience with enviable precision. Or maybe they did know because they seemed to do their best to push him and Angelique together. Even Sarge was making it difficult for Angelique to completely avoid Blake.

He circumvented the rudimentary front desk, Angelique following him into the treatment area.

"Hey, Dad." Blake headed straight for his father.

His dad—early seventies, tall and slender like Blake, with gray wavy hair—was hunched at an old metal table, organizing vaccine syringes. His aging father turned affectionate eyes on him and stood to give Blake a hug. With a warm embrace, Blake gave him a slap on the back before releasing him.

"Thanks for coming, son. The measles outbreak has gotten worse, and a few cases of whooping cough showed up in a neighboring reservation. I'm trying to nip it before it spreads too far."

"Anytime, you know that." Blake stepped aside so Angelique wasn't blocked from view. "Dad, this is Angelique Barbetta."

She extended a hand with choppy movements, her steely self-confidence wavering.

"Nice to meet you, Dr. Holloway."

The fluorescent overhead lights cast a yellow hue over the room, making it look even more dismal than it really was, but Angelique looked stunning. In any lighting, any clothing—even in creepy puppet slippers—or no clothing at all, Blake couldn't get enough of her. She was like an addiction that had him totally hooked regardless of the consequences.

"Likewise," said Blake's quiet, introverted father as he clasped Angelique's hand between his.

Ludy, his half-Hispanic, half-Native American stepmom, came out of the medical supply room and waved.

"Hey, Ludy."

A little portly around the middle in her older age, Ludy shuffled over to hug Blake.

She looked at Angelique. "You brought new help this time." Ludy patted him on the cheek. "Good boy."

"Ludy, this is Angelique. She's assisting me tonight."

"Excellent, I have a station set up for you back here." She crooked a pudgy finger and led them to the back of the clinic.

Blake let Angelique go first, following close behind. Her intelligent eyes took in the desolate conditions as she scanned every inch of the clinic.

Bingo. A swell of satisfaction blossomed in his chest.

"The shuttle will be here with the first load of patients in a few minutes," Ludy said over her shoulder. She led them into a makeshift exam station, one of several since the room was divided by mobile partitions instead of solid walls. A papered examination table sat catty-corner, ready for a new patient. A few chairs lined the walls, along with a desk, and a long table was already set up with boxes of vaccines and various medical supplies.

Blake withdrew his personal prescription pad from a pocket and tossed it on the desk.

"Each vaccine is in a different color box," Ludy explained to Angelique, pointing to the portable cabinet pushed against one wall. Two rows of colorful boxes were lined up. Prefilled by the manufacturer, the syringes were tagged with the same color label as the box, so they were easily distinguishable.

Ludy walked to a row of cabinets across the room, grabbed two pairs of scrubs, and rejoined them at the station. "Here." His stepmom handed one pair to Blake and one to Angelique.

Reluctantly, she reached for the worn blue hospital scrubs and shot a doubtful look at Blake. He gave her a slight nod and a reassuring blink of his eyes.

She took the scrubs.

"Thanks, Ludy." Blake motioned for Angelique to follow him. "We'll go change and be right back."

Blake took Angelique's elbow and led her down the hall to a back office. He closed and locked the door. Pulling his shirt over his head, he said, "The scrubs are sterile, and in case there's a spill or a bleeder, your clothes won't get ruined." He tossed his shirt to the side and unbuttoned his pants. When he glanced at Angelique, her face had gone pale.

"What's wrong?" He sat down on a chair to untie his hiking boots.

"There might be blood?" She swallowed hard.

He chuckled. "We're just administering vaccines, not performing thoracic surgery. The blood will be miniscule, but it can get on your clothes if you're not careful."

With both boots off, he stood and unzipped his jeans. Angelique's gaze followed their journey downward, and heat blazed to life in Blake's chest. And his groin. He stopped the descent of his pants before revealing the incriminating evidence.

He motioned to the scrubs in her hand. "You have to change, too."

"I . . . I'm not sure if I can help you with this." She was still looking at his crotch.

"I'm pretty sure you can completely cure the problem I've got at the moment."

Her gaze flew to his.

"But now isn't the time."

"I mean the vaccines!" Her face glowed a deep neon pink.

Sweet. Nope, pink definitely wasn't tacky.

"I'm not a nurse."

Blake shook his head. "You're just going to hand me cotton swabs and alcohol and dispose of the used syringes when I'm done. That's it. Nothing that requires a license." He slid his jeans all the way off and laid them across a chair. Her eyes caressed over him and grew even darker, cloudier, as though she liked what she saw.

He pulled on the scrub bottoms and sat to put his boots back on, but she still just stood there. With both boots tied, he rested his elbows on his knees and frowned at her.

"What's wrong?"

"I can't change in front of you."

He chuckled. And frankly, seeing her so vulnerable, so out of her element, so unable to control the unfamiliar situation was potent and heady. "I've seen every inch of you already, babe."

Her hand went to her chest. "We were in the dark, so you really didn't *see* me." She twirled her index finger in a circle, indicating for him to turn around.

He sighed. "All right." He stood, grabbed the scrub top, and turned to face the wall.

"Thanks. And don't call me *babe*."

"Why not?"

She hesitated. "Because I find it . . ."

A turn on?

". . . disturbing."

He blew out a laugh. After cinching the drawstring at his waist, he pulled the scrub top over his head and listened to the rustling of fabric against skin as Angelique undressed and pulled on the scrubs.

"Okay, I'm ready," she said, and Blake turned around.

From her onyx eyes, shimmering with uncertainty, to her black silky hair, all the way to her red polished toenails, Blake had never seen another living soul make a pair of worn-out old scrubs look so unbelievably stunning.

"All I have is UGG boots." She rolled one bare foot onto its side and sucked her bottom lip between her teeth.

"I'm sure Ludy has something you can borrow." He jerked the door open and charged through it to start the night's work. It was either that or kiss her senseless right there in the back room of his dad's clinic.

The bolt of yearning lodged in Angelique's chest somewhere in the vicinity of her thumping heart grew larger with each little patient. Ludy led a young mother and her small boy into the exam cubicle and handed a file to Blake. The two-year-old's arms clasped around his mother's neck, he held on for dear life.

Angelique would never have a child of her own, clinging to her for security. The sting of loneliness smoldering inside her rose a notch as the parade of needy children continued through the evening.

Angelique showed the mom where to sit, and the boy's eyes rounded. He snuggled into his mother's embrace as Blake read his file.

Blake hadn't just played her heartstrings like a violin. He'd conducted them like an entire orchestra. How could she possibly help take Blake away from the people who needed him so much? And to rob Blake of the sheer joy he so obviously gleaned from volunteering here would be almost criminal. There was no recognition, no accolades, no news cameras around to splash his selfless efforts across the tabloids like a philanthropic celebrity. As far as she could see, Blake didn't ask for anything in return. Not one thing.

"This little guy needs the green one," Blake said to Angelique, indicating which vaccine. "Green like a dinosaur." He growled and waved two mock claws in the air, his elbows drawn into his body like a *T-Rex*. The two-year-old giggled while Angelique retrieved the syringe and a swab and handed both to Blake. His fingers closed around hers as he took them from her, and even through both of their latex gloves, a jolt of electricity shot up her arm, zinged through her chest, and tingled in the far reaches of her female anatomy.

Seated on a wheeled stool, he looked up at her, his own fevered reaction apparent in his eyes. Angelique turned back to the cabinet to grab a box of rubber finger puppets, the prize for each kid after the trauma of getting needled in their tiny arms and tushies. She cringed and nearly cried every time one of the tiny patients squalled from the stinging stick of a needle.

"Sorry, little guy, but this is going to pinch a little." Blake swabbed the little cherub-faced boy's arm and glanced at his mother. "Ready, Mom?"

The boy's mother squeezed her son close and cooed into his ear. She nodded to Blake.

Capturing a fleshy part of the boy's chubby arm, Blake administered the vaccine, and the toddler let out a squeal. "Sorry, buddy," Blake said, rubbing the red mark on his arm with the swab. "It's all over now. And you know what? I hope I have a little boy just like you someday."

Angelique bristled because he'd said the same thing several times tonight. Each declaration of his desire for children had driven a nail deeper into Angelique's heart.

Blake gave the mother a consoling smile. "He may get irritable for a few days. Give him lots of liquids and no sugar until he feels better."

"Here you go, sweetie," Angelique said, putting the box of finger puppets in front of him. "Why don't you pick out two, since you've been our best patient."

Of course she'd said that to every one of the kids who came into the clinic tonight. How could she not? Each one had been cuter than the last and softened her heart a little more every minute she'd spent at the clinic. Watching Blake shower each little patient with adoration had turned up the heat on the block of ice that used to be her heart. By the time the sixth busload of impoverished children had come and gone, so much love and compassion pumped through Angelique's heart she thought it would burst.

Tears shimmering in the little boy's eyes, he picked yellow and blue rubber toys and clutched them in his tiny hands like gold. His mother left with her son hiccupping over her shoulder.

"That was the last patient." His stepmom came in from the waiting room. Ludy hadn't slowed down the entire evening, and fatigue lines showed around her eyes. She set two bags on a chair. "Here are your clothes. Go on home. You've done enough for one night."

"Are you sure you don't need help cleaning up?" Blake asked, tossing the last used syringe into a red biohazard can.

Ludy shook her head decisively. "Your father and I can manage."

Blake's dad appeared in the doorway of the makeshift treatment station. "We'll take care of it. I've disrupted enough of your evening."

The elder Dr. Holloway slid a white doctor's coat off, and Ludy took it from him, the two communicating with nearly imperceptible body language and able to anticipate the other's thoughts and actions. A toasty sense of contentment slid through Angelique, making her long for the same thing with . . . her gaze swiveled to Blake, and her lungs locked.

"Thanks for your help," said Ludy, placing lids on the boxes of leftover vaccines.

"Hopefully, this will contain the outbreak." Dr. Holloway gave Blake a bear hug. "Dinner in a few weeks at our house?" He looked at Angelique. "Bring Angelique with you."

"I . . . well . . ." Angelique looked from Dr. Holloway to Ludy, their expectant stares dealing the final blow to her thawing heart, and it puddled at her feet. "I'll try. Thank you for the invitation."

Blake's face lit with pride, and a seed of hope sprang up from the depths of Angelique's soul. A seed she knew would be choked by the bitter weeds that had already taken root there because of the things she could never have.

Chapter Fifteen

Angelique spent most of the drive home deep in thought about the clinic, the people who needed Blake, especially the kids. They pulled up in back of Angelique's cabin. The back porch light cast a glow over the back side of the house.

"I'll walk you to the door." Blake slid the gearshift into park and killed the engine.

She grabbed his forearm and held him in place.

"How is the clinic funded?" It was the first time she'd been able to speak since leaving the reservation. Completely overwhelmed by the selfless compassion Blake and his family showed to the children of a poor, obscure community long forgotten by . . . well, everyone, had rendered her speechless—a rare occurrence indeed. Angelique's mind had raced at warp speed during the ride home, searching for words of praise, but everything seemed too shallow. And hypocritical.

Blake sighed, scrubbing a hand over his face. "There's no short answer."

"I want to know," she murmured. "And now is the best time." *It's your last chance to state your case before I make ground meat out of your lawyer tomorrow.* And this might very well be the last night Blake would be willing to speak to her at all. Angelique found herself hoping Blake could change her mind. There was nothing she could do to stop the development company, even if she resigned from the case, but at least she wouldn't have it on her conscience.

Her gaze raked over the beautiful man behind the wheel. Maybe she'd have Blake Holloway.

"Then I'm going to need a beer." Blake gave her a half smile. "Would your parents mind?"

"They went back to Albuquerque. Nona had a doctor's appointment." She reached for the door handle. "It's my cabin, anyway. I don't have to ask their permission."

They grabbed their bags of clothes from the backseat and let Sarge out. He shuffled outside, took care of business, and promptly trotted in carrying a stick between his teeth. Blake stood at the bar, and Sarge dropped the stick at his feet.

"Sorry, buddy, no playing fetch in the house." Blake bent to scratch Sarge's head.

Angelique retrieved two beer bottles from the fridge and shut it with a foot. "At least it's not my—" She snapped her mouth shut, her cheeks burning. She found a bottle opener in a kitchen drawer and popped the tops.

Coming around the bar, she headed into the den and turned on a lamp. Blake followed her, and she handed him a bottle. They sank into the plush leather sofa, both exhausted from the long night's work at the clinic.

"Cheers." She held out her bottle, and Blake bumped longnecks with her before drawing on the icy contents.

"Want a fire?" Blake asked. "I could build one."

Without a word, Angelique grabbed the remote off the side table, pointed it at the fireplace, and clicked a button. A gorgeous crackling fire instantly appeared.

Blake threw his head back and laughed. "You're such a city girl."

"Hey, I drive a four-wheel-drive SUV," she said defensively, but really, she couldn't disagree with him.

He gave her a sidelong look. "It's a Lexus."

"My firm wanted me to have convenience." She shrugged.

Blake looked around. "They must've wanted you to have luxury, too. This place isn't your average weekend cabin. It's a house that could be lived in year-round."

"So is yours." She drew on her beer, the tension in her shoulders releasing a little more with each drink. "It's just older than this one."

"It's good for a bachelor like me, but when I have a family, it won't be big enough."

She tensed. Stared at her bottle, mesmerized by the opaque brown glass. Of course he wanted a family. Kids. Something she could never give him.

"Did I say something wrong?" He tilted his head, trying to get her to look at him.

She shook her head, unable to force a smile. "No. Not at all." No, wanting a family was perfectly understandable. The role of family man would fit him, and he'd probably slide right into it like a tailor-made suit once he found the right woman. A woman who wasn't a walking health hazard with a malformed genetic code.

He studied her for a moment. Pulled on his bottle of beer again and swallowed. "The clinic is funded by a federal grant."

Her head swiveled toward him.

He lifted a shoulder. "You wanted to know, so I'm telling you.

The meds and supplies are paid for by the grant. Most of the tribes are reclusive. They won't travel too far off the reservation for help, so we bring help to them."

"So your dad and Ludy survive on their retirement savings?"

He nodded. "A modest retirement. Practicing in a small town like Red River is more of a calling than just a profession. It pays enough to live a decent life, maybe even provide for some extra luxury items. My dad put enough retirement away over the years to be moderately comfortable, but he's by no means wealthy. That's why I took out loans to pay my own way through med school."

Her eyes flew wide. Her parents had footed the bill for everything. She walked out of UNM law school without a single debt. That was a big part of the reason she worked so hard at her job, to show her parents some gratitude and not take their help for granted.

"Dad offered to help with the costs, but I wouldn't accept it." He took another gulp of beer, set the bottle on the table, and slumped down into the posh leather to stare into the fire.

"And if your current office . . . ceases to exist?"

"The developers are offering us a fraction of what our businesses are worth. The amount won't even cover the loan I took out to pay for the building and update the practice when I bought it. I won't have the capital to open up somewhere else in town, plus I've still got student loans. I'll be forced to move back to a big city where I can make some real money. I'll be miserable, but at least I'll be able to pay off my debts without declaring bankruptcy like most of the other business owners who are caught in the web. When the bank calls in their small business loans, most of Red River will fold. It was a brilliant plan by the developers, actually. And it's working like a charm. The modicum of resistance we've been able to cultivate stands little chance against them. It's a David and Goliath scenario."

"David won, remember?" She wasn't sure why she said it, but it just slipped out, and Blake turned a surprised look on her.

"And the clinic? How will all of this affect your dad's free clinic?" Angelique dreaded the answer because she was pretty sure she already knew what would become of it. The tip of a very sharp invisible knife hovered at her chest.

He drew in a heavy sigh and folded one arm behind his head, his free hand resting on a muscled thigh. "The grant was based on both Dad and I offering our medical services. Volunteers are hard to come by anyway, so with me gone, he'll likely lose the grant."

The knife penetrated, sinking into her chest with a twist. "I'm . . . I'm sorry."

His head rolled to the side, and his blue eyes stared into hers. He reached for her cheek and caressed it. His tender touch sent a shiver racing over her as his skilled fingers traced down her neck to outline her collarbone.

"Are you?" he murmured.

His touch quickened her breath. And those eyes. Those eyes made her heart skitter and skip. She nodded as his thumb found her lips and traced them. "Yes, I really am."

And right in that moment, just this one last time, she wanted to be with him. Wanted him to transform her into a whole woman again with his sweet lovemaking. Just once more she wanted to feel him against her, in her, rocking her world.

His thumb made another circle around her lips, then rested on the bottom. She pulled the tip into her mouth and suckled.

A faint groan whispered through his lips. He laced a hand behind her neck and pulled her on top of him so she straddled his hips. His hardness pressed between her legs, and every bit of air squeezed from her lungs. Instinctively, she moved against him. Her insides liquefied as the friction of their hips moving in unison built to a seething volcano at her core and wrung a desperate gasp from her.

He pulled her mouth to his, but she pushed against his chest so their noses brushed.

"This is a bad idea." She swallowed, trying to convince herself more than him. "I'm crossing some unprofessional boundaries."

"Then let them get another attorney," Blake whispered against her mouth.

"It won't matter. The next attorney will win, too."

"We'll worry about that tomorrow." He pulled Angelique into him and consumed her mouth with his.

She opened for him, and his tongue stroked over hers. Soft like velvet, but strong enough to crush her willpower into dust. Her fingers laced into his hair and pulled his head back, exposing his neck. Her mouth left his probing tongue, and she feathered kisses across his jawline to his ear. A nibble and a suckle of his earlobe made a guttural sound escape just before he sucked in a sharp breath.

One of his hands slid under her scrub top, kneading up her spine. The other cupped her butt and pulled her tighter against his hardness. They both let out a startled gasp.

Mouth open, breath ragged, she stared down at him.

"That's what you do to me." His words came out as a low growl. "Every time I see you, I want to take your clothes off and make love to you so hard and so long that you'll never want another man but me."

She wanted to say that there *was* no other man for her except him, but then his mouth was on hers again, his tongue commanding hers, his hands owning her body. His mouth dropped to her neck, and she wrapped both arms around him. Clutched him to her so the moment would be etched into her memory. So the feel of him would be imprinted on her mind forever. He covered her pebbled flesh with hot, wet kisses until she gave in to the power of his touch and let out a hushed sob of pleasure. He smiled against the sensitive skin where her neck met her shoulder.

Grabbing for his scrub top, she tried to pull it over his head. Impatient and desperate to touch him, she reached for the drawstring around his waist. He laughed and held her hand still.

"We need to shower first."

Her brow furrowed, her breathing heavy with desire.

"We've been seeing patients. It's more hygienic if we wash off." Grabbing her by the hips, he stood her on both feet and took her hand. "Where's your room?"

She pointed to the loft. "I . . . You go first."

With a shake of his head, he pulled her against him. "I was hoping we could shower together."

Resting her head against his shoulder, she stared into the fire. "Can the lights be off?" Her voice cracked, and her words sounded meek. She hated meek. It was just a more polite way of saying weak.

He stroked her hair and placed a gentle kiss into it. "If you want, but I've got a better idea."

She listened to the strum of his heartbeat under her ear. It soothed and steadied her.

"Do you trust me?" he murmured.

She did. Her head bobbed up and down. "I shouldn't. Not after the way you've used my panties against me, but I do."

"Then let's go upstairs."

Blake took off his scrub shirt and laid it on a chair by the fireplace in Angelique's room. Her master suite consumed the entire loft. A large seating area in front of a gas log fireplace—he stifled an eye roll—gigantic king-size bed, and a bathroom almost as big as his den.

Steam and the scent of vanilla began to filter from the bathroom, where he'd instructed Angelique to get in the shower and turn toward the wall before he got in. He blew out a breath. She was so beautiful. So damn beautiful that it hurt to look at her sometimes, especially when he couldn't touch her. That she was still so self-conscious about her body made his chest ache.

A few of Blake's patients had gone through breast cancer. They'd dealt with the fear that it would reoccur, the self-image doubts it created in a woman's psyche. Some suffered problems with intimacy afterward, most struggled in some way or another for a time. A small percentage never recovered emotionally. It had to be all the more difficult for a young, beautiful woman like Angelique who still had so much life left to experience.

Sitting on the loveseat, he tugged off his boots and socks, then stood to pull off the rest of his clothes.

Her ex had probably made the mental battle even harder by screwing a girl who was barely legal while Angelique was sick. Blake raked a hand over his face. Gabriel was the rubber boob, not Angelique. Blake's stomach knotted every time he thought of her going back to Albuquerque to work for a guy who had treated her worse than the dirt he wiped off his expensive Italian shoes.

She was young, smart, the toughest woman he'd ever met, and the most beautiful. And the only woman he'd ever wanted to beg to stay with him. He just had to get *her* to see how special she was.

He walked to the fireplace and flicked the switch next to it. Voilà, a picturesque fire instantly appeared behind the glass. He chuckled and headed into the bathroom.

Flickering candles were scattered around the bathroom in asymmetrical groups, yet each seemed in its perfect place—talent only creative women and gay men possessed. The overhead lights were turned off, but the candles cast a warm glow through the bathroom and shadows danced on the tiled walls. A corner tub with jets looked as though it'd never been used. That would be remedied soon, if he had anything to say about it.

Two plush brown bath towels sat on an ornate brass stool next to the shower door, perfectly folded. He stepped over to the shower and placed a handful of gold squares on top of the towels.

"Can I come in?"

"Yes," she said in a small voice, but it still echoed off the shower walls.

He pulled the frosted glass door open, and the sight took his breath away. Her back to him, she washed the last shampoo suds from her long black hair. Water cascaded over a defined yet feminine back that angled into a slender waist, dimples appearing just above her shapely bottom. The remnants of suds mingled with water cascaded down long, graceful legs. A thin gold chain adorned one ankle, and he wanted to lick the water droplets from every inch of her body. From the red tips of her flushed ears, all the way down to her polished toes.

He pulled in a jagged breath and stepped into the shower.

His broad shoulders blocked the steamy water, and a shiver raced over her, her skin pebbling.

"Come here." He laced one arm around her waist, the other around her collarbone to caress the opposite shoulder, and pulled her back against him.

"Oh!" She sucked in a breath when the evidence of his arousal nudged her from behind.

He smiled against her ear.

He angled their bodies so the water reached over his shoulder and cascaded down her front, and she warmed against him yet still quivered. Anticipation mingled with uncertainty flowed off her in pulsing waves.

He held her close, stroking her shoulder and the flesh just below her belly button. Coaxed her body into following his in a gentle, rhythmic sway as the water heated their skin and soothed their senses. Finally, the tension in her body slacked, and she relaxed into him.

"You're so sweet, Blake." Her voice shook, and he peeked around to find a tear trekking down her already wet cheek.

"Hey, what's wrong?" He nuzzled the side of her neck. "I may not have sexual superpowers, but I've never brought a woman to tears either."

She didn't laugh. "Be serious." This time a small sob escaped. "I don't cry." She sniffed. "I'm not a crier."

"Uh-huh, so you're not crying, but tell me what's making you not cry. We're standing in the shower naked together—I think it's okay to share."

She took in a deep, ragged breath, both her hands covering his. "After the mastectomies, Gabriel couldn't stomach . . . intimacy with me. He avoided me at bedtime, left the room when I got undressed, never came into the bathroom when I showered. When I was feeling better and was done with most of the reconstruction, I tried to . . . entice him. He . . ." Her voice cracked.

"Shh, babe," Blake whispered into her hair. "He's not worth it."

"No, you wanted to hear this. And it's not really about him. I mean it is, but it's not. Shit." She swiped under her eyes.

Blake kept the gentle sway of their bodies going, one arm still draped around her collarbone, the other around her abdomen. "I'm listening," he said. A gentle sob rippled through her, and she trembled against him.

He wished the hot water could wash away every bit of damage the illness and the idiot ex had inflicted on her mind and body. Unfortunately, he knew healing that kind of wound wasn't so simple. Now she was finally talking, opening up about the hurt and pain of her circumstances, and he wanted her to pour out her fears, her worries, so he could help carry them. Then he planned to make love to her half of the night, and spend the other half with her wrapped in his arms.

"When he touched me that night, he looked like he might be sick. He couldn't even get it . . . well, you know, he couldn't perform."

Blake tightened his hold around her.

"The next week I went back to work. One night I forgot some files and stopped by the office late at night. I walked in on him and the Cheerleader. Trust me when I say he had no problems getting it up with her. It was just me who he found repulsive."

Blake's stomach pitched at how much that must've hurt. How it must've shattered her already fragile self-image and been a setback to the emotional recovery a person goes through after a tragic illness.

His fingers caressed down her belly and stopped just above the curls. "There's not an ounce of repulsiveness in your beautiful Italian body. You're a knockout." He pulled her against his swollen member. "He didn't deserve you."

Instinct took over, and Angelique's bottom rubbed against him. He groaned, his erection throbbing against her backside. The curve of her ear flushed as he showered it with wet, suckling kisses, and her fevered skin burned his lips.

"I feel like a hideous monster."

She gasped when his fingers sank into her soft curls and found the nub hidden in her cleft, already throbbing with desire. For him. She wanted him as much as he wanted her, but for how long? Would her desire for him come to an end when the case was over?

"Never thought any man would find me attractive again," she breathed out in a desperate whisper as his fingers gently worked the pulsing nub that went molten under his touch.

"You were wrong." *So wrong.* Blake feathered his tongue and mouth down her neck and nipped her shoulder, leaving a trail of pebbled skin in his wake.

She'd probably never been more wrong, because Blake couldn't think of anything *but* her. How much he wanted her in his bed, wanted to share his life with her, wanted to snuggle in front of the fire with her during the cold winter nights. He was even compromising the trust he'd built with his friends here in Red River by keeping her purpose a secret just to have more time with her. But she obviously wasn't interested in the same thing. The way she stiffened and audibly sucked in a breath when he'd mentioned kids and a family had communicated her lack of maternal desire.

Unless he could coax that maternal desire out from under her steel armor the way he had her sexual desire. At the moment, her sexual desire was alive and well and hopefully about to gasp out his name.

His finger shifted into a circular rhythm. Within seconds she was doing just what he'd hoped.

"Blake."

He smiled. "What?" he murmured against her ear and reached for her slick opening from behind.

Another deep moan escaped her, and satisfaction swelled in his chest.

"Yes!"

Never turning her toward him, because it was up to her to take that step and allow him to see and touch her breasts in the light, he threaded one hand on top of hers and braced their palms against the shower wall. His other arm still laced around her middle, he dipped his knees and slid up and into her wetness with one stroke. Her liquid heat clenched around him, and she shuddered and arched back against him.

"You're so wet, baby. So ready for me."

Her heated flesh undulated around him, and he moved inside her, bending his knees and thrusting upward, over and over. And over. Until her body tightened around him, and she shuddered, murmuring his name again on a strangled, desperate cry.

She collapsed back against him, and he chuckled. "I forgot something."

"Wh . . . what?" she asked, barely coherent.

He opened the door, still holding on to her so she wouldn't puddle onto the shower floor. The fact that she responded to him so completely, with such raw emotion made his chest expand. Withdrawing from her, he reached for a gold square and ripped it open with his teeth.

She let out a frustrated sigh. "Hurry," she said, eyes still closed and voice breathy.

He laughed. "So bossy." He rolled it on with one hand and positioned himself behind her again.

"You're just now figuring that out?"

He entered her again, and she lay back against him, her satiated body pliant under his touch. Her tall frame molded to his. One of her hands gripped his thigh, her fingers flexing into his flesh. It drove him on, urged him to take her to the brink again and again while he had the chance. While she'd let him into her head and maybe even into her heart.

Still bracing her other hand against the wall, he took her sweet earlobe between his teeth and sank his teeth in a fraction until she gasped. "The minute I laid eyes on you I knew you'd be just as bossy with your clothes off as you are with them on." His hips rolled into her from behind with even, confident strokes. "You're everything I dreamed of and so much more."

With the hot water drenching them, he made love to her until her body clenched around him again, and this time, he rode the wave over the edge too.

Chapter Sixteen

Angelique wanted tonight, the time she had with Blake, to last a lifetime. It was a dream she didn't want to wake up from.

When Blake stepped out of the shower, he'd kept his back to her, so mindful of her insecurities over her body. Once they dried off and wrapped themselves in soft bath towels, he took her to bed and made love to her all over again with just the fire casting a glow across the room. Both lying on their sides with him behind her, he'd anchored a strong arm around her middle and held her against him, bringing her to the brink of ecstasy, then pushing her over as she arched against him.

Jeez, how many times had she called out his name tonight? And had she really begged for more? Surely she imagined it, because Angelique Barbetta didn't beg. Except that she had. Quite loudly, in fact.

But at the moment, snuggled into the nook of Blake's arm, she didn't much care.

She traced and explored the hills and valleys of his chest with gentle fingertips. "Tell me about your mom."

He drew in a deep breath and let it out. "There's not much to tell, really."

"What was she like?"

He smoothed a hand over his face. "After having me, she miscarried several times. It destroyed her. She suffered from depression and just drew so far into her own shell that no one could reach her. Not even me or my dad. When Dad finally left, I wanted to go with him because living with Mom was so lonely, but I felt guilty about leaving her alone. She was just so sad all the time." His hand fell heavily back onto the bed. "I stayed because I felt sorry for her."

Angelique's hand stilled against Blake's chest. If he felt sorry for his mom, did he feel the same way about Angelique because she'd been ill?

"What?" His arm tightened around her.

"Hmm?" she asked.

"You just tensed." His warm palm slid down her arm. "Why?"

She bit her lip and gave her head a gentle shake. "Nothing. It's just . . . tell me about her cancer."

He sighed and stroked her hair. "Are you sure you want to hear this? You already know how it ends." His voice thickened with sadness.

"I'm sure."

"I honestly don't know much. She kept it to herself. She was a nurse, but she'd lost several jobs over the years because of her dark moods. My dad always sent money to take care of us. She didn't tell me about her diagnosis until the very end. I'd been in medical school and then the long hours of residency. She said she didn't want to worry me." He shook his head against the pillow. "She'd given up on life a long time before she got sick. I don't think she even tried to fight it. It was like she wanted to go."

Angelique let out a gentle sigh against his firm chest, their bodies tangled together with the soft down comforter and fire keeping them cozy. The rhythmic rise and fall of his chest coaxed her into a euphoric dreamlike state, not quite asleep and not quite awake. "What was it like for you?"

The ebb and flow of his breathing stopped, and his chest under her fingertips went still, like he couldn't breathe.

"Lonely. My whole life with her was lonely." His voice was faint in the darkness.

"I'm so sorry." She placed a gentle kiss on his chest.

He put a finger under her chin and tilted her mouth up to meet his, then brushed a warm kiss across her lips. "Let's talk about something else." He wrapped his hand around the curve of her neck. "Like how good you taste," he whispered against her mouth before seizing it with a deep, luxurious kiss.

His stomach rumbled.

She giggled. "I think you're hungry for the taste of something besides me."

"That's debatable." He tried to lay another kiss on her, but she pulled back.

"Seriously, I can make something to eat. How hungry are you?" Her hand caressed down to the roped muscles over his abdomen.

He laughed and smoothed a palm down her ribs to rest in the curve of her waist. "Starved. I think we burned more calories tonight than an Olympic swimmer."

"I've got some fettuccini in the fridge." His muscles danced under her wandering fingertips.

"Sounds good," he said, his voice thickening. "But if you keep that up, we'll burn another few thousand calories first."

She laughed and pulled her hand away. "You stay here. I'll bring a tray up." Rolling out of bed, she walked to the large walk-in closet for a robe, her back to him.

She slipped on her kimono and cinched the belt, then walked back into the bedroom. Blake lay in bed, rolled up onto an elbow. The sheet had slipped low, and the firelight danced over his muscled torso.

"Need help?"

Oh, yeah. She needed his help, but not in the kitchen.

"Nope. I got it." She stopped at the door, one hand on the frame, and looked back at the beautiful man in her bed. He was everything she needed in a man—kind, loving, reliable. Yet completely the opposite of what she'd always thought she wanted. Red River and its country doctor were quickly redefining her idea of ambition and success. She smiled. "Be right back."

His grin was mischievous. "I'm not going anywhere."

She drifted down the stairs, and her fingertips played along the rustic wood banister. She let Sarge out of the pantry and opened the back door for him. He darted outside for a potty break while she went back to the kitchen and dished out pasta onto a plate, popping it in the microwave. After digging around in the pantry, she found a small serving tray and loaded it with two sets of utensils and napkins. The microwave beeped, and she added the steaming plate of fettuccini to the tray and uncorked a bottle of red wine.

As she poured the wine into two stemmed glasses, the door creaked.

"All done, Sarge?"

A glass in each hand, she turned toward the tray and stifled a scream, her heart leaping into her throat.

"It's not just Sarge," said Gabriel.

Her heart thundering, she set the glasses on the tray and sagged against the bar. Sarge scampered into the kitchen, with his long, thin tail wagging.

"Sorry to startle you, but the door was open." Gabriel pushed it closed with a click.

Angelique rubbed both temples, then looked at the clock over the microwave.

"What are you doing here, Gabriel? It's two thirty in the morning." She could barely keep her tone civil.

"I needed to see you." He glanced around the cabin. "Nice place. The firm really put you up in style."

"What do you want?" she ground out.

He sighed, giving her a coy smile.

"You know I really hated the way things ended between us, Ang." He walked around the bar and joined her in the kitchen.

"You looked pretty happy to me with Ciara's ankles around your neck. The noises you were making weren't sounds of agony either." She crossed rigid arms over her chest.

"That was a mistake. A lapse in judgment. Couldn't you find it in your heart to forgive and forget?" He took a step toward her.

"Don't come near me." She stepped back. "What's this really about, Gabriel? Stop playing games and get to it."

He ran a hand through his hair. "I think Ciara was after me from the beginning. She played on my sympathies when you were sick."

No kidding.

"It was her fault. She threw herself at me." He stepped closer again. "But it's over now. I've broken it off with her, and you and I can be together again."

Unbelievable. He actually believed his own bullshit.

"Uh-huh." Angelique pursed her lips. "And what about your baby, Gabriel? Did you forget that little detail?"

"I'll take care of the baby." He hesitated. "If it's even mine. I've asked Ciara for a paternity test when it's born."

"So you thought you could drive up here in the middle of the night and, what . . . I'd jump into your arms and welcome you into my bed? Is that it?"

She backed into the cabinets as he closed the gap between them. Putting a hand on her forearms, he caressed down. "Come on, Ang. We were good together. Once you're done here, you'll be a partner. In a few years we can own that place and push the old dead weight out."

She might actually need her own attorney because she was about to commit a violent crime. Teeth clenched, she drew in a breath.

"First of all, we were never good together. It just took me far longer than it should have to figure that out. Secondly, you had no business driving up here unannounced. I've got company." She nodded to the tray loaded with a service for two.

Shock registered in his expression, then possessive anger, and his fingers tightened around her arms. "You're not the country bumpkin type, Ang. He's just a stand-in for me while you're here, and you know it." He leaned in to kiss her, but she put her hand up to cover her face and tried to push him away. Gabriel jerked on her arms.

"Ouch! Let go!"

"Third," Blake said from the stairs, "take your hands off her, or you'll have a hard time driving back to Albuquerque with two broken arms."

Gabriel let go of Angelique and took a step back. The color drained from his face.

She rubbed at her stinging arms.

Wearing nothing but blue hospital scrubs slung low on his narrow hips, the Y of his toned abs appeared just above the cinched drawstring as he stood there, defending Angelique's honor. Again. His muscled chest flexed, his hands clenched into fists, and Angelique's heart did a dance.

Gabriel's mouth mutated into a sneer as he turned back to Angelique "What do you think will happen to your partnership when the firm finds out you're sleeping with the enemy?"

She swallowed, and her hand involuntarily fluttered to her chest. She *had* thought about it. Many times. And she'd known from the beginning that getting involved with Blake may not be illegal, but it was certainly professionally questionable. But she hadn't been able to stop, because . . .

Her gaze locked on to Blake's darkening blue eyes.

Because she was falling in love with him. This man that she couldn't have. Couldn't selfishly deprive of the family he wanted. He had so much love to give, and she couldn't stand it if he grew to resent her for taking away his chance to have kids of his own someday.

Gabriel smirked. "Yeah, I did some checking." Gabriel glanced at Blake. "Did you consider that he's using you to help his own case?"

Angelique's attention snapped back to Gabriel. His audacity, his accusation stabbed at the sliver of doubt that she'd been trying to ignore.

Unsure, she looked at Blake. Even if he was exploiting her feelings for him, he was still twice the man Gabriel would ever be. She'd seen proof of that at the clinic.

Gabriel turned beady eyes back to Angelique. "As soon as the case is over, he'll toss you out like a pair of worn-out shoes."

Blake growled.

Gabriel's hatefulness severed her last thread of patience. She drew back and slapped him square on the cheek. He stumbled back, grabbing at the red handprint left on his face. Blake flew down the stairs and had Gabriel by the throat in just two long strides.

"You had your chance, and you fucked it up. Now she's mine, and I'm not going to let you hurt her anymore."

Gabriel clawed at Blake's hands for release. "Call off your dog, Ang, or I'll file charges on you both."

"You're the one who's trespassing," Blake seethed.

"This place is rented in the firm's name, and I'm a partner. Technically, I have every right to be here."

"Can I hit him now?" Blake asked Angelique through clenched teeth, and Gabriel's eyes rounded.

"No, babe, he's not worth bruising your knuckles. Let him go so he can slither back to the hole he crawled out of."

Blake's face relaxed, and he glanced at her like he was seeing her for the first time. His blue eyes caressed over her face, and she let her lips curve into a warm smile.

"He's nothing to me, Blake," she said as though Gabriel weren't even in the room.

Blake let go of Gabriel with a push.

Gabriel stumbled back and then straightened. "I need the money and the files back, Angelique."

Ah, no more Ang? Good.

"If they're not returned by the end of the week, I'll have to go to the partners with this," Gabriel said, smoothing his Ralph Lauren sweater. "Who do you think they'll believe? An employee who is up here living large and sleeping with our rival? Or me—an invested partner who bills more hours than the other partners combined."

Except me. The last three years Angelique had billed more hours than anyone else at the firm, which put a partnership well within her grasp. Until she was diagnosed and had to take an extended medical leave. Until her ex decided to accuse her of corporate espionage and embezzlement. Until she endangered a relatively open-and-shut case by sleeping with the opposition.

She drew in a pained breath. Unfortunately, Gabriel was right.

He was desperate, and she knew better than anyone that he'd do just about anything to save himself.

Blake growled. "Are you sure I can't hit him?"

Without another word, Gabriel darted for the door.

"Give my regards to everyone at work," Angelique called after him, but the door slammed shut before she could finish the sentence.

She and Blake stared at each other for a second.

"You called me *babe*," said Blake.

"You called me *yours*," Angelique countered. "No one's ever defended me like that."

Blake stared at her. "Do you want to be? Mine, that is?"

Yes. Yes, she did. She swallowed, her hand moving to the sash at her waist. She tugged on it until the bow untangled and fell free. His eyes glowed with a new flicker of desire. Fear sent razor-sharp spasms straight to her heart, but she couldn't stop.

She refused to look away, even though she was scared of what might register in his dreamy sapphire gems. Revulsion? Pity? Before the weed of doubt racing through her could take root, she brushed it off. With a miniscule sway of her shoulders, the robe slid off and pooled at her feet with a swish.

Blake's lust-filled gaze sank to her chest, and his lips parted. Then his stare slid down her flat tummy to the black triangle below her belly button, then up to her breasts again.

"I don't know why you're so self-conscious." His voice had gone all husky like he had gravel in his throat. "You're perfect."

Stepping free from the robe, she walked to him. Gently, she took both of his hands in hers and guided them to her breasts. Instinctively, his palms cupped them, his fingers flexing and kneading.

"Take me upstairs," she whispered. *Because yes, I want to be yours.*

Unfortunately, people didn't always get what they wanted.

Something long and wet poked at Angelique's lips. Eyes closed and brain still misty with sleep from the long night of perfect lovemaking, she pushed the probing thing away and snuggled deeper into the covers.

"Not again, I'm too tired." She barely got out the words before sleep started to overtake her again.

The cold, slippery shaft nudged at her lips again.

Without opening her eyes, she smiled. "You liked that, hmm?"

A restrained bark had her cracking one eyelid. She lunged away from Sarge's slimy nose and long snout, wiping her mouth with the back of her hand.

"Blah!" She tried to spit the dachshund's germs from the tip of her tongue, and then she glared at him. "Really? That's the wake-up I get?" She looked around the empty bed with its rumpled sheets, still heavy with the scent of sex. "I was hoping for something"—she looked at Sarge's nose and smiled—"longer."

Because the object she'd been dreaming of just a moment ago was talented in a way that most women fantasized of but few actually experienced. The way he'd made love to her, stroked her, brought her to climax time after time was . . . a natural wonder. Yes, a seven-inch wonder of the world.

Rubbing sleep from her eyes, she looked around the room. Blake's clothes were gone, but a note sat on the bedside table. She reached for it, seeing his handwriting scrawled across the front. He'd addressed it "Babe," not "Angelique."

She pulled her bottom lip between her teeth, drew her knees to her chest, and unfolded the note. It said he had early patients and didn't want to wake her. Sarge had been walked but not fed. The last sentence was an invitation to come to his cabin after work where they could further explore how best to use the words *more* and *yes*.

She laughed.

And he'd signed it "Dr. Tall, Dark, and Hot-some." Angelique drew in a sharp breath. How did he know she and Kimberly had dubbed him that? She narrowed her eyes at the note. That rascal. Gossip really did travel at lightning speed in this town, and the trees must have ears.

Sarge scampered across the bed and settled next to her. She scratched him on the head, and he rolled onto his back, legs straight up in the air.

"I know how you feel." She looked down at him and thought of how she'd laid herself open to Blake, both physically and emotionally. Every time he'd touched her last night, she'd practically fallen on her back and spread her legs in anticipation. After the way Blake had defended her, challenged Gabriel, then made love to her all night, she couldn't help but respond to every touch, every breath, every delicious word he whispered while he brought her to . . .

She counted on her fingers. Seven, if she remembered correctly.

Yep. A smile spread across her face, and warmth spread through her chest. Dr. Tall, Dark, and Hot-some was the seventh wonder of the world in her estimation. Maybe she should call Guinness World Records, because really, the man needed some sort of award for his mad skills between the sheets.

A beep sounded, and her phone vibrated on the nightstand. She snagged it and read the reminder that was displayed on the screen. Her appointment with Blake's attorney this morning at ten o'clock. Right. Dream over, back to reality.

The warmth in her chest turned to ice, and her arms and legs, which had felt limp from a full night of heady sex, went rigid. She fell back on the pillow and threw an arm over her face.

Blake's affection, his gentleness, the powerful hold he had over her seemed to seep away like a thick fog burning off under the scorching rays of a full sun. Could Gabriel be right? Could Blake have manipulated her heart to gain an advantage? As ruthless as Angelique could be in the courtroom, she'd never slept with someone to win. But she wasn't stupid. Or naïve. She knew it happened.

She lay there, settled into the sheets that still held the scent of their lovemaking, torn between a career that she'd worked for her entire adult life and a love that might not last forever.

Chapter Seventeen

Angry clouds hung in the sky, a winter storm threatening to roll into the Red River Valley several weeks too early as Angelique made the forty-minute drive over to Angel Fire to meet with Blake's attorney. She eased her SUV into a gravel parking lot in front of the old stucco building labeled "Angel Fire Public Library" and parked in between an old Chevy in need of a new paint job and a beat-up stepside truck.

She'd done this a thousand times, faced down an adversary of inferior skill. Today was no different. Except that it was.

Turning off the engine, she surveyed the smattering of buildings that made up the village of Angel Fire. If she'd thought Red River was a one-horse town, Angel Fire didn't even have an old donkey to ride. If you blinked, you'd miss it. But it was safer to meet here than in Red River where everyone would figure out she was the evil attorney sent to modernize their town.

The opposing attorney had communicated with her via e-mail, claiming his cell phone was lost and his landline was temporarily out of order due to a mix-up with the phone company. She suspected he just couldn't afford one. Slow to return her e-mails, he finally admitted to using a computer at the public library because he didn't have his own. More excuses were offered, which Angelique assured him weren't necessary.

She retrieved the Red River Resort Development file from her briefcase one more time. Thumbing to the second page, she memorized the attorney's name.

Mr. Fred Tipton.

She pulled out the document titled New Mexico Historic Preservation Division that listed detailed instructions on how to preserve land and buildings by having them listed on the New Mexico State Register of Cultural Properties. After studying it for a moment, she sighed and closed the file. This would've been so easy. So easy to dispose of this poor guy like a used Kleenex and go back to Albuquerque where the firm would've been waiting with open arms and a corner office.

If only she hadn't let Red River's sentimental beauty wiggle its way into her hardened heart. If only she hadn't let Red River's hospitable citizens inject enough tenderness into her heart that it doubled in size like the Grinch in her favorite Dr. Seuss story. If only she hadn't let Red River's country doctor—who looked like a *GQ* model and had the charm and personality of a Peace Corps volunteer—completely own her heart.

"If onlies" were for people who lost.

She chewed on her lower lip and stared at the front door of the old library building. Her partnership was waiting right inside. All she had to do was walk in and take it. Then the case would simply be about pushing the paperwork through until the business district was safely owned by the resort developers and they broke ground on the new facility.

Propping an elbow against the door, she bit her fingernail. Blake was a good man. The best she'd ever met. As scary as it was to take another chance, terrifying to put her heart in someone else's hands, she cared too much for him to finish her work here. She'd blown into town, intending to keep to herself during the three months it would take to help her clients dismantle Red River. Instead, it had taken a fraction of that time for Blake and the rest of the townsfolk to dismantle her killer courtroom instincts and cast-iron will.

Letting go of the partnership she'd worked so hard for wouldn't be easy, but maybe it would be worth it. And there was that whole clear conscience thing. Even if she and Blake couldn't clear the multitude of hurdles in their way to have a future together, she could leave Red River knowing she'd done the right thing. A clear conscience might be nice to have since she'd have nothing else left.

Returning the file and the document that would sink her case and her future at Riggs, Castillo & Marone to the briefcase, she got out of the car. Dressed in a black pencil skirt, a white button-up blouse, and a wool houndstooth blazer, Angelique walked across the parking lot, gravel crunching under her expensive black heels. Her normal work clothes seemed foreign and uncomfortable now, and she adjusted the waistband then pulled on the lapel of her blazer. When had these shoes started to pinch? She blew out a breath and reached for the door. Probably about the time Red River started to feel like home, and the Merrell hiking boots she'd bought at the Red River Mercantile shop became her daily choice of footwear.

Pulling open the glass door of the old library building, she squared her shoulders, ready to deliver the final blow to her career.

With few windows, the interior was dark and eerie. A moldy smell hung in the air, the dusty shelves adding a staleness to the atmosphere. The few bookshelves that lined the walls were ransacked and disorderly. An elderly woman read a book behind the front desk and didn't look up.

Angelique moved her Oakley sunglasses to the top of her head, cleared her throat, and stepped up to the desk.

"Hello," she said. "I'm here to meet a Mr. Tipton."

The old woman pointed to a back room without looking up.

"Thank you."

Angelique headed in the appointed direction, maneuvering around several scarred wooden tables, and stopped just outside of the cracked door.

She drew in a breath, planted a professional but cool smile on her lips, and charged into the room with an air of commanding authority befitting a CEO of a Fortune 500 company. Or a Secret Service agent about to take a bullet for the president. She had to at least play the part, even if she was about to give up her ace in the hole.

Angelique's steps faltered, and she wobbled on her black stilettos, nearly falling right on her face. Blake and his attorney rose to their feet, and Blake stepped around to help her. She backed away and smoothed her skirt.

"You all right, babe?" Blake used the term of endearment so easily. So smoothly. As if he had no idea that it would undermine her professionalism.

The other man—if she could really call him a man—smoothed back his greasy comb-over. His leer slid over her, then settled on her chest.

"Are you a peace offering from the other firm?" Mr. Aqua Velva's bloodshot eyes dropped to her crotch.

"What are you doing here?" she asked Blake, unable to hide her shock.

Blake's expression blanked at her steely tone. "Uh, trying to save my town and my livelihood. You know that as well as anyone."

Aqua Velva's brown suit was a few sizes too small, the buttons of his dress shirt strained against his midsection, and a double chin jiggled when a smile slid over his puffy lips.

"The resort people." Aqua Velva rubbed his hands together. "Trying to buy us off, huh?" He licked his lips.

A fire hotter than Three Mile Island lit in her pitching stomach and burned through every ounce of charity she'd felt a few minutes ago. The stench of cheap cologne stung her nose and throat, and she had to swallow twice to force out more words.

"You weren't supposed to be here. You said you had patients," Angelique said to Blake, her teeth grinding.

"I decided to reschedule them, and I have every reason to be here." Blake stuffed both hands into his khaki dress pants, his blue eyes clouding to gray.

"You lied."

"No, I didn't, and it's my ass on the line, Angelique. Why wouldn't I do everything I can to save my business and the life I'm *trying* to build here?"

Her breath hitched. "Is that what last night was about? Softening me up so you'd have an edge?"

Blake's jaw went slack. He shook his head and blew out a fake laugh.

"I have to say it's tempting, Dr. Holloway," Aqua Velva interrupted.

Blake's forehead wrinkled. "Someone care to tell me what this is about, because obviously I'm missing something."

Angelique shook with a burning rage that threatened to incinerate everything in the room. Gabriel may have been right. Blake just might've used her to help win his case. He had *lied*. Made love to her like she was the center of his universe, then *lied*. The element of surprise was a powerful strategic weapon in any battle—be it in the courtroom or in warfare—and often garnered a sizeable advantage for the person savvy enough to wield it.

She almost laughed at the irony. That's exactly what she would've done a few weeks ago before Blake, with all of his compassionate country doctor charm, had her surrendering her career, her common sense, and her heart.

She zeroed in on Aqua Velva. Something hard stabbed at her chest, and all the air was sucked right out of the room. The dank surroundings melted away, and only the prey in her crosshairs remained. This blemish on the butt of society was the enemy, and she was going to drop him like she would big game on a safari. One shot. Fast and clean.

Blake said something, but it didn't process through the correct neural pathways that were short-circuiting with rage. His voice was distant and fuzzy, drowned out by the blood pounding in her ears. With slow, decisive steps, Angelique walked to the table. Her voice low and dangerous, she chose each word carefully.

"I'll tell you what this is about, *Dr. Holloway.*" Her granite stare never wavered from Aqua Velva.

Blake went still as she stared his attorney down. The poor lighting glinted off the beads of sweat across Aqua Velva's receding hairline.

"I don't do business with slime," Angelique said through clenched teeth. Then she *did* turn her stare on Blake.

Aqua Velva sputtered.

"And I don't play fair with someone willing to stab me in the back."

"That's really rich, Angelique. You work for people who are trying to screw *you* over, and yet here you are still doing their dirty work while accusing me of not playing fair." He crossed both arms over his chest, his voice grown steely. "You're a smart woman and a good attorney. How can you work for scum like that?"

"Wait." Horror slid over Aqua Velva's pasty face. "There's no bribe?"

"A bribe?" Blake's confused stare went from Angelique, to Aqua Velva, then back to Angelique.

A ruthless smile turned up the corners of Angelique's lips before her gaze slid back to Aqua Velva. "Unfortunately for you, I'm not your perverse fantasy come true." Her tone was formal and razor sharp. "However, I am your worst nightmare." She donned her granite mask. "I'm going to destroy you in the most painful and humiliating way possible. So why don't you go home and fantasize about that."

"You weren't kidding, were you? You really will do anything to win." Blake's tone had gone low and hollow.

Her nuclear stare stayed firmly planted on Aqua Velva. "The hounds of hell couldn't pull me off this slimy bastard before I tear out his jugular."

She turned on her heels and strode to the door. Blake called her name, but his callous tone didn't resemble the sweet, smooth voice that had slid over her like hot fudge just last night. This voice bit at her ears and sliced across her skin like razor blades.

She kept walking. Long, sure strides carried her away before he could hear the sob that she was trying so hard to choke back.

She hurried across the parking lot. Her eyes stung with hot tears. Blake called to her from behind. She broke into a run, stilettos and all, unlocked her SUV with the remote, and peeled out of the parking lot with Blake's arms flailing in her rearview mirror.

───

The road blurred through Angelique's steady stream of tears until finally she pulled onto the shoulder and dialed Kimberly's number.

"Hey!" Kimberly practically yelled into the phone. "I was just about to call you. I'll be in Red River late Friday night and we can start our baking mission early Saturday. Plus," Kimberly rattled on, "a baking class is on the bucket list, so we can mark that off. *And*"—Angelique was getting dizzy—"fencing or alligator wrestling is next on the list. Take your pick. I actually found an alligator farm close to the Colorado border."

"Kimberly," Angelique said, her voice breaking.

"What is it, sweetie? Really, alligator wrestling isn't that dangerous. It's mostly for show. They're like giant lizards trained to let the customers win."

"Blake's attorney is the guy from the casino. The one who thought I was a prostitute." She choked, her throat closing up.

Kimberly let out a long, low whistle. "Whadaya know? Was there anything left of him when you were done?"

"Blake . . ." Her voice shook. "Blake was there."

"So he kicked the guy's ass, right?"

Angelique blew out a shaky laugh and explained what happened all the way up to the part where she'd run out of the library so Blake wouldn't see her crying like a little girl. She wouldn't give him the satisfaction of seeing her cry over the way he'd so masterfully manipulated her into believing he wanted her . . . for her.

He'd make a great attorney.

"Blake couldn't have known about the casino, hon." Kimberly's voice was soothing.

"I know, but Gabriel was probably right. I think Blake's interest in me may've been because of the case." Her voice cracked again. "How can I be so good at my job and suck so hard at choosing men? I'd actually planned to give Blake's attorney the one piece of information that could save Red River."

"Which means you'd lose, and you never lose." Kimberly whistled again. "You must have it bad for the good doctor. Losing the case could get you fired, but leaving that firm full of good ol' boys wouldn't be the worst idea you've ever had."

"That's just it. I didn't care about the firm or my career. I wanted to help Blake, until I walked into that room and saw him standing there after he'd specifically told me he had patients." After he'd made love to her all night under false pretenses. "Aqua Velva just accelerated my sizzling fuse. If using me was Blake's plan . . ." If distracting her with great sex and incredible abs was part of his scheme. ". . . it worked beautifully." She squeezed her eyes shut and pressed the palm of one hand against her forehead where a dull throb beat at the inside of her skull.

"So what are you going to do?" Kimberly asked.

"I have no idea." And Angelique didn't because the same cold hollowness that'd gutted her when she was diagnosed now crept back in to choke out the love she felt for Blake.

Chapter Eighteen

Angelique picked up the phone several times to dial Blake's number, only to toss it back on the counter. If he hadn't been using her, wouldn't he have called by now? She sat on the back porch wrapped in a blanket and watched the sun sink lower while nursing a glass of red wine.

Funny how much she missed him, even though she'd never really had him to begin with. They never had a future together. Well, yes, she'd had a momentary lapse in reality by thinking she might actually be able to stay in Red River and be happy here. With Blake.

Stupid, stupid, stupid. She'd known from the start that getting involved with Blake was a dead end. He was a family kind of guy. Had said so on more than one occasion. She wasn't. Well, she *was*, but she wouldn't go there. So this . . . *thing* she'd had with Blake was better off over sooner rather than later. *She* was better off. Right?

She took another sip of wine to warm her against the autumn chill. The snowcap on Wheeler Peak was getting thicker each day, a sure sign that winter would be here soon and fall would be over. Just like everything else in her life, including her partnership. It was the end of the week, and if Gabriel hadn't already gone to the partners to ruin her career, Angelique was about to ruin it herself.

Blake's lack of communication was proof enough that he'd been playing her. His presence and the identity of his attorney had shaken her to the core. No way had Blake not noticed. Yet, he still hadn't tried to contact her either by phone or by taking the five-minute walk across the footbridge to knock on her door. The old Angelique would've said, *Game on*, and followed through with the threats she'd issued to Aqua Velva, attorney at law.

The new Angelique didn't have the stomach to destroy this wonderful little community of quirky, loveable people, even if Blake *had* duped her on their behalf.

She looked down at the Red River Resort Development file sitting in her lap. The firm had e-mailed and called several times since her meeting with Blake's attorney, but she'd ignored them all. If she was going to go down, she might as well go down with panache.

Setting her wine glass aside, she pulled out the New Mexico Historic Preservation document. With a red pen—fitting for Red River, this place that had somehow become so important to her—she scribbled a note across the top.

Kimberly Rasnick, Attorney at Law, is expecting your call. (505)555-8263

Act fast. Can only stall so long.

She hesitated, chewing on her bottom lip, and looked at the black thong sitting on the side table.

You can throw these out. I never wore them, anyway. It was the only way I could get Sarge to deliver the note.

She hesitated again, considering the sign-off. *Love* would be the right word, then her name. But she couldn't force her fingers to form the letters. Finally she wrote, *All the best*, and left her name off.

Rolling the note into a small tube, she wrapped her black thong around it—the very thing that had brought them together in the first place—secured them with a rubber band, and called to Sarge, who was currently sniffing around a pine tree.

After making sure the package was secured between his teeth, she shooed him away and went inside to leave a note for Kimberly. Coop had called and asked her to fill in for Ella in tonight's volleyball match, and Kimberly would likely arrive while she was gone.

So that was that. No man, no partnership, and she was about to lose her first case. On purpose. A case she should've been able to win blindfolded. She might even be out of a job, but somewhere along the winding road through the Red River Valley, she'd lost the desire to return to Albuquerque at all. All the things she thought she'd wanted when she first got here seemed distasteful and unfulfilling now. She had no idea how she was going to move forward, or what the next step in her life would be.

Unless, of course, Gabriel really did try to pin his missing company funds and client files on her. That would make the next step in her life pretty clear. She'd need an attorney to start building her defense. Even though Gabriel had no proof, he was a good lawyer and could make her life miserable . . . correction, *more* miserable than he already had.

She scribbled off a note to Kimberly and went to lean against the windowsill. Bundling her sweater tighter, she stared out at the yard littered with autumn leaves. A gusty breeze sent colorful foliage tumbling across the lawn, and sparse snow flurries drifted past the window, melting the second they touched the ground.

She had made a lot of money at Riggs, Castillo & Marone. Financially, she could take her time figuring out her next move—or use her savings to pay for her defense if necessary.

But the only scenario that made her heart skip with joy was living right here in Red River with Blake.

She released a weighty breath.

Too bad that was the only scenario that wasn't possible.

Blake's jaw tightened when Angelique took the court with Coop.

She'd warned him. She'd told him several times over that she was a good attorney and that she'd win this case. He shouldn't be so disappointed. And angry. Angry that she'd behaved exactly like she said she would from the very beginning.

Stupidly, he thought he'd peeled back just enough layers to glimpse the real Angelique. The Angelique with a heart and the ability to care about people instead of wins.

When she'd flipped the Vicious Switch the moment she walked into the library conference room, it'd been a shock. Of course, Fred Tipton accusing her of some sort of bribery would've ticked off anyone. After Angelique stormed out, he'd whirled on Fred and demanded answers, but Fred became suddenly tight-lipped and evasive. Then he recommended that Blake try bribing the bank owners, which got Mr. Tipton fired on the spot.

Tipton had handed over the case file to Blake, which consisted of no more than five pieces of paper. Mostly correspondence from Angelique and her law firm. Obviously, Tipton knew how to put together a legal case about as well as Blake did.

Which left Blake and his fellow business owner friends doomed.

They had no attorney, no money to hire another one, and Angelique was about to get what she wanted. Another win. He hoped it was worth it to her, because she'd lost his respect in the process.

Just before leaving for the game, he'd heard a scratch at his back door and knew it was Sarge. He couldn't even bring himself to pet her dog, so he left the scratch unanswered until the little dog wandered away.

Now Angelique was in her pure form. Iron mask, steel countenance, sheer competitiveness etched into her determined stance. And she played the part of a champion well. With no emotion at all, not a single flinch in her concentration, she and Coop wiped the floor with the other team, then wrung them out like an old dishrag.

He couldn't watch it anymore, because he really just wanted to shake her by the shoulders and tell her to grow up. Instead, he stomped off the bleachers and headed for the door.

As he walked past the crowd toward the door, Ella called out his name. He stopped and found her in the crowd, two rows up in the stands.

"Uh, Doc," she said, her voice a little bewildered.

"Ella, everything all right?"

A hand on her rounded belly, she stood and looked down at the pool of water at her feet. Then she looked back at him, eyes rounded with fear, and shook her head.

The crowd gasped.

Coop ran toward them just as Ella bent over in the throes of a hard contraction.

Blake and Coop were at her side in two strides. "Okay, breathe, sweetheart." Coop's voice was shrill. "Okay, okay." His eyes went wild. "Okay . . ."

Right. Coop was going to be a lot of help.

"Ella, how long have you been having contractions?" Blake kept his tone calm.

The pain subsiding, she found her voice. "A while, but I thought they were Braxton Hicks." She doubled over again and groaned against the pain.

Blake looked around, and his eyes landed on Angelique. He ignored her and moved on to Lorenda. "Lorenda, call 911." She nodded and pulled out her phone. Then he found Miranda in the crowd. "You're on crowd control."

Miranda put two fingers in her mouth and let out a sharp whistle. The chatter ceased, and she shouted, "Everybody out! Lady having a baby." The crowd moved toward the door, and Miranda herded them out.

Blake returned his attention to Ella, whose face crinkled under another contraction. Coop was frozen with fear.

"Ella, help is on the way," Blake tried to soothe her.

Lorenda shook her head at him and held the phone away from her ear. "There was a logging accident. Dispatch is diverting my call to Taos. It'll be thirty minutes."

Hell. The contractions were already coming so fast the baby would be here by then.

Ella yelped in pain and clutched at her lower belly.

He retrieved his keys from his pocket and tried to hand them to Lorenda, but she was on the phone. Angelique was the only person left without an assignment. "Go to my clinic. In the storage room there's a portable gurney. It's not that heavy, so you should be able to carry it on your own. Double-time it."

She didn't hesitate. Snatching the keys, she nodded and took off at a dead run.

In less than eight minutes they had Ella in Blake's office on a clean examination table. He instructed Lorenda and Angelique to hold up Ella's legs.

"You can do this, sweetheart," Coop said, standing at Ella's head and holding her hand as she bore down and pushed.

"The baby's crowning," Blake assured them. "Come on, Mom, keep pushing."

Ella grunted and screamed, then she panted for precious air.

"Just a few more pushes and you'll get to see your new baby," Blake encouraged her with a calm voice.

She pushed hard and screamed when a slimy head popped out into his gloved hands.

"Okay, great, Mom. No tearing. Now we gotta get the shoulders out, so can you take a deep breath and push as hard as you can?"

Ella shook her head and sobbed, sweaty hair plastered around her face.

"Sure you can, sweetheart. Come on." Coop kissed her temple.

"You can do it, Ella," Lorenda assured her friend.

Blake glanced at Angelique and did a small double take at the wetness that shimmered in her eyes. The softness. The longing.

Ella let out another wail of pain, and Blake tore his gaze off Angelique.

"Come on, Ella, push for us," Blake coaxed her.

One more long grunt mixed with groans, a few cuss words and a scream, and the Wells family became a family of three.

Holding the little bloody creature in his hands, Blake smiled. "It's a girl." His voice was a little shaky. He'd delivered a few babies during his residency. It'd been a while, but was no less incredible, the miracle of a new life never ceasing to choke him up. "You did good, Mom. I hope I have a kid half as beautiful as her someday."

The infant started to wail, and Ella wept while Coop hugged his wife tight, showering kisses over her head.

"Angelique, grab the fresh blanket I laid out, and hold her so I can tie off the cord."

"Um . . ." Angelique's stormy eyes went wide.

Blake gave her a stern stare. "I need to deliver the placenta."

She grabbed the blanket and let Blake lay the baby girl in her arms.

He retrieved a box of sterile instruments from a drawer, ripped the plastic off, and tied off the umbilical cord. "Now bundle her up in the blanket tight while I finish with Ella."

Turning to Ella, Blake asked, "You good, Mom?"

Ella nodded, still weeping.

"As soon as the placenta is clear you can hold your daughter, okay?"

Ella nodded and wept some more. Coop even swiped at a tear.

And that's what Blake loved about his job. Not the ego of being a doctor, not the prestige, not the money, because hell, he didn't make that much in Red River. It was moments like this that made it worthwhile.

Angelique turned back to them with the baby girl nestled in her arms and handed the bundle to Coop, watery eyes glistening under the lights. Not enough for actual tears to fall, but enough to make her turn to the wall and pull off her gloves.

Huh.

Ms. Badass Attorney's maternal instincts were kicking in, and she wore her thoughts and her mushy emotions right there on her black Nike sleeve. Unbelievable. He'd seen a glimpse of her softness. Way more than a glimpse. He'd seen all five feet nine inches of bared softness up close, flush against him and murmuring his name. But this, this raw yearning that was so apparent when a woman wanted a child, was unexpected because she didn't seem to have a maternal bone in her entire lush body. And it was nice because he'd imagined Angelique having his baby, imagined this very scenario with Angelique in the throes of childbirth.

Until she vowed to destroy him and everything in his life.

Sirens sounded in the distance, and Blake finished up with Ella and covered her with a blanket.

"Miranda's outside flagging down the EMTs," Lorenda said. "I'll go hold the door open for them."

"No." Angelique still faced the wall, but her voice was hard. "I'll go. I'm leaving anyway."

Chapter Nineteen

The doorbell tinkled as Blake entered the Ostergaards' bakery the next morning. But even the tasty aromas coming from the shop couldn't squash his dark mood. He'd been a happy man just a few days ago, thinking he might have a future with Angelique. Thinking she might choose him over a client and actually use her legal prowess to help save Red River instead of level it.

Now he had to figure out another plan because his previous one had disintegrated just about the time Angelique turned on him in the meeting, and then he'd had to fire his attorney. The truth was, he wasn't exactly sure what to do next. Not sure there *was* anything he could do. But he couldn't keep the truth from his friends any longer. It was time to tell them how bad the situation really was. Maybe one of them could come up with a better way to handle things, because he'd screwed it up royally so far.

The shop was empty, but the sounds of clanking pots and pans came from the back room. Blake walked to the counter and perused the brimming display cabinet.

The Ostergaards' selection hadn't been this extensive since Mrs. O was diagnosed. She must be feeling better. That was good news in this little town where everyone celebrated one another's victories and grieved one another's tragedies.

And that made Blake feel even worse about his failure. Angelique and her client would deliver a damaging blow to the Ostergaards and the rest of the proprietors along Main Street. They'd trusted him, and he'd let them down, all because he couldn't keep his mind or his hands off of a certain strong-willed, leggy Italian girl from the moment she'd snatched her black thong right out of his hand.

After delivering Ella's baby, he'd spent the rest of last night pacing the floor of his cabin. He'd walked outside a few times to go bang on her door, only to decide against it. Reasoning with her seemed pointless. If she still couldn't see that loyalty to her law firm was completely misguided and misplaced, that she was on the wrong side even if she did win, it was because she didn't *want* to see it. So did he really want to see *her* again?

Dammit, yes he did. So he'd wallowed in self-pity all night, hoping Sarge would show up to play a new round of Mystery Panties. Even better, Sarge's owner could've shown up in said panties and given him an explanation as to what her problem was. Unfortunately, he hadn't seen hide, nor hair, nor panties of either of them.

How pathetic was he, anyway? Pretty pathetic because he couldn't stop thinking about the woman who came to Red River to dismantle his life and in general rip his A-fibrillating heart from his chest.

"Ah, zee first customer of zee morning." Mr. Ostergaard came from the back to stand behind the counter. "Vhat brings you out on a Saturday morning, Dr. Holloway?"

"Morning, Mr. Ostergaard. It's my weekend to help out at the free clinic." *And I need to tell you what a screwup I am.* "How's Mrs. O?" Blake asked, fully expecting a good report.

Mr. O's expression dimmed, and he shook his head. "Zee chemo is very hard on her. She's home resting."

Confused, Blake glanced over the full display of fresh pastries. Then Mr. O must be doing double time.

"Vhat can I get you, Doctor?"

"How about . . . six of those." He pointed to the cream cheese Danishes. While he was here he might as well pick up something for the rest of the crew because Kaylee and Nadine had volunteered to help out today, too. Racking up brownie points with those two never hurt, especially since he was probably going to have to lay them off soon. Keeping a staff was a little difficult when you didn't have a business left. "And how about six of those." He pointed to the cinnamon rolls, and cleared his throat. Stuffed both hands in his pockets. "Uh, listen, Mr. O, I'm calling a meeting to discuss the resort project Monday morning in my office. Can you be there?"

"Of course," said Mr. O.

"And can you help me pass the word to all the other business owners? There's something I need to tell every—"

"This is the last tray." Angelique hurried out of the back room, holding a pan of pastries with two oven mitts. She stopped short. Even though she wore an apron, she was still covered in flour. Her hair was pulled back, and a coat of flour or maybe powdered sugar had settled over the black silky mess. White smudges streaked one cheek and her forehead, which now wrinkled at the sight of him.

Mr. Ostergaard hustled over to her and took the tray. "Zank you, dear. Business vill be good this veek because of you and Kimberly." With tongs, he dished the hot pastries into the display cabinet.

Angelique just stared at Blake, while Mr. Ostergaard disappeared with the empty pan into the back kitchen.

"Hi," Blake said. Because what else *could* he say?

After he pulled Gabriel off her, she'd made love to Blake like he was the only man she'd ever want again. But the next day, she'd turned into a barracuda, renewed her threat to destroy them all, then showed up here the very same week to . . . *bake?* For the very people she was trying to put out of business?

She wiped both hands on the apron, which made a bigger mess. "Hello." She turned to go to the kitchen.

"You're working for the Ostergaards?" Blake said it more like an accusation.

She half turned back to him but couldn't meet his eyes. "Just helping out a little since Mrs. O is sick."

With the back of one hand, she swiped at her forehead and managed to smudge even more flour across her olive-toned skin. The stark contrast was, well, pretty. Because everything she did seemed attractive to him. She could roll in flour and all he'd want to do is lick it off.

"I know what it's like." She kept her tone even. Emotionless. "It's the least I can do before I leave Red River."

The thought of her leaving felt like someone punched him square in the solar plexus.

But what the hell was she doing here? *Baking?* Did she play the Good Samaritan to all of her victims before tearing their hearts out?

"Now who's Florence Nightingale?" He didn't even try to stay the sharpness of his tone.

Mr. O came barreling back in the room with a noticeable skip in his step.

"Okay!" Mr. Ostergaard reappeared and stood in front of the counter. "Now, vhat else can I get you?"

"Can I borrow your new help for a minute?" He gave Angelique a challenging look, and she narrowed both eyes at him.

"I've got to clean up the kitchen." Angelique took a step back.

"It'll only take a minute. We really should speak in private." He glanced at Mr. O, then turned a sly smile on her. "About that library thing." *Bingo.* She blanched. She still didn't want Mr. O to know the truth. So that was mean of Blake. Kind of like blackmailing her with her panties, but he was way beyond caring at the moment. He should've already told the Os and everyone else in Red River who Angelique really was and why she was here. He'd kept it a secret too long, mostly for selfish reasons, but also because he didn't want them to dislike her before the town had a chance to prickle her conscience. Before he was able to get to know her and see where it might lead.

"I don't think there's anything left to say." She refused to back down. So like her. One way or another he was going to find out what was going on in that stubborn, gorgeous head of hers.

They stared each other down like an old John Wayne movie. Or like Doc Holliday and Wyatt Earp shooting it out with outlaws at the OK Corral. Blake almost snorted, cleared his throat. *Get a grip.* Whatever the case, this Doc Holloway wasn't going down without a fight. To the death. Cheese Danishes and gooey cinnamon rolls blazing.

He took out his wallet and placed some bills on the counter as Mr. O rang up his order and handed Blake the box of pastries. He set the pastries by the cash register and walked around the counter, straight to Angelique.

Her onyx eyes flew wide as each step drew him closer, and her lush lips formed a little O. Before she could protest, argue, scowl, or run, because that's what the hardheaded woman was likely to do, he wrapped her in his arms and hauled her against him. He pulled her within a breath.

Blake glanced at Mr. O again, and Angelique's eyes issued a silent plea.

"You can't have it both ways forever," he whispered and nearly choked on the hypocritical statement. That's exactly what he'd been doing—having his Italian cake and enjoying the taste of it too. Selfish as it sounded even to himself, he'd wanted to keep both Red River *and* Angelique. But she obviously still didn't see him as a priority over her career or that law firm full of vipers back in Albuquerque.

She tensed, swallowed, but didn't struggle against him. "You got what you wanted."

He didn't have any of the things he wanted. "Not by a long shot."

Her eyes flitted to Mr. O for an infinitesimal fraction of time, then landed on Blake again. Her chin notched up. "I can't give you anything else."

"Is that how you really feel, Angelique?" His gaze dropped to those plump lips, and then he gave himself a mental slap. Now wasn't the time to give in to how much he wanted her. Only her. Any way she'd have him. She'd likely see it as weakness.

"Yes, that's how I feel. So let me go." Her voice wavered, and a glint of something softer raced across her face. Then it was gone.

He wanted to stop her absurd talk with a hot, demanding kiss. Instead, he set her away from him. "Then I guess we're done."

He nodded good-bye to an open-mouthed Mr. Ostergaard and strolled out of the bakery with a box of fresh pastries under his arm.

Blake thumbed through the keys on his key chain as he climbed the steps to his back door. His brain fuzzy from working all day at the free clinic while thinking of a frustrating, flour-caked attorney, he dropped the keys. Drawing in a weary breath, he pinched the bridge of his nose.

Get over it. You knew she was trouble from the beginning.

When he bent to pick up the keys, something in his periphery caught his eye. He wandered to the wooden post that supported the porch roof and kicked a stray paper bag away that had blown in from somewhere unknown.

His brows bunched as he eyed the foreign object that had been lying on his porch under a piece of trash for no telling how long. He picked it up, snapped off the rubber band, and held up . . . *black thong panties?*

A smile cracked his face wide open and spread all the way to his center as he examined the same pair of panties he'd had the privilege of holding the first day he met Angelique. Nice. Sarge was back on panty patrol.

"Good dog," Blake mumbled, as he unfolded the piece of paper. He owed Sergeant Schnitzel a dog treat. Blake would buy the dog a whole box if his owner would come to her senses.

Finally getting the paper smoothed out, Blake's eyes scanned the page.

He turned around and headed back to the truck. If he hurried, he could make it to the market before it closed because he owed a certain weenie dog the biggest box of Milk Bones he could find.

That evening, Angelique drove through Red River and headed back to the cabin, with Kimberly nursing a few superficial teeth marks on one hand. Angelique shook her head. "How about we take a break from the bucket list? It's getting hazardous to our health."

"Okay, so maybe alligator wrestling wasn't the best idea on the bucket list," Kimberly huffed.

Angelique rolled her eyes. "Ya think?"

"They were supposed to be tame!" Kimberly crowed.

"You're lucky you have a hand left." Angelique sighed as her SUV climbed another hill, the evening sky turning a pale shade of lavender.

"That's the last time I try to give a giant lizard a treat."

"You still haven't heard from Blake?" Angelique asked Kimberly, chewing her bottom lip. He'd ignored her note, her *gift*, then made it clear they were over this morning at the bakery. But why wouldn't he call Kimberly and take the help she was offering? Kimberly's skills as an attorney had to be far superior to Aqua Velva's. A rock would offer better legal representation, so what was Blake's problem?

"No." Kimberly shook her head. "Sorry, sweetie."

Angelique knew exactly what Blake's problem was. Her. And maybe Kimberly was guilty by association.

She'd deflected several calls from the firm, but she couldn't hold them off any longer. They wanted an update, and they'd have some pretty stern questions as to how and why this case went so far south; she might as well start speaking Spanish and set up a law office in Puerto Vallarta.

She'd never written a resignation before. First thing tomorrow she'd have to figure out how because the partners would surely demand one. Actually, she'd be lucky if they allowed her to quit with some dignity instead of firing her. And she still had to deal with Gabriel and his asinine accusations.

She sighed. Maybe she could buy out that alligator farm she and Kimberly had just come from. Raising alligators seemed like an honorable profession. Society needed more alligators, right? And only one of them had snapped at them for real. They were fairly docile and well-trained creatures. A bucket of fish entrails and they'd be eating out of the palm of her fingerless hand.

Angelique slowed, flipped her blinker up, and turned right into her drive. Her brows knitted together. "My parents are here." She pulled to a stop next to her parents' sedan. "They didn't tell me they were coming back so soon."

Kimberly suddenly found something out the window very interesting. "Oh, look. A cute little squirrel." Kimberly pointed to absolutely nothing.

Angelique rolled her eyes. Kimberly never referred to anything as cute without at least two expletives attached, turning it into an insult. "You didn't need to call my parents. I'm fine."

They parked and walked up the porch to the door. "I've got to go back to Taos tomorrow as soon as we're done at the Ostergaards', so I called in reinforcements."

Her dad and Nona descended on them the second she and Kimberly walked through the door, the aroma of some sort of exquisite Italian dish filling the cabin. Food was her mother's answer to just about any problem. Many Barbetta family crises had ended with a trip to the tailor to let out waistlines. Thank God for yoga pants. When cannelloni and zeppole made an appearance, you could bet money that something catastrophic had gone down like the Yankees losing the pennant. Or a daughter diagnosed with breast cancer.

"Hello, beautiful." Angelique's dad gave her a peck on the cheek. "We came for a quick visit. Kimberly left a key under the mat for us."

"I see that." Angelique set her purse down on the counter. "What's the occasion?"

Her mom, bent over waist-deep in the fridge, pulled her head out of the produce drawer. "Can't we come see our daughter just because we love her?"

"You can come see me anytime you want, but I think Kimberly lured you guys up here under false pretenses." Angelique eyed Kimberly with a suspicious glare.

Kimberly walked to the stove and peeked into a simmering pot. "I have no idea what you're talking about." She slurped spaghetti sauce from a well-used wooden spoon.

"Stop that, young lady." Mom skittered over and swatted Kimberly's hand, snatching the spoon away. "You know better than to do that when I'm cooking."

"Yes, ma'am." Kimberly tried to sound contrite but failed. She pulled a pitcher from the cupboard. "I'm spiking the lemonade," she announced.

"So what's this we hear about you losing your first case ever?" Her dad sat down at the table.

"Gee." Angelique glowered at Kimberly. "Good news travels fast."

"Technically, she's not going to lose," Kimberly said. "The case will be dropped."

"It's still a loss, but if I'm going to lose a case, I'm glad it's this one." Angelique sighed. Even if Blake didn't want her anymore, it was still worth it. She wasn't exactly sure when it had happened, but Red River and its band of misfit residents had changed her whole perspective on how she wanted to practice law. How she wanted to *live*.

"So does that mean you're coming back to Albuquerque soon?" Nona asked, sniffing around the stove. "There are plenty of eligible men there. It's time you settle down like your brothers and pop out a kid or two."

Angelique sent Kimberly another sharp-ass glare for obviously sharing her man problems, too.

Kimberly shrugged.

Angelique rubbed the corners of her eyes, bleary from getting up at the crack of dawn. "I don't need a man, Nona." *Unless the man is Blake Holloway.* Yes. Yes, she so needed that particular man. "And I'm not planning to have kids."

"Oh, honey, you don't know for sure if your kids will inherit the gene. Nona and I both had breast cancer, too, and we didn't let it stop us from having a family."

"And look how well that worked out." Angelique pointed to both of her breasts. "There wasn't a lot of genetic testing data when you two had it, so of course your illness didn't affect your decision to have kids."

"We also have much better early detection methods now that weren't available in our day," her mom countered.

"But you had no way of knowing your genetic code was faulty. I *know* I'd be putting my children at risk. What kind of mother would that make me?"

Her mother sighed. "You're missing the point, dear. We're all still living." She swept a hand across the room, indicating herself, Nona, and Angelique. "You know that thing called modern medicine? It actually works, and my life wouldn't have been complete if I hadn't had you kids."

Nona nodded, taking a seat at the table. "At least modern medicine can make 'em look real. In my day they slapped a wooden boob on us and sent us on our way. Try finding a man with that."

Angelique's dad groaned.

"Well, we just want to see her find a nice man without having to use online dating." Nona shook her head at Angelique's dad. "My friend Edna signed up on one of those senior citizens' sites in Boca Raton, and it didn't end well. They all just wanted her body."

Kimberly scoffed and stirred the lemonade. "This from someone who picks up strangers at the Health Shack between Calcium Support for Brittle Bones and the Colon Cleanse section."

"Actually, it was the ginseng and black cohosh section for a stronger libido, and at least they offered to buy me dinner first." Nona pretended to put a hex on Kimberly with the index and pinky fingers of one wrinkled and bony hand.

"You two shush already." Her mother gave Nona and Kimberly her best Kitchen General I'm-about-to-storm-the-beachhead stare.

Angelique sank both hands into her hair and sagged against the counter. "Will there ever come a time when . . . cancer . . ." She stumbled over the word because she hated it. Just speaking it made her angry. "When it doesn't control my life?"

Her mom took a deep breath. "Sweetie, the doubts you're having, they're normal. It'll get easier with time, but you're worrying about possibilities that are beyond your control. I know you don't want to be a victim, but you can never stop being a survivor."

Angelique put a hand to her forehead as a throb started at the center of her brain. "After your mastectomies, did you ever feel like you were going crazy?"

Her mother looked thoughtful. "Well, there was that one time when I thought I was bipolar, but it turned out to be menopause." She waved a dismissive hand in the air before adding a plate of browned meatballs to the sauce. "The point is you have to go on and live your life. Otherwise, you're letting cancer win, even if it never comes back."

There was that "winning" thing again. Oh, her mother was so good at pushing the right buttons.

Her mother dropped a wad of spaghetti into a pot of boiling water. "*You*. Who hates to lose more than the Yankees hate the Red Sox." Her mother used a large spoon to tap the pasta down into the boiling water.

Angelique rubbed her temples. "The truth is, I'm not sure what I want to do. Kimberly may be filing some papers for me first thing

Monday morning." If Blake would just take the help they were offering. "It'll probably take a few more days to wrap things up here." If she was lucky. "Then I'll have to explain all of this to the firm." Right before they fired her.

"You can stay with me in Taos for a little while if you want," Kimberly offered. "I could use your help with a few cases, and getting certified as scuba divers is next on the bucket list. It'll be faster if you stay close."

"I thought we just agreed no more bucket list for a while?" Angelique said.

"I agreed to no such thing," Kimberly huffed.

Hell's bells, Angelique didn't have anything better to do. Or wouldn't in a few days when she was unemployed. Why not? Scuba diving in a landlocked state at eight thousand feet of altitude might be an adventure. And skydiving out of a perfectly good plane was looking better and better.

Her mother patted her hand. "All we're saying, dear, is that it'll be okay. Things have a way of working themselves out."

Well, frick. So far nothing in her life had worked itself out. And she wasn't expecting that to change anytime soon.

Chapter Twenty

Angelique and Kimberly spent Sunday morning baking enough pastries to fill the Ostergaards' display case for the week. Helping out Mr. and Mrs. O had been cathartic, since Angelique's time in Red River was coming to a close.

She and Kimberly hugged good-bye in the parking lot. Kimberly drove back to Taos to work on an important case, and Angelique went back to her cabin.

When she entered the kitchen, Angelique froze. Her mother broke eggs into a bowl, and her father sat at the table working a crossword puzzle.

And Blake stood over the kitchen island—*her* kitchen island—attacking vegetables like a samurai warrior. Obviously, he wasn't experienced at dicing produce because she'd never seen a tomato cut into the shape of South America.

He glanced up and did a double take. Angelique's heart skipped. She stopped in the doorway, frozen like a deer in his headlights while she drank in the heated look of desire that shone in his eyes. Her insides liquefied.

"Hello, dear." Her mother started to beat the eggs with a whisk. "Look who stopped by with a box of dog treats for Sarge."

His eyes slid down her flour-caked body. A tingle started between her legs and quickly escalated to a slow burn when Blake's gaze climbed back up her body inch by slow, sensual inch.

Okay.

She cleared her throat since her parents were in the room. Didn't look like he was too mad at her. He looked . . . hot . . . and his smoky eyes said he wanted to be doing her instead of the vegetables. So why did it take him so long to show up after she'd given him the keys to his quaint little kingdom with that legal document?

"All done baking for that nice German couple in town?" her mother asked.

Angelique nodded. "Yes, Mother."

She turned her simmering voice and scalding stare on Blake. "So you just stopped by, Dr. Holloway?" She lifted a shoulder and waved a hand in the air rather dramatically. Or insanely, she wasn't sure which. "Just stopped by and made yourself at home in my kitchen with my parents." Her volume cranked up several notches. "I mean, you think you can pop over and what? Borrow a cup of sugar whenever you want?" She damn well wasn't talking about sugar, and he knew it. "Because I gotta tell you, Doc, I'm getting a little tired of giving you things that you don't appreciate."

Her mom's whisking slowed, and both of her parents eyed her and Blake.

Blake just kept chopping, as cool as one of the cucumbers he was hacking at. But when he stole glances at her in between whacks, his eyes blazed with heat. "Oh, I appreciate everything. Very much, in fact. I brought Sarge a thank-you gift."

Angelique folded her arms and cocked a hip. "I sent a message to you a few days ago."

"It just reached me late yesterday. I didn't want to show up empty-handed, so I had to hunt down a box of treats. Your mom was kind enough to invite me to stay for Sunday brunch."

"We're having omelets, so can you set the table, Angelique?" her mom asked.

Hell's bells, she couldn't do this, couldn't deal with Blake in front of her mother. She looked at the flour caked under her fingernails and drew in a breath. "Give me a minute to clean up." She retreated to her room where she could regroup and think for a minute without Blake making her drool and heat in places that shouldn't be heating this early in the morning. With her parents under the same roof. Over omelets.

When she reappeared in the kitchen, freshly showered and dressed in running clothes, Blake's gaze took another inventory of her. The sweltering look in his eyes turned the heat between her legs into liquid fire.

Her mom yammered, while issuing kitchen orders to her dad that went promptly ignored as he concentrated on the crossword puzzle. A polite nod and a blank look gave away Blake's inability to keep up with her mother's verbal gymnastics. If he didn't already regret bringing Sarge the treats, he would as soon as Mom commanded him to—

"Here, Blake." Her mom retrieved an apron from the drawer and handed it to him. "Put this on."

Aaaand there it was. Frilly kitchen armor. Certain to strike fear into the heart of any man.

Blake hesitated, his brow furrowed. Reaching for the apron, he looked at Angelique. She shrugged, because really, what else could she do? It was the price he'd have to pay for both ignoring her and for Mom's home cooking. There were certain unwritten rules in the

Barbetta family, and Mom calling the shots in any kitchen was one of them. Punishable by an empty stomach if broken.

Served him right, because she still didn't know why he'd shown so little interest in the sacrifice she'd made for him and Red River. Okay, she'd made it for herself, too, but that was beside the point at the moment.

Angelique had to hand it to the guy. He tied the apron around his waist without so much as a flinch. Only the slight flush of his face showed his discomfort.

Nona walked in still in her robe. She took her sweet time looking him up and down through thick lenses. "Finally a classy choice with the hired help. That Kimberly person was of questionable moral character if you ask me. When did we hire a cook?"

Angelique nearly burst. "Oh, for the love of God." She grabbed five placemats and turned on her grandmother. "You know exactly who Blake is. Stop pretending to be senile just so you can get away with being obnoxious."

Nona headed for the coffeepot with a harrumph. "It was worth a shot." She turned back to Blake and stared at the frilly apron around his midsection. "Really, Dr. Holloway, if you're going to be part of this family, you've got to know when to put your foot down."

Be part of their family? "Nona!" Angelique hissed. Heat, and not the sexy kind that inspired fantasies of Blake wearing nothing but a stethoscope, crept up Angelique's neck. She was going to threaten to have Nona banned from bingo night at the senior center. Nona was already on the center's watch list. After the incident with the fire extinguisher and the male strippers who showed up during a square dancing class in full firefighter's gear, a single anonymous phone call would totally work.

"For God's sake, Nona," Angelique warned. "Blake just stopped in to leave some dog treats and have breakfast."

Nona stirred cream and sugar into her cup. "Dear, if a man will wear a lavender apron for your mother, then he wants to be a permanent fixture in your life." Angelique and her parents all hissed at Nona simultaneously.

Blake's Ginsu chopping slowed.

Oh God in heaven, please make her stop.

"What?" Nona asked. Lifting up one slightly cupped hand, she gave it a sharp twist through the air. The old Italian neighborhood way of saying WTF.

"Um, standing right here," Blake said.

Angelique wasn't sure if the look of sheer terror that spread across his face and made his eyes bulge out was because of the apron comment or the permanent fixture comment or the fact that her family was scarier than the Munsters.

Her dad looked up from his puzzle and stared at Blake over the reading glasses perched on the end of his nose. "Welcome to my world, Dr. Holloway."

"That's it!" Angelique had obviously reached her breaking point, because she tossed the placemats down, grabbed Blake's arm, and hauled him outside, slamming the door behind them. She was even hotter when she was angry.

She towed him down the porch stairs and around the side of the cabin where inquiring minds couldn't see them through the windows, and spun on him.

She just stared at him, her breaths uneven and urgent. "How could you hire scum like Fred Tipton?"

"That was the first time I'd met him in person, and Tipton was the only attorney we could afford. You've known our financial situation from the beginning." Shifting his weight, Blake closed the space between them so that his inner thigh brushed the outside of hers.

"He offered to pay me for sex." She hugged herself.

"*What?*"

"When Kimberly and I went to the casino a few weeks ago. He's the guy who thought I was a prostitute."

Blake's fists clenched. "That's what he was talking about?" He scrubbed a hand over his face. "When he said you were a bribe?" His voice grew strained as his teeth ground together. "So that's why you turned so vicious on a dime? It wasn't just to win, it was because of Tipton."

She twisted a handful of his gray thermal shirt into her fist and nodded. At least she was touching him. He liked that. Had been afraid he'd never feel it again.

"I should've done more than fire the bastard."

Her gaze locked with his, the anger draining away. "You fired him?" Big black eyes rounded, and her expression turned soft. Vulnerable.

And that's all it took to finish wrapping him completely around one of her long, slender fingers. He loved those fingers. Especially when they slid through his hair, flexed against his chest, and wrapped around his . . .

He cleared his throat. He brushed her creamy cheek with the pad of his thumb, the softness of her skin a sharp contrast to his calloused fingers. He nodded. "Yep. And just in time, too, because the small business proprietors of Red River have retained legal representation from a Ms. Kimberly Rasnick of Taos, New Mexico. I called her cell a few minutes ago. She's a kick-ass lawyer because she's found a way to save us."

Angelique twisted his shirt tighter and tugged gently, looking down. "I didn't want you to see me like that. You know, at the meeting when I turned into a shark with razor-sharp teeth. It was humiliating after how . . . intimate we've been. You're the only person I've ever cared about *not* seeing how brutal I can be when I'm working. When I'm with you, I don't want to be . . . as strong as I usually am. I've never even let myself cry in front of any man except you."

The softness of her hair tickled his lips, and he pressed them against her temple. "There's nothing wrong with letting someone else be strong for you once in a while."

"It's weak. Like wearing a pink ribbon."

He let out an easy laugh. "Nothing about you is weak, Angelique."

"And I've never willingly let anyone win until I met you." She tapped her fisted hands against his chest. "Damn you. I used to see my courtroom demeanor and competitiveness as my biggest strengths."

He pulled her into his arms and planted a kiss on her forehead, breathing in the soft scent of the soap she'd just showered with. "You *were* like a really well-dressed Rottweiler."

She blew out a choked breath and buried her face in his chest. Nice. Right where he wanted her. Next to his heart.

"You were pretty hot, by the way. Except for the part where you said you would destroy me in the most painful and humiliating way."

"I was talking to your slimy lawyer."

"Tipton *was* creepy. Even creepier than your puppet slippers."

She jabbed Blake in the side.

"Ouch," he said with a laugh. "You can kiss that and make it better if you want."

She jabbed him again.

They swayed to the breeze for a moment, wrapped in each other's arms.

"Thank you," Blake finally said, caressing the silky hair at the back of her head. "I know how much giving me that document must've cost you."

"You're welcome," Angelique whispered.

He tightened his arms around her. "How did your firm handle the news?"

"They don't know yet. I'll have to tell them first thing in the morning. Kimberly is filing the papers tomorrow as soon as the county clerk's office opens."

"I'd drive to Taos and bring her Tipton's case file tonight, but I'm not sure it would help," Blake said. "It was almost empty."

Angelique shook her head. "Already taken care of. I gave Kimberly everything she needs." Something akin to fear threaded through her words, something he'd never heard from her except when it came to her health. "If the firm ever finds out, nine kinds of hell will break loose."

"The firm doesn't need to know, and neither do any of Red River's business owners." Blake stroked her hair. "Everyone still thinks you're here on vacation, and that's the way it can stay." He pressed a loving kiss to her cheek. "What will happen when you tell your bosses tomorrow?" he asked, but he could guess without her having to explain.

"Well, my partnership is gone for one, and I'm not sure I'll have a job there anymore."

Blake sighed against her temple. "Stay here. With me." That would make him happy, he just wasn't sure if she could be happy here in a tiny little town. But he really wished she would at least give it a try.

"It may not end with me losing my job and partnership." Her grip tightened around him. "Gabriel's accusing me of some pretty bad stuff. If the partners take his side—"

"Which they likely will, I assume?"

She shook her head. "I just don't know. I can't imagine how they'd pin it on me, but I seem to be the easiest target. It could go either way."

"So we'll deal with it together. And I wouldn't mind being a part of your family, even if Nona is a little frightening."

Angelique pushed back to look at him. Her forehead creased, and new tears filled her eyes. "You don't want to be with me, Blake. I know you want a family, so don't deny it. I don't want to have kids. I'm scared I'll pass my toxic genetics down to them, and I couldn't live with that."

With a finger under her chin, he tipped her head up and angled it just right. Brushing a kiss across her plump lips, he tasted her sweetness, a sweetness she didn't even know she possessed, and then he deepened the kiss. Slow and sensual, he drank in her heat until a small sound of her pleasure escaped and he absorbed it, letting it reverberate through him. He smiled against her lips when she moaned, and pulled her trembling body flush against the firmness of his.

The contrast of her curves molding against his hardness drove him crazy with want. Her kiss became a little more aggressive. Raw need singed him everywhere she touched, as her hands did a dance all over him. Exploring. Touching. Massaging. She grabbed for the hem of his shirt and found his bare flesh. His muscles bunched when her cold fingers flexed against him, heat coursing through his chest and gathering below his belt. This time *he* moaned. He broke the kiss.

"Come on," he whispered urgently against her lips. "Let's go to my place."

She started to protest, but he cut her off with another demanding kiss. Because really it seemed the only way to win with her. Either kissing her senseless or blackmailing her with her own panties.

Speaking of . . .

His hand sank way south of the border, then eased around to stroke the soft stretchy material between her legs. She shimmied against him with a groan. *Perfect.*

"What color are they?" he murmured against her throat, rubbing between her legs. Her fevered desire heated his fingers. That should keep her mind occupied with something other than disagreeing with him.

"Wh . . ." She swallowed hard, her breath hitching. "What?"

"Your panties?" He increased the pressure of his strokes until she went a little weak in the knees, and he snaked an arm around her waist for support. "Tell me."

"I don't remember," she whispered, her head falling back, giving him more access to her creamy neck. Her hands clutched at his arms and shoulders.

"Liar," he said against her ear, sending another wave of shivers through her. He released her waist, inched his fingers under the soft fabric of her sweatshirt, and found the sensitive spot over her ribcage that turned her on so much. Her skin pebbled, but heated at the same time. As he caressed with just enough friction, a moan slipped from between her pliant lips.

"My . . ." she gasped. "My parents are inside."

He stroked the delicate skin down to her waist then up over her slender ribcage again, her body warming to his touch more with each pass. "Precisely why we're going to my cabin. Otherwise, I'd undress you right here and make love to you on the grass." His thumb moved in a circular motion between her legs, and her breaths turned ragged. Urgent. Evidence of her growing need moistened his fingertips. "What color?"

She swallowed again, falling against him. "I'm not wearing any."

Fuck's sake. He was already aroused, but that caused a surge of lust to bowl him over like a wave hitting a sandcastle on the beach. He gritted his teeth, and without a word—because he couldn't speak without losing it right there—he pulled her across the bridge and into his cabin.

Angelique grabbed for the bottom of Blake's shirt as they stumbled through Blake's back door, him kicking it shut with a thud. Biting threads of pleasure coiled inside of her, begging for release. She lifted the hem of his thermal pullover, and he peeled it off so fast it was like ripping the wrapper off a piece of yummy candy. Candy she'd like to taste with slow, savoring licks and bites.

He let her go long enough to lock the door. When he turned back to her, her eyes took a nice vacation down the hard planes of his chest and ripped abs. The dark line of hair that disappeared under faded Levi's that hung so low on his hips the V at his groin made her mouth water.

She ate him up with her stare.

He advanced on her with the stealth of a lion and a stare so hungry it made her coil even tighter, like a spring at its breaking point. Her breath caught as he came to a stop so close to her, his breath warmed her cheeks. He didn't touch her, didn't reach out for her. He just stood there looking down at her with a sultry look that communicated his desire to have her, each of his ragged, hot breaths washing over her prickling skin.

"Your room's over there?" She nodded toward a door to the left of the fireplace.

"Uh-huh," he said, as she backed toward it, him following her step for step.

She backed through the door and turned to look at the room. Not much there besides a bed with a handmade quilt over it in deep red and brown hues and an old dresser. Not surprising for a single guy, but now the place was his to keep for as long as he wanted to live here. He could transform his rustic bachelor pad into a real home, and that thought caused an incredible warmth to sweep through her.

She never imaged losing would feel so good. "The bed looks comfortable," she said, as he came up behind her and put his hands on her waist and his mouth on her neck.

"It is. Brand new." His wet kiss, coupled with a nip of his teeth, sent a tremble through her. "Now you," he said, his voice gone all husky with lust as he pulled at her sweatshirt.

Not a good idea. This wasn't a good idea. Okay, so it felt good. Really, really good at the moment, and it would probably feel much better in another minute or two. But still not smart.

She told herself to bolt. To walk away while she could still salvage some remnant of her heart. A few minutes ago when she'd told him she didn't want kids, he didn't respond. And if he couldn't face that now, then he certainly wouldn't be able to deal with it in the future. But her hands didn't obey, and she turned, splaying her fingers against his chest. Her palms slid over the hard muscles that were encased with smooth, masculine skin. When they brushed over his nipples, the skin tightened and his pecs flexed.

Lowering her head, her mouth closed over one of the buds, and his breath hissed out. She smiled against his chest. Rolling her tongue over the nub, she gently pulled on it with her teeth, and his hands sank into her hair. So she paid the other side due attention, earning her another hiss accompanied by a moan.

"Take your shirt off," he said, fisting a hand in her hair and gently pulling her mouth up to his. "You're so beautiful, I want to see you."

With a quick lift and toss, her college sweatshirt sailed across the room, and his greedy stare licked over her black lace bra. He started at her ear, nipping and teasing down her neck until his hot, wet kisses reached the lace strap. With gentle fingers, he pulled the strap off her shoulder, exposing the tender skin to his very thorough mouth. A shudder rushed over her, pebbling her wet skin. Her bra fell loose with a twitch of his fingers, and he cupped both breasts.

"Your body is beautiful, Angelique. I love touching you," he said as he pulled her bra off and tossed it aside.

His mouth found hers, soft and warm and loving. When a sigh escaped through her parted lips, his tongue slipped in and it was like a little slice of heaven on earth. He pulled her hips against his, and the hardness that pressed into her belly almost made her weak in the knees. Well, actually it *did* make her knees go weak. She swayed right into him, in fact, molding around him like melted chocolate over a strawberry. One of his hands wandered south and found its way home, eliciting another shudder from her.

His talented fingers had her workout pants pushed down just past her waist, when he froze. Pulling away so that their noses nearly grazed, he looked into her eyes.

"You lied."

Wait. "What?" she said, trying to think through the foggy lust that had settled over her.

"You said you weren't wearing panties." His fingers snapped the elastic band at the top, and a sweet sting coursed through her bottom. "You lied."

"Well, you were playing dirty by touching my . . ."

When she hesitated his lips turned up, and wickedness winked in his blue eyes. "Yeah?" he teased her to finish the sentence.

Of course she didn't give him the satisfaction. ". . . by the *way* you were touching me."

He chuckled. "You didn't seem to mind."

"No, but that's not the point."

"I've got a point for you." He gently eased her back toward the bed. "Lie down and I'll show you."

She ignored him. "The way you touched me gave you an unfair advantage, so I had to do *something*."

His eyes glinted. "Ah, always looking for a strategy to gain the upper hand." He nipped at her bottom lip, and more arousal speared through her. "Trust me, when we're done here, you'll feel like the winner. I'll make sure of it."

She laughed. "Okay, but you first." With quick fingers she had his jeans and boxer briefs sinking over that lovely ass all the way to the hardwood floors. *Mmm. Hard wood.* This may not be such a bad idea after all. At least for now.

Before he knew what she was doing, she pulled him to the bed and pushed him down onto his back. Kicking the rest of her clothes off, she climbed up his body one slow inch at a time, her tongue taking a playful journey all the way to his mouth. After a hot, sensual kiss, she started to descend again, until she reached the intended destination and took him home with slow, sultry strokes of her tongue.

His breathing became labored, and his fingers threaded into her hair as he rode the wave of bliss that she tried so lovingly to provide for him.

When she was done, he pulled her up to lie against him. The cool morning air chilled her skin, and a little shiver raced over her. He pulled the quilt over them and wrapped her in his arms. His chest rose and fell, and she traced the sculpted angles of his chest with the tip of one finger, her legs and feet entwined with his.

"Will you stay?" One hand caressed her hair, the other trailed down her spine, with light, gentle flicks and back up again.

She wanted to. Loving Blake was so different than it'd been with Gabriel. More passionate, more emotional, more give and take, more . . . more of everything.

It took her a second to open her eyes and give him a sobering look. She shook her head. "Blake, I know you want a family. I couldn't ask you to settle for less."

"I don't care about any of that." He tried to nip at her bottom lip, but she pushed him away.

"When we were at the free clinic and then when Ella's baby was born, I heard you say you wanted kids."

He pulled in an exasperated breath. "Angelique, I'm supposed to say nice things to my patients. I *do* want kids, but I want you more."

"You say that now, but later on you might change your mind." Her stomach knotted. "I couldn't live through another man that I love pushing me away because of how cancer has changed my life."

His hands stilled against her, and the entire length of his body went rigid. "Maybe you should give me some credit and stop comparing me to the shallow prick who broke your heart." His tone was sharp and stabbed at her heart. "Or is that the problem? Are you sure you're not still in love with him?"

Gabriel Schmabriel. She loved Blake. "I'm positive."

"You just said another man you love. Does that mean you love me?"

Yes. She hesitated.

"Because I love you, Angelique."

Her heart soared, and her eyes filled. *Good Lord, what's wrong with me?* She had never let herself cry in front of anyone. Not even during her illness, not when dealing with the aftershock of losing her real breasts, and certainly not when she caught Gabriel with the Cheerleader. She'd kept it to herself, dealt with it privately, refusing to let anyone else see her weakness.

"God help me, I've tried not to love you because I don't know if I can make you happy." He rubbed his eyes with a thumb and index finger. "I'm not sure *you* know what will make you happy. But I do love you."

"I love you, too." Her voice was a whisper.

And with a smooth movement that made her breath hitch, he rolled her onto her back and moved over her. When his impressive erection settled between her legs, she let out a small gasp of anticipation, which he swallowed with a hot kiss. Her need spiked again, and it churned and lapped inside her, begging for him. All of him.

As he nudged her thighs farther apart, she wrapped both legs around his waist. Her body cried out for more where his erection touched her, liquid heat jolting through her all the way to her core.

You should walk away from me. "You're right, I don't know what will make me happy." *Or if you'll stay happy with me. Only me.*

Staring down at her, he pushed halfway inside her, and she arched into him. Her body already reacting, tightening, quivering. Her lungs seized as the coil tightened, pleading for more of him. He lowered his head and sank his teeth into her neck with just enough pressure to bend her to his will.

He was so good at that anatomy stuff.

"This seems to make you happy. Why don't we start there?" he said with a raspy voice as he placed a kiss on the same spot where his teeth had just been.

It took every ounce of willpower and courage she had to open her eyes and look at him, but she did it. His body rigid with renewed desire, his face as beautiful as an angel's. With a palm on his cheek, she stroked his day-old stubble. "Eventually this won't be enough. I'm scared *I* won't be enough. What if you want more?"

"What if I don't?"

And with that, he plunged inside her to the hilt, filling her body with his pulsing flesh. Flooding her mind with pleasure and desire. She urged him on, her hands traversing every inch of his back and bottom and neck and shoulders. Pulling him deeper, clamping around him like a vise. And he didn't disappoint. Somewhere in the cabin next door, two omelets went cold and untouched as he took her fast and urgent until his name tumbled through her lips, and a fierce orgasm splintered her body and her mind into a thousand shards.

Chapter Twenty-One

Angelique wasn't sure how much time had passed, or what time it was. All she was sure of was that she could lie in Blake's bed, wrapped around him for the rest of her life. Her heart zinged with a burst of warmth when a light snore drifted from the beautiful man whom she clung to.

But then a gust of reality blew away her daydream, and an arctic chill filled her chest, weighing her down.

She could chance it. Chance a future with Blake. Trust that he'd never tire of just her. Hope that he'd never grow distant and regretful because he'd settled. But somehow she didn't think so. She'd seen his face when Ella and Coop's baby had slid into his hands. Saw Blake's admiration when Ella, Coop, and their new infant were loaded into the ambulance, all clinging together as a new family.

She looked up at Blake's sleeping profile and appreciated his honed jaw. His beautifully formed features. There were worse things than taking a chance on a man like him, and the benefits would certainly be worth it for however long the relationship lasted. But could she live through the heartbreak of watching him become distant and disconnected if someday he decided he wanted more than just her?

She didn't think she could. Cancer, mastectomies, reconstruction, and Gabriel's betrayal would be like a lazy stroll through the park compared to Blake falling out of love with her. Gently, she tried to extricate herself from his grasp so she could dress and slip out without waking him. As she rolled toward the edge of the bed, his sinewy arm snaked out and hooked around her waist.

"Are you trying to sneak away?" He rose onto an elbow.

Yes. "No, of course not."

She clamped her eyes shut for a second before turning to face him. Mistake. Big mistake. His soft blue eyes lured her in again, and she let him pull her back against him. They lay on their sides facing each other, him still reclined on one elbow, her supporting her weight with one hand.

"Then stay a little longer. This is nice." He nodded, glancing at the rumpled bed that had been perfectly made when they arrived. His eyes took in her nakedness, and he ran his big, warm palm up her arm. "I'll start a fire in a little while, and you could cook something to eat. I'm starving after all the physical activity." He gave her a playful grin.

She pinched him. "So you're using me for food?"

He lifted one shoulder. "You're using me for sex, aren't you?"

She laughed. "Well, you *are* much more satisfying than Harley." And oh, heavens, he had to be. She'd never actually used Harley, but still. The way Blake . . . his stamina . . . the multiple . . .

He scowled. "Who the hell is Harley? And just how many exes do you have, anyway?"

She gave him a wicked smile. "Not telling. And Harley is a battery-operated gag gift from Kimberly."

"Oh, hell no. Harley's got to go. I've already ousted your Audi-driving, Rolex-wearing ex-fiancé *and* my maintenance man, Clifford. I'm definitely not competing with the Energizer Bunny."

"I should remind you that you beat Clifford by default just because it wasn't his weekend to clean your office when Gabriel showed up in town the first time."

"There's such a thing as being in the right place at the right time." He fell back on the pillow and slid an arm under the back of his head. His sculpted biceps flexed, and his dreamy blue eyes stared up at her through long, shuttered lashes.

Oh, hell's bells. Darn those mesmerizingly beautiful eyes and sinfully long lashes that any woman would kill to have. And the incredibly well defined arms, too. They were just too much for her to resist. Way sexier than Clifford the maintenance man.

His gaze slid down to her breasts. The very same breasts that she'd wanted before the mastectomies but had made her feel like the bride of Frankenstein afterward—yes indeed, those were the ones. Instead of revulsion, a spark of lust ignited in his baby blues, turning them almost purple.

She sighed, her engine starting to rev again. Who needed Harley? She loved this gorgeous man, and he was right here. Waiting for her.

"My parents are visiting. I should get home. It's kind of rude to leave guests alone for too long."

He blinked the sleep out of his eyes, and her heart melted a little more. Pretty soon, she'd be nothing but a puddle at his feet.

"I'll go with you."

"You don't have to." She put a hand to his chest, the steady rhythm of his heartbeat pulsing into her the same way his cock had. A wave of terror hit her.

"What?" he asked when her expression changed.

"I don't think we . . . one time we didn't . . ." Her eyes rounded at him. "We got so crazy, I think we forgot to use a condom once." Her hand went to her mouth. "Oh my God. What if . . ."

His hand tightened around her waist and drew her closer. "Would that be so bad?"

No. It wouldn't. She stared at him, wide-eyed at the thought. Nothing would make her happier than having a baby. His child. But no.

"Babe, I'm a doctor. I know the statistics. Just because you have the gene doesn't mean our children will have it."

Our children. Her heart thundered. "There's at least a fifty-fifty chance a daughter *would* inherit my defective genetics."

"Even if she does, it's not a certainty that she'll actually develop breast cancer. We can keep a close eye on it."

Having children with Blake seemed like a dream. A dream that would complete her life. But the risks . . . what if their children couldn't beat the odds the way she had? "You sound like my mother."

"Then your mom's a smart lady."

"I didn't mean it as a compliment." Angelique pushed at his chest, but he held her tight.

He brushed the back of his finger down her cheek. "Worrying about it won't help."

Closing her eyes, she put her hand over his and cradled it against her cheek. His roughened skin against her softness stoked the smoldering heat inside of her, and it flared.

She took the tip of his finger between her lips and suckled. A gentle growl reverberated in his chest.

"You won't get to see your parents until tomorrow if you keep that up."

"They might prefer Clifford over you if they knew what you've been doing to me." She sank her teeth gently into the pad of his finger.

He drew in a ragged breath. "I'm pretty confident your parents and Nona are on my side, so forget Clifford."

She squeaked when Blake pulled her down and rolled on top of her. Wrapping herself around him, she nipped at his bottom lip. "Make me," she whispered.

At her words, his cock grew thicker and hard as granite against her inner thigh. *"Damn,"* he said on a half moan, grinding his hips into hers.

He closed his eyes, and he pressed against her again. His rock-hardness against the soft, wet folds of her sex made the sensations climbing inside her arrow straight to her core.

"If you're sure you wouldn't rather have Clifford as your boy-friend." He reached for a gold square on the nightstand, and had it rolled on before she could respond.

She giggled. "I guess I can give up Clifford if you give me a reason."

"Stay another hour, and I'll make sure you never think of Clifford again."

A cry of ecstasy ripped from her as he drove into her deep and hard.

The sun made an appearance over Wheeler Peak, burning off the early morning fog and providing some warmth to the crisp atmosphere. Finishing up her morning run, Angelique turned onto her drive and slowed her pace. As she approached the house, she stalled to a slow walk to catch her breath before making the call that would change the course of her life.

She wiped sweat from her brow with a forearm and headed around to the back door, where she took off her shoes. Who was she kidding? Her life had been forever changed the second she let Blake Holloway touch her.

Sarge greeted her just inside, and she scooped him up. Planting a kiss on the top of his head, she scratched him behind the ears. "Hey, bud. You miss me?"

Her mother flew into the kitchen wearing a colorful velour warm-up suit. "Hi, sweetie. We're going to the Gold Miner's Café for breakfast. Nona has a date. Want to come along and eavesdrop for entertainment? We sit at a different table, and she tells the guy that I'm the maid and your dad's the chauffeur."

"Why does that not surprise me?" said Angelique.

Her mom shrugged. "She's an old woman. We humor her."

Angelique shook her head and set Sarge back on the floor. "Sounds fun, but no thanks. I've got to call the office while you guys are out." Walking to the pantry, she filled Sarge's bowl with kibble and gave him fresh water.

Nona walked in reeking of Final Net and wearing gold metallic sneakers. Oy vey. Dad was next, mumbling something about troublesome mothers-in-law. He pecked Angelique on the cheek just before her mom shooed them all out the door.

Her mom grabbed her purse, but she came to a stop next to Angelique. "Are you going to be okay, dear? I can stay with you."

Angelique smiled at her mom. "Thanks, but I need to do this on my own."

Her mom sighed and gave her a hug. "All right, but if you need us, you can reach us on my cell." The horn honked. Her mom rolled her eyes and said something in broken Italian that couldn't be nice.

Angelique's heart warmed as she watched her obnoxious, loving, busybody family drive off.

The landline rang, and Angelique snatched it up to look at caller ID. A wave of relief washed over her, and she answered it.

"Hey, Coop. How's the new mom and baby?"

"New mom speaking," Ella said, her voice bleary.

"Well, hey there, new mom. How are you?"

"Crazy from sleep deprivation. If I ever go to work for the CIA, I know how to torture someone. It totally works. I actually agreed to host Thanksgiving dinner at my house next month for both my family and Coop's. At the same time."

"Oh, wow," Angelique said.

"I know, right? Hey, can you play volleyball tomorrow night? I'm not up to it yet, and it's the last game before the league playoffs."

Angelique would likely be homeless by then, because the firm was probably going to evict her in the next five minutes when she called them with the news. Even if they didn't fire her on the spot, she was ready to quit, and she'd have to move out of the cabin anyway. Blake probably wouldn't mind if she stayed at his place.

"Sure thing, Ella."

"Great! You've been a real lifesaver, Angelique. So how much longer will you be in Red River?"

"Um. Not sure."

"Any way we can talk you into staying permanently?"

Angelique wouldn't have thought so a month ago. But now? Staying here with Blake sounded dreamy. If she wasn't in prison.

She chuckled. "We'll see."

A baby cried in the background. "Nap time is over," Ella said, frazzled.

When they clicked off, Angelique stared at the phone. Took a deep breath and dialed her office number.

The receptionist answered on the second ring.

"Hi, Marie. This is Angelique Barbetta. Is Clarence in?" She might as well start at the top with the senior partner.

"Can I tell him what this is regarding?" The receptionist's melodic voice streamed through the line.

"It's regarding the Red River Resort Development case."

The receptionist put her on hold, and Angelique braced herself for the firestorm.

"Angelique." Clarence's voice boomed in her ear. Even though he was approaching seventy, his very presence still commanded authority and respect.

"Clarence," Angelique said.

"I expected you to return my calls sooner. Our client isn't getting good vibes. Says there's been no communication from you. Typically, I'd take your side."

Sure. Like when you looked the other way after Gabriel turned the firm upside down by knocking up the Cheerleader.

"But I have to say, I've been disappointed in the lack of updates from you."

"About that." Angelique swallowed. Took a deep breath. "We're going to lose this one, Clarence."

He went silent, and so did she.

Finally he spoke, his voice low and threatening. "Do you want to explain how you've let this case spin so far out of control?"

"The property owners are filing paperwork as we speak to have the buildings listed on the state historic register. They will be protected by historic preservation laws. There's nothing we can do to stop it."

There's nothing I want to do to stop it.

"And does the property owners' new momentum have anything to do with you losing your professionalism and getting personally involved with one of them?"

Angelique closed her eyes. Gabriel had already ratted her out.

It has everything to do with it almost slipped from her mouth, but she trod lightly. With any luck she wouldn't end up disbarred on top of everything else. "Look, Clarence, I've been rethinking my career at Riggs, Castillo & Marone—"

"As well you should. We gave you this case because it was an easy win. So you could ease back into work after the long absence you needed. It should've been child's play for someone with your skills. But . . ." His tone took on a edge of condescension. "Let's just say you're still not up to your usual standards."

She stiffened. Cancer *had* changed her, but Red River had changed her more. In a way that the men at her firm would never understand.

"I'd hoped the time away from Albuquerque would bring back the shark in you now that you're healthy again. Get you back on your game."

"You mean this should've been an easy kill to get me enamored with the taste of blood again?" Her hands started to tremble.

"Exactly. It appears I was wrong."

Totally wrong. Angelique was nothing like the woman they'd sent here. Instead of blood, her tastes now ran more for delicious German pastries and a certain country doctor who made her mouth water every time she looked at him.

"I've made you and the partners a lot of money, Clarence, attracted high-profile clients to the firm, and when I was down, you let Gabriel kick me." She seethed more with each word. "You wanted to get me out of the way so I wouldn't make waves for your golden boy, nothing more. No matter how easy this case was supposed to be, you knew it was nowhere near my area of expertise. Tell me, Clarence, did you know Gabriel was screwing my legal assistant while he was engaged to me?"

Clarence's guilty silence set off her already shredded nerves. He wasn't stupid. The reason he was senior partner was because he made it his business to know everything that went on in his firm.

She blew out a strained laugh. "Of course you knew. You just didn't care."

"The other partners and I expect you back here by the end of the week," Clarence said, his tone cold as the snowcapped mountain peaks outside her cabin. "You've got some explaining to do."

"What else can I say, Clarence? The resort isn't going to happen. The case is closed."

"The case over our missing client files and money is just getting started. See you in a few days," Clarence said, and the line went dead.

Chapter Twenty-Two

Ms. Nelson clung to Blake's arm as he opened the door of exam room B and led her into the hall. Except for a short break so he could tell his business friends the good news, his entire Monday morning schedule was filled with Red River's elderly female population. As much as he enjoyed hearing stories of their weekly pinochle shenanigans where they drank highballs and pretended it was plain Coke, he really wanted to get done with patients and call Angelique.

After they spent most of yesterday in bed together, he was pretty sure she'd stay in Red River and give it a chance. Give *them* a chance. A smile crept across his lips. He wanted to seal the deal while she was being so agreeable. Plus, she said she was calling her firm this morning, and he didn't want her to be alone all day.

He had to be honest with himself. He just wanted to be with her, period.

"Maybe you should take my temperature again, Doc? I'm coming down with something, I'm sure of it."

"We've taken it four times, Ms. Nelson. Drink plenty of fluids and stay warm. The temperatures are dropping. I hear our first snowstorm of the year is supposed to hit this weekend."

She sighed her disappointment as Nadine scurried down the hall and came to a halt in front of them.

Nadine's jet-black hair was pulled back into a severe top knot, and her thunderous expression was even more pronounced. And frightening. He stilled, Ms. Nelson still clamped to his arm.

"Everyone is up in the apartment waiting." Nadine nodded toward his office at the end of the hall and folded her arms with authority.

"What's wrong?" Blake couldn't imagine what had Nadine so irritable this early in the morning, unless the Ostergaards ran out of sticky buns before it was Nadine's turn to order. That usually caused a near riot.

She tapped her foot. "Maybe Kaylee can help Ms. Nelson to the front?" Nadine widened her eyes at Blake and even stopped smacking her gum. *Oh, no.* It must be serious.

"Kaylee," Blake called to his assistant, who'd just stepped out of exam room A. "Can you see our favorite patient to the reception area, please?"

"Sure thing, Dr. Holloway." His exhaustingly enthusiastic nurse bebopped over. "Anything you need."

Nadine pried Mrs. Nelson's bony fingers off of Blake's arm and handed her off to Kaylee. "Okay, young lady, you have a seat out front, and I'll be right with you."

Kaylee guided her to the front, chattering the entire way. When they disappeared around the corner, Nadine's black penciled-on eyebrow rose so high it almost disappeared into her hairline.

"What?" Blake asked, a little scared of the answer.

"Better bring your neighbor some Kevlar when you get off work." She pointed to the ceiling where the majority of Red River's business owners were waiting for him. "They're pissed."

Blake's mouth turned to gravel. "Excuse me?"

Nadine refolded her arms across her chest. "I knew something was off about her. I mean, really, she used the name Angie Marone here in your office, but at the volleyball games she goes by Angelique Barbetta. She really played us for fools, didn't she?"

Blake closed his eyes and pinched the bridge of his nose. *How did they find out?*

Nadine smacked her gum twice. "It sucks that you've had to live next to her. I hope she didn't sucker you into becoming her friend while she was stabbing you in the back."

When his eyes popped open, Nadine stared back at him with both penciled eyebrows cocked high.

"It's a long story." One he'd hoped he'd never have to explain.

"Okaaaay." Nadine smacked her gum again and waited for more.

He let his eyes drift shut again.

"Oh, no. You like her. As in *like* her—like her." Nadine's scowl turned to compassion, and her voice changed to that tone he'd heard her use when her six-year-old skinned a knee. "What can I do to help?"

He sighed. "Nothing. This is my fault. I'll handle it." He turned to go up to the apartment but stopped. "Nadine, it's not what you think. Angelique isn't what you think. I'll explain later, but can I count on you to keep an open mind and maybe even give her another chance?"

Nadine kept her tone neutral, but she gave him a you've-been-played-like-a-schmuck look. "Go have your meeting, Doc." She turned and stalked down the hall.

His stomach tightened as he climbed the stairs.

This was supposed to be a victory meeting where he announced that they'd won the case. Red River would stay untouched, and their way of life would stay unchanged. And no one would ever know why Angelique really came here. All they needed to know was why she decided to stay. So who gave her up?

He paused at the door and drew in a breath before pushing it open. He had to do some damage control with the owners. Their town, their buildings, their businesses being saved should soften their hearts. Maybe he could explain *how* they won, and this tight-knit community of people who argued one minute and then fiercely defended one another the next would forgive him and Angelique. But offering up that information could get Angelique in even more trouble than she was already facing.

With his hand on the doorknob, he hauled in a deep breath.

He'd handle this. Force them to see that turning on the woman he loved wasn't necessary. Then he'd go see Angelique on his lunch break. She deserved to know that she'd been outed, and he didn't want her to hear it from anyone but him.

Thank God there were no cops around, because Angelique did twenty over the speed limit trying to get to Blake's office. She might be facing a legal battle of her own, but after the phone call with Clarence, her future seemed so clear. Why hadn't she seen it sooner?

She sniffed under her arm. Okay, a shower would've been nice in her *immediate* future before she did zero to ninety to see Red River's most eligible hottie. But after her morning run, she'd been distracted by her parents, then Ella's phone call. Then she'd decided to get the call to the firm over with before she lost her nerve.

Blake didn't seem to mind any of her other flaws, so she'd make it worth his while if he could overlook this one lapse in personal hygiene. She had news!

Blake was worth a risk. Her own heart was worth it, because her heart would be broken and useless without giving a relationship with him a chance. She had to hope and believe that they could face any obstacle together and overcome it. Together.

Her heart skittered, and her eyes moistened. Cancer was in her past. Blake was her future. And if illness reared its ugly head again, she had faith in Blake to weather that storm with her.

And losing? The call to the firm had sealed her first legal loss, but she didn't feel like a loser. Her ambition had always driven her to the next goal, but no matter how many goals she reached, how many victories she claimed, they never seemed to fill her with contentment. Today she didn't just feel like a winner. She felt like a champion, only not in the way she always thought she would.

She was in love. With a man who loved her back, more than he loved himself. And somehow helping the small business guys in this little town seemed a whole lot more fulfilling than defending high-profile criminals and getting her name and picture on every news channel and paper in the Southwest.

After a stop at the market for champagne—which raised a few eyebrows from the clerks since it was barely nine thirty in the morning—she'd grabbed a nonalcoholic bottle and headed to Blake's office. She pulled into a parking spot against the curb in downtown Red River.

Not long ago she'd sat in this same spot covered in poison oak and wondered why the people of this town were so attached to these dilapidated old buildings. Now she saw the charm. The history. The sense of community that flowed through this town, and she loved it. Wanted to be a part of it. Hopefully forever.

She pulled down the visor and looked at her bedraggled hair, the ponytail hanging loose from her run.

Gah!

She tried to smooth it out, but gave up and dug into her purse for perfume. Rummaging through the contents, she grabbed the tube of breath spray. With two squirts to the mouth, she looked at the bottle.

What the heck.

Lifting one arm, she squirted the minty scent onto her microfiber sweatshirt, then repeated on the other side. She tossed it into her purse, grabbed the bottle of champagne, and hopped out of her SUV, clicking the remote over her shoulder.

———

Blake turned the doorknob and walked into his old apartment. All of Main Street's proprietors stood around the bar that separated the kitchen from the den. Fred Tipton's case file was open on the counter. Empty. The pages distributed among some of the business owners, the others looked over their shoulder and studied the documents that had Angelique's name all over them.

Shit. This was even bigger trouble than Blake thought. *He* had outed Angelique.

Early that morning, he'd run up to the apartment to make sure it was presentable for the meeting. He tossed the file onto the counter and went to check the bathroom. That's when Kaylee popped in and told him the first patient of the day was having trouble breathing. He rushed downstairs, and sure enough, one of his elderly regulars was having an asthma attack.

He put the nebulizer on her, got the attack under control . . . and never thought about the file again.

Mr. Ostergaard was the first to speak, his German accent thickened with grief. "Zhis cannot be true. Angelique vas such a nice young voman."

Blake rubbed the back of his neck and went to stand by the window. He leaned against the sill. This was going to be bad, and it was his fault.

"I can't believe she pretended to be here on vacation." Page in hand, Cooper Wells looked up. "Ang was my friend. We went to high school together."

"Coop, come on," Blake said. "You know she's still your friend."

The owner of the Shear Elegance Salon across the street tapped a manicured nail against the Formica countertop. "With friends like that we don't need enemies. Frenemy, that's what she is."

A murmur of agreement circled the room.

Blake adjusted the stethoscope that was draped around his neck and shoved both hands in his pockets. "It's not what it looks like. I called this meeting to tell you the new resort isn't going to happen. Our buildings will be listed on the State Register of Cultural Properties. We have a new attorney filing the papers right now. Every building in Red River's business district is safe. Our businesses are safe. Our lives are safe."

He would've thought his friends would be happy. Crazy happy. But no, their expressions told him they felt betrayed and wounded on the most personal level. That's how Red River was. They stuck together. They treated newcomers and even tourists like their own, until someone made the mistake of crossing them.

"She iz not velcome in my store anymore," Mr. O said.

Blake raked a hand over his freshly shaved jaw. How could he fix this without giving up even more information that could damage Angelique's future? "Look, I felt the same way when she first moved here—"

"You knew all along?" Coop's look of shock turned to suspicion. "Oh, wow," he finally said. "You two are . . ."

Gasps rippled through the small crowd.

"You didn't tell us because you're sleeping with her?" the owner of the seamstress shop said.

His brain whirred to find a way to make them understand that Angelique had become one of the good guys during this whole ugly mess.

"How convenient that she lives next door to you," Joe said.

He turned to look out the window. "I didn't tell you for a few reasons." He couldn't break doctor-patient confidentiality, but if he played the sympathy card, maybe they'd give Angelique a break. "Angelique had a lot of the same health issues my mom had. I *am* a doctor, so don't hold it against me for having sympathy. I thought I could help her through the mental and emotional block that goes with her particular health problem. You know, get close to her."

"Um, Doc," Coop said from behind him.

Blake didn't turn around. "No, let me finish. It's time I tell you guys the truth." He kept gazing out the window at the people ambling down Main Street and tried to explain from the beginning. Then he'd explain all the way to the end about how she was a wonderful person and how much he loved her. "I wanted to give it some time, see if I could change her mind. Our attorney wasn't exactly a legal genius. He didn't stand a chance against a lawyer of Angelique Barbetta's caliber, and I was trying to tip the scales in our favor."

"And you did a magnificent job." Angelique's voice was lethal.

He spun around.

There she was, standing in the doorway with a bottle of champagne. Beautiful. Hurt. And angry as hell.

Angelique's heart hit the floor like a brick. There was Blake, the man she loved. The man she thought loved her back. Telling Red River why she'd come here, how he felt sorry for her, how he really did use her.

"Angelique, I wasn't expecting you." Blake's expression blanked.

"Obviously," she whispered, still trying to process the scene. Hatred oozed off of everyone in the room, even her old buddy, Coop.

"You are a hypocrite." Mr. O glared at her. "You come to my zhop and bake vhile you deceive us."

One of the women hissed at her.

"Poser," someone said just below a shout.

Out of breath from hustling up the stairs, Nadine appeared in the doorway. "Sorry, boss." She panted, trying to catch her breath. "*Ms. Marone* slipped past me while I was helping a patient." She gave Angelique a testy glance.

"It's okay, Nadine. Go back to the front desk," Blake said without taking his eyes off of Angelique.

Nadine grumbled and disappeared.

"Angelique, I was just trying to explain to everyone—"

She held up a hand to silence him, and her entire body started to tremble. "Yes, I heard you, Dr. Holloway. From the part where you used my breast cancer to manipulate me."

A hush fell over the room, and all the air disappeared like it'd been sucked up by a vacuum. She gasped for breath.

Blake shook his head. "You don't understand." He ran a set of fingers through his hair.

"Oh, I think I understand perfectly." How on earth could she have been so wrong about another man?

The onlookers stood in silence and watched the freak show, with her as the star.

Blake started toward her, but she took a step back, and he stopped.

"After what I've done for Red River. What I've been through." She closed her eyes, giving her head a shake. *No, this couldn't be happening again.* "After all I've given up for you, you had to lie to me again yesterday morning? You couldn't just leave me be?"

"No! It wasn't like that." He held a hand out and took a step toward her, but she backed away. He stopped and calmed his voice. "I know it looks bad, but it's not what you think."

Angelique's voice shook. "I get it." Boy did she ever. "Me giving you the information you needed to win wasn't enough. You kept me occupied with promises for the future and talk of love until the papers were safely filed." A sob nearly escaped, but Angelique bit it back. She'd chosen the wrong man twice. For different reasons, she hadn't been enough for either of them. "Your strategy was quite brilliant, Doctor." She held up both hands in defeat. "You win."

Blake turned to the openmouthed crowd. "Could you guys wait downstairs? Angelique and I need to talk."

"No." Angelique couldn't hold back the tears much longer, and damned if she was going to let a single tear fall in front of them. Blake was no different than Gabriel or the other partners at her firm. They used her the way they needed, then moved on. "No, we don't." She set the bottle of champagne on the breakfast bar, blood rushing to her ears with a thundering, steady beat. "This is for all of you. Congratulations on your success." She turned and headed for the door.

"Angelique, wait. Please." Blake closed the space between them, putting a hand on her shoulder.

She pulled out of his grasp and whirled on him. "Don't touch me." Her voice was low. Dangerously low. She should've known better, but she'd damn sure never make the same mistake again. "I'm done here."

"Let me explain, babe."

She backed through the door. "I'm not your babe." She swallowed, trying to keep it together for just another few seconds. "And as it turns out, I'm not the only bottom dweller in Red River."

Angelique took the stairs two by two, hot tears starting to flow before she reached the bottom. Nadine called out, "Good riddance" as Angelique raced through the waiting room, through the glass door, and out of Dr. Tall, Dark, and Hot-some's life forever.

Chapter Twenty-Three

Blake explained every detail to the crowd of angry business owners—
even the part about how Angelique had ruined her career for their
sake. He swore them to secrecy, kind of a joke in this town. But a
reminder that his medical training had taught him how to stop a
beating heart, in a way that even the best forensics experts would
identify as natural causes, seemed to work. They listened, agreed
that what happened in his apartment that day would stay in his
apartment forever, and then they all went back to their work.

Blake had Nadine reschedule the rest of his patients so he could
find Angelique.

He felt like such an ass.

He dialed her cell as he got into his truck and tore out of the parking lot, the off-road tires squalling against gravel. He got her voicemail without the phone ringing once, a sure sign that she'd declined
his call. He hit Redial and got Angelique's voicemail again. Then he
dialed the landline. No answer there either. So he kept hitting Redial

until he finally got to his driveway and pulled in without hardly slowing down.

The truck had barely stopped rolling when he threw it into park and jumped out. He flew across the footbridge and knocked on Angelique's front door.

Mr. Barbetta answered, a pointed look on his face.

"I'd like to see Angelique, Mr. Barbetta."

"She doesn't want to see you, son."

"I know she's here, sir, her SUV is out front. Can you please tell her I'd like to speak with her?"

Her father's scowl deepened. "I don't know what happened between you two, but she's pretty upset. I think it best you leave her be for a while."

That was the problem. She might never want to see Blake again. He wanted to explain now.

Nona walked past the door and tried to put a hex on him. Thank God Kimberly wasn't in town. He'd likely limp back home half the man he'd been when he arrived on Angelique's doorstep.

Blake scrubbed a hand over his jaw. "Could you give her a message for me?"

Mr. Barbetta gave a reluctant nod. "I'll try."

"Tell her I'd at least like to explain. I owe her that."

He headed back over the bridge, the sky clouding over with the first storm of the year rolling in. How did he screw this up so bad? Losing Angelique wouldn't just stun him. It would be a crushing blow that he wasn't sure he could recover from.

His weight landed on the loose board that he still hadn't fixed, and it gave way, making him stumble. He stopped and looked back at her cabin. Now he had all the time he needed to fix the bridge and every other item on his long repair list, thanks to Angelique. But time, this cabin, the practice, his volunteer work—none of it meant anything without her in his life.

He picked his way over the rotted spots and walked toward home.

He had to find a way to get through to her before she packed her bags and left.

Only the business owners of the historic district stopped to give Angelique an awkward stare when she walked into the Red River Community Center Tuesday night. No one else seemed to notice her. They probably hadn't heard the gossip yet, but another twenty-four hours would remedy that. Her heart punched at the wall of her chest, but she lifted her chin.

Ella and Coop waved from the stands, their baby bundled into Ella's arms. Coop climbed down and jogged over to Angelique.

"Thanks for coming, Ang."

She stuffed both hands in her microfiber hoodie and scuffed at the gym floor with the toe of one running shoe. "I'm surprised you wanted me to, Coop. After what I heard yesterday, I didn't think you and Ella would ever want to see me again."

"We can talk about it later." He squeezed Angelique's shoulder. "Ready to play?"

Damn right she was. Pummeling a volleyball might relieve some stress. Especially if she pictured it as Dr. T, D, & H's head. She zipped off her hoodie, tossed it in the corner, and set her keys and phone on top.

With a fist bump, she looked at Coop. "I'm ready to win."

Coop blew out a laugh and led her onto the court.

It didn't take long for Angelique and Coop to put away another win for Team RRC. She played hard, trying not to think of the two dozen or so phone calls from Blake she'd deflected, the voice-mails he'd left that she refused to listen to, or the message Blake had relayed through her father. Because every time she let her thoughts wander to Blake, his betrayal was like a kick in the gut. Worse actually. It was like he kicked her in the heart, ripped it from her body, then doused it with gasoline and set it on fire.

After she and Coop shook hands at the net with the losing team, she followed Coop off the court. Glancing at the far end of the bleachers where Blake sat amidst his family members and staff, Angelique beat back hot, angry tears and several unbecoming words.

She wiped the sweat from her face with a towel and took a seat with Coop and Ella in the stands.

"Drinks are on us at Joe's after the last game, Angelique," Ella said, handing the baby to Coop. He cooed at his infant daughter, and Angelique's heart squeezed.

She shook her head. The situation was already awkward enough. "Can't. I have to pack." "I'm leaving early tomorrow morning."

Ella and Coop exchanged a look.

"We were hoping you'd stay this week. I think we can win the league championship," Coop said.

"We need you, Angelique. You guys kicked ass out there," Ella said.

"Hey, you said *I* couldn't cuss around the baby," Coop scolded his wife while rocking the baby in his arms. "How is that fair?"

Ella raised an eyebrow at him. "When you go through twelve hours of hard labor, then you can cuss all you want around our kids."

"Your hard labor lasted less than twenty minutes," Coop dead-panned.

Ella shrugged. "It felt like twelve hours." She waved a hand dismissively, before letting the baby grasp her finger. "Besides, it was like pushing a grand piano through a keyhole, so I still win."

Angelique really liked Ella, but . . .

"Why would you guys want me to stay?" Angelique asked. Blake had exposed her. "Aren't you angry?"

Coop held a finger to his lips. "Not here." He leaned in to whisper. "But Doc told us what you did for us."

And the hits just keep on coming. Blake didn't just reveal her initial purpose here. He was broadcasting evidence that could destroy her completely. How could she ever practice law again if it was common knowledge that she'd helped her client lose?

Her chest squeezed, making her heart thump in a sickly rhythm.

Her phone dinged, and she pulled it from her pocket. She tapped the new text from Kimberly, and it popped onto the screen.

Spoke to lawyer I know in Albuq. There's rumbling about your firm. Rumors of Gabriel having a meltdown. Lots of clients bailing.

Angelique thumbed a response into her phone.

What kind of meltdown?

Within five seconds Kimberly's response dinged.

Dunno. Friend said partners at RC&M are scrambling for damage control.

Great. Whatever crisis Gabriel was having, he'd likely try to blame that on her, too. Angelique typed a quick message telling Kimberly to keep her posted and dropped her phone back into the pocket of her hoodie.

The ref blew the whistle for the next game, and Blake and his cousin, Perry, emerged from the crowded bleachers to stand on the sidelines. A hush settled over the stands as Blake and Perry pulled off their black sweatshirts to reveal . . .

Angelique stifled a gasp. They wore matching hot-pink athletic shirts with a breast cancer ribbon outlined on the left shoulder. Blake and Perry turned around so the crowd could read the backs.

Perry's said "Fight Like a Girl" in big, bold letters. Emblazoned across the back of Blake's shirt was the phrase "Someone I Love Is a Survivor." The crowd roared. Several catcalls rang out from amidst the crowded stands.

Coop put two fingers in his mouth and whistled. "Hey, Doc! Love the new team shirts."

Blake and Perry jogged over. Blake nodded to Coop, but then his eyes settled on Angelique. "It's my new favorite color." His gaze locked with hers. "From now on, I plan to wear pink every day in October so breast cancer survivors know how much I care."

A wave of female "awws" rippled through the crowd.

Sitting a few seats over, Mrs. Ostergaard wiped at her eyes. "Zhat is a good young man."

He's a shit. Angelique bit back the words. She hated pink. Hated ribbons. And Blake knew it. At the moment, she especially hated him for putting her on the spot in front of all these people after what he'd done. When her hands started to tremble, she looked away.

The ref blew the whistle, and Blake walked backward onto the court until the ref bounced the ball to him. He waited for the opposing team to take the court, and the match started.

Coop leaned over to Angelique. "Nice shirts, huh?" He said it like he was talking about the weather. Angelique ignored him.

Perry sent the ball flying out of bounds and lost the serve. Blake gave him a brotherly slap on the back, and the other team took possession of the ball.

"You know, Doc must really care about the person he's wearing it for." Coop spoke in his best nonchalant tone. "Never seen him do anything like that before."

Right. Good to know Dr. T, D, & H didn't make a habit of seducing his rivals to get what he needed. Didn't sink their careers and break their hearts when he was done with them. That made Angelique feel so much better.

In fact, being his only victim made her feel like a freaking princess.

She thought her heart might implode. With a rub of her chest, she willed the suffocating pain to go away. It didn't.

Coop leveled a knowing stare at her. "He's a good guy, Ang. That's all I'm saying."

Angelique drew in a breath and found Blake on the court again. As much as she wanted him to have a good excuse, a reasonable explanation, she heard what she heard in his apartment. So had Coop. There was no denying the evidence.

She stood. "I've got to go."

Ella spoke up. "Angelique, please stay."

"I've got a lot to do before I leave town tomorrow. I'll see you guys around, okay?" Against Coop and Ella's protests, Angelique jumped from the bleachers and hurried out of the gym.

As far as she was concerned the subject of her future with Blake and Red River was closed, and she was marking it off as a loss. And much to her horror, she was getting too good at losing.

"Mom! Will you let Sarge outside?" Angelique called downstairs early the next morning as she tried to finish packing the last of her things. She went into the bathroom and started to fill a large cosmetic bag with makeup and toiletries.

Her mom whistled for the dog from downstairs, and Sarge's nails clipped against the stairs as he scampered down them.

Angelique looked around the expansive bathroom. She'd settled in here like it was her home. This cabin *had* become her home, and leaving it seemed . . . wrong. She'd come here to fill a void created by her illness. Instead of another win that would catapult her into a partnership at one of the most prestigious law firms in the Southwest, that emptiness had been filled by a charming little town full of neighborly and warm people who'd do anything for one another.

That vacancy in her soul had also been occupied by a man. A man who had turned her heart upside down by looking at her naked, surgically altered body with desire instead of distaste. A gentle man who had covered every inch of her body with sensual kisses, finding the spots where she still had feeling after the surgeries had damaged so many of her nerve endings. Zeroing in on them with his mouth and fingers so she enjoyed each sexual encounter as much as he did. More, actually. Every time they'd made love, he made sure she was satisfied many times over before he took his own pleasure.

How could all of that have been a lie?

Her lip trembled, and she bit at it, looking in the mirror. She couldn't wrap her mind around Blake's dishonesty. It simply rocked her world and tilted it off its axis.

Suck it up, Barbetta.

She squared her shoulders and tossed more makeup into the bag just before her lip started trembling again and tears slid down her cheeks. She sank onto the vanity stool and dropped her head into her hands.

Handing the victory over to Blake had made her so incredibly happy. She'd wanted him to be the hero. For the other business owners, for his dad's clinic, for Red River. For her. It'd cost her a hefty price, but she'd been glad to pay it.

She had no idea what to do next. Now she had a whole new open, throbbing wound in her soul to fill up again. But how?

And that was just the problem, wasn't it? She wasn't sure she *could* move on without Blake.

She pushed herself out of the small vanity chair and headed downstairs to see how much progress her parents had made.

"Hello, sweetie." Her dad gave her a peck on the cheek. "You almost packed up?"

Angelique nodded. "How's it going down here?"

"We've packed everything that you designated as your belongings." Her mom closed up a box. "It wasn't much." Mom glowered at Nona. "We should double-check every box and your grandmother's suitcase before we leave. A few stray items made their way into the to-be-packed pile."

"It was just a candy dish, and I thought it was Angelique's." Nona harrumphed, wheeling her small suitcase to the back door.

"It was an expensive piece of Nambé, and you knew perfectly well that it wasn't Angelique's." Her mother rolled her eyes.

"I'll lock the boxes in the car until we leave." Her dad grabbed a box and headed for the door. "Just don't give Granny Klepto the keys, or the state troopers might stop us before we leave the county and arrest us for theft."

Nona plopped down in a dinette chair. "If they're good-looking, I wouldn't mind being frisked."

Her dad groaned in disgust as he walked out the back door.

"Where's Sarge?" Angelique asked.

Her mother frowned. "I was busy packing, so I opened the back door and let him wander out on his own. I guess he hasn't come back yet. Why don't you see if your father can go look for him?"

Angelique shook her head. "I'll go." She slipped on her UGG boots at the back door and grabbed a jacket off the hook. "It's really getting cold." She peeked out the window as she slipped on the warm fleece. "Looks like it's going to rain or snow. I'll right back."

Snuggling deeper into the down jacket against the cold morning air, Angelique walked toward the footbridge. Getting closer, close enough to see the full expanse of the bridge, her heart stuttered. A large section of the old wood planks was splintered, leaving a gaping hole on the left side of the bridge. Half the railing on that side was completely gone too, with several large, broken timbers dangling over the edge of the bridge.

"Sarge!" Angelique yelled.

A tiny brown head and long snout popped up over the bank of the stream and whined.

"Come on, boy!" She clapped her hands.

He tore toward her, shivering and covered in mud, but when she tried to pick him up, he whined and backed away.

"What's wrong, Sergeant Schnitzel?" She tried to coax him to her again, but he barked and ran in the other direction, disappearing over the bank again.

Angelique climbed up the small incline and called to him again when she crested the top. She stopped stone-cold in her tracks, her heart lurching. She tried to scream but nothing came out, her throat closing up so tight she could hardly pull in air. The stream water lapped at a large swatch of hot-pink fabric. Nestled between two large boulders, a limp body floated and gently shifted with the rhythmic pulse of the water against the rocks.

Chapter Twenty-Four

"Blake!" Angelique found her voice as she splashed into the water. Her boots sank into the muddy stream bottom, and she had to slog through it. "Blake!" He was lying faceup, and his skin had gone a pale gray.

Tears spilled over, and for the first time in her life she didn't care. Didn't worry about looking weak. She couldn't lose Blake. Just knowing he was in the world made it a better place.

Sergeant Schnitzel barked and turned frenzied circles on the bank. Finally, he dove into the water too and swam after Angelique. By the time she reached Blake, the cold water had reached her chest.

"Blake, I'm here." He didn't move. A steady flow of blood spilled from a gash in his forehead and disappeared into his curly, wet hair. With two fingers she checked for a pulse and sent a thank-you heavenward. Thank God he hadn't fallen facedown. She eased him out of the stone crevice and hooked both hands under his arms, tugging him toward the bank. Sergeant Schnitzel swam at their side, like he was helping rescue his buddy.

One of Blake's eyes cracked open. "Angelique?" His voice was weak and his body shivered.

"I'm here." The muddy bottom and waterlogged boots slowed her progress, but the water made his large frame buoyant enough for her to tow him toward dry ground.

He struggled to stand but howled in pain and fell back on her. She pushed her full weight against him to keep from going under.

"Just float while I pull you to land." Angelique started toward the bank again.

"I fell in," he moaned.

She tried to keep her voice steady. "Yeah, I noticed." She struggled against the mud, her steps cumbersome.

"I was bringing Sarge home." His teeth chattered as he spoke, and his eyes fluttered closed again.

Still swimming in circles next to them, Sarge barked at the mention of his name.

Okay, that was good news. Then Blake couldn't have been in the water that long because she'd asked her mom to let Sarge out not more than ten minutes ago. Still, the paleness of his skin and the way he was trembling sent a wave of terror rioting through her body.

"I think my leg's broken." The shivers raking his body deepened. "I couldn't get to the bank," he mumbled, his eyes still closed.

"Good thing for you I'm strong, because we're almost there." She managed to drag him onto dry land, his legs still hanging in the water. He winced. Sarge climbed out onto the bank and shook stream water off, whining at Blake's side.

Blake put a hand on Sarge's head. "Good boy," he managed to say through chattering teeth.

"Yeah, he kind of led me to you." Angelique pulled off her sodden jacket and put it under Blake's head. A rush of relief hit her like a brick wall. She sagged over him for a moment and let more tears flow as she rested her forehead against his chest.

"He brought me more of your panties." Blake's shaking hand patted his pants pocket. His eyes closed, and a soft smile curled up the corners of his pasty, white lips.

Angelique nearly growled. "You're half-dead in the stream with a broken leg, and you're happy about having my panties in your pocket?"

His smiled broadened, but he didn't open his eyes.

"Oh, for God's sake. Maybe I'll just leave you two panty conspirators on the bank to fend for yourselves." She tried to push herself up to a stand, but Blake's hand closed around her wrist.

"For the record, your panties make me happy no matter where they are, but most of all when you're in them." Now his eyes did open and locked with hers. "Or not in them. Either way it's a win-win for me."

Her breath hitched, because even in his current condition, he still looked at her like she was the most beautiful woman he'd ever seen. Like he wanted to climb in bed with her and stay there all day. And that's when she knew that she couldn't live without him because he . . . he was her other half. Without him she couldn't be whole.

"I need to go get help, okay?" She ran a muddy hand over his cheek. "I'll be right back."

"Promise?"

She nodded. "Promise," she said just before his eyes fluttered shut again.

His leg hurt. Almost as much as the throbbing cut on his head.

Angelique fussed over him like a mother hen. Actually, like a lioness protecting what was hers. The paramedics even flinched a few times when they tried to tell her to move out of the way. It was kind of nice. And a little funny when she mowed down one paramedic with a sharp-ass glare for trying to remove the heavy quilt she'd pulled off one of the beds in her cabin and tucked around him. All the blood drained from the poor kid's face, and he backed away, letting Angelique pretty much have her way. Smart guy.

Blake couldn't help it. He watched her in action and smiled, even though his leg and head hurt like hell. He'd love to see her in the courtroom someday. As long as she was on his side.

As the paramedics loaded him onto a gurney, Angelique's family bustled around him, trying to help. Mr. and Mrs. Barbetta both hissed at Nona when she asked the paramedics to take off their shirts and pose for a picture with her. She may have even mumbled something about making a video with her smartphone.

That was a little creepy. Blake shook the thought from his mind.

When he was firmly strapped to the gurney, a temporary bandage on his head and a brace on his leg, the paramedics wheeled him toward the ambulance. Refusing to leave his side, Angelique grasped his hand in hers. The gray sky shadowed her mud-streaked face, and she shivered.

"Angelique, you should go change into dry clothes. You can meet me at the hospital."

She shook her head. "I'm staying with you."

What the hell. He had her undivided attention "Fellas, can you give us a second? I need to talk to Angelique in private." The paramedics stopped.

"Really?" Angelique's brows rose. "Now? Here?" She motioned to his leg and the gurney.

"Yes, yes, and yes." Blake nodded to the paramedics, and they stepped a few feet away.

She sighed and looked around at the overcast sky. "Okay." She gave in. "But make it snappy. We've got an ambulance to catch."

"I didn't mean to give you up. I accidentally left the file out, and the others read it before I got to the meeting. By the time I walked up to the apartment, it was too late. I had to scramble to turn the situation around and get them to see that you were on their side."

His heart squeezed when Angelique's eyes filled with tears because he knew how much he'd hurt her. She sniffled and looked away.

"You told them *everything*."

"It was the only way I could get them to listen, Angelique. I wasn't trying to hurt you."

She drew in a breath. "If that information ever gets out, it could cause me a lot of trouble."

"It won't get out. I promise." He stroked her cheek. "They know who saved their town and they're grateful."

"What about what you said about me and your mother . . . our health. I'm not just a pity case to you?" She pulled a plump lip between her teeth.

"*Pity?*" Blake half snorted. "Angelique, you evoke a lot of emotions in me, but pity isn't one of them."

Angelique gave a small laugh and swiped at a tear. "Are you sure? I couldn't stand it if you wanted to be with me because you felt sorry for me. You know, because of your mom."

"You're nothing like my mom. You're a fighter. God help me, you're like an MMA champion, always ready to step into the ring and take me on." He tugged her down so that her hand rested against his chest and her face was close to his. "Maybe that's why I love you so much. Will you mar—"

A horn double beeped as a black four-door Mercedes pulled into Angelique's drive. Her expression darkened, and she tensed against him when she looked up.

"Frick," she murmured under her breath and stood.

The Mercedes pulled to a stop next to Angelique's car, and both front doors popped open. Two men got out, a little overdressed for Red River in Blake's opinion.

"Clarence. Robert." Angelique acknowledged both of them with a stony expression.

"Angelique." Clarence, the older of the two with silver hair and a medium build, greeted her. "Obviously, we've caught you at a bad time."

"Yes, you have. Blake needs to get to the hospital. I'll be out of the cabin today, if that's why you're here."

Blake tightened his grip around her hand. She was planning to leave today? He glanced at her SUV, his jaw twitching. He'd been in so much pain he hadn't noticed her trunk open with boxes and luggage loaded in the back.

Robert, late forties with black hair and a hint of gray at the temples, shook his head. "We're not here to run you out. Just the opposite."

"Excuse me," Blake interrupted. "Who the hell are you two?" He could guess, which was why he had no intention of being polite.

Angelique pulled in a breath. "This is Clarence Riggs and Robert Castillo. The two senior partners at my firm."

Ah. He guessed right. And if he remembered correctly, Marone was the last name on the company letterhead. As in Gabriel "the Douchebag" Marone.

"Look." Angelique's expression turned icy. "We'll have to do this some other time, gentlemen. Blake's hurt. If you'll still be in town later, I could meet you."

Oh, hell no. He wasn't about to leave her alone with these two jokers. "I'm good." Blake propped his free arm under his head, refusing to let go of Angelique's hand. "Right, fellas?" He glanced at the paramedics before returning a steely gaze to the men who'd already stabbed Angelique in the back. If they'd expected her to work side by side with Gabriel after what he'd done, no telling why they were here now.

"Right, Doc," the paramedics agreed. "We're good."

"Blake, you need to go to the hospital," Angelique pleaded with him.

His grip tightened around her long, slender fingers, and he caressed the empty spot where he wanted to put a ring. "I'm not leaving you alone with them."

"I'm perfectly capable of handling this on my own." Her eyes flashed at him.

"I'm well aware of that." Really? Were they really going to argue about this *now*? "I'm still staying."

She studied him for a second, then turned to her bosses. Correction. Former bosses, if Blake had anything to say about it, and he really, really wanted a lot to say about it.

"What's so important that the two managing senior partners had to drive all the way to Red River to say it?" Angelique's posture went rigid, and tension poured off of her in waves.

Clarence cleared his throat. "I was a little hard on you the other day when you called, Angelique."

"Ya think?" Angelique said, her tone as frigid as the water she'd just pulled Blake from.

Good girl.

"Losing this case and such a big client was a shock. I'm sure you can understand," Robert added.

Angelique's expression stayed detached, but her chest rose and fell in quick succession. Blake caressed the inside of her wrist with the pad of his thumb, her racing pulse thrumming under his touch.

"Cut to the chase, gentlemen. I'm busy." Her words were like steel, and Blake couldn't hold back a faint smile. *Go get 'em, tiger.*

Clarence and Robert exchanged a look. "We came up her to deliver some good news in person," Robert said.

"And what would that be?" she asked, clearly skeptical.

"Gabriel has resigned from the firm," Robert said, pasting on an artificial smile. "We're offering you a full partnership, effective immediately."

Huh? Angelique had to blink a few times to process what Clarence and Robert had just offered her. Everything she'd always wanted. At least until a few weeks ago when the man on the gurney next to her stomped up to her cabin door and called her a bottom dweller after rescuing her dog.

"What do you say, Angelique?" Clarence beamed with pride. "An even bigger salary than you make now, with no ceiling. An expense account and a company car. Most importantly, your name would be on the door." He stuffed both hands in his pockets, his chest swelling.

When she didn't respond with a resounding yes, his brow furrowed. Robert fidgeted and glanced at his partner in crime.

"So what brought this on?" Because she knew darned well they weren't making this very attractive offer out of the goodness of their hearts. They'd obviously forgotten with whom they were dealing. When she negotiated deals for her clients, she could smell a rat from the next county. There was definitely a rodent or two trying to steal the cheese from the mousetrap.

Robert spoke up. "You've worked hard, Angelique. You deserve it, and we're getting a fine attorney as a partner."

"Uh-huh. Tell me why Gabriel's out and I'm in, because I know it can't be a lucky coincidence." Blake's hand tensed around hers at the mention of her ex's name.

Robert sputtered. Clarence rubbed the back of his neck. Yep. Their whiskers just twitched. Angelique planted a fist on her hip and leveled her infamous cast-iron stare at them. And waited. A silent, deadly stare was one of her best negotiation tactics.

A few moments ticked by. Clarence deflated, and Robert stared at the ground.

Worked every time.

"Gabriel's girlfriend took the files and the money. She wanted us to think it was you," explained Clarence. "Apparently, she cleaned out his bank account as well and skipped town after he broke it off with her. He's . . ." Clarence cleared his throat. "He's not dealing with all of this very well. He's decided to move back east and join a firm there after he's had time to . . ." Clarence shoved his hands in his hands in his pockets. "After he's had time to regain his composure."

Blake stroked the top of her third finger.

"And?" She wasn't going to let it go so easily.

Obviously tired of being in the hot seat, Clarence looked to Robert.

"Word of Gabriel's emotional instability has gotten out, and we're losing clients," Robert said.

"Many of whom I handled cases for, right? I did most of the legwork while Gabriel took the credit, and now you need my help to keep them." It wasn't a question, and Angelique kind of enjoyed watching them squirm.

Robert's eye twitched. "You're a good attorney, Ang—"

"Great," she interrupted him. "I'm a great attorney."

Blake's thumb stroked the inside of her wrist, sending a tingle up her arm.

"Right, Angelique," Clarence said. "You're a great attorney, which is why we want you as a partner. So what do you say? How does Riggs, Castillo & Barbetta sound?"

Her breath caught in her chest. Blake's caresses stopped, and everyone watched her. Waiting.

She turned to Blake. "What were you saying before they pulled up?" She tossed her head in the direction of Clarence and Robert.

"Are you sure you want to do this in front of everybody?" Blake asked her, his expression guarded.

She nodded. "You started it, now let's finish it here and now."

He drew in a breath, and his fingers started to move over her hand again. "I don't want you to work for these clowns." Blake shot a glowering look at Clarence and Robert. "They don't deserve you. But whatever you decide, wherever you want to live and work, I'll go with you." He hesitated and looked down at her hand. "If you'll marry me."

Her mother squeaked a small cry of joy, and her father put an arm around her shoulder.

The air rushed from Angelique's lungs, but her heart filled with joy. "You'd do that?" Her lip quivered and she drew it between her teeth for a second. "You'd leave Red River?"

"For you I would." He nodded. "Only for you."

Robert clapped his hands together. "Then we have an arrangement that makes everybody happy."

"Not so fast." Angelique held up a finger to shush Robert, but she kept her eyes on Blake. "What if I said I don't want to be part of Riggs, Castillo & Barbetta, but instead I'd rather live here with you and be Angelique Barbetta-Holloway?"

Blake's mouth curved into a smile. "Seriously? I have to say all that every time I introduce you?"

She arched a brow at him.

"I love the name Angelique Barbetta-Holloway," Blake said. "It's very elongated just like your dog."

She laughed, and Blake tugged her down until his nose grazed hers. "I love you," she whispered against his mouth just before he placed a gentle kiss on her lips.

Clarence cleared his throat.

She broke the kiss and smiled down at Blake. "Gentlemen, the answer is no. I was just offered a better partnership."

Her parents threw their arms around each other in a full-body hug. The Red River paramedics clapped, and then Nona asked them to check her heart with their stethoscopes. Angelique didn't know what Clarence and Robert did next, and frankly, she didn't much care.

"Is that a yes to my proposal?" Blake asked.

Angelique nodded, feeling the smile on her face all the way to her toes. Winning really was the best, and she'd just hit the lottery.

"Good." Blake grimaced. "Then can we go to the hospital now? My leg is killing me."

Chapter Twenty-Five

"Happy Thanksgiving!" Angelique said over the melee of loud family members when Kimberly stormed through the front door, a bottle of red wine in her hand.

Angelique grabbed the wine so Kimberly could hug the Barbetta horde who had descended on Blake's cabin for the holiday. In the almost two months that Angelique and Blake had been married, she'd managed to redecorate, repaint, refurnish, and remove Harry the giant moose head so they could host both the Barbettas and the Holloways for their first Thanksgiving dinner together.

"Marriage really agrees with you," Kimberly said, bending over to give Angelique's nephew a wedgie. He ran off screaming to his mother. "I've never seen you glow like this."

She and Blake had a quiet ceremony at a Victorian inn just off Main Street. They'd exchanged vows in front of the inn's picturesque window while snow blanketed the mountains during Red River's first big storm of the season. Her mother still hadn't gotten over Angelique's refusal to have a big Catholic wedding.

Angelique had a feeling her mother would forgive her soon enough. Angelique was about to deliver news that would most certainly wash her mother's irritation away.

Several aunts who had filtered in from Long Island and Boca Raton crowded into the kitchen to make turkey with all the traditional trimmings. All of them barked orders at once, vying for control. Angelique's niece hung from Blake's neck and her nephew was wrapped around his leg, while he cheered at a televised football game.

"Word of advice," Angelique said. "Stay out of the kitchen. Kind of scary in there." They glanced at the female Italian kitchen generals and laughed.

"I think I've died and gone to Sicily," said Kimberly.

Angelique introduced her to Blake's dad and stepmom, who looked a little scared in their quiet corner of the den.

"Hey, I could use your help with a couple of new clients," Kimberly said.

"You asking me to be your partner?"

"Maybe," Kimberly teased. "As long as my name's first on the door."

Blake swooped in for a kiss, a kid still hanging from his neck. "Hey, Kimberly," he said after pecking Angelique on the lips.

"Hey, big guy." Kimberly slugged Blake on the arm. "I'm starving." She hitched up her leopard-print belt and looked at the kitchen. "I'm going in." She joined the fray of New York accents sputtering Italian words every other sentence.

Sliding both arms around Angelique's waist, he pulled her close. "She's a brave girl."

Angelique giggled. "You're holding up pretty well." She peeked over Blake's shoulder at her in-laws. "I'm not sure about your folks, though."

He glanced over his shoulder and smiled. "My parents will get used to it." He kissed her.

"Eww!" Angelique's niece squealed, dropped to the floor, and ran off.

"Sarge has a gift for you." He brushed another soft kiss across her lips.

"For *me*? Is he bringing me *your* underwear this time?"

Blake laughed. "Go find him and see."

Angelique hunted down Sarge, finally finding him curled up on their bed in the master bedroom.

"Hey, Sergeant Schnitzel." She scratched his head and he rolled over onto his back, all four legs sticking up in the air. A hot-pink dog tag glinted up at her, and she picked it up, running a finger over the new charm dangling from his collar. The words "I love you" were inscribed across it.

Angelique smiled, her heart doing a dance. Rummaging around in the nightstand, she found a pen and a scrap of paper. With a flourish, she scribbled down a note telling Blake to meet her in the bedroom, retrieved a brand-new pair of panties from her lingerie drawer, and secured them with a hair rubber band.

"Here, Sarge." She held out the bundle to the dog. "Bring these to Daddy." Sarge clamped his long snout around the lace and jumped from the bed, tail wagging. Angelique lay back on the bed and waited, her fingers laced behind her head and legs crossed at the ankles.

Within a minute, the door swung open and Blake smiled at her, a lazy, sensual smile. "Are these for me?" He held up the swatch of hot-pink lace between two fingers just like the first time they'd met.

"Uh-huh," Angelique said as he trekked toward her. "I went shopping just for you."

His blue eyes blazed, turning a deep shade of purple. Starting at her ankles, he climbed up her body until he came to rest on his side, looking down at her. "When do I get to see the rest?"

"How about a new pair each day as long as they still fit." She slid her arms around his neck.

His forehead wrinkled with confusion.

Releasing his neck, she grasped his hand and laid it on her abdomen. "Sarge is going to have a playmate."

Blake blinked at her, his jaw slack.

"I have an appointment with Ella's obstetrician next week, but I think I'm about six weeks along."

Blake swallowed, and a nearly indiscernible wetness shimmered in his eyes. And oh God in heaven, those glistening blue eyes stole her breath. "You're happy about it?" He looked deep into her eyes.

She nodded, her heart filled with love. "I'm happy." With the back of a finger, she stroked his cheek and down his neck, admiring this man she loved so much.

And then he was kissing her, which was fine because she couldn't think of anything else she'd rather be doing right now except . . .

"Why don't you lock the door, and I'll show you today's pair. They're a different shade of pink."

He smiled against her mouth. "Perfect." He nipped at her bottom lip. "My favorite color."

The End

Acknowledgments

I owe a heartfelt thank-you to the town of Red River, New Mexico, especially Katy Pierce, Steve Heglund, Fritz Davis, and Ron Weathers. While the characters and establishments in my novels are formed solely from my imagination, the real people and places of Red River are no less wonderful. I've taken some creative liberties, but in real life, Red River is one of the most magical places on earth.

Thank you to my brother, Ricky, who gave me the idea for the canine character in this story, and to my sister, Shurla, for naming him.

A huge thank-you goes out to my critique partner, Shelly Chalmers, whose imagination never ceases to amaze.

And last but certainly not least, my deepest gratitude to my editors, Kelli Martin of Montlake Romance at Amazon Publishing and Melody Guy, the entire Montlake team, and my agent, Jill Marsal of the Marsal Lyon Literary Agency.

About the Author

A 2014 Golden Heart® finalist, Shelly Alexander grew up traveling the world, earned a bachelor's degree in marketing, and worked in the business world for twenty-five years. With four older brothers, she watched every *Star Trek* episode ever made, joined the softball team instead of ballet class, and played with G. I. Joes while the Barbie Corvette stayed tucked in the closet. When she had three sons of her own, she decided to escape her male-dominated world by reading romance novels and has been hooked ever since. Now she spends her days writing steamy contemporary romances while enjoying the arid climate of the beautiful Southwest.

Photo © 2014 Frank Frost Photography

DEC 0 3 2015